"You'll just have to trust me, Janine."

Luc's voice was smoke and velvet.

"Let me see my vases," she insisted. What's the worst that he could do? Say no? Close further in on her?

He started to smile, a dangerous spark in his gaze. "For a price."

"A price?"

"Dinner."

"Dinner?" Good God, was he asking her out on a date?

"So we can discuss the security of the exhibit."

She eyed him warily. "Only if I see the vases right now."

"That can be arranged." He reached into his pocket for the key, and his eyebrow tilted upward. "Trust me," he said again.

"Is there any reason not to?"

A low, sexy laugh was his only response.

"Roxanne St. Claire packs a punch with her debut novel *Tropical Getaway*. In-depth characterizations and an intriguing plot make this book hard to put down. Ms. St. Claire is definitely one to keep an eye on."

—The Word on Romance

"*Tropical Getaway* twines mystery and romance into a realistic and interesting tale. St. Claire's debut book would be great to read while looking out the window over snow and ice, dreaming of the sun-drenched isles of the Caribbean."

—*Old Book Barn Gazette*

"Roxanne St. Claire's debut is a steamy mixture of intrigue, passion and red herrings. Set in the exotic locales of the Caribbean, *Tropical Getaway* is the perfect escape for a cold winter night."

—AOL Romance Fiction Forum

"Captures the essence of paradise, tosses in some heated passion, and meshes it into a compelling suspense. . . . The setting is perfect; the romance, one of the best; and the suspense will have you on the edge of your seat!"

—Romance Reader's Connection

"*Tropical Getaway* sucks you into the story from the moment you read the prologue. The pages just keep turning and before you know it you are so engrossed in the story you forget everything around you."

—ARomanceReview.com

ROXANNE ST. CLAIRE

FRENCH TWIST

POCKET BOOKS
New York   London   Toronto   Sydney

An *Original* Publication of POCKET BOOKS

 POCKET BOOKS, a division of Simon & Schuster, Inc.
1230 Avenue of the Americas, New York, NY 10020

ISBN: 0-7434-7729-4

First Pocket Books printing February 2004

10 9 8 7 6 5 4 3 2

POCKET and colophon are registered trademarks of Simon & Schuster, Inc.

Cover design by Jae Song
Photo of Eiffel Tower © Craig Aurness/Corbis

Manufactured in the United States of America

For information regarding special discounts for bulk purchases, please contact Simon & Schuster Special Sales at 1-800-456-6798 or business@simonandschuster.com.

For Dante and Mia,
my children, my treasures, my *raison d'être*

Acknowledgments

A heartfelt *merci beaucoup* to:

Elizabeth Anderson, a talented writer and genuine friend, whose keen insights, helpful suggestions, and rich outpouring of smiley faces are shining through on every page. Thanks for helping polish the Plums to high gloss finish, 'Zie.

The City of Versailles webmaster, who generously offered precise details and conducted personal fact-checking to ensure the accuracy of all things pertaining to his great city and Palace. *Avoir la paix,* Gregory.

Former FBI Agent James Vatter, for providing a wealth of information about investigations of art crimes committed by U.S. felons on international soil. Any inaccuracies regarding the workings of law enforcement in this area are mine, not his.

FRENCH TWIST

Prologue

As he picked the lock, Nick Jarrett hummed Mozart's Piano Concerto in A Major. An extraordinary melody. Complex, dynamic, a bit irreverent. No wonder he liked it. He glanced down the empty hotel corridor—no one in sight. His fingers moved to the sprightly minuet of the second movement. A simple matter of pick, pluck, and run.

Even though his client thought the script on this job should read pick, pluck, *murder,* and run.

But Nick had no intention of killing anyone. He was a thief. Sometimes a liar and occasionally, when pushed to the wall, a cheat. But not a murderer. This was Karim Benazir's idea of a test.

The pick vibrated the key shaft and released the six-pin lock with a tiny ping.

Nick hated to be tested.

If he'd followed Benazir's commands, there'd be a man sleeping in this hotel room. Nick had been instructed to put a bullet in the guy's head before emptying the safe of the half million dollars worth of diamonds that waited there.

Of course, Nick had arranged things differently. He'd still get the diamonds and a healthy percentage of the take, but nobody would die tonight. In fact, he'd just passed the portly businessman in the restaurant downstairs, enjoying a bowl of lobster bisque.

Benazir wouldn't be happy. But the dethroned Indian prince could climb into a hole in hell if he expected anything more than the usual burglary services.

Nick inched the door open, stepping into the ink black suite as lightly as the tune that played in his brain. He paused, held his breath, and listened. Silence. Without making a sound, he strode across the marble floor of the living room toward the bedroom.

The room darkeners had been pulled so that not a single sliver of the lights of Manhattan peeked through. Surprising, but not a problem. He'd been born with exceptional night vision. He'd also been born with natural coordination, dexterous fingers, and titanium nerves. All ideal qualities for his chosen profession. Or, more precisely, for the profession that had chosen him.

He placed a latex-gloved hand on the ornate closet door handle and opened it. Behind the clothes inside, he inched his fingertips along the wall until he felt the hard surface of the safe. It required just nine twists of his wrist to get it right. This was too easy.

A fine chill danced down his spine. This *was* too easy. But as his left hand curled around the bag of jewels, he ignored the inner voice. He was nearly finished, and he'd be home drinking a bone-dry martini in fifteen minutes.

There was just one last task to complete the job. His last job, ever.

He pulled a felt-tipped marker out of his jacket pocket with his free hand and bit the red cap with his teeth. Using the inside of the closet door as his canvas, he swiftly sketched the familiar elongated body. Several slashes on either side represented the fingerlike appendages. A final flourish completed the segmented, curved tail and its venomous stinger.

As always, the Scorpion had left his mark.

The cap still in his teeth, Nick eased the safe closed and pushed the closet door with his shoulder. As it snapped shut he heard another sound, and suddenly the room was bathed in light.

"FBI. Don't move."

Nick bit hard on the pen cap as the bag of diamonds fell from his fingers and hit the floor. *Son of a bitch.* He'd fallen right into a trap.

"Hey, Nick." He could have sworn he heard a chuckle in the familiar voice. "You're under arrest."

An image of his mother and his sister flashed in Nick's mind as he made an abrupt decision. He had to die. But before he did, he'd turn the tables on Karim Benazir and put the bastard away for good. Then the only two people who mattered to him would be safe.

A quiet breath shuddered through him. Now he was ready to face his captor, ready to give Tristan Stewart the satisfaction of holding a gun to the head of the Scorpion.

You win, buddy.

Nick turned and stared into the hard gray eyes of the FBI agent he'd successfully eluded for years. He didn't think about the prick Benazir, or the trap that he'd waltzed right into with his "flawless" night vision. He didn't dwell on the fact that, at thirty-four, his life was about to end. He thought only of his mother, Gabrielle, and his sister, Claire. They'd be miserable and betrayed and confused—but they'd be alive.

Ignoring the two other agents who flanked Tristan, Nick held his arms out from his body, gripping the open red marker so hard that the ink stained his rubber gloves.

He was, quite literally, caught red-handed. The irony made his lip curl around the pen cap still trapped in his teeth. His gaze locked on the man who had made a career out of searching for the Scorpion.

Could there be any sympathy in his heart? After all, Tristan had eaten plenty of meals at Gabrielle Jarrett's kitchen table, and he'd never been able to conceal his adoration of Claire.

The agent looked victorious but wary, as though the thief would once again disappear into thin air.

If only he could.

Nick tilted his head and spat the cap onto the floor. "Let's make a deal, Tris."

The steel eyes flashed just enough for Nick to know he'd get his deal. Nick Jarrett was about to die. The Scorpion had to be squashed. And someone else would live and breathe in his place.

CHAPTER
One

H oly hell. Her Plums were missing.

Janine Coulter blinked against the blinding May sunshine reflected off hundreds of Venetian mirrors. Even in the chaotic cavern of light, glass, and enough gilded fleur-de-lis to eliminate world hunger, she could *feel* that her precious Pompadour Plum vases were not in Versailles' famed Hall of Mirrors.

"Monsieur le Directeur, where are the Sèvres vases?"

Henri Duvoisier started to smile, but then must have remembered he was French. "How astute of you to notice, Dr. Coulter. We are not including them in this area of the exhibit." At her intake of breath, he lifted a bony shoulder. "We have been advised against doing so."

Janine closed her eyes, digging deep for every ounce of diplomacy and patience. This was a test. He resented her because, in his eyes, she was a novice, an American, a woman, and an intruder.

"Advised?" This would be a battle of wills, but her will was steel. Hadn't she proved that by her sheer determination to assume the position of exhibit curator? "By whom?"

He didn't respond.

She looked directly into Henri's limpid blue eyes. "The vases are the centerpiece of the exhibit, *monsieur,* and our plans call for them to be in the middle of the hall." She turned and crossed the polished parquet, the staccato tap of her high heels echoing off the marble walls and richly painted ceilings. "They were supposed to be right here."

She stood below the massive portrait of Madame de Pompadour. If little bourgeoisie Jeanne-Antoinette Poisson could march into the most splendid palace in France and convince the surly court that she deserved to be the king's mistress, certainly one unwelcome art history professor from UCLA could handle Versailles' embittered director.

"We have altered the design of the exhibit because of security issues, Dr. Coulter," Henri said.

Was there a French equivalent to "I don't give a shit"?

She squared her shoulders and matched the haughty expression captured in Boucher's famed image of *la Pompadour*. "I wasn't apprised of these security issues."

Henri cleared his throat and suddenly sent a beseeching glance over her shoulder. Someone else had entered the hall. She didn't hear footsteps, but she sensed a presence. She turned to follow Henri's gaze.

At first she couldn't see anything but a shadow against an arched window at the very end of the hall. Then the shadow became a silhouette of a man as he silently approached.

"That's because you were unavoidably detained." The English words, buried in a smoky baritone and rich French accent, echoed through the massive hall.

He strode toward her with all the assurance of the three Bourbon kings who'd played God in this very room. They had been tall enough to look down on their subjects, dark enough to be the focal point of every portrait, and handsome enough to have their legendary libidos constantly satisfied.

This man could be a direct descendant. And then some.

His eyes, nearly as black as his thick, straight hair, glinted as he gazed at her. A shadow of stubborn whiskers in his hollow cheeks balanced the dark slash of brow. Everything about him—from the elegant thousand-dollar suit fitted to his wide shoulders, down to the rich Euro loafers—screamed control, perfection, and superiority.

Not only did he have the drop-dead looks of French royalty, he had the 'tude to match.

Janine tilted her face up to him, something a five-foot-seven-inch woman in heels rarely had to do.

"Ah, Luc." Henri's voice startled her; she'd forgotten he was in the room. The museum director murmured something indecipherable while he shook the new arrival's hand.

The corner of the man's mouth curled, and he turned to Janine, sweeping a glance over her and lingering a moment longer than necessary on her legs. Maybe the spunky skirt was a little too L.A. hip and not enough Paris couture?

His eyes narrowed a fraction. "Evidently you were unable to be involved in the last-minute decisions, *Madame la Curator.*" His English was flawless, softened by a French accent. "I understand you had urgent personal business keeping you from joining us."

The musical cadence didn't mask the little dig. Whoever Luc was, he knew, like everyone else, that she'd been delayed because her wedding had been scheduled to take place the week before. And like everyone else, he would soon realize that she had no ring, no new last name, and no husband in tow.

For the millionth time, she cursed Sam Benjamin and the ground the cheating, lying bastard walked on.

She held out her hand. "I'm Dr. Janine Coulter."

With a slight bow of his head, he engulfed her hand with a large, strong grip. "Luc Tremont."

"Luc is our *spécialist de la securité,*" Henri explained. "A consultant, as you would say, whom we have hired to control the security of the Pompadour exhibit. And yes, Luc, this is the newly appointed *Madame la Curator,* our distinguished guest from the *Université de Californie,* Janine Coulter."

A shower of resentment sparked at her nerve endings. She hadn't been told a thing about a security consultant.

"The pleasure is mine, *madame.*" A decidedly un-French smile revealed perfect white teeth. His handshake relaxed as one of his fingers lightly moved over her skin. More resentment sparked. *Something* sparked. She withdrew her hand.

"From California," he said, in a tone so soft it could be

considered seductive . . . or mocking. "But your beautiful name is so French. Janine."

Szha-neen. It sure never sounded like that before. She shook her head and tried to respond in his language to be polite and demonstrate her fluency, but every syllable she'd ever known eluded her. Damn. "No, not French. Just . . . American."

She crossed her arms self-consciously. This was probably part of their sabotage strategy. They sent this hunk to sidetrack her, make her stumble on the job, steal her attention from her responsibilities. Who said the French weren't effective warriors?

"We were so sorry to hear of the passing of Dr. Farrow," he said.

The familiar dull ache settled around her heart at the mention of the man whose death she'd yet to accept. "Thank you. His death was a tremendous loss for the art world and for the university."

But she didn't want to discuss her friend and mentor. Or the fact that she'd persuaded the French minister of culture to give her Albert Farrow's coveted assignment. She'd defended her position enough; she was the curator and she wanted the Plums.

"Monsieur Tremont, do you know where the Sèvres vases are?"

He extended an arm toward an artful arrangement of porcelain under a portrait of Louis XV. "Some are right there, *madame,* and there are still more in the *Salon de la Guerre.*"

She'd already been through that area of the Hall of Mirrors, nearly a football field away. No vases. Not the ones she wanted. *"Non, monsieur.* The Pompadour Plum vases."

She heard Henri stifle a moan at the phrase. The American media had dubbed the three exquisite vases "the Pompadour Plums" after they had been found in the dusty basement of a French château a year ago. The purist French historians despised the catchy description of the matchless purple porcelain that had been the subject of such great debate in the art world.

Luc Tremont regarded her from under thick, dark lashes. "It's my strong recommendation that we limit the viewing of the Sèvres to one of the anterooms, guarded twenty-four hours a day. I'll allow entrance by invitation only."

He'll allow entrance?

"I don't think so," she responded. "The vases are the heart and soul of the exhibit."

"There are nearly a hundred other artifacts on display," he countered.

"None as precious as the Sèvres." And none as closely tied to Madame de Pompadour, the exhibit's namesake. "They are the whole reason people will come to this exhibit."

"Surely they will want to see all of the treasures of Louis XV's Versailles."

He was clueless, this big French security guard. "Monsieur Tremont, do you realize that in the history of all mankind, there has never been a piece of soft paste Sèvres porcelain produced in that color? Let alone three matching vases, all with Pompadour's image and name?" She purposely used the let-me-spell-this-out-for-you tone that she saved for freshmen. "All three bear *Madame's* actual signature written in gold. They are *priceless.*"

"Precisely my point." A glimmer lit his midnight gaze. "Professor."

A sudden, uncomfortable warmth spread through her, but she continued her argument. "They're the reason more than a million people around the world will file into museums like this one," she insisted. "It would be like exhibiting King Tut without the sarcophagus. We can't deny visitors the chance to see the Pompadour Plums."

"*Madame.*" Henri cleared his throat. "We are not using that expression."

She ignored him, her focus unwavering on Tremont. "Why would you do something so counterproductive? This is rare. This is huge. It has to be shown to the world, not just a select few."

Tremont took a few steps closer to her, invading her breathing space in that totally French way. But somehow, with him, it was more . . . *invasive.* "There have been very specific threats to the exhibit, *madame.* I don't think you want to take the chance of losing the vases before they have traveled the world."

Of course not. If anything went wrong, her trial run would end as fast as she could say *au revoir*. But she wouldn't let this guy steamroll her. "Why don't you let me in on the security issues, Monsieur Tremont, and then we can come up with a plan that meets your needs and mine?"

"*Madame la Curator.*" A hint of condescension was artfully buried in the musical accent. "There have been rumblings in the underground world of art trading."

So, word on the street said there would be a hit. "I don't have a problem with armed guards and increased museum security," she responded, "but I refuse to remove the Sèvres vases from the main exhibit."

"I'm afraid you have no authority to *refuse* anything."

"Sorry, but I do." She gave him a sweet smile. "Perhaps we can discuss this with the minister of culture, who *gave* me the authority to do what I want with my vases."

He winked at her. "They belong to France."

Damn. She could have bitten a hole in her lip. "I mean *Madame*'s vases . . . the Sèvres vases."

With one strong, sure hand on her shoulder, Tremont guided her away from Henri, leaning close enough for Janine to feel a whisper of warm breath on her cheek. The French—personal space was irrelevant to them. "*Madame*. Doctor. What do you prefer that I call you?"

She couldn't resist. "Janine."

"Janine." *Szha-neen*. It was absolutely *sinful* the way he said it. "There is more than I am telling you."

A shiver skated down her spine, but that was due to his serious tone, *not* his sexy pronunciation.

He moved his hand down her back, leaving a trail of heat in its wake. "Surely you understand that there are those who will stop at nothing to own such a magnificent piece of history as Pompadour's vases."

"Of course there are thieves who would want them," she said impatiently. "But hiding them in another room? Offering a viewing by invitation only? Such extreme measures will only detract from the exhibit."

He shook his head. "Not when lives are at risk, Janine."

"Whose life is at risk?" she scoffed in disbelief.

"Yours."

Luc knew his trump card would get her attention. He could think of a number of other ways to do so, some more appealing than others. Like claiming her pretty little mouth in a world-class demonstration of a French kiss. That would also satisfy the annoying itch that started the moment he laid eyes on the California girl.

"My life is at risk?" As the blood faded from her face, her alabaster skin revealed the faintest dusting of freckles, noticeable only because of the reflected sunbeams bouncing around the *Galerie des Glaces.* Sunlight suited her. She belonged in the sun. On the beach, sparkling on the sand somewhere. She was so bright and fresh and . . . American.

Behind him, other staff members had entered the Hall. Although the palace was closed to visitors in preparation for the gala that would launch the exhibit, there were still many faces he didn't recognize. Or trust.

"Why don't we walk outside for a few moments?" he suggested. "We can talk privately."

Her sky blue eyes flashed, but she consented with a nod. Before Henri could attach himself to them again, Luc led Janine through a gallery that opened onto the *Cour de Marbre.*

He paused as they stepped onto the intricate pattern of gray and white marble. Beyond it rolled the emerald lawns of the gardens, dotted with multicolored flowers, gushing fountains, and priceless sculptures.

As always, the singular beauty of France simply left

him homesick. But he held out his hand to share the scene. *"C'est magnifique, n'est ce pas?"*

She cast a quick glance at the view and barely inhaled enough to enjoy the fragrance of orange blossoms that floated on the breeze. Tucking her handbag under her elbow, she crossed her arms and locked an insistent gaze on him. "I'm not here to take a tour, *monsieur.* I'd appreciate an explanation of what you just said."

The color had returned to her fine-boned face. She had no way of knowing he wasn't just another anti-American Frenchman who resented her arrival, so he forgave her the little jutting chin. He knew enough about her situation to understand.

"Not a tour, I promise. But I find that hall a bit suffocating, *non?* In May in France, there's never a reason to be indoors."

She gave the grounds another cursory glance and then trained her blue eyes on him again. "Can you tell me exactly what you meant in there?"

"Oui." Three uniformed tour guides stood smoking a few yards away. Versailles had ears, and eyes. That was his biggest problem. "While we walk, *s'il vous plaît."* He headed toward the matching pools that anchored the entrance to the gardens.

Although his gut instinct—backed up by a thorough background check—cleared Dr. Coulter from any suspicion, he still had no intention of telling her the truth. Raw ambition may have been her motive for muscling in on the curator's job when the old man killed himself, or she might have been sent as a plant. Or simply a distraction.

He took another surreptitious glance at her long, lean calves. His weakness for a magnificent pair of legs was known to only a few, but those few included at least one man who'd like to see him dead.

He opted for the obvious explanation. "There's a great deal of anti-American sentiment in France, as you undoubtedly are aware. There are those who'd prefer that the curator of the Pompadour exhibit be a French citizen."

"I'm qualified for the job, and the minister of culture agreed." Her cool tone left no room for discussion. "Certainly your anti-American sentiment doesn't include killing visitors to your country?"

"Not usually." He smiled at her as a breeze lifted a strand of her platinum blond hair from the loose knot at the nape of her neck, and she hastily tucked it back. "Although we've been known to insult them into leaving."

She responded with a soft, musical laugh that reminded him of a wind chime. "I can handle that."

"I've no doubt you can."

He remembered the grainy photo he'd seen on the UCLA faculty web site. He'd been searching for potential cracks in security when he discovered that the curator-to-be was more than a hotshot art history PhD who'd worked closely with the famed Albert Farrow. She was also a knockout.

And she remained unmarried, despite a delay for her wedding. He'd have to find out why.

"You've assumed a very high-profile position in an important and controversial exhibit for Versailles, indeed, for all of France." He tilted his head toward her and lowered his voice. "And, of course, there are those who firmly believe the Plums are nothing but a hoax."

She groaned and looked at the sky. "Lord, save me from the anti-Pompadour crowd. They were the bane of Albert's existence—and mine. They are idiot conservatives who would keep Louis's mistress out of the history books completely if they could."

He laughed softly. "*Mais oui*. A Monica Lewinsky of her time."

Her eyes sparked in response. "That is so wrong—she changed the course of history. She was as powerful as a queen and just as influential as the king she loved."

"But as you say, she rarely merits more than a paragraph in French history books."

"This exhibit could change that," she insisted.

"Then you understand why you are the focus of so much attention, Janine."

She shrugged it off. "I didn't want the attention. I'm here because the Pompadour Plums are one of the most significant finds of the twentieth-century art world. I worked side by side with Albert Farrow to prove their existence. To great personal and professional expense, I have convinced Claude Marchionette, the minister of culture, that I'm the best person to keep those vases front and center in this exhibit."

Precisely where he didn't want them to be. "And you are to be congratulated on that coup. I'm sure it will elevate your stature considerably in the art and academic world."

Her eyes darkened to match the water in the ornate fountain behind her. "Who hired you anyway? Henri Duvoisier?"

He nearly laughed. *"Non."*

"But he's the top of the food chain at Versailles."

"I was retained from outside the museum hierarchy." She wasn't stupid; in a minute she'd run up the "food chain" and figure it out.

She frowned. "The *Réunion des Musées Nationals* is the only authority over the museums, as far as I know." She stared at him, the stray hair escaping again. "Claude Marchionette?"

"Precisement." He resisted the urge to touch that silky strand, watching it dance in the breeze.

Her jaw dropped. *"You* were hired by the minister of culture, too?"

"He has given me carte blanche to protect the exhibit. Even if that means altering it."

"Then he's given two people carte blanche," she said, with a wry lift of her brow. "And surely you know that security doesn't drive the design of an exhibit, it's the other way around."

He nodded. "I am sensitive to that. I'm a specialist, brought in for very specific situations such as this major exhibit. I'm well-trained to protect priceless treasures."

"What kind of training?"

He recited his résumé casually, glossing over dates and years as if modest, not purposefully vague. He managed to sound as if he had experience in museums all over the world and enough education to be considered "intelligent" by the elite French standards.

"Do you require references, *madame?"* he asked, unfastening the single button of his suit jacket and slipping his hands into his pockets.

"I'll talk to the minister."

"You do that." Because a conversation with Claude Marchionette wouldn't change a thing.

As they reached the stone barrier around an enormous fountain, she stopped and studied the sculpture at its center.

"It's the Greek goddess Latona," he commented.

"Yes, I know." A hint of a smile crossed her face as she gazed at the spray that burst from the open mouths of dozens of gilded frogs.

"Do you find her amusing?" he asked.

"Not her, all the frogs."

He chuckled. "Never let it be said that the French can't laugh at themselves."

She turned and unexpectedly put a hand on his arm. "Listen, I'm not on a mission to change French history or the way it's recorded." Color rose in her cheeks and her eyes sparkled. "I'm just partial to porcelain, especially the Plums. And I'm the last person who would compromise their security. Couldn't you please consider moving them back to the main exhibit?"

Keeping the Plums separate from the rest of the exhibit was critical to Luc's success on this job. It was the only way the whole event could be choreographed and completed without endangering lives. "I'm sorry," he responded. "We can't make it easy for a thief."

And yet, that was precisely what he was doing.

She held his gaze for a long moment, all plantinum blond and blue-eyed determination. He could stare at her all day. If she'd been sent to distract him, then his nemesis knew him far too well.

She stepped away, and he followed her around the base of the fountain in silence, admiring the way her trim little suit fit from behind.

"Are you supposed to baby-sit me, as well as the vases?" she finally asked.

"To some extent. Although it appears the Pompadour Plums will be less of a challenge than the curator."

"You've got that right." She tossed a glance over her shoulder, her lips lifted in a hint of a smile. "You can't lock me up in a viewing room and allow visitors by invitation."

"That's not a bad idea," he shot back. "Just you, me, and your vases."

Her expression melted into embarrassment. "Sorry about that. I really didn't mean to call them mine."

This time he didn't fight the urge. He lifted the shiny lock of hair and tucked it behind her ear with a teasing smile. "I'll keep your secret, *Madame la Curator.*"

A tiny crease formed on her brow as she opened her mouth to speak. Then she pressed her lips together.

"What is it?" he urged.

"Nothing. You just . . . you just don't seem very French."

His gut tightened. *"Pardon?"* He let his gaze drop over her face and down her torso in proof that he could caress the opposite sex with a smoldering gaze as well as the next Frenchman. To confirm that he was as French as croissants and champagne. "Why would you say that?"

"For one thing, you smile."

"Just trying to make you feel at home." He dipped his head close enough to catch her sweet, floral scent. "Janine."

She flushed again when he said her name. "And you have no qualms about making eye contact."

"How could I look away from such a lovely woman?"

She rolled her eyes. "Yeah, you're French."

"But of course." He would have to be very careful with this all-American beauty. Very careful indeed. If her real mission was to distract him, she'd already succeeded.

CHAPTER
Two

By the time Luc Tremont escorted her back, Janine had figured out that the engaging and flirtatious Frenchman was a master of the art of saying nothing. She escaped him at the museum offices, feigning an appointment.

Making her way through the maze of closed doors to her tiny, windowless office, she dropped her handbag on the desk and fell into her chair. God, she'd been here a whole day and still hadn't even *seen* her vases.

Her vases? She sniffed and slid her jacket over the back of the chair. They *were* her vases; hers and Albert's. They'd spent their careers working to prove the vases existed, and then . . . The pain was still fresh. Why, after all those months and years of work, when the Plums were finally discovered, why would Albert inexplicably end his life?

She knew all the pat answers that floated around: that he'd buckled under the pressure of his critics, that he'd given in to the Alzheimer's that had begun to tear at his brain. No one seemed to give credence to her theory that it was not suicide. So, here she was, in France. Doing the only thing she could do to continue his life's work, and hers: showcasing the Plums to the world.

And now, even that was compromised by the rather unnerving Luc Tremont. He'd certainly managed to unnerve her out by that fountain—but not with idle threats.

With boudoir eyes, a velvet voice, and his better-to-eat-you-with smile, all contained in one super-sized package. He'd make any red-blooded female dry mouthed and stupefied. *Jus you and me and your vahses, Szha-neeeeen.* And she'd blushed like a schoolgirl.

The unfamiliar double ring of her desk phone made her jump. Her first call in her new job. She cleared her throat and answered. "Janine Coulter."

"Hey, Jay-nine."

Oh, hell. "Hello, Sam."

"I thought I'd hear from you when you got the flowers."

The ones she snipped the tops off and dumped into the trash can in her hotel room? "I didn't accept them from the concierge."

"Those were Sterling Silver roses, Janine. It took me two fucking days to find them in France."

Yeah, right. It took his secretary two hours. "I'm very busy, Sam. What do you want?"

"I can be on a flight this afternoon." He paused, for drama, no doubt. Everything Sam did was for effect. "We can get married in Paris. Just say the word."

"Shelby." That was the word: the actress he'd betrayed her with.

"Oh, Christ. How many times do I have to tell you? She's desperate; she knows the network's going to fire her. She came on to me."

She came, all right. Janine had heard every moan and gasp when she'd walked through Sam's front door, holding the final guest list in one hand and two tickets to Paris in the other. She could hear Shelby projecting, like a good theater-trained actress, all the way from the bedroom.

"Apparently I didn't make this clear when I left. We're done. Over. *Fini*. What part of that don't you understand? There's a lot going on here, and I need to concentrate."

"I told you you'd be in over your head when you went after this job."

"Thanks, Sam. Your confidence and support are touching. I'm *not* in over my head. Even Albert, before he died, told me I could have handled the job as well as he could."

Sam responded with that disgusted little snort-cough he always made. "Oh, come on. Albert Farrow was a certifiable freak show in purple pants, and he proved it by blowing away what was left of his brains."

"Shut *up,* Sam." The pain was too fresh, too real. But that wouldn't stop Sam from trivializing it; no doubt he'd already pitched Albert's life story as a movie of the week to TNT. "He wasn't crazy."

"But you were, to ditch me and take that job."

"Ditch you?" She sucked in a breath and squeezed the

phone tighter. "You did the ditching when you took that woman into your bed. Listen, I've staked my entire reputation to get here, and I intend to do this job without distractions from you."

"Bag the teacher voice, Jay. I get your point." The long distance crackling stopped momentarily. Had he just hit mute? The static started again with his next word. "I just didn't think your going after this Plum thing was such a good idea."

"You thought it was a swell idea a week ago. A honeymoon in France and the possibility of my being out of town for most of a year. How convenient for you."

"Jay-baby." He took another long, dramatic pause, and she heard something rustle in the background. "You just had so much hit you at once." Was that the click of a keyboard?

She almost laughed out loud. He wasn't going for *impact* with long, staged pauses. He was reading his e-mail, skimming a script, and probably scanning his PDA for a phone number, all while trying to woo her back. The epitome of West Coast multitasking.

"Yes, I did, Sam. My dear friend died tragically, on the verge of realizing his lifelong dream. And I stepped up to the plate to make sure that dream stays alive. And then my fiancé decided to boink a stupid, has-been actress five days before he said 'I do' to me. Yep. That's a lot."

He muted her for a few seconds and then came back on the line. "She's not stupid."

"Madame la Curator! Vous êtes ici."

Surprised, Janine looked up to meet the dark gaze of

Simone de Vries. "Thank you so much for calling, Sam. Good-bye." She dropped the phone in the cradle and smiled at the woman in charge of Versailles Security. *"Oui, madame.* I'm here."

Simone stepped into the office and closed the door behind her. "Are you finding everything you need?"

"Oui." After the morning she'd had, she couldn't bear to start the polite dance of small talk the French insisted on before every real conversation. The hell with protocol. "I've just met the new security consultant. You didn't mention him at the exhibit planning meeting this morning."

Simone looked suitably regretful. *"Pardonnez-moi, madame.* I forgot. He will be here during the exhibit month as part of the security staff."

Luc Tremont hardly considered himself *staff.* "He told me you were conducting an investigation into some threats."

Simone frowned and shook her head, her stiff brown hair not moving with the gesture. "You should concern yourself with the art and the guests, and I will worry about the security."

"Do you agree with his plan to keep the Sèvres vases in a safe room apart from the exhibit?"

Simone raised an eyebrow along with her shoulder. "That is *une necessité."*

"I don't think it is in the best interests of the museum or the exhibit." Janine purposely kept her English slow and plain. "I plan to speak with the minister of culture to get them reinstated, at least for the gala. The president of France will be here."

"Non." Simone squished her face into an unattractive network of lines. "We will not do that, *madame.*"

We? Who is this *we?*

"The president will be on the private invitation list to see the vases at the gala," Simone assured her. "Do not worry."

"But I am worried, *madame.* There will be hundreds of other guests on Saturday, not to mention the thousands of people who'll be expecting to see them while they're on display at Versailles."

"Ah, oui. C'est une désappointement." She looked down her long nose at Janine, a haughty French version of "too bad, so sad."

"It is more than a disappointment, *madame,*" she said quietly. "It's a travesty."

"Madame la Curator. You are new to our museum, and you are . . . perhaps unaware of some of the problems that we are facing. There have been a number of serious thefts recently. By chance, have you heard of the pieces missing from the Louvre and the sizeable turmoil that has caused?"

Of course Janine had heard of the Louvre thefts and had read all the reports placing blame squarely on the lax security at that great museum. "Yes, *madame.* But I have every confidence in your security efforts."

"Merci." Simone's smile was tight at best. "But our experience tells us that when there is a noticeable increase in thefts, it means that the underground markets are rich at the moment. There are wealthy, greedy collectors who are looking to add treasures to their coffers."

"I understand that. I just believe this step is too drastic and extremely detrimental to the exhibit."

Simone leaned forward and lowered her voice. *"Madame. Ecoutez, s'il vous plait.* There is a very dangerous and daring thief moving about France *maintenant."*

"I'm sure there are many thieves, *now* and always. Certainly you can use twenty-four-hour guards, alarms, and other protective measures."

Simone slowly shook her head, a warning in her dark eyes. "Nothing would stop the Scorpion, *madame."*

"The Scorpion?" Janine tried not to laugh. "He's been dead for years."

Simone's eyes narrowed. "There is a rumor that he lives."

Janine couldn't resist a mocking smile. "There's also a rumor that Elvis is alive and well and performing in Switzerland."

"You will not be making jokes if the vases disappear, *madame."* Simone was dead serious. Did she really believe it? "I'm expected in Henri's office *tout de suite."* She turned to leave, pausing as she placed her hand on the doorknob. "I strongly urge you to cooperate with Monsieur Tremont. He is very well regarded." Then she left.

Janine stared at the closed door. "Thanks, sweetie. So nice to have a girlfriend at work."

She lifted the phone to call the minister of culture's office.

The Scorpion? These people obviously believed in ghosts.

When he turned onto the rue de Rennes in Saint-Germain, Luc realized that he'd been thinking in English for the entire hour it had taken to navigate the insane traffic from Versailles to Paris. He parked his car and pocketed the key, muttering his favorite French curse. He couldn't allow himself the luxury of thinking in English. Not yet.

But if all went as planned, then he'd finally be able to indulge in that luxury, and many others he'd feared he'd never enjoy again. He'd risk anything for that. He was about to risk *everything* for that.

Slipping through the late lunch crowds on the boulevard Saint-Germain, he replayed the conversation with the pretty American curator. She might look like the girl next-door, but his thoughts weren't exactly neighborly. In *any* language.

Too bad he had such a monumental task in front of him. Too bad she was American. Too bad he'd be gone before she even adjusted to the time change.

All around him, tourists and locals soaked up the spring afternoon at the cafés that lined the main avenue of the Left Bank. Luc sidestepped a group of sightseers on their way into the Musée Delacroix and tossed some money in the box of a street musician. Tuning out the distant whine of a siren and the hum of humanity around him, he concentrated on finding a man waiting at the Café Clairmont.

The irony of the name wasn't lost on Luc. As he crossed the crowded rue Bonapart he spotted his contact, wearing blue-lensed sunglasses and a Red Sox baseball cap pulled low. Luc didn't miss the subtle significance of the hat choice, either. It wasn't part of their prearranged code; it was just a reminder of who had the power in this twisted relationship. Reading *USA Today,* Tristan Stewart looked as much like a bumbling foreigner as an FBI agent could.

As Luc walked by the café, Tristan dropped a few Euros on the table and stood, his newspaper fluttering in front of Luc.

"Ah, *pardonnez-moi,*" Tristan said, butchering even that simple phrase.

Luc picked up the paper and handed it to him. *"Voici, monsieur."*

"Merci."

"De rien."

Tristan adjusted his baseball cap. *"Parlez vous en Anglais?"* He fell into step with Luc on the street.

Luc maintained the funereal expression of a put-upon Parisian. *"Un peu."*

"Would you happen to know how I get to the Eiffel Tower?"

The Eiffel Tower meant they had specific new information. Had he asked for directions to Notre Dame, Luc would have continued his stroll alone. *"Oui.* I'm going that way."

They walked silently for a few minutes, toward the river.

"We're on," Tristan announced quietly.

Luc made no outward reaction. *"Bien."*

A stunning redhead sauntered by, and the platinum sheen of Janine Coulter's hair flashed in Luc's mind. But like any good Frenchman, he stared at the redhead, and she responded with the icy nonlook that acknowledged his compliment.

"I've pleaded your case," Tristan finally said.

Luc's gut squeezed as he waited for the next sentence. This was it. Life or death. Yes or no. "And?"

"He agreed."

Luc resisted the urge to shout in relief. "Of course he did."

Tristan burned him with a warning look. "You gotta pull this off, man. Exactly like you said you can. And I don't know how the hell you plan to do that, because you're walking right into a trap."

"Trust me."

"Right." Tristan tried to cover up the word with a cough. "Our sources confirmed that it's going to happen on Saturday night, just as we expected. At the gala."

Bon Dieu, he had work to do today.

Tristan slowed his step and looked sideways at Luc. "If anything goes wrong, *anything,* all bets are off."

"Nothing will go wrong." Not for him, at least. But Luc felt a tug of sympathy for the lovely curator; her party was going to be a disaster.

They were nearly at the river, the blue black waters of the Seine churned by the strong spring wind. "I will give you who you want, and then you will give me what I want," Luc said. "But I need the time and space to get the job done my way."

Tristan nodded. "As long as I don't wind up looking like an idiot for agreeing to this."

Luc started to smile. *Here comes a Tristan Truism: Go out on a limb, and you fall.*

"Don't fuck this up, man."

Luc laughed softly. "Not the platitude I was expecting, Tris."

"There's a lot at stake, and I'm not just talking about your personal needs."

This went so far beyond personal *needs*. But he didn't correct Tristan. "I know what's at stake."

"I'm betting *everything* that you can do this."

Then they were both betting everything. Luc could just hear the wheels in Tristan's head. *Fool me once . . .*

They reached the edge of the Invalides section of the city and paused at a stone wall along the river. "Weren't you looking for the *Tour d'Eiffel, monsieur?*" Luc pointed toward the spire in the sky. "There it is."

As Tristan looked, Luc leaned close enough for his whisper to be heard. "We both know the Scorpion can't stay hidden much longer."

CHAPTER
Three

Janine lost all track of time as she drafted her speech for the gala in French. A hungry rumble from her stomach finally convinced her to quit.

No one had stopped into her office to say good night. Just like no one had invited her for the standard three-hour Euro-lunch. And forget about dinner.

She looked at her watch. It was damn near eight o'clock and she *still* hadn't seen her Plums.

"Let's see, I can hide in here and have a pity party. . . ." She closed her laptop with a clunk. Sliding the top drawer of her desk open, she lifted the newspaper clipping she'd placed there that morning. It was a silly gesture, but she wanted Albert with her somehow. "Or I can find your Plums and feel better," she said to Albert's smiling black-and-white photo.

Except for the soft echo of her heels on the wood floors, the deserted building was dead silent as she left the business offices and headed toward the center of the great palace. In these gilded halls she could almost smell the perfume of courtesans, the heavy fragrance of flowers and musk that they'd used to cover their humanity.

Goosebumps jumped to attention along her bare arms, reminding her that she'd forgotten her jacket. She paused at a vestibule outside the endless array of baths, libraries, galleries, and meeting rooms of the king's chambers.

Which one of those splendid rooms housed her vases?

And where the hell were the guards? Was security in this place so lax that someone who hid in the palace until the tourists and staff left could roam about freely? Could anyone touch priceless art and furniture, climb up and take a nap in the king's bed if he felt like it?

She crossed the loggia and tried to open one of several doors. It was locked. But the next swung wide without so much as a click.

"Yes," she whispered with self-satisfaction.

The glow of early-evening light slipped through the only window. But she knew she'd entered the Cabinet of the Dogs. The kings had kept their favorite *chiens* in here, enclosed in gold-and-white kennels. No one with a drop of French blood in him would place the vases in the *Antichambres des Chiens*.

Across the parquet, another door stood open, inviting her to step into the world-famous Clock Cabinet, an enormous study where all of the kings had carefully timed their every movement of every day.

She paused at the pedestal with a bronze statue of Louis on horseback in the center of the room, and studied the gigantic Passement clock along one wall. They weren't in this room. She just knew it.

Across from her, a glass-topped table stood by the entrance to one more room . . . the private bedroom.

That's where *she'd* put the vases. Where Jeanne-Antoinette Poisson practiced her most effective influence over the king.

As she stepped toward the bedroom, she heard something.

A soft, breathy . . . whistle. A *melody*.

Her heart stopped, and then kicked into double time. Who on earth was whistling in Louis's bedroom? She listened intently, closing her eyes to focus on the sound.

Was that *Mozart?* Possibly. Certainly the kind of tune Jeanne-Antoinette might have hummed while preparing for a late-night tryst with her king.

Should she march in and face . . . what? A ghost? A guard?

As much as she wanted to see the Plums, she didn't particularly relish an encounter with a surly French night guard. Not even one who whistled classical music.

Still, she had every right to be there. Clearing her throat, she called out, "Is anyone there?"

The whistling stopped immediately.

Taking a step into the room, she peered into the shadows, her gaze moving over the tables and heavily embroidered canopy over the bed. The room was empty.

But who'd been whistling?

An unearthly sensation of being watched sent a shiver up her back. Without stopping to analyze it, she turned back to the doorway, darting back into the Clock Cabinet on the balls of her feet to avoid broadcasting an audio trail. She retraced her steps through the anterooms and out the door she'd first entered, snapping it closed behind her.

Her heart thumped so hard she couldn't hear anything, and she cursed herself for being a ninny. There were no ghosts in this palace.

A hair tickled her face, and she jerked backward with a gasp. Damn, she was being ridiculous. She'd imagined that noise. Could it have been the wind? Not blowing Mozart through a crack in the window. But *were* the vases in there?

Another sickening thought curled through her. Not a ghost. Not a guard.

A thief.

She'd never forgive herself if they were stolen and she'd been this close to preventing it. What was she thinking, running away? She twisted the handle. This time, it jerked against her palm. Wasn't this door unlocked a minute ago?

She crouched down to peer into the mechanism, squinting one eye and shimmying the brass lever.

The stray hair blew across her cheek again, and goosebumps rose along with her fear. Something, someone was right behind her, breathing against her neck, warming her skin!

"That lock can't be picked."

Janine shot to her feet, her head banging into something hard. She heard the smack of teeth hitting teeth on the impact. Whipping around, she stumbled back against the door and saw Luc Tremont.

He rubbed his chin, a wry glimmer in his eyes. "Ouch."

She flattened herself against the door, the ornate carving digging into her back. Her chest rose and fell with each desperate attempt to get air back into her lungs. Blood sang in her head as she looked up at him. "What are you doing here?"

He tilted his head to the side and lowered his lids enough to peer out from underneath his lashes. "I might ask the same thing, Janine."

"I wanted to see the vases."

"You should have asked me this morning."

"I want to be sure they're still there."

A crease formed between the dark slashes of his eyebrows. "Why wouldn't they be?"

She stared into his eyes, so black that she could hardly see the pupils, and said the first thing that popped into her head. "The Scorpion."

Did he blink? *"Excusez?"* he asked casually.

"I—Simone told me—I heard that . . ." She shook her head, coherence slowly returning to her numb brain. "Never mind. I went to see . . . to find the vases, but I heard something and got scared."

"What did you hear?"

"Mozart." It was the best she could do with scrambled brain cells.

He frowned and took a step closer, eliminating all but a few inches between them. "I meant what did you hear about the Scorpion?"

If she took a breath, her breasts would actually touch his chest. He was so *substantial,* in a pale blue cotton shirt opened at his throat. At the edge of his collar, she could see the hint of a pulse throb.

She could almost taste the air trapped in the tiny space between them.

"What did you hear?" His repeated demand was gentle, as though he was coaxing a child.

"Nothing but rumors. You know, gossip."

Still he didn't move, and she plastered herself harder against the door. His gaze held her as effectively as if he pinned her with his muscular arms.

Why was she letting him intimidate her? She raised her chin and glared at him. "If you don't mind, I need to be sure the Plums are okay."

"They are fine."

"How do you know?"

His blistering gaze dropped over her face, settling on her mouth for a millisecond, then sliding down to her chest. A ribbon of response curled inside of her, winding all the way down to knot low in her stomach. Way, way too low to qualify as *fear*.

"You'll just have to trust me, Janine." His voice was smoke and velvet.

"Let me see my vases," she insisted. What's the worst that he could do? Say no? Close further in on her?

He started to smile, a dangerous spark in his eyes. "For a price."

"A price?"

"Dinner."

"Dinner?" Good God, was he asking her out on a date?

"So we can discuss the security of the exhibit."

She eyed him warily. "Only if I see the vases right now."

He reached into his pocket and pulled out a single key. "That can be arranged."

"Assuming no one has taken them."

"Oh, no one has taken them." His eyebrow tilted upward. "Trust me."

"Is there any reason not to?"

A low, sexy laugh was his only response.

Luc memorized the image she made, flushed and trapped, her long, blond hair spilling out of its confines. Her delicious lips parted as she struggled to breathe. Some night when isolation and solitude gnawed at him, he'd remember the pretty girl from California and imagine the things he could do with her against a wall.

He finally let her step away, so he could unlock the door.

"Where'd you hide them?" she asked.

"In the bedchamber." He placed a hand on her back, liking the damp heat that seeped through the fine material.

She sidestepped his touch. "Who might have been in there? I could have sworn I heard someone."

"Security." They turned the corner of the Clock Cabinet and then entered the enormous bedchamber. And this was the *intimate* bedroom. He had little tolerance for the egos of the kings.

"Where are the Plums?" she asked immediately.

He tsked emphatically, distracting her while he

checked the position of the cabinet lock. "Patience, Janine, patience."

She strode toward a bank of electrical switches that had been blended into the woodwork.

He caught her hand just before she touched the wall. "If we turn the lights on, we'll have sixteen security guards up here with guns drawn in a minute. Spare me the trouble."

She pulled out of his grip. "Fine."

Walking to the massive armoire, he pulled out a second key. "They're in here."

"It doesn't seem so all-fired secure," she commented, moving closer to him. "Anyone could take a whack at that cupboard and get them out."

"Have some faith in our security, Janine."

"I got through half the palace and no one even saw me."

He doubted that was true, but didn't bother to explain the network of miniature cameras they'd recently installed. He tugged at the door of the chest and opened it. The three vases, two about twelve inches high and one about eighteen, stood side by side.

Well, Dr. Coulter, let's see just how good you are.

She gently nudged him aside to stand in front of the vases. He allowed her the space, carefully watching her expression. Her gaze traveled over the center vase, a smile tugging at the corner of her lips.

"They're extraordinary," she whispered, reverence deepening her voice. Everything male in him responded to that soulful inflection, imagining how she would make gentle demands of a lover.

She lifted her hand to the vase, and he stopped her. *"Non."*

Anger flashed in her eyes, and her delicate jaw set. "I want to touch them."

Of course she wouldn't be satisfied until she actually had her hands on them. He'd have to take the chance of removing one. He gripped the middle vase by the narrow neck and pulled it out, holding it up for her to examine.

"The color is awesome, isn't it?" Her fingers grazed the handle, then caressed the magnificent glaze. "It's just amazing for soft paste."

Even in the dim evening light, the smooth indigo and violet tones were evident. And he'd seen these under the harsh light of day. They were nearly perfect.

With two hands, Janine eased the vase higher as she bent down to see under the base.

"This is precarious," he lied. "I could drop it."

She laughed. "You wouldn't dare."

This was the final test: now he'd discover whether she was a hired distraction or an innocent one. He watched her eyes narrow as she squinted at the base. She wore almost no makeup, except for mascara to darken what were undoubtedly pale lashes. A natural blond.

"Please, can you bring it over to the light?" She glanced at him.

"It's awkward." He'd rather not stand in the window and broadcast their presence. At her look, he angled the vase toward the window.

She leaned closer, the beginnings of a frown forming.

With the tip of her fingernail, she scraped at a gold-leaf rose petal. He heard the tiniest gasp.

"Is something the matter, Janine?"

Slowly she straightened, a look of horror in her eyes. "This is not a Sèvres vase." She took a step back, crossed her arms, and glared at him. "This is a fake."

Sacrè Dieu. She *was* that good.

CHAPTER
Four

The vase trembled in Luc's grip, and Janine was certain he was about to drop it on the hard wood floor. She almost reached out to grab it, in an instinctive response to protect something so beautiful, fake or not. But he just shook his head, letting out a long, low whistle.

"Very impressive work, *Madame la Curator.*"

She blinked in confusion. "What? You knew?"

He carried the vase back and set it between the others, adjusting it so that its design—a continuum with the other two—faced forward. "Did you really think I would hide priceless vases protected only by a three-hundred-year-old lock?"

"Was that some kind of a test?" She slammed her hands on her hips to keep from throttling him.

He grinned. "You passed."

"Where in holy *hell* are my Plums, Tremont?"

His laugh surprised her. "They are not in holy hell, I assure you." He laid a casual hand on her shoulder. "They are hidden. They are safe. You have to—"

"No." She dodged his touch. "I don't trust you. There is no reason why the curator of this exhibit can't see those vases. Right now."

He studied her for a moment, then held his hand toward the door. *"Après vous, madame."*

"Where are we going?" she asked, without moving.

"To the vases." He gently nudged her forward. "But we will have to take a circuitous route because there are hidden cameras all over Versailles, and no one knows where I've put the vases."

Irritation washed over her. He was too much. "Where *you've* put them?"

"I trust no one, Janine." His mouth lifted in the beginnings of a smile. "But I will trust you." The pressure on her back increased ever so slightly, his hand large and warm. "If you will do the same of me."

She followed him to another anteroom, this one darker and smaller than the others.

"You know so much about this palace," he said as they walked. "Surely you are aware the kings of Versailles had many places to hide. For their own safety, which was constantly at risk."

"Of course." She reached back to her early education to remember those hiding places. She was the expert in French art and history, she should know them all. He was just a glorified guard.

They moved through an oversized bath chamber and then the ostentatious library beyond it. Through another open door, they arrived at "the new rooms" and the decor changed dramatically to simpler design—still gold, but with less flamboyance in the artisan's handiwork. This was not Pompadour's area of Versailles, and her absence was tangible. The rooms grew colder, somehow, with the loss of the fleur-de-lis grandeur.

When they reached Louis XVI's game room, Luc approached a paneled wall next to the ornate marble fireplace. They'd come to the end of this wing of Versailles.

"A secret door," Janine said softly.

"Absolument." He eased a side table away and reached behind the gilded frame of the mirror above the fireplace. She heard something click, and sure enough, a wall panel opened soundlessly toward a darkened hallway.

She choked back a laugh. "Who knew?"

"Almost no one."

As they stepped in, she blinked to adjust to the darkness. Very little light came in behind them, and the hall turned into a black hole at the far end.

"I had no idea this was here," she exclaimed in a whisper, rubbing her arms at a chill of surprise. "I can't believe it."

He slid the door closed behind them, and Janine flinched at the sound. Instantly, he draped his arm over her shoulder, pulling her to his warm side with a reassuring tug. "Stay next to me."

She wouldn't dream of arguing. It was ink black and impossible to see. She inhaled the musty smell that clung to the stone walls, mixed with Luc's heady, masculine scent.

"I can't believe there's a passageway in Versailles that I don't know about," she murmured, almost afraid to speak aloud.

"This was built as an escape route for the king in case

of attack. It remains a well-kept secret." Without so much as a stumble, he eased them around a corner she hadn't even seen, then guided her down three unexpected steps.

"Are the Plums in here?" she asked.

"No. They are on the other side of this passageway."

She automatically extended an arm to keep from bumping into a wall. "I hope you don't carry my vases through the dark like this."

He laughed softly, stopping to do something she couldn't see. Suddenly, soft light spilled into the hallway as he opened a small door.

Over a raised threshold was the second-story gallery of the Royal Chapel.

Janine broke into a slow, surprised smile as they entered it. "Well, they're certainly *not* in holy hell."

Immense stained-glass windows lined the walls, casting a soft glow and a hundred eerie shadows. Janine approached the stone-and-gold balustrade along the upper level and paused to take in the cavernous church. It was so stunning, so perfect, she almost couldn't breathe. She'd always loved this awesome cathedral, tucked away in the corner of the palace.

"Balance," she said softly.

"Pardon?"

"Absolutely everything is in perfect symmetry." She held out a hand to indicate the relief painted on the curved ceiling over the gold organ and the altar below it. "The art is balanced in color and form, the columns a perfect blend of traditional and classical." She leaned further over the railing to see the dramatic layout of glistening marble along the center aisle. "Nothing is even slightly off-kilter here."

His hands locked on her waist. "You will be, if you go any further, Janine."

Szha-neen. He practically whispered it in her ear, threatening her . . . balance. She turned, forcing him to remove his hands or allow his protective gesture to transform into something far more intimate.

He took a single step back, holding her gaze as he let her go.

That ribbon wound tighter inside her stomach. "Where are the vases?"

"Hidden behind the altar."

Her eyes widened.

"Too sacrilegious for you?"

She let her breath out in a little laugh. "Well, it *is* the place where kings were married and princes were baptized."

"And now it is the place where your vases are hidden." His wink was devilish. "You should approve of my ingenuity." Taking her hand, he led her toward the stone stairs and the first floor of the chapel. "Come with me."

It was eerie to travel the same route as a king to his coronation or a queen to her marriage. Janine gazed at the columned archways that lined the aisle, imagining throngs of French men and women, honoring their monarchs, praying to their God. Luc's feet made no sound; her heels tapped the marble.

It suddenly felt very much like a wedding.

"Oh." She hadn't meant for the little exclamation to

escape her lips, and she swallowed the sudden lump that formed in her throat.

"Are you all right?" he asked, laying a solicitous hand on her back.

Damn Sam Benjamin and his empty promises. "This much beauty always overwhelms me."

He walked around the three curved steps below the enormous gilded altar and approached a two-foot-high iron railing. In one swift move, he was over it and turned to her. The sacred area was meant to be entered from a room behind it. "Would you like some help?" He glanced down at the fitted skirt that stopped a good four inches above her knee.

"I can handle it." She hiked the skirt up her thighs to avoid tearing the fabric, straddled the railing, then brought her other leg over. She looked up to see him watching her—and her legs—with an amused expression.

Her tummy twirled again. "I hadn't planned on hurdling barriers in a cathedral today."

"Clearly." He smiled, then approached the golden door of the tabernacle, used to house the Holy Communion.

"In the *tabernacle?*" Her quick laugh echoed through the church. "Are you hoping that the fear of God will keep a thief away?"

"The only thing a thief fears is getting caught," he said. "There won't be any visitors in this church while the exhibit is open. We'll bring the vases to the king's bedroom every day. When you close to the public each night, the counterfeit vases will be in their place. And the Plums will be here."

She stood a step behind him, watching him work two separate locks. One with a key, the other a combination lock that he artfully covered as he spun it in alternating semicircles. While he worked the locks, her gaze traveled over the breadth of his back and the snug fit of the chambray cotton over his muscles, tucked neatly into the narrow waist of his pants.

Good God. She was standing under Jouvenet's *Descent of the Holy Spirit* admiring the backside of a security specialist who chose the tabernacle of the Royal Chapel as the secret hiding place for rare art.

What had gotten into her?

The door unlatched with a resounding snap, but Luc held it closed, as though waiting for precisely the right moment to reveal the treasure.

"Do you really think this is the smartest place to keep these?" she asked, forcing her attention away from his impressive torso.

"A thief will work to find his way into the room where the vases are kept, and he is most likely to do that in off hours. If there was nothing there, he would start searching for them. But if he sees the replicas, he will take those."

"And then what? A trio of forged Sèvres vases is on the gray market?"

"Until someone proves they are fakes." He turned to her, a lock of hair falling over his brow. "But if something should happen to me, then you will know where the real Plums are."

"What could happen to you?" She fought the urge to touch that fallen lock.

He gave her a cavalier shrug. "Who knows?"

"You're full of it." Surely other people knew where the vases were. Certainly Simone de Vries was in on his big secret. She tapped his arm. "Let me see them."

He opened the door with a flourish. *"Voilà, madame. Your Plums."*

Her fingers grazed the cool porcelain. All three had handles of gilded bronze ormolu shaped into profiled busts of Madame de Pompadour. At the center of each was a unique image made entirely of "jewels" that were actually drops of translucent enamel over stamped foils.

She knew by the Sèvres artisan's imprint that they'd been created early in Jeanne-Antoinette's reign as mistress. Each image depicted a different moment in the young woman's relationship with King Louis XV. Meeting him in the woods during a hunt, being courted at a masquerade ball, and the most stunning of all: her presentation to the queen, the wife of her lover. That was the central vase and unquestionably the most beautiful. The scene itself had launched the outcry of disbelief when the vases were found. Why would the king's mistress commission a vase to commemorate such an awkward moment? But Janine, and Albert Farrow, had understood.

"It tells you everything you need to know about this woman," Janine said quietly.

"That she feared nothing," Luc agreed.

She couldn't resist a smile. "Exactly. Meeting the queen was her pivotal turning point." Janine ran a finger over the pretty face on the painting. "Getting the king's devotion was easy. But when she won over his wife, she achieved true acceptance. And power. She knew it, and that's why she chose to memorialize that moment with this vase."

"She's holding Louis's medallion in her hand," he noted. "A symbol of who controlled whom, no doubt."

"I don't think so," she said, stroking the glaze with one finger. "That medallion is the equivalent of a wedding ring to her. It elevated her from mistress to . . . legitimate." She dug her fingernail into the soft paste of the base, with just enough pressure—the amount of pressure was key to the process—to lift any black specks left from an imperfect firing. There were none. The gold leaf remained impenetrable to the slightest demarcation. She looked up at him victoriously. "These are definitely my vases."

"How can you tell?"

"That's a trade secret." She straightened the vase. "One that takes years to learn."

A touch on her chin surprised her as he turned her face toward him and tilted it up. "Then here's another one. You cannot tell anyone that these are here. No one. Promise me that you will not."

The intensity in his eyes took her breath away. Her conversation with the minister of culture that afternoon had verified that Luc Tremont, and his unconventional security strategy, were a done deal.

"I have spoken to Claude Marchionette," she said. "I understand I have to follow your lead."

"Then we should celebrate." He lowered his head toward her, and for one frozen second, she thought he was going to kiss her. A trace of his scent teased her. It wasn't aftershave or cologne, it was . . . him. Refined, enticing, and intense. "We've made such progress today, Janine." His gaze dropped down to her mouth.

Good Lord, he was something. But the last thing she needed was a flirtation and fling with the security consultant. She was on shaky enough ground having stepped boldly into Albert Farrow's difficult-to-fill shoes. Squaring her shoulders, she took a step back. "I appreciate your letting me in on your big secret."

His laugh was smooth as silk and sexy as sin. "I haven't even begun to let you in on secrets. And, Janine, you must answer a question that has me burning with curiosity."

"What is it?"

He lifted her hand and held it between them. "Where is the diamond ring that delayed your arrival in France?"

Her heart flipped. "I flushed it down the toilet."

"I was thinking of having dinner at le Potager du Roy," Luc said, kicking the Alpha Romeo into third gear as he drove away from the palace. It wasn't as romantic as Les Trois Marches, but romance would lead to seduction. And although her obvious expertise had cleared her of suspicion, he knew better than to indulge in the temptation. If he did, she would deserve an explanation for his inevitable disappearance next week. An explanation she would never receive.

Unless something went very, very wrong at the gala on Saturday night.

"Letourneur is a formidable chef." He glanced at her long, lean thigh, tanned and toned, just as he would expect from a California girl. He imagined how those legs would feel wrapped around him, how sweet her skin would taste to his tongue.

"I'm sure I'll love it," she said.

Yes, you would, *ma belle.* Yes, you would.

"Did you grow up in Los Angeles?" He knew she hadn't, but wanted to see how much she'd reveal.

"A few hours away, in Porterville. It's a small town not too far from Bakersfield. Have you ever been to California?"

His memory flashed on one very lucrative assignment that had taken him to L.A., followed by a drive up the awesome coast highway to another job in San Francisco. "No," he lied smoothly, and grinned at her. "But I understand they think they can make wine there."

She rewarded his humor with a light laugh and flipped her long hair over her shoulder. She'd abandoned the effort to keep it back before they left Versailles. The effect was stunning. Even in the darkness, her hair shimmered, falling damn near to her waist in varying shades of ivory and wheat.

"You don't look anything like an art historian," he mused. "How did you pick such an unlikely profession?"

"I went to UCLA to study theater, under the mistaken notion that I could be an actress."

He stole another glance. That piece of information hadn't been in her file. "You certainly have the looks for the job. What was mistaken? You can't act?"

"Actually, I wasn't bad. Not Meryl Streep, but I could deliver a line." She crossed her legs, and he watched her thigh muscle flex.

"So what happened? Why are you a curator of an art exhibit and not in the movies?"

"Because delivering lines is such a tiny part of it. I hated the phoniness, the back-stabbing, the cutthroat competition. Then I took baroque art history as a mick and—"

"A mick?"

"A class so easy, even Mickey Mouse could pass."

"I like that." He chuckled. "So, was it?"

"No. But I discovered something I loved. Artists I respected. Dead ones, with no agenda." She laughed. "So I moved down campus and found my calling with Sèvres porcelain and Dr. Albert Farrow." Her voice dropped with a sad note.

He nodded sympathetically. "His death was a real loss."

"You have no idea." She stared out the window as he pulled into a side street near the restaurant.

"But it is our good fortune that his replacement is so qualified."

"You and Claude Marchionette seem to be the only two people in France who agree with that."

"But that didn't stop you from going after the job."

"Nothing could have stopped me," she said quietly. "I knew if I didn't fight for the position, someone else would get it, and the vases could disappear into obscurity, victims of those who'd prefer they'd never been found in the first place."

"How did you convince the minister to let you have Albert's job?" He remembered being surprised at the time of the announcement and immediately suspicious of the replacement.

"I got on a plane, flew to France, and pleaded my case." She shot him a narrow-eyed look. "I can be very persuasive."

"I bet you can." He maneuvered the Alpha into a parking spot. "And you obviously know your way around a piece of porcelain."

"Thanks to Albert Farrow." She stared straight ahead, her tone flat. "Really, I had total support from the minister. And as you know, his support is all one needs around here."

He smiled at the dig, and then asked, "Pardon me if this is a delicate subject, but why did Dr. Farrow kill himself?"

"I don't think he did."

"Excuse me?"

"It appears that I'm alone in that regard. It just . . . well, it just was so shocking to me." She paused for a minute. "He'd spent a lifetime trying to prove the Plums existed, and then they were unearthed by a couple of rich New Yorkers who bought an old château and cleaned out the basement. He was joyous after all the years of defending an indefensible position." She smoothed the material of her skirt. "But, he'd also been . . . sick. Forgetful. In the early stages of Alzheimer's."

"Certainly scary enough to make a person want to give up."

"That's what the police thought."

Luc filed the information as he turned off the ignition. "Why was his position indefensible?"

"Everyone knows you can't produce a color that rich and rare in soft paste, and hard paste deposits of kaolin weren't found until 1768. These vases predate that by ten years, proving that Madame de Pompadour was responsible for one of the greatest breakthroughs in art history." She paused for a moment, looking out the window. "If it weren't for Albert's firm beliefs, for his fanatical interpretation of ancient records from the Sèvres factory, no one would have ever known about the Plums. No one would have paid any attention to them when they were found, if Albert hadn't paved the way. He not only fought to prove their authenticity, he was the driving force behind this entire exhibit."

The passion in her voice tugged at his heart when he thought of what would happen on Saturday night. "That's the reason its success is so important to you."

"I wrote my doctorate thesis on the Plums and have dedicated my career to using them to establish a new and controversial time line for the history of porcelain making." Her blue eyes flashed at him. "I have many reasons not to want them hidden from the public."

"I'm sorry that you dislike how I've arranged the exhibit."

"I hate it," she stated simply. Then a little smile lifted the corner of her lips. "Plus, if I screw up, they'll boot my behind back to L.A., and I really don't want to go there until my ex-fiancé gets run over by a truck."

He laughed out loud. "Another noble reason."

He got out and rounded the front of the car, still smiling. Opening her door, he offered his hand to help her out onto the cobblestone sidewalk, his gaze on those perfect legs as she climbed out.

He didn't let go of her hand. "You will be a great

success in Versailles," he said, lifting her fingers to his mouth. She would be; it just wouldn't be immediately obvious to her. "I promise you will be the champion of the art world."

He almost wished he could tell her the truth, to save him from those moments when she would hate him in the next few days.

She looked up with an enticing plea in her eyes. "Then put my Plums back in the Hall, Luc."

"I will," he promised. "Eventually."

She started to say something, but he silenced her with a finger to her mouth. "It will be much better this way, believe me." Her lips felt tender and warm under his finger. What would those lips feel like under his mouth? "I will not let anything happen to your vases."

"Would you please stop calling them that?" she asked.

He slid his finger over her chin and under her jaw. He felt her swallow and touched a tiny vein tripping in her throat.

"Luc."

His name, even spoken in her throaty whisper, suddenly sounded so hollow. The need to have her call him by his real name suddenly kicked him in the stomach. He felt a voracious hunger, stirring his gut and making him hard.

He opened his hand and cupped the narrow column of her neck, his thumb settling on the translucent skin that dipped between her collarbones. "So tell me, Janine Coulter. When you threw your diamond ring down the toilet, was it a broken heart or a change of one?"

She attempted a valiant smile. "Both."

"Ah." He took a deep breath, loving the sweet, clean fragrance of her, slowly moving his other hand to her shoulder, turning her into him. "Do you know what the French do for a broken heart?"

She held his gaze as he traced the V neck of her silk top.

"They kiss it and make it better." Nothing, absolutely nothing, could stop him from taking his kiss. He placed his lips gently on hers, keeping his eager tongue at bay. The kiss was over in a few seconds. "For your broken heart."

He could feel her quivering just before she backed away. "I never said *mine* was broken. Just changed."

"Touché, ma belle," he said with a laugh. He wrapped her under his arm and closed the car door behind her. "Now come and enjoy our French cuisine and wine, and tell me all your secrets."

He suddenly wished very much that he could tell her his secrets, too.

Tristan Stewart watched the intimate exchange from a darkened car less than a block away and rolled his eyes. "Always the player. Ten minutes with a pretty woman and he's kissing her in the street."

The other FBI agent sitting next to him laughed softly. "Ya gotta hand it to the bastard," Paul Dunne said. "The guy's got a pair."

Tristan nodded, watching Luc curl a possessive arm around the good-looking American curator.

"I mean, shit," Paul continued. "It took a major set of *cojones* to move those damn vases that quickly. He had to miss two walks of a guard and at least six cameras."

"Yeah. He avoided half the security in Versailles, hid the real vases, planted the new ones, and still managed to pick up a chick on the way." Tristan watched Luc disappear into the shadows with Janine Coulter.

"He's the best there is," Paul said. "That's why you use him."

That was one reason. The other was that Tristan had made a pact with the devil five years ago.

"So, we gonna stick around and see if the guy gets laid, or what?" Paul took a sip of cold coffee and spat it back into the cup. "Cause if we're bettin', I definitely have my money on Tremont to get some tonight."

Luc would never seduce an American girl; it would be too much like going home. And it would be against his code of ethics. Tristan bit back a bitter laugh. The most celebrated thief in recent history, and yet he had his code of ethics.

He dumped his own cold coffee out the window. "Nah. Let's go."

CHAPTER
Five

Janine stood in the center of the king's bedchamber, surrounded by the ever-serious faces of her French colleagues as they stared at the stage designed to exhibit the Pompadour Plums.

Henri shook his head and toyed with the frames of his glasses, scratched his palms nervously, then folded his hands and tapped his fingertips together.

Janine didn't know whether to laugh or scream as he fussed and fidgeted like a kindergartner who had to go to the bathroom. But every time she looked at the three splendid vases on their snow-white draping, she really just wanted to cry. The gala would start in two hours, and the wrong vases were on display.

Henri had given her no indication he knew they were staring at forgeries. Her gut instinct told her to say nothing.

But when, oh God, *when* would the switch be made?

Simone de Vries barreled into the room, two security guards in tow. She was already dressed in a conservative navy gown for the gala, her helmet of hair looking as unyielding as ever. *"Où est Luc?"* she demanded of Henri. Then she glared at Janine and repeated in English, "Where is Luc?"

Janine had been asking herself that for three days.

"Je ne sais pas, madame," she answered. "I have not spoken to him." She'd last seen Luc after their dinner at Le Potager. He had taken her back to her hotel, walked her into the lobby, and air-kissed her cheek good night. Then he'd disappeared into the night.

Over dinner he had deftly kept the conversation light and easy, letting Janine tell him about her classes and students and her whirlwind preparations to come to France after Albert died. No discussion of her failed engagement. Much to her relief, there was no more kissing her broken heart to make it better. At least, she thought she was relieved. What else would she call the flutter in her stomach every time she turned a corner at the palace and thought she might see him . . . and he wasn't there? Good thing she wasn't counting on his protection from threats, real or imagined.

"He has something very important to do," Simone announced.

Oh yes, he does, Janine thought with a rueful glance at the woman. He has to switch the vases. No doubt she knew that, too.

"Please find me the minute he arrives." Simone swept out of the room.

Henri ran a hand through his hair and tugged at a stray whisker of his mustache. "There's nothing more to be done in here, *madame,*" he finally said to Janine. "We have to hope for the best."

She gave him a reassuring smile. "Don't worry, Henri. Everything is ready." Except the centerpiece of the exhibit. She looked at her watch. The doors opened in less than two hours. She had just enough time for one more check of the Hall of Mirrors before returning to her hotel room to change.

She paused in the main entrance of the Hall, under the massive banner that proclaimed the name of the exhibit: Pompadour! Mistress of the Enlightenment!

Blinking back an unexpected rush of emotion, Janine took in the beauty of the room. A thousand lights shimmered off the endless wall of mirrors. Through the graceful curve of the Palladian windows, the sun set over the gardens of Versailles, shooting fingers of scarlet and gold over the greenery and casting a celestial glow over the magnificent art.

No doubt the room looked exactly like this the evening Jeanne-Antoinette had been presented to Louis's court. Only on this night, instead of a king and hundreds of courtiers, the palace would host the president of France and hundreds of dignitaries, historians, diplomats, and the upper crust of French society.

Janine might not have as much at stake as Pompadour, but she had plenty to prove. Although she had no king waiting to take her to his bed to celebrate the triumph, no lover anticipating the thrill of a first tryst.

An unexpected face flashed in her mind—one with penetrating dark eyes and an alluring smile—and a shiver slid up her spine.

Driving to the hotel, she indulged in remembering the kiss Luc had stolen. The way he wrapped her up in that incredible voice, as smooth and sweet as hot caramel. She frowned as she parked in front of the Hôtel Trianon and handed her keys to a valet. Mr. Smooth better get the flippin' vases in place before the president showed up. That's *all* that mattered.

An undercurrent of excitement buzzed through the elegant lobby of the Trianon. Dignitaries and guests lounged at tables in the bar and gathered in small groups under a massive chandelier. Stiletto heels clicked along the black-and-white marble floor, and a potent mix of perfumes permeated the air. Beside men in stark formal wear, France's A-list women posed *Vogue*-like in an array of stunning gowns.

Her own selection was a black floor-length dress, professional but attractive. Not nearly as attractive as the amazing strapless column of white silk with a daring slit that she had chosen for her wedding, though. In a fit of self-pity, she'd thrown it in her suitcase when she'd left for France. Maybe sometime in the next year she'd have the desire to wear it for a formal event. But not tonight. Not yet.

Janine stuck the card key in her lock with a determined push, but the door swung open before the card made contact. It hadn't been latched. She blinked at the late-afternoon sun shimmering through sheer curtains.

Taking one tentative step inside, her hands rose to her mouth to trap the scream that threatened. The bed was stripped to reveal a slashed mattress. The armoire doors hung open, every drawer yanked out, their contents dumped onto the floor. Cosmetics and toiletries were strewn and smashed by the bathroom door. On the closet door, her black gown hung exactly as she had left it that morning.

Except for a scarlet shadow across the bodice.

Mesmerized, she took a few steps closer. It was almost impossible to see on the black silk, but it was there. A red pattern of some kind, made with paint or a marker. A long streak with slashes of lines coming out from it and . . . a tail. An animal? A bug?

At the double ring of the room phone, she let out a little shriek. Leaning into the doorway, she managed to see most of the bathroom. It looked empty.

The phone persisted.

With a shaking hand she lifted the receiver, half expecting a creepy warning and heavy breathing.

"Janine?" *Szha-neen.*

The sound of his voice nearly undid her, a sob choking her. "Oh, my God, Luc."

"What's the matter?"

"My room. Someone's . . . been . . . here."

"Don't move. I'll be right there. I'm in the lobby."

She dropped the receiver, staring at the scars in the mattress and imagining what kind of weapon could do such destruction. Who would do this? Why?

Thank God he'd called her.

I'm in the lobby.

What the hell was he doing *there?*

"*Sacré Dieu.*"

Janine jumped at the sound of his voice.

Luc stood in the doorway, a scowl darkening his

expression as he stared at the mess. He closed the space between them in two strides. "Are you all right?"

She hugged herself and nodded, not trusting her voice. He folded her into his chest and murmured soothingly in French. She gave in to the comfort of his embrace, then looked over his shoulder. "What—what's on my dress?"

He followed her gaze, breaking their contact and walking slowly to the closet. "*Merde*," he muttered, taking the fabric in his hands. "That fucking bastard."

The last curse was decidedly not French. "What is it? Who are you talking about?"

He yanked the dress off the hanger and rolled it into a ball, tossing it angrily on the floor. "*Rien*," he spat.

"Nothing?" She choked on the lump of fear still blocking her throat. "It doesn't look like *nothing* to me."

"Someone is trying to scare you, Janine."

"With a child's drawing of . . ." The realization kicked her in the chest. "A *scorpion?*"

"Something like that." He turned to her. "We've got to get you out of here. I'll contact security and have the room taken care of."

"But—but the gala. I have to be there in an hour."

"You can change in my room. I have one here for the night."

"Wait just a second." She held up two hands and resisted the urge to stamp her foot in frustration. "What the *hell* is going on?" Squeezing her eyes shut, she remembered the vases. "And why aren't the real Plums on display?"

"No." He shook his head and looked around the room. "Not now, certainly."

"Why? What does this have to do with it? Was somebody here looking for the vases? And what about that scorpion?" She pointed to the dress on the floor. "What does that mean? Wasn't that guy caught and killed years ago?"

He didn't look at her. "Yes. He's dead. This is . . ." He closed his eyes and sighed. "This is someone doing a damn poor imitation. Whoever did this is an idiot who knows nothing about . . . nothing."

He enclosed her hands in his large, warm fingers. "You must listen to me, Janine. The president of France will not know the difference. No one will, except you and me. And one or two others in the room, whom you won't even realize are there."

Frustration burned in her. Nothing made sense. Not this invasion of her room, not having fake vases on display for the gala, not his nonexplanations.

"After tonight," he said, "I promise that only the real Plums will be on display. And you can move them back into the Hall."

She couldn't fight with this force of a man right now. She just had to get through this night. Taking a step back, her gaze traveled over the magnificent tuxedo he wore.

"God damn it," she muttered. "Now what'll I wear?"

"Don't you have another gown?"

She looked over his shoulder, into the far recess of the closet. The plastic dress bag hung untouched. Somehow, the intruder had missed it. Then she closed her eyes and blew out a breath of pure defeat. "Yeah. I have one."

*   *   *

Luc took Janine to his room, avoiding her questions with vague answers, grateful that the impending gala demanded her focus and attention.

"All right," she told herself, as she dropped her purse on the bed and carried a small tote bag into the bathroom. "I can do this."

"Of course you can," he agreed, hanging her dress bag over a chair. "It won't do any good to lose your focus tonight, Janine." Nor for him. At the first signal, he would have to move instantly.

Through his peripheral vision, he could see her in the doorway of the bathroom, pulling a brush and hair dryer from a bag. In less than two seconds, he opened the purse she'd left on the bed and removed the room key that he'd seen her drop into a side pocket. Then he turned back into his closet, took a small leather satchel, and hustled to the door.

"I'll be back in half an hour, Janine. Is that enough time for you to dress?"

She stepped out of the bathroom and touched the dress bag, a strange look on her face. "Yes. That'll be fine."

Closing the door firmly behind him, he slipped down the stairwell and back to her room. Using her card key, he let himself in.

Something was very wrong with this picture. He didn't put anything past Karim Benazir's hired hands, but this just didn't fit the pattern of the last few weeks. Scooping up the black dress from the floor, he stuffed it into the bag. He checked the door that adjoined the next room to make sure it was locked. Then, in the hall, he pulled out a tiny screwdriver and slid it into the lock, scraping the card-reading mechanism. He slipped the *Ne Pas Déranger* sign on the door and left. No one would—or could—disturb this crime scene now.

In the parking garage, he hid the satchel in the trunk of his Alpha and flipped open his cell phone. At Tristan's curt greeting, he cleared his throat and put on the rich New England accent that he saved for the control freak FBI agent, just because it pissed him off to no end. "You need to get some housekeeping done in Janine Coulter's room at the Trianon."

"What happened?"

"She had guests. You don't want hotel security on this. Get her another room for tonight. I won't be able to take care of her."

He disconnected without waiting for a response. They never bothered with the slightest formality. It wasn't an attempt to be covert, and it sure wasn't because of the years they'd played rugby, swapped homework, and cut school together. They were both just too honest to pretend they felt anything but gut-level loathing for one another, no matter how badly they needed each other.

He gave Janine enough time to shower and dress and put on whatever makeup a woman that beautiful would think she'd need, then knocked lightly on his hotel room door before he entered.

She'd been staring out the window but turned at the sound, her pale hair flowing like a drape of satin over her arms. It left her bare shouldered and swathed in white. A goddess, in every sense of the word.

The white material clung to her, tight enough to hug

the womanly swell of her breasts and sheer enough for a man's imagination to easily visualize what was underneath. It made him ache with instant arousal. He'd better get used to it. With her in that dress, he'd be hard anytime she was around tonight.

She didn't waste a moment on pleasantries. "Did you get security in the room? Do they have any idea who was in there? Did they look for fingerprints?"

"Yes. No. No."

"No *what?* No fingerprints?" Her cornflower blue eyes, lightly dusted with some kind of sparkly shadow, narrowed in demand. "I want to talk to security."

He shook his head and took a step toward her. Against the white of her dress, her sun-kissed skin glowed like she'd been polished. "The gala starts in a few minutes. They have had some break-ins in the hotel. Security thinks this is another of those."

He couldn't stop himself from running a finger over her shoulder and touching a lock of hair. A flush deepened her cheeks, but she didn't sidestep his touch. His gaze dropped to her bodice and traveled down the elegant dress. *"Tu parais ravissant."*

"Thank you." Her own gaze darted briefly over him. "Ditto. In English."

He grinned at the reluctant compliment. As she reached for a beaded evening bag on the bed, a dramatic slit in the side of her dress revealed a taut, tanned thigh. He sucked in a heated breath.

"I can't find my room key," she said. "I must have left it when I packed."

"You won't need it."

At the tone of his voice, she looked up and their gazes locked. "Excuse me?" Slowly she straightened, the swell of her breasts expanding as she drew an indignant breath. His pulse danced in response. "I certainly *will* need my own room."

His lips curled in a half smile. Oh, it would be fun to tease her. To seduce her. To completely undo her. "I have arranged for your belongings to be moved to another room, and you can pick up a new key later tonight."

"Oh. It appears you've thought of everything."

"Not everything." He raised an eyebrow toward the slit. "I hadn't thought of a limousine, and you might have a bit of a challenge getting in my car."

She smoothed the fabric over her legs. "I'll manage. I have a job to do."

And so did he. And when it was over, Luc Tremont would disappear.

What a shame. He'd have enjoyed just one taste of this woman. Just one journey over her silky skin, to inhale her delicate scent and bury himself in her glossy hair and sexy body. To hear her beg for his hands and mouth and body, and call out his name, his real name, in her musical American voice.

Nick. Nick.

But that was a sound Nick Jarrett would never hear again.

CHAPTER
Six

The echo of six hundred self-important voices, the ring of crystal champagne flutes, and the strains of a small orchestra resonated throughout the magnificent palace. Janine imagined the night when Louis XV donned branches as his masquerade and mingled with his guests, looking for the young Parisian woman rumored to love the woods. She smiled at the image of the king disguised as a tree.

"What amuses you, Janine?" Luc leaned too close, his husky voice sending delicious vibrations down to her toes.

She shrugged, her bare shoulder brushing against the sleeve of his tuxedo jacket. He was always so *near*. "History amuses me," she answered, and looked up at him. How had he managed to notice her expression, when his own gaze never left the crowd? "And of course, I'm pleased at the success of the gala."

He spared her a quick, skeptical glance. "It's far from over."

But they had made it through the first hour without incident. Luc looked away, and she followed his stare to a man with dark blond hair and steely gray eyes. He wore a tuxedo, not nearly as well-tailored as Luc's. His arms were folded across his broad chest, his expression impassive as he stared right back at Luc. Then his attention shifted to her. She shivered under the man's intense scrutiny, which lacked the warm appraisal of most of Luc's countrymen.

"He's not French," she muttered softly.

Luc cleared his throat and smiled. "Not in the least."

"Do you know him?" she asked.

"We've met." He put a possessive hand on her lower back and guided her in the opposite direction. "The reception line for the president is forming. Aren't you expected to be in it?"

Damn! She'd lost track of the time. "I'll find Henri and take my place." She paused as he fell into step with her. "Don't tell me you're in the reception line, too?"

"I could be. If you need protection." A slight smile played at the corner of his lips. "Be careful, *ma belle.*"

"Of what, *monsieur?*" She matched his sotto voice.

He grazed her shoulder with a fingertip. "A beautiful woman must beware of the *dragueurs.*"

"*Dragueurs?*"

"The relentless Frenchmen who target American women," he explained. "They are everywhere."

"I thought you were watching for thieves."

"I am watching everything," he assured her, so close she could practically taste the subtle spice of his aftershave. She imagined the scrape of his whiskers against her cheek. Her throat. Her breasts. "Especially you."

"I'll be fine, thank you. I don't need your supervision."

On the contrary; she needed to get away from him. She hadn't come to France to flirt.

His smile widened to a predatory grin, and she swore he knew what she was thinking. "I'm never far," he said softly.

"I've noticed." She turned toward the line and ignored his soft chuckle, her nerves stretched to their limit.

Why was she so anxious tonight? Was it Luc, making scrambled eggs out of her brain?

No. She was just unnerved by the significance of the night, the size of the crowd, the pressure to perform. Not to mention the ominous message left in her hotel room by a supposedly dead legend, and the fact that Henri had "accidentally" distributed the old programs that still had Albert's name on them. She'd approved a new version, but he'd blamed a printing glitch. Forged vases and a palace crawling with the media and the French version of Secret Service didn't exactly relax her, either.

Luc was just another distraction. A big, gorgeous, flirtatious, sexy distraction who made her feel like he wanted to rip her dress off and eat her for dinner.

Squaring her shoulders and tilting her chin, she stopped to say hello to a young woman who worked for the Ministry of Culture, but a dark-skinned man with piercing black eyes forced himself in front of her.

"Madame Coulter, excusez-moi de vous déranger." His tone

was frosty enough for her to know the polite words surely preceded an intrusive question. A quick glance at the press credentials that hung around his neck confirmed it. *Le Figaro* was a right-wing newspaper that had been outspoken in its disdain of the choice for curator of the Pompadour exhibit.

Dealing with the media was part of the job, but she didn't have to like it. *"Une question seulement. En Anglais, s'il vous plaît."* He was her height, which allowed her to stare directly into his eyes. He reminded her of one of her more arrogant students, about to dispute a grade.

Stroking a wispy goatee, he inhaled slowly, either preparing for the language switch or getting ready to pounce. "Could you please tell me why the Plums are not . . ." As he paused to search for a word, Janine flashed on what he might say. *Why the Plums are not real?* But that was ridiculous. He couldn't know that.

" . . . on general display for the guests who have paid thousands to see them?" the reporter concluded.

Janine gave him a tight smile. "They are readily available for viewing in the anteroom."

"Was this your idea, *madame?*" The reporter tightened the space between them. "I saw the original plans of the exhibit prior to your arrival, and the vases were right there." He pointed to the very spot where Janine had stood and made her plea to Henri just a few days earlier.

"It's not unusual to alter the layout of the exhibit to accommodate the traffic flow, Mr.— Mr.—" She glanced at his badge. "Mr. Surjeet. They are far more secure this way."

"Is there a specific security concern?" he asked.

Of course the media would be looking for the news that had nothing to do with *art*. "Security is always a concern when treasures as priceless as the Pompadour Plums are on display."

"Would you be kind enough to take me to the Sèvres vases now, *madame?* Perhaps highlight some of the details with your noted expertise?" Sarcasm and accusation dripped from the question. But instead of kick-starting a self-defense mechanism, a tingle of apprehension danced through her. God, she was a mess tonight.

"I'm so sorry. I'm expected in the reception line now." She started to turn away.

He put an unwelcome hand on her arm. *"Why* aren't the Plums in plain view?"

"I've already answered that." She dropped her gaze to where his olive brown fingers squeezed her skin. "They are simply being guarded. *Excusez-moi, s'il vous plait."*

She pivoted in the opposite direction before he could respond. She could almost swear he'd been testing her about the imposter Plums, but that was utterly impossible.

Taking her place in the reception line, she greeted the first of several hundred people, shaking the gloved hand of a bank president's wife and reciting her prepared greeting. *"Bon soir, madame. Bienvenue à Pompadour."*

Two hours later, her cheeks hurting, her feet aching, and her hand feeling like it could drop off her wrist with one more shake, Janine said her simple phrase to the last person in line. She scanned the six hundred guests as they milled about the Hall of Mirrors. Where was Luc?

Probably in the king's bedchamber guarding the faux Plums.

The public address system crackled with the announcement that the president was about to make a brief address. Janine checked her watch and fought a wave of annoyance. What was going on? They were twenty minutes early.

She began to work through the crowd toward the stage and podium. They had rehearsed this presentation repeatedly that afternoon, and it was timed to the minute. Following the first announcement, she was supposed to take the stage and introduce Claude Marchionette, who would present the president.

She resisted the urge to elbow people out of her way, her heart sinking when she heard the nasal tones of Henri Duvoisier. What was he doing up there? She stopped and listened.

Giving *her* speech, that's what he was doing! The *snake*.

And since the program had Albert's name listed, no one would question why she wasn't speaking. Damn him.

Maneuvering behind a petite woman, she could do nothing except watch the older man read from her very own notes that she'd placed on the podium. It was so outrageous. She'd been sandbagged.

The image of her slashed mattress and defaced gown burned in her mind like an eerie negative photo. No; perhaps she'd been *warned*.

To march up there now and muscle him out of the

way would only make her look foolish, although every cell in her body wanted to do so. Anyway, he was already reading the paragraph about international pride. *Which meant he'd skipped the section on the Plums.* The slimy little weasel.

He finished to polite applause and turned the microphone over to the portly minister of culture. Marchionette's voice boomed over the hushed crowd, but Janine didn't need to hear his speech again. She'd heard it three times today. She turned on her heel, fury fueling her steps.

She moved to the back of the Hall and saw Simone de Vries speaking rapidly to a uniformed guard. As she approached them, Simone turned and left the Hall. Janine caught the eye of the guard.

"Excusez-moi. Have you seen Monsieur Tremont?" she asked him.

"Madame de Vries just asked the same question," he replied. "I saw him about an hour ago, near the gaming room."

"Merci, monsieur." The gaming room? Where the passageway to the chapel was hidden. Could he have gone to see the Plums? To finally make the exchange? As she crossed the Hall, she pictured the mirror and hidden door. Could she figure out how he opened the passageway, and then navigate her way through the dark?

Pausing under an archway, she glanced toward the stage where the minister extolled the French president's unwavering support for the arts. But she didn't see the man at the podium, because her gaze was caught by icy gray eyes. This time, the man didn't seem quite so menacing. She could have sworn he raised an eyebrow, and the slightest hint of a smile lifted his lip.

Who *was* that man and why did he seem so interested in her? One of Luc's *dragueurs?* She saw his mouth move as though he spoke to himself. Or into a hidden microphone.

Oh. Not one of Luc's *dragueurs*. One of Luc's henchmen.

She left the Hall of Mirrors, heading straight for the grand vestibule outside the king's suite. It was empty, as every guest had crowded into the Hall in anticipation of the president's speech. Two impassive guards flanked the entryway to the bedchamber. Only one let his gaze sweep over her. The other took his responsibility very seriously, staring straight ahead.

A thunderous ovation burst from the Hall of Mirrors. The president must have taken the podium. She continued toward a hallway that ran alongside all of the rooms.

"Where are you going in such a hurry?"

Spinning around, she met the beady eyes of the *Figaro* reporter. She hadn't heard him approach her over the applause. "What do you want?"

"*Pardon, Madame.* You are anxious to go somewhere, *non?*"

She nodded and tilted her head away from him. "*La salle de bain.*" Surely he wouldn't follow her to the bathroom.

"*Madame,* I must ask you, how closely have you looked at those vases?" He took a step toward her. "I seriously doubt their authenticity."

She inched away. Did he mean the forgeries, or was he

simply another critic who thought the whole concept of the Plums was bogus? "There is nothing to doubt."

"Perhaps you could prove that to me right now." Again he crept closer. "Perhaps you will show me the markings and allow me to examine the underglaze."

If he was smart enough to know what an underglaze was, maybe he really did know something about porcelain. His sneaky eyes narrowed, and a band of moisture formed above his thick upper lip. No, this guy was more smarmy than smart.

"I'm afraid I can't, *monsieur*." He'd literally backed her into the hall. She couldn't even see the guard—and the guard couldn't see her. "If you'll excuse me," she held up her tiny purse as though it could stop him. "I'm certain you can examine the vases from the viewing station, as all the other . . ." Her gaze dropped pointedly to his media badge, but there was nothing around his neck now. Her throat closed up. "As the other *reporters* have done."

"I am not like the others." He reached into his jacket pocket, and she expected the identification badge to appear. "As you can see."

The flash of steel kicked a breath out of her lungs. She stared at the knife, and then looked into his eyes.

Lives are at risk, Szha-neen. Your life.

She pivoted on her heel and ran. Another round of applause rose from the Hall of Mirrors, lasting as long as it took her to reach the door to the Library. A sudden, muffled pop in the midst of the clamor halted her midstep.

What was that sound?

The quickening thump of her own heartbeat blocked out the ovation. Behind her, footsteps echoed. She shoved her handbag under her arm and scooped her dress up to her knees. At the end of the hallway were the double doors to the Gaming Room.

The secret passageway.

As she ran, she heard another dull thud. Almost like a gunshot . . . with a silencer.

Holy, *holy* hell. What was going on out there?

Blood pumped through her ears as her heel slid on the Gaming Room's polished parquet floor and caught on the edge of an Oriental carpet. She stumbled to the marble mantel, pounding it as she willed herself to remember the trick to the hidden door.

"Damn. Damn, come on!" The bag slipped out from under her arm as she used both hands to shove a heavy table next to the fireplace aside. Standing in front of the gilded mirror above the mantel, her quick breaths fogged the glass as she jammed her trembling hand behind the frame. She slid her fingers up and down as Luc had. At last she hit a metal dial, and she turned it to the right until it clicked. The paneled wall next to the fireplace opened.

She dove into the darkness of the passageway and jerked the panel back in place. It latched with a definitive clunk, leaving her in the cool blackness of Louis's safe haven.

Even with a silencer, Luc heard the gunshot and knew the heist had begun. He was already in position in the Council Chamber, behind the ornate closet doors, watching a tiny monitor transmitting video from two different cameras hidden in the king's bedchamber. At the moment of the thunderous applause, four men approached the door, and with each shot fired, Tristan's well-rehearsed guards fell as though they hadn't been wearing bullet-proof vests. Exactly as planned.

From the upper corner of the screen, he could see four men enter the room. Two dragged the guards' bodies into the room, then left, closing the doors behind them. On watch, no doubt. The two remaining men moved directly to the exhibit. The video was grainy, but he could make out their features well enough to know he'd never seen them before. Of course, he didn't expect Karim Benazir himself to show up—just his lackeys.

One by one, they rolled the vases in thick burlap. Take care, he silently warned. The longer those Plums stayed intact, the longer they could relay the information he needed. When they'd finished, one of them stared for a moment at the white silk material Luc had insisted be part of the exhibit.

Come on. *Draw.*

After a moment, the thief pulled out a red marker.

Luc lifted the tiny microphone to his lips as the thief sketched a clumsy scorpion. "Bingo," he whispered.

"A scorpion?" Tristan sounded almost disappointed, but it could have been the static.

"You hate it when I'm right."

"I don't know if you're right yet."

"You will soon." Luc smiled into the microphone. He liked symmetry. And irony. Benazir thought he was luring the Scorpion and getting a priceless treasure at the same time. In truth, the Indian was setting himself up and getting worthless junk vases.

"Don't screw this up, Luc."

"Keep your suits away for five days, Tris. Then you'll get what you want."

And so would he. Not a full pardon, and no chance of resuming life as Nick Jarrett; the director wouldn't consider it. But he'd get a new life, a new name, and a new home on American soil. That would be his reward for taking Benazir's bait and risking his life to get the bastard back in jail.

"You're gonna need some help," Tristan warned.

"I'll call you if I miss you." Luc had to make Benazir think he was working alone, zealously trying to prove that this new Scorpion was an imposter. If Benazir thought he was working with the FBI, the dethroned prince would vanish. The safety of Switzerland was just a wide, open border away.

Another loud ovation burst from the Hall of Mirrors as the two thieves nonchalantly opened the doors.

"They're leaving," Luc said. "They're outside the chamber with the vases under their arms."

"Ballsy bastards, aren't they?"

Luc grinned. It was exactly how he would have done it. No doubt the four of them formed a tight group that hid the vases between them as they strolled out the front door of the palace.

"Hold your position," Tristan ordered. "Give them plenty of time."

"I'm leaving now," Luc announced.

"Just wait a goddamn minute."

Luc reached into his ear to take the transmitter out, but wasn't fast enough.

"Your girlfriend is missing."

"What?" His gut tightened.

"The American curator. She got squeezed out of the speeches and left fuming."

He swore under his breath. "Was she alone?"

"I saw a reporter hounding her."

A reporter? Would Janine take a reporter to see the real Plums? Damn, he shouldn't have shown them to her. But he'd wanted her to be the hero, to produce the real Plums after the "heist." It was the least he could do after wrecking her big night.

"Why didn't she give her speech?" He'd thought she'd be safe while all this was going on. She'd be up on the podium, in front of thousands of people and under the watchful eyes of the French Secret Service.

"Seems the museum folks had other ideas."

The guards on the ground finally stood, evidently getting the "all clear" whispered in their ears from someone else.

"I'm leaving," he told Tristan. "Give me five days, and I'll give you Benazir."

Without waiting for a response, he tugged the earpiece out and opened the closet doors. He took the side entrance through the king's privy and into the darkened Clock Chamber, then continued through the connected rooms.

She *wouldn't* have taken someone to see the Plums, would she?

The minute he stepped into the Gaming Room, he

noticed the table that blocked the panel to the passage-way had been moved. He certainly hadn't left it that way.

Oh, God.

As he approached it, something caught his eye on the Oriental carpet. A small white handbag.

Son of a bitch. She *did*.

CHAPTER
Seven

The brilliant craftsmen of the eighteenth century had managed to create a completely soundproof chamber. Dark and creepy as hell, but safe from that scary little man and his knife.

Janine leaned against the rough wall and gave into the weakness in her legs. Sliding down, she felt the surface snag her silk dress. She closed her eyes and shuddered. She'd lived in L.A. long enough to know the sound of a gunshot, silenced or not.

As her breathing returned to normal and her heart stopped racing, she remembered her purse. Oh, *hell*. Why didn't she just leave a sign for the reporter? *This way, whacko. Behind the secret door.*

What if he found the passageway? Maybe she should go deeper, to where the hallway curved. At least she'd be out of sight if he did get the door open.

She stood unsteadily. Holding out her hands in a classic blind man's walk, she tiptoed along the stone floor. After what seemed like an eternity of creeping forward, her hands hit the angle of the wall. Yes. The turn. As she began to navigate around it, she heard a scraping sound from behind her, and a soft light glazed the curved wall just as she slipped behind it.

Someone was in the passageway with her.

If that reporter caught her and . . . Fear skittered down her back. No one would hear her scream. They might never even find her. Her heart hammered so loud, she was sure it would give her away.

Reaching into the darkness, she found the handle of the chapel door, gave it a hard push, and practically tumbled over the threshold into the shadowy church. Closing the door behind her, she kicked off her shoes and snatched them up by the ankle straps. The marble floor chilled her bare feet as she scampered toward the balustrade and looked down into the sanctuary.

"Oh, my God." She clutched the railing.

Forty feet below, the tabernacle door stood wide open. It was impossible to see inside from her vantage point, so she tripped down the stone steps in the back of the church and ran up the aisle toward the gaping golden case.

No. *No.*

Her Plums were gone.

She reached the altar, panting for air, searching for an explanation. Luc must have moved them. He'd been gone during the whole reception line. He'd moved them. He *had* to. What the hell—

"What the hell?"

Janine spun around at the echo of her thoughts and looked straight into the face of Luc Tremont.

White, hot fury exploded in his head. He stared at the empty tabernacle and swore again, not even caring if his French accent was lost. Taking the three stairs in one stride, he jumped the gate and approached the altar.

If Benazir was responsible for the theft upstairs, then who the hell masterminded this one?

"I thought no one else knew they were here."

He heard the accusation in Janine's voice, but when he turned, he only saw devastation in her eyes.

"No one did." Only Tristan. And if he found this hiding place empty, *all bets were off*.

Tristan would only see that the priceless artifacts, hidden by Luc's own hand, were missing. A neat confirmation of the suspicion Tristan held for five years: that Nick Jarrett, the former thief turned FBI undercover informant, obviously wasn't as "rehabilitated" as he claimed.

Luc glared at the spot where the Plums had stood. He could claim he hadn't led a thief to the vases, but nothing he could say would change Tristan's convictions. He'd never get his five days. He'd never get Benazir. He'd never get *home*.

He only had one option. He had to find the vases fast, and return them. Then he could get back on Benazir's trail. He had five days. He could do it.

"Luc," he heard Janine say. "We have to get the Plums."

He ran a hand through his hair and finally focused on her. "I will."

She'd managed to climb the railing and get behind the altar with him. "How?"

"I placed a tracking device in one of the vases." He

blessed the gut instinct that made him insure against exactly this kind of foul-up.

"Who the hell are you, James Freaking Bond?"

He closed the tabernacle door. "Just doing my job. I'll find them. You," he looked at her, "are not going to say a word about this to anyone."

"What?" She practically spat the word. "Of course I am. This is a serious crime."

Only one lock remained on the door, and he started to clamp it closed.

She grabbed his arm. "What are you doing?"

"No one needs to know they are missing, Janine." It would be a while until Tristan even checked their agreed upon hiding place for the real Plums. By then, Luc could have found and returned them. "No one needs to know they've ever been taken."

He saw the doubt darken her eyes. "Why wouldn't we tell the police about this? How could *you,* Mr. God's-Answer-to-Security, not report this?"

"Because by the time the French police and gendarmerie and DST untangle their red tape and figure out who's supposed to investigate this, your Plums will be so deep into the underground that you won't see them for another two hundred years." He scanned the marble floor for the other lock.

"And how will you know they're the real Plums once you find them?"

"I'll know. I've got a track—"

She grabbed his shoulder. "I'm going with you."

He stared at her for a second, noting the fire in her eyes and the set to her jaw. Then he lifted the altar cloth to see if the lock had fallen under there. "No, you're not."

"Oh, yes I am." She shook the cloth out of his hand.

"Forget it."

Her expression softened to a plea. "I won't be able to live with myself if anything happens to those Plums, Luc."

Was she *serious?* "Look, you have no idea what you're getting into. No idea what just went on upstairs. There was another theft. The forgeries were stolen. Guards were shot." Not hurt, but she didn't need to know that now.

"All the more reason for me to go with you. The cops will be focused on that theft, and there will be two sets of vases out there, and only I can tell good from bad." She looked so damn pleased with her logic. Which, he had to admit, was sound.

"I work alone," he said simply, turning away to search for the missing lock.

"So where should I tell the police you went, after you—supposedly the only person who knew where the real vases were—discovered they were missing?"

He stopped hunting and glared at her. "You won't tell them anything."

"Not even that you"—she pointed to the tabernacle— "destroyed the evidence?"

He scowled. "What are you saying?"

"That I can make you look guilty as hell." She held onto the altar for balance as she calmly slipped a shoe on one foot. "You need me." She slipped on the other shoe.

A siren wailed outside and someone shouted. Damn it, every exit would be blocked by police and security in a matter of minutes. He didn't have time to negotiate with a willful woman, but leaving her behind would guarantee Tristan would discover the missing vases.

He took one last look at the tabernacle and grabbed her hand. "You'd better be able to run."

Before she could ask why, he rushed her out the exit he knew was concealed under the sixth station of the cross.

From his penthouse suite in a far corner of the Royal Parc Evian hotel, Karim Benazir lifted his head from the massage table and stared at the serene waters of Lake Geneva. But he didn't see the moonlight dancing over the famed crescent-shaped body of water, or the reflection of Evian-les-Bains' glittering casino lights. He was picturing the events taking place three hundred and fifty miles away in another luxurious setting. He had the best people in the world working in Versailles, but still, he longed to be in the middle of the action.

Of course, he would never compromise his newfound liberty by appearing in public. Not yet.

"You must relax, Your Highness." Larinna's voice in his beloved Sanskrit tongue interrupted his thoughts. He let her ease his head back into the fleece-lined opening of the bench. She continued her ministrations, a little harder, a little deeper into his taut muscles. He let out a satisfied breath. He'd missed this during the five years he'd just spent in hell.

Impatience made him lift his head again, unable to

stomach the waiting, his sharp gaze taking in the sur-
roundings.

"Are you satisfied with the accommodations, sire?"

He grunted. Rich draperies pooled around the floor-
to-ceiling windows overlooking the lake. Magnificent
frescoes covered the walls.

This was how he was meant to live. It was in his soul.
Literally, in his blood. It was bad enough his own people
had turned him out in favor of democracy, but then Nick
Jarrett had destroyed the second empire Karim had built.
And he had to pay for that.

As though on cue, the gentle trill of a phone cut into
his thoughts.

He hoisted his girth from the massage table, vaguely
aware that he'd nearly toppled Larinna, and grabbed a
cell phone on the bed. "Yes?"

"The Scorpion has struck."

Karim breathed steadily, letting Claude Marchionette's
thick French permeate his being. Praise Allah, he'd done
it. He dropped onto the bed and glanced down at his
naked body, his cock already arched from the massage.
"Do we have both sets?"

"Of course we do, Karim."

Disgust rolled through him at the use of his first
name, but he didn't bother to chastise the Frenchman.
They still needed each other. "How did you find the genuine vases?"

"I placed a very good woman in charge of security,"
Marchionette boasted. "Now I have completed my job. I
expect the same from you, Karim."

Karim despised the subtle threat, but managed to

control his response. "In a matter of weeks the counterfeit vases will travel through the usual underground and quickly be revealed as fake."

"And you will destroy the real vases," Marchionette reminded him. "The world will only know that one set ever existed and that set is a forgery. As you know, this is the only reason why I would jeopardize my career and life to assist you. The Plums must be destroyed."

As if he would ever ruin such beauty. "Of course. You may consider it done already." In fact, the Pompadour Plums would join the other priceless art he collected and would someday be given a place of honor, when he managed to reseat himself on his throne. But they had another purpose, first. Scorpion bait.

He hung up without giving the self-important French bastard an opportunity to threaten him again. Loathing rolled through him. That's what Nick Jarrett had stolen from him: not just his freedom, but respect.

The Plums were a bonus, really. As much as he wanted them, he wanted the Scorpion more. It had been easy enough to put his organization back in place from that minimum security/maximum discomfort hellhole of a jail. But his spirit hadn't been moved to action until the day that he received a letter from France. A single page, bearing the four most motivating words he'd ever read: Nick Jarrett is alive.

Oh yes. The Scorpion still lived and breathed. In France, working for the government of the United States. On art crimes—what a joke.

He stroked himself absently while he tried to erase the impudent tone of Marchionette's voice from his memory. That idiot hadn't thought of any of this. All he did was agree to make it easy, and his price was stupidly low: destroy the real Plums and let the fakes be "discovered." If the man had any balls or brains, he'd want money, too.

Karim was the genius behind this plan. He'd figured out a way to get the FBI to produce the imitation vases he would sell on the black market. And he'd even ensured that if the genuine article was tracked and found, there could only be one perpetrator of the crime: Nick Jarrett. All the while, the Scorpion would be crawling directly to him, on his belly, stinger out. To be crushed.

And if not, there was always Plan B. B for *Boston*.

The phone rang in his hand. When he answered it, he could tell immediately that something was wrong. Surjeet's voice never cracked.

"What is it?" Karim demanded.

"There is a problem, Your Highness."

Had he lost the vases? "What?"

"The Scorpion is not alone. I followed him, and he left with the American curator."

Karim spat out a curse. The only person in France who could tell the vases apart in a matter of minutes. "She was supposed to have been under Marchionette's control," he rasped.

"I tried to distract her, but she knew where the vases were." Surjeet cleared his throat nervously.

Why? Why would Nick Jarrett compromise himself and bring a woman along? His gaze moved to the generous body of his own traveling companion, who stood a few feet away. Of course. Jarrett would use a woman for the same reason he did. Protection.

"Does this change anything, sir?" Surjeet asked.

"Not yet. Deliver the vases as instructed, quickly. You may not have much time." Karim mentally reviewed his plans and the placement of his men. "The Scorpion will be closely watched, don't worry."

"What about the American?"

He could not take the chance of the esteemed Dr. Coulter getting her hands on the vases and ruining his plans. "Do exactly what we discussed with the vases." He watched his cock harden as an idea formed. "Then I want her out. Gone. It should be easy to make it look like the Scorpion killed her."

Without waiting for Surjeet to respond, he dropped the phone on the floor.

Larinna stooped to pick it up, then held out the bottle of massage oil. "Would you care to continue, Your Highness?"

He muttered a Sanskrit word under his breath, as he stroked and engorged himself. Yes, a woman could be used for many things. How ironic that the Scorpion and the Prince had so much in common.

CHAPTER
Eight

Janine hoped Luc knew what he was doing, because it looked like they were trapped between a sea of limousines and six hundred drunken gala guests. Around the perimeter of the main building, uniformed guards, police, and plainclothes Secret Service had formed a blockade.

"Will they let us out?" she asked.

He shot her a threatening look. "No questions for a few minutes, all right? Just follow me." He led her toward a two-foot-wide pathway between the chapel and the main entrance of the palace. She cursed her high heels as she jogged to keep up with his long strides. Along the shadowy walls of the west wing, he moved so quickly, she nearly stumbled. When they reached a steep set of stairs to the gardens, he stopped suddenly.

"Can you manage these?" He sounded doubtful and ready to dump her in the nearest fountain.

She peered down into the massive labyrinth of gardens beyond the steps, then bent over to slide her sandals off. "Of course."

As they darted past a series of geometric pools, an icy spray misted her, sending a chill over her skin. He didn't seem to notice as he slowed and scanned the landscape.

"Now where?" she asked, rubbing her arms with a shoe in each hand.

"This way. Into the trees."

L'Orangerie was the only section of the gardens not bathed in decorative lights. He tugged her deeper into the dense orange groves, the sweet fragrance of citrus and pomegranates nearly suffocating her. Dirt and stones stabbed her bare feet. A sharp branch scraped her bare arm; her hair and dress were snagged every few feet by twigs. *Where was he going?*

They zigzagged through the grove until she saw the lights of the pièce d'Eau des Suisses, the fountain at the edge of the palace grounds. The only thing left was an impenetrable wall of shrubbery that surrounded the gardens.

"How are we going to get out?"

"Through the exit," he said, as calmly as if they'd chosen a more traditional departure. "Straight ahead."

Tucked in the middle of the ten-foot-tall barrier of foliage was a waist-high iron gate that probably functioned as a service entrance. He shook it once, clattering a thick metal chain. Without another word, he braced himself on the gate and hurdled it in one smooth movement. Turning, he reached for her.

"Hold your dress," he commanded, sliding his hands under her arms and hoisting her up with the ease of a parent lifting a child.

The opening led to a narrow street lined with

wrought iron gaslights, a row of sandstone homes, and a few parked cars. The suburbs of Versailles. He guided her to one of the cars and opened the passenger door.

"Get in," he said.

As she slid onto the cold seat, a jagged tear in the leather scratched her exposed thigh.

Tossing his jacket in the backseat, Luc jumped in and yanked down the visor. Slapping it back in place, he reached in front of her and snapped open the glove box. He patted the inside quickly, then swore softly. Bending over, he reached under his seat, feeling around with his eyes closed.

"*Voilà,*" he said, producing a key and stabbing it into the ignition.

As he whipped the Volvo out of its parking spot, she asked, "Was this waiting here for you or did you just steal it?"

He merely drove down the main boulevard, loosening his bow tie so it hung open from his shirt collar. His dark hair flirted with his collar, and his powerful arms and chest seemed overwhelming in the small space of the car.

Janine forced herself to look away from the compelling image he made. Better to think about what she was doing, not who she was doing it with. "Where are we going?"

He took his eyes off the road long enough to let his gaze slide all the way down her dress, then back to her face. "You ask a lot of questions for an uninvited guest."

She plucked an orange twig out of her hair and flicked it onto the floor. "Yeah? Well, you run pretty fast for someone with nothing to hide."

He didn't respond, his attention frozen on the rearview mirror. "We have company."

"Who?" She rolled down her window to get a better look at her side view mirror. A white car had appeared, perhaps half a mile behind them. "Who is that?"

"The Police Nationale. Close your window."

She did, but kept an eye on the mirror. "It's okay. You're not speeding or running red lights; we haven't done anything wrong."

His eyes never moved from the mirror.

"Have we?" Janine looked again, seeing the blue light bar across the roof of the car. It wasn't on . . . yet. Luc kept the speed steady and watched the rearview mirror, his expression taut and intense. Her heart dipped. "You just stole this car, didn't you?"

"Do you want to find the Plums?"

She glared at him. "I'm going to assume that's a rhetorical question."

"Then you must do precisely as I tell you." He turned a corner and the police car followed. "Believe me, we do not want him to request the *carte grise*. We do not want him to ask for registration, insurance, or identification or *anything*. Is that clear? We want him to leave us alone."

His tone left no room for an argument.

"Okay." The lights were closer. "How do we do that?"

"Take off your dress."

She felt her jaw go slack. "What?"

"Take off your dress." He repeated the words slowly, as though she couldn't understand plain, ridiculous English requests. "Someone may have reported you as missing after the theft. You are a suspect. They will detain us for hours."

"A suspect? That's ridiculous." She shook her head and looked at the reflection of the car again. They were no closer. "Anyway, they won't recognize me."

"Every minute, the Plums get further away and out of our reach." He waved a hand toward her. "They'll be looking for someone fitting your description, wearing a long white dress. It's your choice if you want to stay and argue with the French police, or get on the road to the vases."

She opened her mouth to disagree, but closed it again. "Don't you think stark naked is just a tad more conspicuous than a simple white dress?"

"Not for what I have in mind."

What did he have in mind? "We didn't *do* anything. We're innocent and we'll explain that to them."

He pierced her with a deadly look. "If they arrest us, you will never see your Plums again. Ever. Believe me."

Fear clutched her heart. It was bad enough if someone took the Plums to sell them on the black market. She couldn't take the chance that someone would destroy them. The blue light of the police car suddenly flashed.

She reached under the arm of her dress and began to slide the zipper down. She had nothing but sheer white panties underneath. No bra. No slip. No significant coverage of any kind. "Don't you dare look," she warned.

A flicker of a smile tipped his lips. "Of course not."

She slid the fabric down her torso. The air blowing through the vents shocked her skin.

"Put it on the floor," he instructed, still intent on the rearview mirror. "Under the seat."

She slipped the material under her backside and down her legs, stashed it as instructed, and covered her bare breasts with crossed arms.

"No." Luc grasped her wrist in his hand. "Put your head in my lap."

She stared at him.

"Janine." His voice was as intense as his focus on the mirror. "Do as I say."

"Is that necess—"

He palmed her head and pushed her into his crotch. She grunted in discomfort as the gear shift lever poked her ribs. "Sorry," he said. "Stay there. We need the element of surprise on our side."

She ignored the order enough to turn her head and peer up at him. With his left hand, he stripped the tie out of his collar and in one yank, popped the tuxedo studs and ripped open the shirt.

"What are you doing?"

"Undressing."

Her face was pressed against solid abdomen muscles, and the back of her head thumped against the steering wheel. But that wasn't the worst part. Under her ear, she felt a very definite bulge. Wasn't this *pretend?*

Steel-like stomach muscles contracted against her face. "We're being pulled over." His perfect American accent stunned her. Flawless, flat, and midwestern.

She struggled to lift her head, but he held her in place as the car slowed and veered to the right.

"Wait," he ordered in that bizarre American English.

"Wait till he's reached the window, then sit up so that he can see you. *All* of you." As he spoke, his fingers fumbled with something in his lap. Good God, he was opening his pants!

She pushed her head against his hand and looked up just as he looked down. "We don't need total realism, okay?"

His eyes glinted for a split second. *"Ne t'inquiétes pas,"* he whispered, French again. But at that moment, she *was* worried.

A blue light flashed in the rearview mirror.

"Wait . . . Wait . . . ," he ordered. "Okay, now." He burrowed his fingers in her hair and gently guided her head up. Just as she cleared the steering wheel, a beam of light flooded the interior of the car and something metal rapped hard against the glass.

Luc lowered the window. "We've been busted, honey," he said with an odd little laugh, the American accent even more pronounced. As he released his hold on her, she jerked out of the light, leaning into the passenger seat.

The policemen saluted.

Janine almost choked, but then another man appeared at her door, wearing a matching blue uniform.

Good God, they were *surrounded*.

The one at Luc's window said something in French, but she didn't catch it. She was too surprised by the goofy look on Luc's face. He suddenly didn't look anything like Luc Tremont. His square jaw had gone slack, his hair mussed.

"Um, Officer." He chuckled awkwardly and struggled

with his fly. "Gee. We're, uh, we are . . . well. I don't speak French, sir. We're trying to find our hotel. The Cheval Rouge. Do you have a clue where it is?"

Suddenly, the light bathed Janine. She blinked, frozen for a split second. *All of you.* Isn't that what he'd said?

She put her hands on the seat and leaned right into the light, offering the policeman a clear view of her breasts and her boldest smile. "Are we in trouble, Officer?" she drawled. She couldn't see his expression, but as he jerked the light away, she could sure see Luc's. A mix of surprise, admiration, and lust.

She leaned into her seat to let him handle it from there, half expecting the other policeman to whip her door open and drop her on the street.

The officer said something else in French, but sounded a shade less intimidating.

Please don't haul me into a French jail naked, she prayed silently. Oh, that would really scal her fate in the art world. Albert would turn over in his grave.

No, he wouldn't. But Albert would turn over in his grave if someone made porcelain dust out of those Plums and eliminated their place in history. What was a little breast exposure compared to that?

Luc squirmed in his seat and tucked his shirt in. "Really sorry, Officer." He grinned at the man. "We're on our honeymoon."

At least he didn't try to pass her off as a hooker. The cop just stared at Luc, and Janine held her breath, waiting for the inevitable. *License and registration, please.*

"Honey. Moon." Luc repeated slowly. He pointed to Janine and then to himself. *"Mar-i-age,"* he said in butchered French. "Last week. Last *Samedi. Nous avons* our *mar-i-age.*"

"*L'hotel n'est pas loin,*" the policeman said pointedly, not returning the smile. "*Allez maintenant.*"

Luc nodded eagerly. "*Oui.* Yes." He turned to Janine. "It's not far. I think he said it's not far."

"He also said 'go now,'" she whispered back.

The policeman illuminated the park. "*Là, monsieur. Tout droit et trois kilometres à gauche.*" Behind her, Janine was aware of the other officer moving to the back of their car.

Luc continued to nod eagerly. "Okay. Good. Over there. Three kilometers to the *gauche*—left? *Oui. Merci.* Really, thank you."

Silently, the cop tucked the flashlight in his belt and placed both hands on the door, his fingers curling into the car. Would he yank it open and demand they both get out?

But he only leaned into the vehicle and pinned Janine with a look of pure disdain. "*Allez.*" He touched the stiff brim of his navy cap, and stepped back.

Luc glanced at her, a victorious light in his eyes, then put the car in gear. He gave a goofy little wave to the policeman, who remained rooted to the spot. In her side mirror, she could see the two men watching them drive away.

Janine finally hugged her knees as they pulled back onto the boulevard.

Luc reached into the backseat. "Very impressive performance," he said, handing his jacket to her.

With a tight smile she slid her arms into the sleeves,

backward for maximum coverage. "Maybe next time we could just be reading a map instead."

He gave her an apologetic smile. "Sorry. Really." Was he referring to his *response?* "You definitely distracted him, though."

He *had* been aroused. The thought sent a blast of heat through her body. "We could have accomplished the same goal by just making out or something."

A smile tipped the corners of his lips. "That *was* something."

The heat flared again, but she willed it away. The Volvo was too small, too intimate for this conversation. "Where did you learn to speak English like that?"

"The cinema," he answered quickly.

As he leaned forward to adjust his clothing, she stole a sideways glance to see his muscles strain the tailored fabric of his shirt. She couldn't look away. But as they drove under the soft yellow light of a streetlamp, her gaze froze on something black and menacing sticking out from the back of his waistband. A sudden light-headedness threatened as she realized what it was. "You're *armed?*"

"I'm a security specialist. I am licensed to carry a weapon."

Lives are at risk. That's what he'd said the day they met in the Hall of Mirrors. *Your life, Szha-neen.*

She dropped her head back against the seat and let out a long, exhausted breath. What a night. "I still can't believe the Plums are gone."

"Neither can I."

She remembered the red slash on her dress and the

warning she'd received from the head of Versailles Security. "Who is this Scorpion, anyway?"

He accelerated through an empty intersection. "He's dead."

"For a dead guy, he's been pretty busy lately."

"It wasn't supposed to happen this way," he said softly.

A distinct sense of unease trickled down her spine. "You knew this was going to happen, didn't you?"

"Not this," he exclaimed, his hand gesture indicating the two of them. "*This* was not part of the plan."

"But there was a plan," she said slowly. "You expected the forgeries to be stolen, didn't you?"

He ran his tongue along the inside of his cheek and kept his attention on the road. "We strongly suspected it might happen."

"*We? * Who's we?"

A car approached from behind, the headlights spotlighting the hard set of his jaw. After a moment, it zipped by. "'We' is Versailles Security," he answered.

"Somehow I can't see you taking orders from Helmet Head De Vries." She shoved her arms deeper into the sleeves of his jacket.

He smiled. "I work for several people."

"*Ooo*-kay." She let out a dry laugh at his evasion techniques. "Why don't you tell me who they are?"

He reached over and almost touched her exposed thigh, but she crossed her legs, shifting out of his reach. "Too much knowledge can be dangerous."

"Look, I know you want me to trust you and shut up, and you probably wish I'd disappear while I'm at it. But none of that's going to happen, Luc." She leaned over the console to make her point. "I have a few questions. Just humor me and answer them."

He shot her a warning look. "It was your idea to accompany me, Janine."

"Yes, it was," she agreed. "But I hadn't planned on stealing a car, getting naked, evading the authorities, or dropping my head in the lap of a man who's, at the very least, armed and dangerous."

"Just armed." This time his hand made contact with her thigh and squeezed gently. "And the car's not stolen. It's borrowed."

He lifted his hand, and she crossed the arms of her jacket and stared out the windshield. Nothing looked even vaguely familiar. "Where did you say we're going?"

"I didn't. Burgundy."

She'd taken enough trips through central France to know this was not the most direct route. After a few minutes, the headlights briefly illuminated a rustic stone marker. *Dijon, 314 kilometers.* Evidently he knew another way.

"Are the vases in Burgundy?"

"The computer that's tracking them is."

"Haven't you heard of a handheld? A PDA? A laptop? It's the new millennium."

Luc shook his head. "Too easily traced."

By whom? She decided not to ask and studied the dark countryside instead. "It's nearly two hundred miles to Dijon," she finally said. "We can't drive two hundred miles in a *borrowed* car."

"Sens is less than a hundred kilometers from here," he told her. "We'll stop there."

"Stop for the night?"

"No. To borrow another car."

She closed her eyes. "What if we're pulled over again?"

Reaching over, he lifted a strand of her hair, letting it flutter onto her shoulder. "Then you know exactly what to do, honey."

He nailed the accent perfectly.

CHAPTER
Nine

An hour later they passed an ancient abbey, its pale limestone walls rising like a timeless sentry above the valley of the Yonne River. Luc knew the landmark well. Bérnard Soisson's château was still a few hours away.

He glanced at his passenger, who hadn't opened her eyes since they'd stopped to refuel in Nemours. Her breathing was far from regular so she wasn't asleep, but the silence gave him a chance to strategize. Which was a challenge, since his mind and body kept betraying him. He kept drifting back to the sensation of her silky hair brushing his crotch, the feel of her breath through the thin fabric of his shirt.

Bon Dieu, how would that feel for real? Once again, arousal clutched him, precisely where her head had been. He exhaled and willed the hardness to subside, but his body wouldn't obey. Desire, hot and intense, shot through him, and he bit back a curse. He had no room for error.

Janine shifted, tensing the muscles of her long, bare legs, wrapped gracefully around each other.

He'd already made an error—she was in the car with him headed to Burgundy.

A car slowed behind him, then passed. He'd seen the same model Peugeot outside of Versailles, but with a different registration number. He had to be vigilant. He had to get control of his mind and his plan. She could help him, it was true. If she didn't distract him to death, first.

The next move was simple: get the car he'd arranged for Bérnard to leave in Sens. He considered calling Bérnard to tell him to expect additional tracking data on another set of vases, but it wasn't worth the risk of having the call traced to his friend's winery. Tristan had no idea the vintner was receiving data.

Not that it was Tristan's style to storm the place and pressure an old man he didn't know, but once the FBI agents realized they didn't have access to the same data— courtesy of Luc's handiwork—they might be mad enough to try and hunt Luc down. Since they couldn't hunt the vases for five days.

Luc ran a hand through his hair and exhaled. He'd explain it all to Bérnard when they arrived; Bernard would love the intrigue. He enjoyed living vicariously through Luc, and he'd never passed judgment. He just accepted the past as past.

As they rounded a wide bend in Route Nationale Six, he glimpsed the lights of Sens. Time for new transportation. He didn't think he'd been followed, but he couldn't be too thorough.

He laid a gentle hand on her shoulder. "Janine?" Her

eyelids immediately flew open. "You need to get dressed."

He leaned over her bare legs to retrieve her dress, the scent of her skin teasing him as he lifted the filmy material from under the seat. He dropped it on her lap. "We are going to change vehicles now."

She looked at the dress and then at him. "How are we going to do that?"

"Quickly and quietly." He lifted a piece of the fabric. "Put it on. I won't look."

"Too late," she said. "You already looked."

He laughed softly. "I think we've established that I'm human." And he'd never forget the picture she made, thrusting her breasts toward the policeman's light. It was brave and smart and sexy as hell.

She maneuvered her feet into the dress and shimmied it up her legs, then plucked at the torn silk. "Well, if this isn't poetic justice, I don't know what is."

"Poetic justice?"

"It was cursed, what can I say? The wedding was cursed from the beginning."

His brows lifted in surprise. "That was your wedding gown?"

"Not anymore." She slipped on her shoes. "I would have just shredded it eventually; this saves me the trouble of deciding between a straight edge razor and a butcher knife."

He raised his eyebrows. "Are you serious?"

"Just human," she responded with a quick smile.

Ahead of him he spotted the Pont d'Arche, a tiny stone bridge near a steep river embankment. From his peripheral vision, he saw Janine slide out of the jacket.

She zipped the dress and adjusted it over her chest. His gaze dropped over the ragged gown. It was torn and discolored and, God, was that blood on the side? It didn't diminish his memory of how she'd looked when he'd first seen her in it a few hours ago. That, along with her *Playboy* pose for the cop, would be stored for frequent future reference.

He smiled at her. "You would have been a stunning bride in that dress." In any dress.

Her gaze turned warm for a second, then she flipped her hand in a dismissive wave. "It's history." She folded his jacket in half and wrapped her arms around it. "Now what, Bond? Got a helicopter waiting for us?"

"Not exactly. But you should get out and go stand by the side of the bridge."

She climbed out and walked in front of the car as he shifted into neutral. The headlights shone straight through the white silk, illuminating the feminine curves underneath. A gust of wind lifted her long blond hair as she strode, giving the vision a dramatic, ethereal quality.

With a flick of the headlights, Luc darkened his private stage. Opening his door, he put one foot on the ground and gave a hard push before he jumped out. The Volvo splashed as it hit the black water, and he heard Janine gasp in surprise.

"Remind me not to let you borrow my car," she said dryly.

He laughed. "All part of the plan, believe me." He took the jacket from her and spread it over her shoulders.

She settled into it. "How far?"

"Not very. A short walk to the cathedral. Have you been to Sens?"

"No." She quickened her step. "Let's sightsee another time, though. I want to get to the Plums."

"Patience, Janine." He paused and listened to the Yonne rush beneath them. The redolent smell of earth and young grapes permeated the dry night air. Burgundy was the one part of France that felt remotely like home. Not that it was anything like the Boston asphalt jungle he'd grown up in, but the wine country was in his blood. Half of his blood, anyway. He put his arm on her back and kept walking toward the graceful trees that had bordered the city's main boulevard for a thousand years. There, he guided her away from the circles of light cast by the gas lamps.

"Are we looking for a particular car, or do you just intend to grab anything that isn't locked?" she asked, as he slowed his step.

"I'm looking for a specific vehicle." But he didn't see it. He searched the dozen or so parked cars in the block that he and Bérnard had agreed upon. There was no black Renault sedan. He walked briskly along the sidewalk and furtively glanced in each. There was no car with a blue umbrella propped on the passenger seat.

"Which one?" she asked with an edge of impatience.

"I'm not sure." Could Bérnard have substituted another car?

"You're going to steal a car, aren't you?"

"No." He kept walking toward the next block. Where *was* it?

She tapped on the hood of an older model Citroën and

put a hand on her hip. "This one's nice. Clean." Cupping her fingers on the glass, she squinted through the window. "Unlocked, too."

"Come on," he said, pulling at her arm. They couldn't wander the streets of Sens at two in the morning peering in parked cars without someone noticing and calling the gendarme.

But the next two blocks yielded nothing. He swore under his breath. This wasn't like Bérnard. His only real friend in France, one of the few people in the world who knew the true identity of Luc Tremont, would never forget their plan. Bérnard knew exactly what was at stake. He'd die before he'd let Luc down.

An icy stab sliced his gut. Without another word, he turned and strode back to the rusting Citroën Janine had first seen.

"You're right," he said softly. "This is the one."

Her jaw dropped as Luc opened the driver's door.

"Get in," he ordered, as he crouched onto the floor and maneuvered his head under the dashboard. He found the ignition wires and touched them together.

Janine opened the passenger door and stuck her head in. "You can't just take this car."

The engine sputtered for a few moments, then growled. "Evidently I can."

He brushed the specks of dirt from his hands, then took the driver's seat. "Sometimes the end justifies the means."

She stood frozen for a second, then folded into the seat with admirable dignity for a woman wearing a tattered wedding gown speckled with blood and pomegranate juice.

"I can honestly say I've never stolen a car before." She turned to him, her eyes bright. "Obviously, you have."

"Obviously."

"This is bullshit," Paul Dunne muttered in disgust, as he fiddled with the sea of meaningless symbols on his computer screen. "I had this working yesterday. We read the data perfectly from the exhibit site."

Tristan watched over his shoulder. Paul could play with the code until his fingers fell off, but Tristan knew he wouldn't get what he wanted. Not for, oh, five days. Yeah, this little snafu had Luc's fingerprints all over it.

Did he really think Tristan wouldn't keep his end of the bargain?

Probably not. They'd never really trust each other. Not again.

"Keep trying," he said, as his pager hummed. Why wouldn't Luc believe him when he said he'd hold off? Why did he have to manipulate everything?

But that was Luc. No, that was *Nick*. A manipulator.

Tristan Stewart lived by a simple rule. Actually, he lived by a lot of them. But one of his favorites was: *You can't trust a thief.*

And where Luc was concerned, he'd broken that axiom right in half.

The pager persisted, and he peered at the number. Oh, great. Rich Ainsbury, the deputy legat who ran the FBI field office in Paris. At two in the morning. It wasn't enough that he'd stalled his own team and the DST; now he'd have to give some bogus explanation to the French liaison.

He punched in Ainsbury's direct line, still cursing Luc. Five freakin' days.

"Any progress, Tris?" Ainsbury asked when he picked up.

"We're attempting analysis of the tracking data now."

Paul looked over his shoulder and rolled his eyes. Tristan shot him a dirty look and turned away.

"How are things going with the DST?" Tristan asked. *A strong offense rarely loses.* It wasn't an obvious preempt; the *Direction de la Surveillannce du Territoire* had jurisdiction over the relationship with the FBI, and he knew that was Ainsbury's primary concern.

"That's not why I called," Ainsbury said. "Something just came in that was flagged urgent and confidential for you."

"Yeah?" He glanced at Paul, who sat at the computer with his arms crossed, fuming at a blank screen. "What is it?"

"Apparently you are supposed to receive immediate notification of a change of residence or status for a French citizen by the name of Bérnard Soisson?"

Tristan's gut constricted. "Yes, I am." Why would the name Bérnard Soisson come up now? That sole connection to his old life was an unconventional allowance the FBI had made for Nick Jarrett—Bérnard was the one person who was approved to know Luc's real identity. Soisson appeared to be just a sixty-five-year-old winemaker, living with his wife in the hills of central France, and Tristan knew he'd had a childhood friendship—more than friendship, in fact—with Gabrielle Jarrett. "What's going on with him?"

Ainsbury cleared his throat. "He's dead."

The first drop of adrenaline trickled through Tristan's veins. "What happened?"

"His body was pulled out of the Armançon River a few hours ago."

"Any evidence of foul play?" He knew what was coming.

"Only if you think a hole in his head from a forty-five is foul."

"Could it have been suicide?"

"Possibly. We're not sure yet."

Tristan ignored the familiar burn in his belly. "Any suspects?"

"His wife is missing. When the gendarmerie arrived to notify the next of kin, one of the winery employees told them that the wife, Lisette, had driven off the previous day and hadn't returned. No one's heard from her."

"Get me a location," he said. "I'm going there."

"Now?" Incredulity raised Ainsbury's usually quiet voice. "I'm sorry if this is a personal friend or something, Tris, but we gotta stay on the Benazir case. You can't—"

"This is related," Tristan said.

"How?"

"Classified."

Ainsbury didn't miss a beat. "I'll have someone call you with the exact location."

Tristan flipped his phone closed and looked at Paul. "Keep working on it. I'm going to follow a lead."

Paul's eyebrows shot up. "What's the lead?"

"Not sure. I'm going with—"

"Gut instinct." Paul nodded knowingly and entered a

new set of useless coordinates on the computer. "And gut instinct is never wrong."

Tristan laughed softly. "You're learning, Dunne."

As he pushed open the door to the chilly spring night, his phone rang again, this time with the address of Bérnard Soisson's winery. He punched it into his PDA and angled the screen in the moonlight to read the map that appeared.

The southern region of the Côte d'Or. He could take a flight to Dijon or drive. Either way, it would take five or six hours to get there.

He wanted Benazir, but he couldn't do a damn thing about that right now. What would it hurt to check on Luc's friend?

It bothered him that an old man living peacefully in the country would die violently. And it bothered him that, if not for the connection to Luc, his death would undoubtedly be an open and shut suicide. But what really bothered him was the timing. Why now?

If it's too strange to be a coincidence, then it isn't one.

CHAPTER
Ten

Apparently Luc had traded caution for speed with the change of cars. He'd abandoned the country roads and opted to fly his stolen car down the highway. Janine had watched for the turn-off for Dijon, but he'd blown right by it and headed south, toward the heart of French wine country. Toward the narrow limestone slope of the Côte d'Or.

She listened to the rumble of the tires on the road, gathering warmth from the jacket that she still wore. He'd cracked his window open, and the fruity, earthy smells mixed with the clean, masculine scent that clung to his clothes. And if that wasn't intoxicating enough, whenever she stole occasional glances at him, her imagination ran as fast as the Citroën.

Every glimpse of the man made her mouth water. And then go bone-dry. Her reaction had little to do with his great looks, or the hypnotic cadence of his French accent. It was the way he moved, the way he attacked this situation, his grace under pressure.

Dear God, what was the matter with her? Since when did Dr. Coulter go for testosterone-loaded supermen who knew how to hot-wire cars and elude the law? Her ex-fiancé had set his Mercedes alarm off every time he tried to arm it. Testosterone? He all but counted the number of wavy brown hairs in his brush each morning.

Luc slid into the right lane at the exit to Beaune and glanced at her. "We'll be stopping at a winery in a few minutes," he said.

She sat up in her seat. "Really? Got a tasting lined up for four-thirty in the morning?"

He almost smiled. "I wouldn't be surprised. My friends, Bérnard and Lisette, are expecting me."

But they weren't expecting her. Evidently that didn't concern him. "Do you think Lisette is my size? I could use a change of clothes."

"She's about your size." He glanced at her and smiled. "But they are wine country farmers, so don't expect couture."

The wool of his jacket scratched her bare shoulders when she shrugged. "I don't need Versace, Luc. A pair of slacks and flat shoes would do the trick."

"I'm sure Lisette can accommodate you," he said, as he turned onto a narrow, rutted road. "They are old family friends." His tone implied that nothing would faze them—not even guests in the middle of the night.

"How long will we stay?"

"Long enough to track the Plums. We can shower and change, get something to eat."

In the moonlight, Janine could see endless rows of vines lining the foothills. An occasional iron gate or low wall marked the perimeter of a winery. Luc pulled into one of those, slowly enough for her to read words carved into a stone marker.

Château Soisson.

"It's not really a château in the truest sense of the word," he warned as the Citroën coughed up the hill and passed some darkened outer buildings. "Just a private country winery."

As they rounded a bend, the headlights fell on a cozy two-story house covered in ivy.

"It's very sweet," she noted, studying the mossy hip roof and weathered shutters. "Very inviting."

"I've always felt at home here," he said softly.

At the personal revelation, she glanced at him. What an odd place for a man like Luc Tremont to feel at home.

The tires kicked up dirt and stones as he drove around the side of the house, under the outstretched arms of an ancient tree. Not a single light burned in any of the arched windows.

"We'll go in through the back," Luc said.

"You mean just walk in?"

He didn't say anything.

"Or shoot off the lock. With you, one never knows," she said, almost to herself.

"These are my very close friends, Janine," he assured her. "I have my own room in this home."

He parked inside an open storage shed in the back, avoiding the gardening tools scattered about. Reaching under the dash, he yanked at something and the engine shut off. "Let's go," he said, closing the doors of the shed behind him.

They crossed a darkened courtyard to a back door. He jiggled the door handle. Kneeling, he reached in his pocket and pulled out a tiny flashlight. Twisting a cap off with his teeth, he flashed a small instrument—a screwdriver?—and slid it in the keyhole. Evidently he had a room, a parking space, but no *key*.

"More breaking and entering?"

"Just . . ." The lock made a grinding noise, then unlatched. "Entering." He flipped off the flashlight and popped on the screwdriver cap with one hand.

He entered first, and suddenly the room was bathed in a soft golden glow. Janine held her breath, expecting someone. The owners. A dog. An alarm. But the spacious kitchen was deserted. A long worktable dominated the center of the room, which was lined with pine cabinets, an ancient gas stove, and a glass-paneled breakfront. All was silent, but for the low-pitched hum of the refrigerator.

"Shouldn't we let someone know that we're here?" Janine whispered.

"Bérnard should be here," Luc said, moving toward a darkened hallway. "And Lisette." He paused and listened, frowning. "I'm going to check the house."

She wanted no part of hanging out in the kitchen alone. "I'm coming with you."

He extended his hand. "Come on."

As they moved through the house he paused to switch on lamps, illuminating polished wood floors with well-worn throw rugs and simple furnishings. They passed a darkened study and living room, then stopped at the bottom of a curved wooden staircase.

"Bérnard?" he called softly, taking the first few steps. He waited a beat, then cocked his head. "Let's go upstairs."

The second floor hallway wrapped around the stairs. At one end was a set of closed double doors.

This time, he knocked. "Lisette?"

Tight-lipped, he eased the door open to reveal a darkened bedroom with an antique four-poster bed taking up most of the space. The rumpled bedclothes looked completely out of place in the otherwise spotless house.

He went directly to the huge antique armoire and opened the doors. "You can get something to wear," he said, indicating it with a nod.

Inhaling the cedar and wool scent of the armoire, she quickly chose a dark flannel shirt, then lightly ran her fingers over the other hangers. She needed sweatpants or something comfortable for . . . whatever she'd be doing. Running.

She took a pair of black jersey slacks with an elastic waist. At the bottom of the armoire, there were a few pairs of flat leather shoes. "Do you think she'd mind if I borrowed some shoes?"

He stood in front of an open dresser drawer across the room. "Take whatever you need. Underwear? Socks?"

It felt so weird to be taking this stranger's clothes. "I'd rather not pilfer the woman's panties, if you don't mind," she said, as she picked a pair of black loafers.

"You were freezing in the car. Here."

She turned and caught a ball tossed to her. Socks. "Fine."

"I'll show you the guest room."

The hall led to another smaller bedroom, this one powder blue and antique oak.

"There's an *en suite* bath," he said. "I'll come back in half an hour. I have some things to do."

When the latch clicked behind him, Janine stared at it for a few seconds. Should she lock it? What a bizarre situation. Alone, apparently, in a little farmhouse in Burgundy. Stealing the owner's ugly clothes and wondering if she should lock the door to keep out . . . who? The missing residents? The man she trusted to find her Plums?

She took a few steps to the door and turned the knob, and a sickening realization squeezed her heart.

She couldn't lock him out. He'd locked her in.

By the time she heard his quiet rap on the door, Janine had washed her face, brushed her hair, and changed into her comfortable, if frumpy, new outfit. She'd even found an unopened toothbrush and brushed her teeth. She sat on the edge of the blue-chenille-covered bed, fighting mad.

"Why the hell are you knocking?" she called. "I can't open it."

The door opened. Luc now wore a dark sweatshirt and faded jeans. Well, he'd said he had a room here.

"Sorry," he muttered. "I didn't realize it locked when I left."

She speared him with a withering look. He realized *everything*. "Do you not trust me? You think you have to lock me up like—like Rapunzel or something?"

"Rapunzel?" He smiled and reached for a strand of her

hair. "You look like Rapunzel with your beautiful, long hair."

Every time he touched her hair, it felt as intimate as a kiss. She pulled her hair out of his reach into a makeshift ponytail. "Please don't do that again."

"What? Touch your hair or compliment you?"

Both. "Lock me up."

"Would you forgive me in exchange for some coffee and breakfast?"

Her empty stomach responded for her. "Possibly."

He slipped his arm over her shoulder and pulled her to his side, his mouth close to her ear. "And, yes, I trust you."

She sidestepped his solid grasp and walked into the hall. "Did you find out where your friends are?"

"No." He started down the stairs ahead of her. "And I had a setback on the vases, too."

"You did?" She slowed her step. "Has something happened to them?"

"I'm not getting a correct read on them. I've found the forgeries, which are traveling along A-5, probably headed toward Germany or Switzerland."

She rounded the corner into the kitchen, momentarily distracted by the aroma of coffee and baked pastries. He pulled a chair out for her. "Hungry?"

"Famished. And the real vases?"

He took a coffeepot off the stove, then carried it to the table and filled two cups. "There's some kind of error reading. It shows the receiver location instead of the transmitter location."

She poured warm cream into her cup and watched the

black transform into perfect café au lait. "Where's the receiver location?"

"Here. Installed in Bérnard's computer." He placed a basket of pastries on the table, the fragrance reminding her that she was starved. "Obviously that's a mistake, and I hope it's temporary," he said as he sat down.

"What do we do? What if you can't get a reading? How do we get them? I thought we'd be able to get them sometime today."

"We'll trace them, don't worry." He laughed softly, took a brioche from the basket, and put it on her plate. "You're such an *American.*"

She broke the pastry, and the buttery crust crumpled, causing a flurry of flakes that she brushed off her fingers. "I suppose that's an insult."

She expected his casual French shrug, but got a warm look instead. "Not at all."

She concentrated on the brioche. "You didn't answer my question. What do we do next?"

"When Bérnard arrives, we'll work on the program. If we have no leads at all on the real vases, I may opt to travel after the forgeries."

He might opt. "What about me?"

This time he did shrug. "We'll have to play it by ear, as you Americans say."

She took a bite of the crumbling brioche, aware that he watched her every move. She dabbed at her mouth with the napkin. "Do you hate Americans like most French people do?"

He sipped his coffee. "I can't speak for the whole country, but no, I don't hate Americans." His gaze dropped to her mouth, and she wiped her lips again self-consciously. "For example, I like you."

Brioche caught in her throat, and she sipped coffee to get it down. "Even though I invited myself along on your chase?"

His dark eyes glinted. He reached across the table and touched her bottom lip. "Perhaps that's why I like you." A sliver of pastry clung to his fingertip. "You missed this."

"Oh." She put her hand to her mouth, to the spot where his fingertips left their invisible imprint.

With his eyes still on hers, he put the pastry crumb in his mouth, and it disappeared on his tongue. "Mmmm." He closed his eyes for a second. "Arlaine is a genius."

She somehow managed to speak. "Arlaine?"

"The housekeeper."

Outside, an engine growled and a bright beam of headlights flashed through the kitchen window.

"That's probably her now." Luc stood and strode to the door, inching its curtain aside.

Janine followed him and tried to get a look over his shoulder. The driver's door of a rusty truck slowly opened with a high-pitched creak. A small figure dressed entirely in black jumped out and started toward the house.

Luc shoved open the door. "Lisette," he called.

The woman froze and stared as he sprinted across the courtyard. "Luc!" Janine heard surprise—no, shock—in the exclamation. *"Que fais-tu ici?"*

What was he doing there? She thought he was *expected*.

They met at the gate, the first rays of sunlight highlighting the older woman's face. Janine could make out plain, angular features and dark cropped hair.

"*Où est* Bérnard?" Luc asked.

She said nothing but shook her head, her expression changing from surprise to . . . something else. Something dark.

"What is it?" Luc demanded in English. "Where is he, Lisette?"

"*Il est mort.*"

The words carried across the morning air, and Janine's breath froze. *He is dead.*

"How?" Luc grabbed Lisette's narrow shoulders and practically lifted her off the ground. "What happened?"

She just looked at him.

"What happened to Bérnard, Lisette?" he insisted, in English.

"Oh, God, Luc," she answered in the same language. "He killed himself."

"*What?*"

"They found him drowned in the Armançon River, with a bullet in his head."

Janine grabbed the doorjamb and felt her blood run ice cold. Drowned . . . with a bullet in his head.

Exactly the way Albert Farrow had died.

CHAPTER
Eleven

A thousand responses screamed in Luc's head. It was impossible. A lie. Bérnard would never, ever take his own life.

Raw, bitter bile rose in his throat, and he fought the urge to punch something. Instead he put an arm around Lisette's shoulder, feeling her frail bones quaking beneath the wool. *"Allons,* Liz. Come inside and get warm."

Janine tried to grab his arm as he passed her. "Luc."

He heard the urgency in her voice, but answered with a harsh look. *No questions, not now.*

Lisette fell into a chair with a sob.

"Tell me what happened." He sat down next to her, clenching and unclenching his jaw to keep from pounding the table. "Tell me, Lisette."

She lifted her head and looked at him, then at Janine. *"Qui l'est?"*

"This is my . . . friend. Janine." He glanced at her, still standing by the door, one hand fisted at her mouth and a storm in her eyes.

Lisette dropped her head into her hands. "I can't believe he is dead," she said softly in French.

Neither could he.

"Luc." Janine knelt down in front of the table. "Listen to me. It's important."

He held up a hand. "Wait, Janine. Not now." He turned back to Lisette. "Tell me exactly what happened."

She kept her face buried in her hands. "He swam out into the river and put a bullet in his head."

Janine gasped, but he ignored her. This just wasn't possible. Bérnard sucked every breath of life with gusto. "I don't believe it," he said, nearly blinded by a flash of rage.

Lisette spread her fingers and peered at him with narrow eyes. "You must believe it. They found him a day ago. He was going to town for lunch and . . . he didn't come home. His bicycle . . . was there . . . and they found him."

He jumped up from his chair, hard enough to nearly knock it over. "Bérnard would never kill himself, Lisette."

Suddenly, her lips started quivering. "They won't let me have him. They are doing . . . medical tests."

An autopsy. His stomach tightened at the thought. The authorities would alert Tristan Stewart, of course, who'd be here in record time to check it out. And if Dudley Do-Right found him here—*with the American curator in tow*—the whole plan would fall apart. He'd broken every rule in the book by involving Bérnard, but he'd trusted the man completely. And he'd needed a contact other than the FBI to make this all work. A sudden ache of loss—and guilt—weighed on his chest.

"Lisette." He sat down next to her again, softening his voice. She'd known he'd done work for the government, that he was involved with art. Beyond that, Bérnard had told her nothing. "I—we—are working on a complicated project, and Bérnard was helping me."

She looked up at him with red-rimmed eyes.

He hated to do this, but he had no choice. He couldn't stay and wait for the transmissions of the data, and he still needed assistance.

He glanced at Janine who leaned against the sink with horror in her eyes. He couldn't trust Janine to read the data; she'd go after the vases herself if she thought she knew where they were.

No. He needed Lisette. Janine would have to go back to Versailles.

"I am using Bérnard's computer to get information that I need, and I must leave soon. I need to be able to contact you over the next few days and have you read this information to me."

It seemed brutally insensitive, and he waited for her look of anger. Instead, she reached over and folded him in her arms. "Bérnard loved you like a son, Luc."

A stab of agony pierced his gut. He would mourn Bérnard terribly. But mourning had to wait a while. He had to get Benazir.

"Of course I will help you." She laid her age-spotted hand on his arm. "I will do whatever you need." She sighed heavily. "Perhaps you can get the horrible medical examiner in Beaune to release his . . . him."

"I will do everything possible, Lisette," he promised. "As soon as this project is completed. But I need to ask you a favor."

She looked up, a question in her eyes.

"When anyone shows up here asking about me, you haven't seen me. Anybody. Even American authorities."

Worry deepened her wrinkles. "Are you in trouble, Luc?"

"Not really," he said smoothly. "Just trying to find something that I've arranged to track on Bérnard's computer."

He heard the sound of an engine, not far away.

"It's Arlaine," Lisette said.

He couldn't see any headlights reflected against the garage. Whoever was driving up the hill didn't want to announce his or her arrival. That would be just like Tristan. "Lisette, I don't want to talk to anybody."

She stood and tilted her head toward the front of the house. "I'll see who it is and won't let them in."

Tristan might worm his way into the house. When his charm failed, he had a pretty effective steamrolling technique. "Bérnard's cellar," Luc said suddenly. No one could find him there, unless they knew the underground room existed.

For a moment, Lisette looked horrified. "You can't go there."

Of course, the memories would be too much for her, too soon. Bérnard's favorite place on earth, his wine cellar. Luc went directly to the oversized metal key that hung near the stove. "You don't have to come down, Lisette. Just pound on the door when it's clear."

Before she could speak, he grabbed Janine's hand and opened the back door, crossing the courtyard.

She stumbled a bit as he pulled her toward a darkened corner of the house, then she stopped and literally dug her heels in. "Listen to me, damn it, it's important."

"I will; just come with me to the wine cellar. We don't have time to stand here."

She shook her head. "Your friend died exactly the same way as Albert Farrow. Exactly, Luc."

Dread pinged up his spine as the realization hit. "You're right."

"It's too weird to be a coincidence."

He heard the slam of a car door at the front of the château. "Come on." He put his hand on her back. "Hurry. We'll figure it out inside."

He'd been to the wine cellar dozens of times with Bérnard, and knew where to push the thick shrubbery aside to reveal a great wooden door. He jammed the key into a giant brass lock. "Watch your step," he warned, as he guided her into the darkness.

"Hello! *Excusez!*" The voice carried across the courtyard. "Is anyone here?" The voice was closer, coming around the back of the château.

Luc closed the door with a thud, blocking out all light, all fresh air, and the familiar voice of his ex-best friend.

"God, I can't see a damn thing." Janine blinked into the pitch blackness and inhaled musty air.

"I'm right here." Luc's powerful arms encircled her, and he pulled her into his chest.

Instinctively she tucked into the hard warmth of him, burying her face in his shirt to block out the mold and dust.

"We're at the top of eight fairly steep stairs." He slowly turned her around. "Step down."

She froze. How could he see? It felt like jumping off a cliff blindfolded.

"Step, Janine. It's about a six-inch drop."

She had no choice. Slowly, she slid the rubber soles of Lisette's black loafers forward, until her foot was off the stone. Then she stepped down about six inches, touching something solid. Exactly as he'd promised.

"Again." He tightened his arm around her, and she did the same, clinging to his hard torso. She took the next step. Then the next. Then the next.

"We're at the bottom now," he finally said.

"Can you turn a light on?"

He let out a quick breath that could have been a laugh. "Electricity is forbidden." He eased her down toward the ground. "Sit here, on the bottom step. I'll find the oil lamp."

There was something about the smell. Decayed earth and rotten air. Janine hugged herself against the cold. "Something stinks."

"That's for sure," he muttered. "As soon as I get the light, I'll open the air vent."

She kept hearing Lisette's words in her head. They found him drowned . . . with a bullet in his head. "This can't be." An invisible weight compressed her chest. "It's just too weird."

From across the basement, she heard scratching and a

hinge creak. Peering into jet blackness, fear tingled up her back. "Are you there?"

"I'm right here. It's not a big room, just a dark one."

She tried to inhale, but her lungs actually hurt. "I can hardly breathe."

"I know. I'll get the vent as soon as I find a goddamn match. I've never come down here without a flashlight."

With the darkness came cold. A bone-chilling, refrigerator cold. "God, this is like being buried alive. What is this place?"

"It's Bérnard's private tasting cellar," Luc said. "Four walls, six alcoves, one table, one oil lamp, two chairs, and about a thousand bottles of the best wine in France." She heard him sigh. "And, somewhere, matches."

She'd never been in such disorienting darkness. Even that passageway in Versailles had breathable air. "Keep talking so I know I'm alive."

He chuckled softly. "You're very much alive. I know they're here somewhere."

She pulled her knees up into her chest and hugged her legs, breathing down the loose flannel shirt onto her bare breasts for warmth.

She tried to listen to the sounds he made, but suddenly all she could hear was a mental replay of Lisette's announcement, pounding in her head. She rubbed her temples and tried to take another deep breath as a wave of dizziness seized her.

Then she heard a different voice in her head. "That man—outside. That was an American. Who was it?"

He didn't respond.

"Luc?"

"Right here." Suddenly a flame flared, flashing orange light on his face. He picked up the glass cover of a hurricane-type lamp and lit the wick. *"Merde,"* he mumbled. "We have only a bit of oil left."

As the golden glow intensified, Janine blinked to adjust. Shadows danced all around, highlighting rows of white cylinders that appeared to be tucked into stone walls.

"Who was it?" she repeated, as she focused on his face.

"It was the FBI."

The chill on her skin turned to ice. "Excuse me?"

"It was an agent from the FBI."

She stood, forcing her wobbly legs to lock. "We were running *from* the FBI?"

He raked his hand through his hair, studying her intently. What lie was he concocting now? Janine could practically hear the wheels spinning in his head.

Trust me, Szha-neen. Trust me.

God*damn* him. "You want to tell me why we were running from the FBI, Luc?"

"I work for them."

She must have misunderstood. "You *what* for them?"

He didn't look away. "I am a consultant, Janine. I was hired by the FBI to supervise the exhibit."

She took a step closer to him. "You were there—at my exhibit—working for the FBI?"

He nodded.

"Are you an FBI agent?"

"No. I'm a hired hand, a specialist brought in for certain situations."

She put a hand on her chest and tried to inhale, but it

just felt like her lungs were filling with dust and cobwebs and dirt. Light-headed, she tried to reach out to the back of a chair, but missed it. He caught her as she stumbled.

"You need oxygen," he said, pulling her toward the steps. "So do I. Come with me to the vent; we can breathe from it directly until the room fills with air."

Nothing fit. Nothing worked. Her brain was shutting down, and the edges of the room got darker.

Was it the lamp or her eyes?

"Just breathe," he told her, squeezing her shoulders and guiding her up the stairs, his own breath sounding as shallow as hers felt.

Then she remembered. Albert. His friend. *Both shot and drowned.*

She swayed and nearly fell, but he held firmly and took her up two more stairs. "If we don't get more oxygen, we're both going to black out."

At the top of the stairs, he released her and started cranking a long, rectangular air vent, letting in slivers of light and blessed, clean air through its slats.

Albert had not committed suicide. He'd been *killed*.

Her legs swayed, and her bloodless head betrayed her by not turning at the same speed as her eyes. She felt drunk and dizzy and weak as she reached for support that wasn't there.

She shook her head to clear it, but it only got foggier. Luc's arms slid around her waist as he pushed her toward the vent, but she stiffened. "Why are you running from the cops, from the FBI, Luc?"

She sounded distorted, like her head was underwater. She could have sworn he paled, but it might have been the flickering light. This man who stole with ease—with style, in fact—was he capable of the truth?

"Now I understand," she said, her voice distant to her own ears. "You're in on it. You're behind the theft of my Plums."

She shook him off when he tried to hold her shoulders, opened her mouth to suck in more air, but there was none. *She couldn't breathe.* She was trapped and dying underground with a man who lied, and *stole*. What else was he capable of?

He pushed her toward the vent again. "You're oxygen deprived. Breathe." He bent so close to her, she could feel the scrape of his whiskers on her cheek as he inhaled deeply himself.

Her head felt so light, it felt *disconnected* from her body. "I hate liars. And you are a liar." She didn't recognize her broken voice. "And a thief."

The light flickered and dimmed. Darkness closed around her. He said something, but the sound was distorted and reverberated in the distance. She could see his face, so close to hers. She could see his mouth move and his eyes plead with her.

Then the blackness came.

CHAPTER
Twelve

She slumped in Luc's arms just as the oil lamp snuffed. Classic hypoxia. How many times had Bérnard promised to update the hundred-year-old ventilation system? Luc folded her into his arms and kept her face toward the vent, inhaling some much-needed air for himself. As soon as the oxygen got back to her brain, she'd wake up.

Sitting down, he brushed her hair away and laid his head on her chest to listen to her heartbeat. "Janine," he whispered.

He pulled her closer into him and curled his hand around her neck. Tracing a line over the translucent skin of her throat, the urge to kiss her slammed into his consciousness. And not a gentle kiss to awaken a fainted Rapunzel. Nothing like that.

He wanted to consume her mouth until her whole body shuddered and rocked against him. But now she shuddered with cold. He ran his hands down her arms and clasped her fingers in his with a silent curse. Her extremities were freezing, and he was fantasizing about waking her for sex on the stairs.

He blew on her hands and lifted her enough to hold her securely with one arm as he maneuvered out of his sweatshirt. He slid it over her, pulling her firmly onto his lap and hoping that he and the shirt retained enough body heat to warm her.

As he pulled her arms through the sleeves, she moaned. "Sam?" The name sucker-punched him. "You lied, Sam."

Sam of the flushed engagement ring, no doubt. The open vent let in enough light so that he could see the color return to her cheeks. He repositioned her so she wouldn't feel his raging erection—she hadn't exactly thrown herself on his lap for pleasure.

"Wake up, Janine."

She groaned and snuggled into him, warming his bare skin. Suddenly she jerked forward, nearly spilling out of his arms. He caught her before she tumbled down the steps, and pulled her back into him. She resisted, stiffening.

"Oh, God. I blacked out." She shook her head and put her hands on her face, taking quick, shallow breaths. "I've never fainted before."

"Hypoxia, Janine. Not a personal weakness." He couldn't help indulging in a reassuring caress of her throat, burying his fingers in the hairs at the nape of her neck. "A very common response to oxygen deprivation. It's like being drunk."

She leaned back, but not out of his arms. "Yes, I felt drunk . . . I still feel . . ." A pink glow highlighted her delicate cheekbones as she dropped her gaze to where she sat. Wordlessly, she inched onto the next step down.

"Try to take slow, deep breaths," he told her, ignoring the empty warm spot she'd left. "In through your nose, out through—"

"You didn't answer me."

"—your mouth."

"Luc." Her voice dropped to a whisper, and she rubbed her temples, warily watching him. "Did you orchestrate the theft of my vases?"

He tried to put his hands on her shoulders, but she shook him off. "No, Janine. You're wasting your energy worrying about it. But—" He paused for a moment and looked hard at her. "I won't argue with you about the coincidence of two bizarre deaths. Something is not right."

It had Karim Benazir's fingerprints all over it, and she had every right to know that.

"I worked with the FBI and museum security to make it easy for the forgeries to be stolen. We are hunting a man who has escaped from a U.S. jail and is building up a massive drug and art smuggling ring." He took her hand and rubbed some warmth into her slender fingers. "I have a plan to get him. If the FBI agent outside knows I'm here and that you're with me, my plan will fail."

"But why is he here?"

"Probably because Bérnard was killed."

She regarded him for a long time. "Do you think this man you're trying to catch killed him?"

"I don't know."

"Do you think he killed Albert?"

He took a deep breath. "Possibly. If we do this right and catch him, perhaps we can find out."

"But why wouldn't the FBI help us? I don't get it."

"Because they don't give a damn about the real vases, Janine. To them, the vases are merely a tool to get to someone far more valuable." He stood and gently pulled her up by the hand he still held. "Let's try this again. I think I can find oil for that lamp, and there's enough air in here now to breathe."

She sat on the bottom stair while he searched.

"Who is this man you're after?" she asked.

"His name is Karim Benazir. About fifteen years ago, a new government in India booted him off his tiny throne in an insignificant province. But he retaliated against his country by building up powerful international art and drug smuggling rings and a money laundering organization based in the U.S. He was caught and captured by the FBI, but escaped prison recently. He has a fairly effective network of paid thieves and assassins who work for him."

"How do you plan to get him?"

"By following a trail," he said vaguely, his fingers passing over Bérnard's favorite brass corkscrew. A dead spider. Matches. And . . . the oil bottle.

No reason to detail why *he* was the person on Benazir's trail. He poured oil into the bottle and lit a match. "Let there be light." It shed just enough light for him to see the surprised look on her face.

"Where's your shirt?"

"On your back, *ma belle*. You were cold."

She touched the sweatshirt she wore, her wide gaze lingering over his bare torso. A hint of color slashed her cheeks before she looked down to the ground. "Thanks."

So, he had the same effect on her that she had on him. The thought warmed him. *"De rien."*

At the top of the stairs, metal scraped.

"Luc?" Lisette whispered into the cellar as a beam of flashlight spilled in front of her. She started down the steps, a bulging knapsack in her arms, a blanket over one shoulder. Her eyes darted between them and around the room, but she didn't stop.

"Is he gone?" Luc asked, moving to relieve her of the bundle and the flashlight.

She nodded, but worry lines creased her forehead. "He was very persistent."

"What did he want to know?"

"About Bérnard's last days. And when I last saw you. I told him you were here at the New Year." That was true. "And that you had spoken to Bérnard since then, a few times."

"Thank you." God, he hated to put her in the middle of this.

"The gendarmerie arrived, also. They wanted to see where Bérnard kept his guns." She shook her head and placed a hand on his arm, then glanced at Janine. "They will come and go all day, so I brought some provisions in case you prefer to stay here."

There was no reason he couldn't be seen by the gendarmerie, but what if Janine had been reported missing? He couldn't take the risk.

"Thank you." He pulled out a chair for her. "Lisette, do you know how to get into Bérnard's computer files?"

She nodded and sat, looking straight at him and not even glancing at Janine. Of course, she assumed the American didn't follow their rapid French. "I do the bookkeeping for the vineyard. I know his password."

Luc walked her through the basics of his tracking program, and she seemed to understand what he needed. She promised to print out everything she could and bring it back later.

"And, Lisette, there is a car in your garage. I need you to remove the registration badges and keep the garage locked all day."

Her gaze flitted to the back of the room again, before she started up the stairs. She looked so anxious, as though Bérnard's ghost could appear at any minute from an alcove of Pinot.

Luc put a sympathetic arm around her as she started up the stairs, then held the flashlight to her feet to guide the way.

"I'll come back as soon as I can," she promised, and left.

When the door closed behind her, Luc put the flashlight upright on the table. Janine had moved into the shadows of one alcove.

"She never speaks to me," she said.

"She doesn't think you'd understand her."

She stepped closer to the circle of white light shed by the flashlight. "She acts like I'm not here. Or that she wishes I weren't."

"Here." He held the blanket out to Janine. "She's in shock. Forget about it."

She waved off his offering. "You need it more than I do."

He put the blanket on the table and reached back into the knapsack. He found another sweater, one he recognized immediately. He slipped it over his head and inhaled the faint cigar smell that clung to the rough wool, giving him the sudden image of his friend's knowing gaze, his crooked smile. Bérnard, who'd loved Gabrielle Sauterville Jarrett . . . until the day he died. Bérnard, laughing and proclaiming, "You should have been my son, Luc."

In the knapsack, he also found a brown paper sack. He opened it and looked up with a quick, teasing smile. "Brioches." He held the bag to her. "You shouldn't drink wine on an empty stomach."

Her jaw slackened, and she bit back a laugh. "I don't want wine. It's nine o'clock in the morning."

"It will warm you." He picked up Bérnard's corkscrew. "And I doubt you'd say no to a 1978 La Romanée Conti Grand Cru."

"Then you'd be wrong." She took the blanket over to the steps, settling under it in a corner.

He shrugged and picked up the flashlight. "You might change your mind if you're cold enough."

The phone rang almost immediately after she'd returned from the wine cellar, yanking Lisette's attention from Bérnard's computer screen. She watched her own hand reach for the receiver. That couldn't be hers, could it? That withered old thing, with brown spots that looked like noble rot on the Pinot Noir? That couldn't be the hand of Lisette Soisson. It looked like it belonged to someone else. To a person who could murder.

Then it must be mine. A rock-hard lump formed in her throat. Her fingers hadn't pulled the trigger, but her hand had killed Bérnard just the same.

She picked up the ancient black receiver, so cold and heavy. Bérnard might have had his computer, but he couldn't part with the old steel telephone that had belonged to his father.

"Allo?"

"Have you given him any information yet?" The thick foreign accent offended her ears.

"Non." She kept all emotion from her voice. She knew what she'd agreed to do. And she knew what it had cost her. He might think she was too stupid to figure out that Bérnard's death was a result of their peculiar relationship, but she knew.

"Have you been able to access the program?"

"Oui."

All she had been trying to do was save Bérnard, to save him from the painful memories of his past. And now he was gone.

"Read me the coordinates."

She read a meaningless string of numbers across the bottom row.

He grunted in response. "Now replace them with these. Listen carefully."

She said nothing, self-disgust filling her. If she did this, she'd probably have two more deaths on her already guilty conscience. All because of her own petty jealousy. All because Gabrielle Sauterville had never really left this farm or her husband's heart.

Ah, *mon Dieu. She* was the one deserved to die, not Bérnard. And not Luc and his American friend. Her stomach turned as she remembered the feel of Luc's comforting hand, his sympathy for her when his own heart was breaking.

"Are you ready?" he growled in her ear.

"Oui." Sacrificing Luc and the woman would be the only way to save her own life. She began to type as he said the numbers, each keystroke changing the information into something entirely different.

Why did Luc have to appear in their lives? She'd been so successful in erasing every trace of Gabrielle from Bérnard's memory. Then *he* showed up. And Bérnard, taking him in like a son, hadn't even had the decency to confide the truth to his own wife. But she'd discovered the truth.

"Did you get that?" he demanded.

"Oui." She read them back to him to prove how cooperative she was being, her mind whirling with guilt and grief.

She'd already manipulated the course of history by destroying all the letters that came from Boston, Massachusetts, in those early years. Pages of apologies and explanations that Bérnard never saw. And then she'd sent that picture and forged a letter so curt and ugly that it had to end any hope Gabrielle might have harbored about seeing her long-lost love again.

That had been enough manipulating for Lisette.

Until that horrible day when a man arrived at the door by the name of Luc Tremont. Did Bérnard actually think she couldn't see the beauty of Gabrielle in her son's eyes? That it wouldn't send her digging for information and an explanation? And when she finally found it, not so deeply buried in his office, what a shock it was.

Not only was he Gabrielle's son; he was a *criminal*, hiding in France. It didn't take long to discover another name in Bérnard's files . . . a man who wanted Luc Tremont out of France as badly as she did. Another criminal. And now, in so deep, she was taking orders from that very man.

"You know what to do," he said, pulling her back to the moment.

Yes, she did. She would take this information to the basement and sentence a man and an innocent woman to death. It was the woman who really made her heart ache. She was young and beautiful. Why should she die, also, because of Lisette's horrible sins?

"And the woman?" the man asked suddenly, as though he could read her thoughts.

"She is here."

"You will receive more directions regarding her. Follow them."

Oh, so many deaths on her conscience. *"Oui."* Even if she didn't follow his directions, even if she'd lied to him, that wouldn't be enough to save Luc's life. Or her own. For surely now that this man had what he wanted, she would not live to see the next harvest.

Janine ate the brioche while she watched Luc examine the rows of bottles, milky white with dust. In the center of the low-ceilinged room, a long wooden table and two chairs sat on a dirt floor. Along the back wall was a simple rack of glassware.

He pulled a bottle from one of the racks, blew on it, studied the label, then replaced it. He took another and brushed some dust off. *"Voilà.* La Romanée. Bérnard's favorite."

"You're really going to drink wine at this hour?"

He glanced up from the bottle with a smile. "Yes, I am." Grabbing a rag that hung next to the glasses, he cleaned the bottle, then placed it on the table and uncorked it. When it was open, he inhaled deeply. "It's so rare, the layers of fragrances this wine offers." He set the open wine bottle to the side while he polished a glass. "It needs to breathe."

"Of course." She took a bite, chewed, and swallowed, still watching him. "You are *so* James Bond."

He chuckled. "You are *so* Californian."

"Not really," she said, brushing the crumbs from her fingertips. "A real Californian would drink with you."

"You will," he promised, with a grin that shot right through her. He picked up the bottle and looked at the label again. "There were only a few thousand bottles of this ever produced. It is the pinnacle of all the *grand crus.*"

As he poured he added, "This particular bottle is quite valuable."

"So, naturally, you stole it."

The corners of his lips lifted. "Bérnard would want me to have it." He walked toward her, taking the remaining space on the step where she sat.

She folded the blanket around her legs and gave his glass a curious look. "So, how valuable?"

He held it to the lamplight, swirling it with the sure hand of a wine connoisseur. "About twenty."

"Oh, come on. That's not expensive. My students drink——" She saw the amusement in his eyes as he inched the glass closer to her.

"Taste it."

The exotic, fruity aroma danced right up her nostrils. She shook her head and leaned away. "Twenty . . . *thousand?*"

"*Santé,*" he whispered just before he sipped. Mesmerized, she watched the bloodred liquid touch his lips. A low moan of ecstasy rumbled from his throat.

"Bérnard was a genius at picking wines the year they were bottled. He invested brilliantly." He looked into the glass as though studying a picture in its depths. "I'll miss him."

He drank again, closing his eyes. With the wine in his mouth, he parted his lips and took in air, then swallowed. "It tastes like the earth of Burgundy. Spicy and rich."

She stared at his slightly open mouth. His lips were so perfectly formed, so inviting, so kissable. He opened his eyes and caught her staring, and that gorgeous mouth slid into a sexy smile. He held the glass to her lips. "You're welcome to taste."

The fragrance of fruit and something almost like licorice floated into her nose, so powerful that she literally felt her tongue react to the scent. Opening her mouth a fraction, she put her hand over his and guided the rim of the glass to her lips, her eyes locked on his.

It was startling at first, almost bitter, tugging at her taste buds. Then the flavors melted around her mouth and she swallowed, the essence lingering after the liquid was gone.

"Wow." She just drank twenty-thousand-dollar wine.

He laughed softly. "Spoken like a true Californian."

She tasted the last of the essence in her mouth. "That's good."

"It's exquisite." Still staring into her eyes, he took another sip, opening his mouth slightly to inhale again before he swallowed. "A bit of smoke. Cinnamon. The blackest of bittersweet chocolate." He raised the glass toward her nose again. "Another?"

"Maybe just, oh, a couple hundred dollars worth."

He smiled and put the wineglass to her lips. Her pulse thumped, and she closed her eyes, giving in to the sensuality of it. As the wine flowed through her mouth, she tried to pick out the flavors he described. "I taste . . ." She ran her tongue over the inside of her bottom lip where some rich residue remained. "Fruit."

"Absolutely." He touched her cheek with the wineglass, rolling it ever so slightly. Her whole body melted with a warm rush. "You taste blackberry and currant and ripe—"

"Plums." They said it at the same second, then caught each other's surprised look and laughed.

Her heart tripped at the sight of his mouth open in a heartfelt laugh. The sound was low and provocative, his eyes bright with their shared joke. As their joint laughter filled the room, his gaze slid down her face and came to a stop at her mouth.

Heat swirled through her at the instant he kissed her.

CHAPTER
Thirteen

Janine tasted exactly like the wine, hot and peppery at first, shocking his lips, then easing into a sweet, smooth, buttery flavor. She opened her mouth, and Luc took it like the thief he was. He swirled his tongue against hers, the heat of her breath and the tannin of the wine fueling the kiss, sending instant electrical sparks through him.

He slid his free hand into the nape of her neck, tunneling into her hair and pulling her closer. He heard the moan escape her lips. Then she started to pull away, which only made him want to deepen the kiss, not stop it.

But he did stop, whispering against her mouth, "I've never seen anything quite like you tasting your first Romanée."

He heard her breath catch.

She backed away, her black pupils nearly obliterating the blue iris, fully dilated from the dim light. No; that wasn't nature's response to darkness. That was her response to *him*. Pure and powerful and real.

She held up a shaky finger and touched his chin, easing him further away. "Hide-and-seek in the dark is enough excitement in one morning for me." Her voice was low, breathless, and dead serious. "Let's hold off on spin the bottle."

Reluctantly, he extracted his hand from her glorious hair.

"I'm not playing games," he said. "I've wanted to kiss you for the last six hours."

She arched one dubious eyebrow.

"Okay." His gaze dropped to her mouth again. "Since I met you."

"Yeah. Well." The cool West Coast indifference didn't hide the reaction that he saw in her eyes. "Don't do it again."

"Yeah. Well." He smiled as he matched her tone. "I just might have to."

For now, he stood and leaned against one of the stone walls.

She tipped her head toward the glass he held. "Where'd you learn so much about wine?"

An image of his mother flashed in his mind, describing the harvest in Burgundy with the same animation and charm another woman might use in the telling of a fairy-tale bedtime story. "Bérnard, of course. He produced some of the best Pinot Noir of the region." He waved a hand toward the alcoves. "And he amassed one of the best wine cellars in the country. There are probably larger collections in the world, but few with the quality you'd find here. He was obsessed with perfection."

Janine bit her lower lip, and sadness darkened her

eyes. "The way he died—exactly, *exactly* the way Albert did. It's bizarre, and it can't be a coincidence, Luc."

He stared into his glass and tried to imagine Bérnard wading into the Armançon River to fire a bullet into his head. "I can't be sure about your friend, but mine was murdered."

She shivered. "Why? Who would do that?"

"I don't know." At her skeptical look, he shook his head. "That's not evasion. I *don't* know." But he certainly had some ideas.

"What was he like?"

"Bérnard?" He glanced at the bottles, the table, the dusty rack of wineglasses, as though the very room should describe its owner. "He was full of spirit; he loved to laugh and eat and drink. He listened to classical music all the time, through a headset he wore day and night. He loved wine and food and art and life." He suddenly remembered a conversation he and Bérnard had about a year ago, and he grinned at her. "He hated California."

"Professional jealousy?"

"Utter intimidation." He tasted his wine again. The Romanée was mellowed by the air now, and even more satisfying. He wanted her to taste it again. He wanted to taste *her* again. "California grape growers finally figured out how to match or exceed some French wines, and he took it as a personal affront."

She pulled her knees up to her chin and hugged her legs, studying him. "You said he was a family friend. Is your family nearby?"

His fictional background was that he'd been born in

Paris of wealthy French parents, educated throughout Europe, all family members deceased. But with determination and a little luck, this false life would shortly transform into a new one.

"My mother was born about a mile from here. Her father worked this vineyard his whole life." Speaking the truth to her felt as good as sharing the wine. "This winery has been in Bérnard's family for nearly two hundred years."

She tucked her chin deeper into her blanketed legs and blew into her cupped hands. "That's really not so long in Euro terms."

"True." He could easily sit next to her, draw her closer, warm her with his own body heat.

"Tell me about your mother and Bérnard."

He grinned. "I like spin the bottle better than twenty questions."

She gave him a warning look. "Answer."

"Yes, Professor." What a sight she must be in a lecture hall full of nineteen-year-old college kids: rapid-firing questions, demanding complete, correct answers, using those amazing legs to distract the boys. The lucky bastards. "I bet you're a force to be reckoned with on campus."

She laughed softly. "Sometimes. But seriously, tell me about your mother and Bérnard."

"My mother practically grew up at this winery. She and Bérnard played children's games in the vineyard and picked and harvested the Pinot Noir every year. Bérnard always planned to marry her, at least that's what he told me. But he had to travel, to expand his education about running the winery, and my mother went to school in Paris, where—"

Good God. He almost said that she'd met an American pilot, and she'd made a stupid mistake. Clenching his teeth, he pushed himself off the wall, setting his glass on the table.

"Yes?" Janine urged. "What happened?"

She got pregnant and, ashamed of what she'd done to Bérnard, she ran off to America with a cheating, lying, manipulative jerk. "She met my father and left poor Bérnard with a broken heart."

"Too bad for Bérnard, but good for you, I suppose."

"You have no idea." He forced a casual laugh. "But don't worry. Lisette was waiting in the wings." And Bérnard never saw or spoke to Gabrielle again, to his lifelong regret. Then, five years ago, Luc had showed up with his strange tale of a secret identity and undercover FBI work. Bérnard had embraced him, literally and figuratively.

"Do Bérnard and Lisette have children?"

"No. Sadly, they don't."

Her eyes widened. "What will happen to the winery?"

"Perhaps Lisette will sell it."

"That seems a shame, after it's been in his family for two hundred years." She brushed some dirt from the stone step where she sat, and looked around. "This is just the type of place the couple from New York bought, the couple who discovered the Plums. They were hidden in a cellar, much like this one."

"That's probably who will buy this. Rich Americans looking to own a piece of history." He seized the change of subject. "So, how did you first hear about the discovery of the Plums?"

She twirled a strand of hair, and a shadow of a smile

crossed her face. "I was leaving Royce Hall after class." The smile bloomed into a full grin. "And Albert came running across the quad, a sight in bright green pants with frogs on them. The frogs were a tribute to France, not a mere fashion faux pas."

"*Naturellement.*"

"Anyway, he came barreling across the grass, waving his arms at me. 'They found them, they found Pompadour's vases!' You'd have thought it was the Holy Grail, he was so happy."

"Why did they mean so much to him?"

She narrowed her eyes as she considered the question. "From an art history standpoint, they're truly significant in the time line of how porcelain was made. A time line that's now completely changed, due to his fervent beliefs."

All this passion wasn't about a time line. "But it's more than that."

Her eyes sparkled in the flickering light. "Yes, it is. They prove that Jeanne-Antoinette Poisson was no mere bourgeoisie mistress. She was a profoundly influential patroness of the arts. She changed the *course* of art history, not just the timing. And she's never been given her rightful due. Not by political or art historians."

She started to say something else, then stopped.

"What is it?"

"No," she shook her head. "Nothing."

"Come on, Dr. Coulter," he coaxed. "I'm enjoying the lecture."

"Once I get started, I can blow through a fifty-minute class without a breath." Her smile tumbled his heart.

"We've got plenty of time." He pulled out a chair and flipped it around, leaning forward on the seat back. "What is it about those Plums?"

"It's not the Plums. It's what they say about Pompadour." She plucked at a thread on the blanket, then looked up at him. "I really admire her. Not the fact that she ditched her husband to sleep with the king. But she was just a lower-middle-class girl with big dreams. And when she realized them, she did amazing things with the power she attained. Few mistresses did anything beyond invent a new sleeve style.

"But Pompadour," she continued, waggling a playful finger at him. "That woman single-handedly propelled literature and painting and theater to the next level. It would have been easy for her to just parlay her gifts—her charm, her influence, her royal lover—into an easy life, one that was all about her clothes and her beauty. That alone would have been a huge step in the world for her. But she was smart." Janine's face lit with something that looked like pride. "Her brains were her secret weapon."

Just like you. He leaned the seat back closer toward her and listened.

"She spent her days grooming Boucher and inspiring Voltaire and discovering obscure porcelain artists. She encouraged them all to push the envelope." A natural flush deepened the color of her cheeks. "She used her tremendous influence to bring talented writers and artists to the world's attention, geniuses who otherwise would have languished in the side streets of Paris."

"And you relate to her."

Janine laughed self-consciously. "I don't know about

that. I respect her, I—I," she paused and thought about it for a minute. "Well, yeah. I guess I do. Believe me, Porterville, California, is about as bourgeoisie as you can get. I wasn't raised in a trailer, but I had plenty of friends who were. So I can relate to someone who looked around and said, 'I can do better. What skills do I have?' Yes." She nodded, almost defiantly. "I do relate to her."

"I understand that." He certainly had his own "bourgeois" childhood, growing up in a run-down brownstone in Southie. Sleeping on a pull-out sofa, so his mother and Claire could have the bedroom. Wanting out. Blaming his father for their poverty. He'd thought the same thing: *I can do better. What skills do I have?*

Janine had looks and brains. Nick Jarrett had dexterity and nerve.

He scooped up the knapsack from the ground and rolled it into a ball. "You should get some sleep." He placed the makeshift pillow on the stair closest to her head.

Later, when it was definite that they only had a reading on the forgeries, he would tell her that she was heading back to Versailles, and that he'd be continuing the journey without her.

"I can't sleep," she said, laying her head on the knapsack. "I'm too keyed up—ouch!" She jerked her head up and grabbed some hair snagged on a Velcro catch.

"Here." He grasped the ensnared lock in one hand. "I can fix it." He eased a long strand through the fibers of Velcro. "Better?"

She rubbed her head where it had pulled. "Thanks." She opened the side pocket of the knapsack and stuck her hand in. "Do you think there's an elastic band or a string in here?"

"Turn around." He put a hand on her shoulders, and she gave him a questioning look. *"Detournez."* He circled his finger in the direction he wanted her to go. "I'll show you a trick."

She obeyed, but kept a wary gaze on him over her shoulder. "What kind of trick?"

He placed his fingertips at her temples and gently swiveled her head forward. "Trust me."

He reached under her hair and lifted it with two hands. God, it was gorgeous. Absolutely straight and thick enough to get lost in, and falling nearly to her waist. He had to fight to keep from tangling his fingers in it and burying his face in the silkiness of it.

"What are doing?" she asked, her voice as tight as the grip he had on her hair.

"This is called a French braid. Are you familiar with it?"

"You know how to French braid?"

He leaned dangerously close to her ear. *"Mais oui, ma belle."* She shuddered, and he chuckled softly. "My mother had to leave early every morning, so I did my sister's hair before school."

He divided it into sections, combing through the length with his fingers to remove any knots. He almost groaned with the pleasure of it. "You have wonderful hair." Long hair and long legs—his two weaknesses in a woman. "Hold still." He wrapped the hair around two fingers and started to twine. "It's like riding a bike, I guess. I haven't forgotten in the thirty years since I braided Claire's hair into submission."

His fingers froze. *Why* did he say her name? What the hell was wrong with him? He scooped a lock and folded it over the rest, then mirrored the action on the other side.

"How much younger than you is Claire? Where does she live?"

"Four years." Truth telling was over. "Paris."

Wheatlike shades of blond were soon intertwined into one flowing rope down her back. He lifted the last section and secured it by tucking the hair back into itself at the nape of her neck. *"Voilà."*

She reached back and touched it with her hand, then turned to him with an unsure smile. "Aren't you full of surprises?"

He grazed her throat with one finger. "Yes, I am."

Her mouth was inches from his. It would have been so easy to steal another kiss; all he needed was the tiniest sign from her. But she turned her attention pointedly to the knapsack, punching it into shape before she laid her head on it. He returned to the chair.

The cellar was suddenly very still and quiet. After a minute she lifted her head. "You're not going to drink all that twenty-thousand-dollar wine, are you?"

He laughed quietly. "We can have it later. And there's plenty more."

She laid her head back down, her eyes wide open. "Where will you be?"

He tapped the back of the chair. "Right here." A good, safe distance from her.

"Don't turn that flashlight off, okay?"

"I'll light the lamp with the oil Lisette brought. We should save the flashlight." He positioned himself so that he could see her and the door at the top of the stairs. "Are you afraid of the dark, Janine?"

"I didn't think so, but it's kind of spooky in here." She adjusted the blanket around her. "What are you going to do?"

Watch you sleep. "I thought I'd figure out a way to get your Plums back."

"Great." She gave him a lazy smile as she put her head down. "You do that."

Janine's eyes burned from exhaustion as she closed her lids, but she ignored the sting. Her head still tingled from his fingertips. Having her hair braided by a man was the most intimate gesture she could imagine . . . except for the wine tasting that preceded it.

What kind of man picked locks and worked for the FBI and put tracking gizmos in porcelain and *braided hair?* What kind of man duped the local police, stole a car, then managed to be tender with a grieving old woman? What kind of man ran like a bandit from the scene of a crime, made her strip naked in the car, and then exchanged wine through the most soulful kiss she'd ever felt?

The kind that sent flashes of pure desire through her body and made her crave more . . . wine.

Stifling a sigh, Janine nestled into her homemade bed. How long would they be here? There were nine hundred and ninety-nine more bottles to spin. But she had no business thinking thoughts like that. She had a mission now, and it wasn't French kissing in a wine cellar.

She tried to imagine the joy of finding the Plums and restoring them to the exhibit. Visualization had always worked for her. When she wanted something very, very badly, she just imagined how it would feel, what it would smell and taste and sound like.

It would feel divine. It would smell like spice and aftershave, taste like mouth-warmed wine and sound . . . French.

"Ohhh." The groan escaped before she could stop it.

Luc laughed. *"Dormez,* Janine."

Yes. It would sound exactly like that.

CHAPTER
Fourteen

J anine."

Szha-neen. The fog of sleep cleared at the feel of a man's hand on her cheek. "What?" She jerked up, the knapsack tumbling down a step. "What is it?"

"Lisette is here." Luc reached to help her to her feet. "We need your help."

"Oh, okay." How long had she been asleep?

The little Frenchwoman peered up from the table, holding a tumbler half full of wine so dark it looked black. She didn't offer the slightest acknowledgment, let alone a friendly hello.

"Bonjour." Janine gave Lisette the brightest smile she could muster, considering she'd been sleeping on stone and dirt for a while.

"Bon soir." No return smile.

Good *evening?* How long had she been asleep? She looked at Luc. His beard was darker, his eyes weary. "What time is it?"

"Almost four o'clock in the afternoon," he said.

She'd slept nearly five hours, the dreamless sleep of the dead.

Straightening her tired back, she walked to the table and sat across from Lisette. Luc crouched between them, his hands on a few scattered papers.

The flashlight stood at the center of the table, casting a ghostly white circle of light on the ceiling and creating odd, long shapes around the room. Luc reached over and put a hand on Lisette's arm, and she responded by taking a deep drink from the tumbler.

"I've found the vases," he said to Janine, an odd glimmer in his eyes. "The forgeries and the real vases. They're together."

She blinked and put her hand on her chest. "How can that be? The same person took them?"

He lifted his brows as though to say, "Who knows?" "At least the same person *has* them. And we now have a location." He tapped a single sheet of white paper, showing a computerized map and a series of numbers along the bottom. "Here."

She glanced at it, then back at him. "Where?"

He held up a hand to quiet her. "We don't need to burden Lisette with the details. She's going to help us prepare to get them, so give Lisette your sizes—everything. Top, bottom, shoes, everything."

She raised an eyebrow and glanced at Lisette. "She's going clothes shopping?"

"Lisette will go to Dijon and buy you the proper attire for where we're going."

"Can't we just go get the vases and leave?" She didn't need the right *clothes* to find the Plums, for God sake.

"We can't stand out. Do you know the French equivalent of your sizes?"

"I—no." She stood and lifted Lisette's flannel shirt enough to show her hips. "Your pants are just a size or so too big, so whatever you are." She held up one finger, then put it down. "Minus one."

Lisette wrote something down on the paper in front of her and asked, *"La chassures?"*

Janine tried to wiggle her toes, but they were jammed into the ugly black flats. "These are at least a size too small."

"Anything else?" Luc prompted.

"And—and . . ." Oh, Lord. She touched her chest self-consciously. "Underwear and . . . a brassiere."

She felt Luc's gaze drop to her chest, but she kept her attention on the other woman. "Thirty-four C," she said, in answer to Lisette's questioning look.

Lisette shook her head. Evidently that didn't compute to a size she recognized. Janine sighed and looked at Luc. "Help me out here."

"Au-dessus de la moyenne," he said, with a sly wink to Janine. Above average. She made a point of watching Lisette write.

Lisette stood suddenly, took the tumbler of wine, and knocked it back in one gulp. Not exactly testing for balance and flavor. Luc reached into his pocket and pulled out a billfold. Without looking or counting, he handed a thick stack of Euros to Lisette.

"Alors," she said, stuffing the money into a pocket of the baggy dress she wore. She picked up a jacket that hung on the back of the chair. *"Au revoir."*

With one glance at Janine, she went up the stairs.

When she opened the door, late-afternoon light peeked through the shrubbery that hid the opening.

"Lisette," Luc called.

She turned slowly. *"Oui?"*

"Merci beaucoup."

She nodded and left.

"She's certainly a woman of few words," Janine said, when the door closed on the inviting twilight.

"I told you, she's in mourning," he said. "Shock and mourning. And she's doing us a huge favor."

Of course he'd defend his friend's wife. It wasn't worth telling him the old lady gave her the willies. She rubbed her back where it had pressed into the steps. "I couldn't possibly feel dirtier."

"We can go back into the house now. You can clean up and have something to eat while Lisette is gone. We'll leave around midnight, so we can arrive when the resort is the most deserted."

"The resort? Where are we going?"

"Lac Léman." The French side of Lake Geneva. "A spa called the Royal Parc in Evian-les-Bains." He frowned at a paper on the table, turning it to face him. "Somewhere in the far western corner of the sixth floor. A lakeside penthouse, no doubt." He looked back at her. "You've never been there, have you?" He sounded concerned that she would say yes.

She shook her head and studied the incomprehensible computer readout in front of him. The only thing that looked vaguely familiar was the map with the half-moon shape of Lake Geneva. "Are you absolutely sure the Plums are there?"

"Oh, yes." He tapped the page with his finger, then looked at her with a strange expression. "My enemy is very, very smart and dangerous."

A drop of anxiety trickled down her sore spine. "He's my enemy, too. I'm convinced this has to do with Albert's death."

He regarded her for a moment. "We're not entirely sure of that."

But she was. And nothing would stop her from going all the way with this.

Suddenly switching to his American accent as he draped his arm around her shoulder, Luc said, "Ready for our honeymoon, honey?"

Her heart flipped. "Is that our cover story, Bond?"

He smiled. "I'm afraid it will have to be. But you have a very memorable appearance, so for us to blend in, you'll have to look different." His fingers drifted to the nape of her neck, warming the skin and raising the fine hairs under his hand. "You might have to do something with your hair."

"From Bond to Sassoon. What do you have in mind? A quick cut and color?"

"If Lisette cannot find a wig, yes." He gave the braid a gentle tug. "Could you live with that?"

It sounded like it would hurt him more than it would hurt her. "Of course. It's just hair; it grows back."

His fingers burrowed further into her hair. "Perhaps we can think of a way to save it."

"Yeah, well." She dipped her head and slipped out of his grasp. "I want to save the Plums, not my hair."

*   *   *

Lisette's hands shook as she climbed into the truck. As she struggled to put the key into the ignition, the passenger door popped open.

Stifling a gasp, she stared at the man whose beady eyes and oily complexion she'd come to hate. "What are you doing here?" she demanded. "I thought you were gone."

The Indian curled his lip at her and slid into the passenger seat next to her, a silver blade flashing in his hand with the same menacing glimmer she saw in his black eyes. "Where are they?"

She couldn't breathe. Would he go to the basement and kill them both?

"In the wine cellar," she whispered, tilting her head toward the side of the house. "Over there."

"Get him out," he ordered. "And keep her down there."

"What?" She put a hand to her chest. The girl would die here? In her own home? In Bérnard's cellar?

He lifted the knife toward her throat. "Get him in the house and keep him there."

So these were the instructions she had to follow. "For how long?"

His gaze slid behind her toward the cellar. "As long as you can."

Shaking her head, she fumbled with the handle and slid out of the car. This was murder. Murder on *her* soul.

Walking to the cellar door, she turned and glanced back at the truck, but the disgusting little Indian had disappeared. Should she run? No. They'd find her. She had no choice but to comply now. Her black soul couldn't be saved, and neither could that girl.

"Luc!" Lisette called, as she opened the cellar door slowly. "Help me, quickly!"

Immediately, she heard his footsteps on the stone steps, and he appeared in the dim light. "What is it, Lisette? What's the matter?"

She gave in to the trembling of her body. "There's . . . someone . . . in the house, I think."

He put a hand on her shoulder and looked past her. "How do you know?"

"I heard something. A noise in the house. I think someone came in the front door." Her mind was spinning as fast as she could tell her lies. "I am so scared, Luc." That much, at least, was true.

Without hesitating, he nodded. "Stay here with Janine." He hustled away toward the house. As soon as she saw him open the kitchen door, she turned toward the cellar.

"*Madame,* Luc has gone to check something in the house. I am going with him. Wait here." Without giving Janine a moment to respond, Lisette slipped out the door and looked at the key in her hand. Should she leave the door unlocked? No, the girl would barge out . . . right into the blade of the Indian.

Her heart pumping wildly, she turned the lock. This was better for her, Lisette told herself. That terrible man couldn't get in, but the poor girl couldn't get out.

Pocketing the key, she dashed toward the house, half expecting someone to jump out of the bushes at her. She jerked open the back door and tried to think of more ways to detain Luc.

*   *   *

Lisette was gone before Janine could protest, leaving her alone in the wine cellar. She'd understood what happened: the woman had heard a noise in the house. Then why not stay here in the cellar until Luc checked it out? A chill skimmed down her arms, regardless of the sweatshirt she wore.

A snapping sound from the top of the stairs grabbed her attention. "Luc?"

She waited, but heard nothing. Picking up the flashlight, she pointed it toward the door, but it remained closed. "Lisette? Is that you?"

She could have sworn she heard the sound of metal scraping. But, then again, her imagination was definitely running on overload. When she thought too hard about it, even the association between Luc's friend Bérnard and Albert seemed absurd. There was no way anyone could make such a wild connection.

Janine waited at the table, holding her head in her hands, as at least twenty minutes passed. How could she be tired again? She'd just slept for hours. Still, her breath became slow and even, and she laid her head on her folded arms. As her eyes started to get heavier, she realized something felt vaguely familiar. She felt . . . *drunk*.

But she hadn't had any more than one sip of the zillion-dollar wine.

Fear snaked through her, shooting just enough adrenaline to give her the strength to lift her head. Peering into the darkness, her gaze traveled to where the vent had been open all day, supplying air and slivers of daylight.

There was nothing but blackness where there should have been an open vent.

It took every ounce of strength she had to push herself up from the table. Dear God in heaven, the vent was closed. How long until she had no air at all?

She called for Luc again, but her voice sounded weak and far away. She managed to get to the steps, but that disconnected sensation was starting again. Her legs wobbled as though she were learning to walk. Stumbling once, then again, she made it up the stairs and reached the vent. It was shut tight. She turned the crank as hard as she could, and it cracked right off in her hands.

Damn it! She poked her fingers against the metal slats, but they were closed completely and sealed around the edges. She pressed her mouth against it, as though she could suck air through the slats, but the rubber-lined edges prevented her from getting a molecule.

A wave of dizziness rolled through her. This was ridiculous. This was fear taking over. There had to be enough air in this cellar for her to survive until Luc came back. Pulling herself up, she struggled to reach the door, but the handle wouldn't move. Goddamn him; why did he always lock her in?

He'd be back in a minute. She tried to take shallow breaths to conserve air, to stay alert and awake.

But the room got darker and her body got heavier, and finally, she just closed her eyes and put her head on the stairs.

He'd been through every room in the house several times, at Lisette's insistence. All was fine, he assured her, anxious to get back to the cellar. Janine wouldn't like being in there alone this long. "I'll keep an eye on things," he told her as they walked across the courtyard. "You just get what you need in Dijon and hurry back."

She looked up at him, sadness giving her eyes a haunted look. "Walk me to the truck, Luc."

He put a comforting arm on her back and quickly guided her across the yard to where her truck was parked. Opening the door, he patted her shoulder. "Go now, Lisette. It's important that we leave tonight."

He watched her drive away, a little ripple of guilt sliding through him. She was just an old farmer, now a widow, and shouldn't be involved in this. He'd have to make it up to her somehow.

As he strode back to the cellar door, he remembered the key. Lisette had it! He'd have to call through the vent and tell Janine to wait a bit longer. Bérnard must have another key somewhere. Otherwise, he'd break into the cellar.

He dropped to his knees, and slammed his hands on the rusted metal of the vent. The slats were completely sealed. He leaned into it and yelled, "Janine!"

How long had he been in the house? And how did the vent get closed? He'd known it to slam shut before; he remembered once it happened when he and Bérnard were in the cellar. But it was only a matter of cranking it open again; wouldn't Janine figure that out?

Kneeling in front of the massive brass keyhole, he peered in. "Janine!" he called again.

Yanking his tiny screwdriver from his pocket, he began to work the lock. Side to side. Front to back. There was nothing standard about the ancient device; it didn't respond to his pick, and he couldn't rake the pins with his scraping technique.

Swearing again, he stood and kicked the door, and then gave the vent a solid smack with his shoe. The metal bent, which would allow some air in the cellar, but not enough, and not fast enough if she was already out. But it would give him some time to find another key.

He stood to run to the house, but suddenly froze. No. He would not leave her out here. This may have been a fluke or an accident . . . or not. Wiping a bead of sweat from his brow, he knelt again at the lock and jammed his screwdriver in. There were no pins, so it had to be an old-fashioned tumbler lock. Just about impossible to pick.

He twisted the screwdriver and closed his eyes to feel the shape of the cylinder, applying varying tension with his fingertips. Damn. A bead of sweat rolled between his shoulder blades. He'd finally met a lock he couldn't pick and someone's life depended on him doing it.

Snapping the screwdriver out of the keyhole, he stood up, stepped back, and pulled out his gun. With one careful shot, he shattered the lock without sending a bullet through the door.

Shoving the door open with a grunt, he almost tripped over Janine's body at the top of the stairs. He dragged her into the evening air, his hands frantically searching for a pulse. Damn, but she was prone to hypoxia. Reaching under the sweatshirt, he flattened his palm over her chest and counted the beats of her heart. With his ear to her mouth, he listened to her intake of breath increase with every gasp.

She would be fine.

But the hairs on the back of his neck stood at attention. Something told him this wasn't a mere mishap.

Scooping Janine into his arms, he then carried her across the courtyard toward the house. By the time he reached the kitchen door, she started to wake up.

She blinked at him. "What happened? How did I get trapped in there?"

He put her in a chair, then reached behind his back for his gun again. "I don't know. I had to shoot off the lock, and while we wait for Lisette, I'm keeping this handy."

CHAPTER
Fifteen

Janine managed to shower and eat the stew that Luc warmed for her. They ate quietly, the lights low, the gun on the table next to him.

They didn't discuss the danger they might be in, which suited Janine just fine. If she dwelled on it, terror took hold. And if he knew she was afraid, he might send her back to Versailles.

"Do we have to wait for her?" Janine kept her eyes on the gun as she asked. "I mean, is it that important, what we're wearing?"

He nodded. "If we stand out, we might as well put a target on our backs. Slipping in unnoticed is critical. And to that end, you need a wig. Or something."

"I'll wear a hat."

"Maybe that would work. I'd hate to see you cut your hair."

"Actually . . ." She smiled for the first time in hours. "My ex-fiancé used to beg me to cut my hair and color it red. It would just about put him over the edge if I came back from France with short, dyed hair after I refused him for so many years."

"That must be your Sam. The liar," he said.

"He's not *my*—" She frowned at him. "How do you know his name?"

"You said it when you fainted."

"Oh, hell." She didn't want to hear this. "What did I say?"

He grinned playfully. "Something like, 'Sam, you're forgiven. If only you'll cough up a bigger, better diamond than the one I flushed away.'"

"Amazing how the lack of oxygen can turn a person into a raving lunatic."

This time he laughed with her, maybe as relieved as she was to not be concentrating on the danger, and the gun. "Is he also an art historian?"

"Not a chance. His idea of art is a movie with subtitles. He can't stand to set foot on the UCLA campus, except to hunt for coeds who want to be movie stars." And he was very good at finding them. "He's a producer. A Hollywood hotshot."

He gave her a disbelieving look. "You're too smart for a guy like that."

"Not smart enough to figure that out for five years."

He scooped a mushroom onto his spoon. "So what made you stay with him?"

"He's very funny and charming, and we had a good time together. We traveled a lot, until he got a big movie deal last year and, well—" He lied, cheated, and made promises he couldn't keep. "Things sort of slid downhill after that."

"But you were going to marry him," he countered. "They couldn't have gone that far 'downhill.'"

She abandoned her stew and looked straight into his eyes. "I was optimistic. Sam offered me the kind of lifestyle I'd dreamed of since I was a little girl in Porterville."

"What kind of lifestyle was that?"

"Comfort. Security. Big-time luxury." She was surprised at how easily she could admit that, now that she'd separated from Sam. "I wanted a *home*. You know, with a curved staircase and a grand piano. It took me a while to realize that the price for the house and husband was way, way too high."

The hint of sorrow in his eyes squeezed some unfamiliar spot in her heart. "Sounds like you figured out that the quality of the husband is more important than the quality of the house."

"You're pretty smart, for a security guard."

He held her gaze for a moment, the compliment warming his brown eyes. "Sam's a fool."

That made her stomach dip, so she looked at the gun again. Just to remind herself *why* she was here, in this château with a devastatingly charming Frenchman.

Headlights pierced through the lace curtains, and he immediately grabbed the gun and stood, the brief moment of intimacy destroyed. Stepping toward the door, he inched back the curtain. "It's Lisette."

Janine joined him in time to catch Lisette's surprised look as she climbed out of the truck. "She probably thought we'd run out before she returned," she said.

He stuck the gun back into his waistband and opened

the door. "Go upstairs and change into whatever she bought. It's time to get out of here."

"Vous êtes très jolie, mademoiselle."

Janine didn't feel so very pretty; she felt completely unnerved—but it was the first civil thing Lisette had said to her. The compliment, issued softly from the older woman as she pulled clothing from the bags she'd brought upstairs, made Janine feel like some kind of French nobility being dressed by her handmaid. No one in France called any woman over twenty-five, single or married, *mademoiselle* anymore.

"Merci," she responded, looking at the array of clothes. "Thank you for getting all this."

Lisette shrugged and smoothed her hand over a black sheath dress. "Luc requested garments of quality." Her English was stilted, but at least she was speaking to Janine now.

"Thank you, again," she said to Lisette, hoping for a return smile. "All of these items will work fine."

Lisette nodded, then crossed her arms. "In the casino," she mumbled, half to herself. "You may need evening clothes."

"I don't think we'll be there that long." They wouldn't be gambling; at least, not at the gaming tables.

Lisette held up one finger. *"Une momente."*

She shuffled out of the room, and Janine opened the last bag. Inside was a black felt beret—sort of like the newsboys' hats that had been popular recently. Lisette must not have been able to find a wig. In a separate bag marked *la pharmacie,* Janine found a small box.

She didn't need to translate the label; the image of a gorgeous redhead with freshly colored hair was universal. *Merlot*. How appropriate—hair the color of wine.

Lisette returned with a package wrapped in tissue stretched over her arms. Janine lifted the edge of it to reveal a beaded cobalt blue gown.

Based on the wardrobe she'd seen so far, it had been many years since Lisette wore anything this stylish. "*Non, non. Merci*. But I don't need your evening gown, *madame*. Really."

Lisette pressed it into Janine's hands. "Please. You will look beautiful in it."

Janine slid the tissue to the top of the dress. "Wow. It's gorgeous." A million tiny blue beads sewn against deep blue satin, a long, V-necked halter top that screamed Marilyn Monroe fifties, and a unique rhinestone clasp at the waist. It could have snagged a fortune at one of the vintage shops on Doheney, in L.A.

"I will not wear this dress, *mademoiselle*," Lisette said, a strange melancholy in her doelike brown eyes. But then, what was strange about heartache on the face of a woman whose husband had just died? "I want you to have it for a special evening with Luc. He will like it. I want him to see you in it."

Oh, God, the woman really didn't get it. She thought they were off on some romantic jaunt to the spas and casinos of Lac Léman. Did she think having dinner with a gun on the table was a vacation? "I'm sure this dress is very dear to you."

"Not really." At Janine's questioning look, Lisette added, "It might bring you . . . happiness."

Janine took the gown, touched by the sadness in Lisette's look, and impulsively, she hugged the little Frenchwoman. She had obviously misjudged her. *"Merci. Merci beaucoup, madame."*

Lisette shrugged off the hug, no doubt mortified by the oh-so-American demonstration of affection to a stranger. *"De rien."*

But it wasn't 'nothing,' and Janine could tell by the look in the woman's eyes. They filled as she looked up at Janine.

"Je regret . . ." Her voice trailed off.

"Pourquoi?" Why was she sorry?

Lisette stepped back and blinked, a giant tear spilling. She laid a wrinkled, sun-damaged hand on her own chest and looked at Janine. *"Je regret,"* she repeated.

This must have to do with Bérnard.

"And I am sorry for your loss," Janine said softly.

Lisette lifted her hand from her bosom and rested it on Janine's face. Her hand was cool and dry, the worn palm of an old woman. *"Vous êtes très jolie,"* she said again.

Very pretty. *"Merci."*

Lisette turned away and busied herself by pulling an ancient suitcase from the closet and opening it on the bed. *"Voilà, mademoiselle."* Then she left without another word.

Janine arranged the beaded gown carefully along the bottom of the suitcase. How sad, that old lady living alone in her château in Burgundy. Grieving her dead husband. Giving away her girlhood gowns.

How very sad.

She changed into cotton pants and pulled on a casual

black sweater. Gathering her hair with one hand, she slid on the black cap, tucking her hair beneath. In the mirror, she adjusted the cap low over her eyes. This would do for now, until she had to chop it.

Then she remembered the feel of Luc's hands in her hair.

Oh, hell. Maybe she could get away with wearing a hat for her entire . . . honeymoon.

CHAPTER
Sixteen

Luc waited until they were almost at Evian-les-Bains to brief Janine on her new identity. Across the sedan that Lisette had produced, she sat tucked into her corner, her endearing little hat pulled low over her eyes.

That cap. *Bon Dieu.* All he wanted to do was rip it off with one hand and bury the other in the hair that came tumbling out.

"Your name is Katie Cooper." He made the pronouncement in accent-free American English. Not the soft New England vowels he grew up with, but it felt almost as good.

She started at the sound of his voice, then laughed. "How do you do that?"

"It's a gift." For the last two hours, driving the winding, narrow roads in the foothills of the Alps, he'd forced himself to think in English. Forced himself to capture the essence of Dr. David Cooper, newlywed surgeon on his extended European honeymoon.

"And I'm your brand-new husband, David."

"Dave?" She choked the name and then tipped the bill of her cap enough for him to see her droll look. "You gotta do better than *Dave,* Luc."

"Don't call me Luc." He said it more sharply than he intended, but a slip like that could be deadly. "It's David, and it matches a credit card in my wallet." At her curious look, he added, "Plus, we want everything ordinary. Nothing conspicuous, nothing that gets noticed."

Her expression grew serious. "Got it. Where are we from?"

"Chi-cah-go." He flattened and drawled the middle syllable just to prove he knew how city natives pronounced the name.

"From one lake to another. That's easy enough to remember."

"Exactly what I was thinking."

She tapped him playfully on the arm. "Which means either we both have great, like-thinking minds or your idea is drop-dead clichéd."

"Humor me. I prefer great, like-thinking minds."

"Great it is, then, Dave. And what do the Coopers do when they aren't jaunting around Europe spending granddaddy's trust?"

"I'm a doctor. You're a lawyer."

"There's an interesting partnership," she mused. "You screw up, I defend."

He laughed, enjoying the volley with her. "I don't think we'll be striking up long conversations with other travelers, but just in case someone asks."

He glanced at her and caught her tucking a stray hair

into the cap. "I can finally put my acting classes to good use," she said.

Eyes back on the road, he read the mile marker and did a quick calculation. "Very soon, too."

"I've heard of the Royal Parc Evian," she said. "It was a summer palace for Edward VII, as I recall. World-famous Gustave Jaulmes frescoes everywhere. Have you been here before?"

"I took a vacation here about ten years ago." *And I relieved an elderly Japanese couple of a hundred-thousand-dollar necklace.* The old cocktail of guilt and regret splashed through him.

He was a thief.

A thief who considered seducing this beautiful woman: this upstanding, ambitious, dynamic professor who wanted nothing more from life than to find her stolen treasures, run her successful art exhibit, and sit on her curved stairs with someone honest and faithful.

And yet, seduction was damn near all he'd been thinking about for most of the last three hours.

"So how does this all unfold?" she asked, interrupting his thoughts. "What's going to happen?"

"I have to see our suite and compare it to where I believe the Plums are. I'll contact Lisette one more time for a final read."

"Are you going to steal them?"

He spared her a quick glance and a wry smile. "In a perfect world, yes."

"And in the real one?"

"We have to be flexible. Just wait and see what happens."

"Got it."

"Don't offer any information to any hotel employees," he warned, as they made their way up the winding drive illuminated by pink and white spotlights. Across the rolling lawns, he saw the peak of the main building bathed in the same spotlights, showcased like a rare jewel on a bed of velvet. "Don't chat with friendly desk clerks or talkative bellmen."

"Friendly desk clerks? In France?" She sniffed. "And no bellman's going to give you the time of day when he sees that decrepit luggage."

He winked at her. "I'm counting on it."

As he slowed the car in front of the entrance, a half dozen valets approached them but didn't open the car door.

"Now don't forget." He unfastened his seatbelt and she did the same. "We're on our honeymoon."

Before she could answer, he reached for her and slid her across the front seat, into his side. He heard her quick, surprised breath.

With one hand, he cupped her cheek, then nudged the bill of her cap higher with his forehead. "So act like you like me."

"I do like you," she whispered back.

"I like you, too." He brought his mouth down on hers and captured it before she could react. He took his time, a lazy, relaxing kiss, exploring her tongue and lips with his until he elicited a soft sigh from her throat.

Oh yeah. He definitely liked her.

He nibbled his way to her ear, clasped her earlobe between his teeth, and gave it a tiny suck. "Just don't call me Luc."

*   *   *

"We found this in the trunk of Luc Tremont's Alpha." Paul Dunne dropped a satchel on Tristan's temporary desk at the Police Nationale office in Versailles. "Open it."

Tristan gave his partner a weary look as he unzipped the bag. "C'mon, man. It's eight o'clock on Monday morning. Hold the drama and tell me what it is."

"Just look."

A ball of black fabric lay inside. He pulled it out. The flimsy little gown meant nothing to him. "So he had a girl's clothes in his car. Why should this surprise me?"

"Look closely."

Tristan let the gown fall open, his hands holding the shoulders. Across the front was a red blotch. "Son of a bitch," he muttered. "I completely forgot about that call."

"What call?" Paul dropped into the metal chair across from Tristan.

Tristan stuffed the gown back in the satchel. "Luc called the night of the gala and told me that someone had broken into Janine Coulter's room at the Trianon. He thought we should check it out and keep security out of it." Now he knew why.

"Let's go." Paul stood and grabbed the satchel.

Tristan frowned and gave a negative shake of his head. He wanted to talk to the American woman alone. "Keep working on that tracking program, Paul. You might still be able to hack into it. I'll go check out the hotel."

"Sure. I thought I had it last night, but hit another roadblock. What did Luc say happened in her room?"

"He didn't. Just that we should check out Janine

Coulter's room before anyone from housekeeping or security got to it. He wanted me to get her another one, which I did, but I never followed up."

Paul rubbed a hand over his thinning hair. "Well, shit, Tris. We've been slightly busy since Saturday night."

He didn't bother to agree. He hated excuses, and Paul knew it. "I bet it's all cleaned up by now." -

"I don't get it, though," Paul said, staring into the satchel again. "Why the hell would Benazir have his people mess up her room and leave the Scorpion's mark? They had bigger shit to pull off that night. And she's not connected to any of this."

Disconnects are sometimes the best connections.

Tristan came around his desk and grabbed his jacket hanging on the back of the door. "I'll tell you this, man, she sure wasn't winning any popularity contests at that gala." He silently cursed himself again for forgetting about Luc's call. "Has anyone seen that woman since Saturday night? Weren't you over at the palace yesterday afternoon? Wasn't she there to inspect the damage?"

"She was definitely not there." Paul followed him out the door. "It's not like you wouldn't notice her."

Tristan snorted. "Luc sure did." And he'd even tried to use Luc's obvious attraction to the woman to slow him down after the theft. But it hadn't helped. Luc had managed to get to the Volvo they'd left for him, and no one had seen any trace of it since that night. Knowing Luc, he didn't go all the way to his destination in it.

Whatever the hell that destination *was,* since no one

had been able to make the goddamn GPS program work yet.

"I'll be at the Trianon," he told Paul.

"Sure," Paul said. "I'll be in hacker hell."

Tristan walked to the hotel, playing with the puzzle pieces all the way. What relation did Janine Coulter have to the Scorpion?

A *Ne Pas Déranger* sign hung on the door of the room number Luc had given him. Could someone else have checked in? Tristan knocked, but there was no answer. He looked up and down the hall, seeing the edge of a housekeeping cart lodged in a room a few doors away.

He found the maid and stumbled through a half-French, half-English story about a lost key and managed to elicit a master from her. When she returned to cleaning, he stuck it in the lock. Nothing happened.

The lock had been stripped. *Damn Luc.*

At the front desk, he waited for an English-speaking manager, tapping the black-and-white marble floor impatiently. At least a dozen familiar faces from the gala waited to check out.

He had to pull out a badge to get help, but when he did, he hit another dead end. Janine Coulter had never picked up the key to her new room and had not checked out of the other one yet.

Tristan flipped the puzzle pieces around in his brain as he got back in the elevator. He hated when they didn't fit.

The maid was still on the floor but, fortunately, in the room next to Janine's. He stepped in and gave her his pathetic stupid American grin as soon as he saw the adjoining door.

"The key didn't work," he said, pointing to the alternate entrance. "Could you help?"

She hustled over, stuck the master key in, and turned away without listening to his *"Merci."*

Tristan slipped into the room and froze.

Security or housekeeping had definitely *not* been in this room. And neither had Janine Coulter, unless she slept on a slashed mattress.

So where the hell was she?

Luc entered their suite soundlessly. When Janine wasn't immediately in sight in either the living or dining areas or on the balcony, his chest tightened a little. He'd left her with explicit instructions: don't let anyone into the expansive penthouse, and don't leave under any circumstances.

For the past two hours, he'd examined escape routes and studied the layout of the casino vis-à-vis the matching penthouse suite at the other end of the main building.

He had programmed the tracking system to let the FBI get a reading on the forged Plums by Thursday morning, so he had three days to lay out and execute the plan. He had to get the real Plums safely out of the room, trap Benazir, and have him ready to hand over the moment Tristan arrived.

Luc now opened the door that led to the two bedrooms. In the smaller, less formal room, the twin beds remained untouched. The canvas bag that he'd brought from Burgundy sat on the floor. Guess he got the little room.

He paused at the other door and listened for the sound of a shower, any sound of life.

"Janine?" No answer. He tapped the door harder, easing it open. "Janine?"

Her suitcase lay open on the giant canopied king-size bed. Of course she'd like this room with fresco-covered walls.

The door to the dressing area and bath was closed. He approached it and called her name again. He'd told her he'd be gone a long time, so he expected her to shower and rest. A glimmer of apprehension sparked in him. He didn't want to walk in on her in the bathroom, but *why* didn't she answer?

"Janine?" An image of her lying on the floor, hurt, bloody, *dead,* flashed in his mind. What if Benazir had been watching? What if he had a plant in the lobby and broke into the room when Luc left?

He turned the door handle and opened it a crack. "Janine, are you in here?" He stuck his head in, politely closing his eyes, but when there was no answer, he looked. A marble tub, empty. A glass shower, empty. On a vanity chair were the pants and top she'd been wearing, panties and a bra draped over them.

He entered and heard a faint, steady hiss.

Luc walked past the shower and around a corner. There, he saw a milky white glass door, the hiss more distinct.

A steam room.

He stared into the thin clouds behind the glass. Condensation frosted the glass, but a rivulet of water streamed down and cleared a path to see inside.

And what a sight it was.

His jaw went slack, and every drop of blood rushed directly to one place in response to the erotic image before him.

She lay on her back, reclining on a long marble ledge. Completely, utterly, indescribably naked.

Eyes closed, one long, tanned leg bent, the other hanging gracefully off the edge, toes pointed to the ground. She had propped one arm under her head; the other fell across her stomach.

His mouth went dry as he stared.

Her whole body was slick with moisture. Her breasts, round and taut and smooth and most definitely *above average,* rose with each even breath she took. His gaze traveled the path his mouth wanted to take, from the smooth pink nipples, down the longs lines of her waist, over the contours of her hipbones and into the golden valley exposed by the angle of her leg.

His fingertips touched the hot, wet glass of the steam room door, itching to take. To steal. To have *that.*

Nick Jarrett used to take whatever he wanted in life. He used to help himself to the beautiful things in this world, including willing women who aroused him to rock hard desire.

But Luc Tremont would not. He took one step backward just as she stretched both arms over her head, then paused as she lazily ran her palms over her sides and up her stomach.

He couldn't move. She arched her back as her fingertips lingered on the sides of her breasts, gently pushing them together, grazing her nipples until they darkened and budded. She'd be furious that he'd been feasting his eyes on every inch of her, acting the voyeur while she imagined herself alone.

Her hips rocked slowly.

Oh. Maybe she didn't imagine herself *alone*.

His cock, already hard enough to cause serious pain, slammed against his pants. She closed her eyes and darted her tongue over her lips. Her right hand traveled lazily down her stomach.

He stopped breathing.

She bent her other leg up onto the ledge and rocked her hips in one sweet, slow motion. She turned her face away, denying him the chance to see how beautiful pleasure made her.

His hands were still on the door. All he had to do was give it a gentle push and he'd be in there, lost in clouds of hot steam. With her already visualizing what he could do to her.

Because he had no doubt whose hands were touching her. No doubt whose mouth she tasted. They'd been inhaling high-octane sexual attraction for the last twenty-four hours. Longer.

Her bottom rose with the first deliberate stroke. Through the mist, he could see her stomach tighten with a quick, shallow breath. He closed his eyes, practically dizzy from need. All he had to do was take what he wanted. Give what she wanted.

I do like you. He could still hear her whispered confession.

All he had to do was—

He turned and left the room.

Cursing as he entered the other bedroom, he quietly

shut the door and locked it. He squeezed his eyes closed, but he still saw her.

Wet and naked and *wanting* him.

But he couldn't seduce a woman as one man, then disappear in a week and become another. Even if he took what they both wanted at that moment, if she ever found out, she'd hate him for what he'd been.

No, he couldn't have her. But that image would burn in his brain forever. He could imagine her slick skin under his hands, her warm breath in his mouth. He could hear her say his name.

Nick.

He dropped his head against the door and let out a long, low moan. He could fight it and try to force it out of his head but nothing could erase that vision, that incredibly beautiful picture of Janine in the steam.

He closed his eyes and surrendered to it.

CHAPTER
Seventeen

P laytime is over." Janine stared at her reflection. "It's time to do whatever has to be done to find my Plums and get them back to Versailles."

She held her hair up to her chin, then dropped it down to her shoulders. Maybe somewhere in between.

She had opened the box of hair dye and read the French instructions, but it would be easier if she cut it first. Her Ritz Spa of a bathroom had a closet full of beauty toys, from a makeup kit to a curling iron, but only a pair of tiny cuticle clippers. They would never work.

Had Luc returned with a more functional pair of scissors?

She'd lost track of time in the steam room and shower. She glanced in the mirror again. She'd lost track of her senses, too.

Grabbing a fluffy white bathrobe, she went out to face her demons. Well, just one demon. With an accent.

"Luc," she called, as she stepped into the tiny hallway between the two bedrooms. "Are you here?"

"Right here." From directly behind her, he opened the other door with a whoosh.

"Oh." She jumped and spun around. In bare feet, she was exactly eye-level with the dark hairs that escaped the open collar of his shirt.

She stepped back and managed a smile. "I didn't hear you come back."

"You were . . . in the bath." His gaze dropped over her robe, lingering on the V neck. "Relaxed now?"

"Totally." *Anything but*. The vestibule where they stood suddenly had no air, no space.

She walked into the main salon and slid open the balcony doors. Stepping out, she gulped in the crisp mountain air, lifted her face to the spring sun, and took in the vista.

One hundred and eighty degrees of Mother Nature's most exquisite artwork, accented by a thousand years of European architecture. She gazed out over the expanse of navy blue water, surrounded by white-tipped mountain peaks and sprawling villages of Swiss timber houses.

"God, this is just amazing," she murmured to herself.

"I was thinking the same thing." He stood right behind her, as warm at her back as the sun on her face.

She glanced over her shoulder and caught his expression. The one that looked like he had a secret. A little playful, a little intense, a lot sexy.

Holy hell. "Did you get scissors?"

He lifted the hair from her shoulder and smoothed it on her back. "I forgot."

He was teasing her, trying to make her comfortable,

make her laugh in the face of danger. He had no idea how vulnerable she was, no idea that he was pressing every feminine button she had.

Or did he?

She turned, brushing against him as she returned to the sitting area that faced the lake. She perched on the edge of a pale green chair.

He followed her, dropping onto a matching settee and spreading his arms across the delicate back. "I thought we could just wait on that haircut for a while."

"I don't want to be a prisoner in this room," she said. "If it's important that I look different, then I'll do what needs to be done."

He nodded, but she could tell he was placating her. Or stalling. "Let me talk to Lisette first. Once I get another read on the location, we'll finalize our plan of attack."

"Oh, I'm sure *we* will."

He leaned forward and rested his elbows on his knees. "I know how you feel about being imprisoned, Rapunzel, but if there's a way I can find those vases and get them out of here without any risk to you, that's my first choice."

"I'm not interested in taking unnecessary risks, Luc. I just want to get this guy. Not just the vases; I want the bastard who killed Albert."

He blew out a long breath and ran a hand through his hair, tousling it. "I just can't figure out the connection, Janine. Benazir was in jail until six weeks ago."

"Albert was killed three weeks ago." Was it only three

weeks? The words made the loss suddenly as fresh as it was the morning one of her grad students tracked her down with the news. "Until now, there was no reason for anyone *not* to think it was suicide."

"Did he own the gun he shot himself with?"

"He didn't own a gun. But in L.A., they're as easy to get as Valium."

"Then who might have killed him? Did he have enemies in the art world? Someone who might want to sway the world's opinion of the authenticity of the Plums?"

"There were detractors, of course. But I don't think anyone would *murder* for the sake of art history." She toyed with the robe ties, and then she remembered the closed vent in the wine cellar. "At least, I didn't think so."

Luc walked to the dining area and opened a compact refrigerator built into the wet bar. "Want some?" he asked, holding up a bottle of Evian water, the familiar label face out.

She smiled and nodded. "When in Rome."

He gave her one and returned to the settee, dwarfing it again as he stretched his long legs in front of him. He took a long, thirsty drink from the bottle.

His muscles flexed. His eyes closed.

Her whole body tightened up. Again. She cinched her robe tighter and tucked her feet under her, forcing herself to look at the view outside.

"Tell me everything you can about Albert," he said, setting his half empty bottle on the table between them.

"That could take a while. He was a very colorful man, and I've known him for a long, long time."

He rolled the bottle's white cap through the fingers of one hand, as smooth as a magician. "Longer than Sam?"

Why would he mention Sam? "Yes, much longer than Sam."

"And what did Albert think of him?"

"He tried his best to like Sam, but they never really clicked." She paused and looked sharply at him. "Sam didn't kill Albert, Luc."

"You sure?"

"Antigun, antideath penalty, antiwar, antiviolence, pacifist Sam? He thought Albert was a repressed oddball who took too much of my time and wore horrendous clothes, but he certainly didn't kill him. If Albert was murdered, I suggest we figure out who killed your friend. The events are too similar for my liking."

Luc held the bottle cap between his thumb and index finger, flipped it, and it appeared in the other hand. A regular David Copperfield. "Repressed? How so?"

"Lots of people thought Albert was locked firmly in the closet—old enough to be thoroughly ashamed of it, and young enough to still be tortured by it. He had grown children from a long-ended marriage, and I . . . I don't know." Janine dropped her head back and closed her eyes. "I hate this subject. I loved him, whatever he was."

"What did you love about him?"

She opened her eyes and looked at him. In all the years they were together, Sam had never asked that.

"Well, he was brilliant and endearing and just plain fun to be with," she began. "I loved how he made me feel about myself."

He leaned forward. "And how was that?"

"Albert thought I was smart, and not just standard-issue bright. When it came to porcelain and Sèvres, he thought I was a damn genius." She tunneled the sides of her hair and locked her hands on top of her head, liking the way the lake air cooled her neck. "How I looked, what I wore, what my parents were or were not, where I came from, what kind of car I drove, how I fit into the Holly-wood scene—none of those things mattered to Albert."

"But they mattered to Sam."

She gave him an incredulous look. "They matter to everyone in L.A., Luc. It's Plasticville, USA. But Albert and I—and a couple of our star grad students—we had such fun not caring about all that. Just loving dead artists and legendary mistresses." She grinned and let her hair tumble back. "Maybe we were all nuts." She took a drink of water. "What else do you want to know?"

"How to tell the real Plums from the fake."

She gave her head a slow, negative shake. "That takes years. Forget it."

He twirled the bottle cap on his thumb like a spinning top, watching it. "What do you mean 'who your parents were or were not'?"

How much information did this inquisitive French-man need? "Oh, that was just an expression," she said dismissively.

"But you used it," he noted. "You said 'who my parents were.' Who are they? Or is it were?"

He wasn't going to let it go. "They're both alive. My parents are . . ." What the hell; did it really matter in this day and age? "My parents never married." She looked at him squarely, defying him to be shocked or disappointed or whatever people were when they found out you are illegitimate. Stupid word.

"My mother was an 'artist.'" She held her fingers out and put imaginary quotes around the title her mother loved so much. "Actually, she was the last of that great generation of West Coast hippies, a holdout for free love until I was born in 1970. I suppose I have my father to thank that I'm not named Zephyr or Harmony."

He laughed, his eyes dancing in the reflection of the sun on Lake Geneva. He had no earthly idea how gorgeous he was.

"My dad came in and out of our lives. Not in a bad way, just in a . . . California way. But over time he became part of the establishment, got a law degree and married a set designer—a woman about five years older than I am. He's all legit now."

Why did she use that stupid word?

"Are you close to him?"

She fiddled with the Evian label. "Close is a relative term in L.A. I think I'm a reminder of his halcyon days. He does occasionally trot me out to cocktail parties at his Malibu Canyon house, but he's got little kids and a different life." She shrugged. "It's a nice life. I'm happy for him."

She shifted uncomfortably. She was the daughter of a couple of unmarried hippies, her best friend a sixty-four-year-old closet gay. Nothing like the sophisticated, chic Parisian women he was used to. And certainly not the worldly, intellectual art expert she'd wanted to project when she stepped off the plane at Charles de Gaulle Airport.

Not that she cared what he thought of her.

"None of this is getting us any answers about our departed friends or the Plums." She stood and started across the salon to the bedroom. "Since I don't have scissors, I can't do anything more drastic than get dressed. But please get in touch with Lisette."

"I'll do what needs to be done."

At the echo of her own earlier promise she glanced over her shoulder and saw that secret, unreadable expression that made her weak. "I'm sure you will. You appear to be a solid citizen with a decent sense of responsibility."

He flipped the cap in the air, appeared to catch it, and then held open two empty hands. "Things aren't always what they seem."

Luc called Lisette on the hotel phone, certain that Tristan didn't have a read on the vases yet. If he was smart enough to put a tap on the Soisson's phone, then he would be smart enough to show up here and get the Plums. Luc was still a few days ahead of Tristan.

Lisette answered on the first ring, the flat tone still evident in her pained voice.

"Can you check the computer for me?" he asked, without identifying himself.

She said nothing for a moment.

"Liz? Are you there?"

"Oh, Luc, *oui. Pardon.*" She almost sounded relieved. He hated putting her in the middle of all this. When it was over, he would spend some time at the château, helping her get things in—

He caught himself. When it was over, if all went well, he'd be living in the United States as a different person. He hoped.

"I have it for you now," she said. She read the coordinates to him, and he compared them to the layout of the resort he had in front of him.

"Are you certain, Lisette?" Something had changed radically in the last twelve hours.

"*Absolument,* Luc."

The Plums had moved. He instructed her to go to another set of coordinates. She read them while he toyed with the pencil and studied the page.

The forgeries had moved, as well.

"*Merci,* Lisette. That's all I need." He put the pencil down and leaned back. "How are you doing?"

She let out a long, sad breath. "*Ça va,* Luc."

He wanted to ask her so many questions. About people Bérnard had talked to, any strange calls or visitors. But he could hear the break in her voice. An interrogation would do her in.

When this was over he'd get the answers for her, regardless of where he lived or who he was. And if he didn't get them, Tristan would. Tristan was a bulldog when faced with an unsolved mystery. And if they could pin a murder on Benazir and get him into a real prison, Tristan would be unstoppable.

When he hung up with Lisette, he recalculated the information and compared it to the resort map again.

Janine came into the dining room, wearing black pants and a sleeveless white top. Her cheeks were flushed with color, and she'd definitely put on some makeup. For him?

"Going somewhere?" he asked.

"Eventually." She looked at the papers on the dining table. "What did you find out?"

He pulled out the chair next to him for her. "Something odd. Look." He slid the resort layout toward her and pointed to a location in a separate building. "They are there."

She leaned closer to the map, then looked up, surprised. "The casino?"

"It looks that way. I'm going down to check it out. There's probably a private room or suite adjacent to the casino, but I can't tell until I get there."

She flattened her palms on the table to push herself up. "I'll come with you."

"No." He put a hand on her arm.

"What if you come face-to-face with those vases? I can tell you instantly whether they are real or not." She started toward the bedroom. "I'll get my hat."

Yes, he'd need her if he came face-to-face with the vases. But what if he came face-to-face with Karim Benazir?

With the hat, he could slip her in and out without too much notice. If Benazir was watching and waiting for him, he'd be looking for a man alone. Not a couple on their honeymoon.

She came back a minute later, the cap pulled low, all hair hidden. "These were in my spa, too." She slid on a pair of pink sunglasses. "How do I look, Dave?"

He folded the map, put it in his back pocket, and dropped his arm around her. "Pretty as a picture, Kate."

CHAPTER
Eighteen

Something didn't fit. Tristan made his way through the maze of closed doors in the Versailles business offices, knocking and inquiring in halting French about the American curator. No one had seen or heard from her since Saturday night. Henri Duvoisier suggested that the curator, who in his opinion was strictly a last-minute stand-in for the great Albert Farrow, must have fled at the first sign of adversity on the job.

But the bright-eyed Ph.D. didn't strike Tristan as a quitter. He knocked on the security director's office door before entering.

"Bonjour, madame."

Simone de Vries jerked her head up and slid off a pair of reading glasses. "Monsieur Stewart," she said without smiling. "Have you any information on the Sèvres vases?"

"No." He glanced at the leather guest chairs, waiting for an invitation. It wasn't forthcoming. "Could I speak with you for a moment?"

She gave a brisk nod, and as he sat, she slid the

papers on her desk into a neat pile, covering the one she'd been holding. "I hope you are working with the DST," she said in excellent English. "They are *very good* at closing in on major losses such as the one we have experienced."

As opposed to the hapless FBI. *Save me from American haters.* "Absolutely," he assured her. "We're working side by side."

"And Monsieur Tremont?" she asked, the whisper of a smile lifting her thin lips. "Is he working on this as well?"

Either she knew he was gone or he'd left his usual mark on the poor woman. No matter their age, nationality, or taste, women fell for that guy. It'd been that way since freaking eighth grade. Tristan simply nodded. "Yes, he is. I am—"

"And where is our curator?"

Who was interrogating whom, here? "Actually, I was hoping to speak with her as well. We've talked to almost everyone else involved with the event. Are you expecting her this morning?"

She arched an eyebrow. "I do not monitor her schedule, *monsieur.* I have not seen her since the gala. Perhaps she has scampered away."

What about Janine Coulter made these people think she'd be scared into leaving? As he understood it, she was the one who'd flown to France after the original curator died, and lobbied for the job. But maybe she *had* bolted. Maybe the ransacked hotel room and the stolen Plums had spooked her. He'd have Paul check all the flights over the weekend.

"How close are you to finding the vases?" Simone asked, an anxious edge to her voice. "They will disappear if too much time passes."

"We're aware of that, ma'am. Everything possible is being done to find the thieves and save the Plums."

She leaned back and crossed her arms. "The loss of the Sèvres *vases,* as we prefer to call them, would be a major setback to the art world, *monsieur.* And a terrible embarrassment for Versailles."

"Of course." That's what she was worried about: her reputation, not the vases. He'd get nothing from this uptight turf protector. "I'd like to stop in Janine Coulter's office, but it's locked. Do you have a key?"

"Oui." She pressed the intercom on her phone, but no one responded. "My assistant will have the key, *monsieur. Une momente, s'il vous plait,* while I check."

When she left the office, Tristan slid the papers over to see what she'd hidden. A letter. He leaned forward to read it. Jeez. French was one thing, upside down French was another.

He managed to read two words. *Ma démission.*

Her resignation? Was the crusty security director planning to *scamper* away? If his memory served him right, Madame de Vries had only been on the job a few months. At the sound of her clicking high heels, he hid the paper and leaned back in his chair.

"Voici," she said, dropping a key in his hand.

He thanked her and headed for the last door in the hallway. The Versailles' staff certainly hadn't offered their guest any great luxuries; the room was tiny, almost airless once he closed the door behind him. The desk was bare except for a closed laptop computer. Would she leave town without her laptop?

He opened the desk drawer and found pencils and paper, a silver hair clasp, and a folded newspaper clipping. Opening it, he read the headline of the obituary. "Celebrated Department Head Commits Suicide." He glanced at the top corner. The UCLA *Daily Bruin.*

Scanning the page, he stopped at the second paragraph. *Dr. Farrow's remains were found in the Stone Canyon Reservoir, a few miles north of campus near Bellagio Road. He had apparently shot himself in the head.*

He could practically hear the puzzle piece snap into place. He picked up the laptop and the article, then checked his watch.

He could be back at the little farmhouse in Burgundy by late afternoon.

But first, he had one more stop to make. Versailles hadn't reopened for tours yet, and he didn't expect anyone to be in the palace chapel at this time of day.

In his opinion, Janine Coulter was officially missing. Was anything else?

Every nuance of Luc's Frenchness disappeared when they stepped out the door of the suite. He said "Hi" to another couple in the elevator, and Janine bit her lip to keep from reacting to the foreign sound of it.

He was just an American guy, draping a possessive arm around her shoulder as they crossed the pristine grounds, making small talk about the lake, the view, the spa.

"So, what's your gambling pleasure?" he asked, as

they strolled under an enormous neon archway that welcomed guests to the Casino Royal. "Craps, blackjack, roulette, slots?"

She looked up as he held the door for her. "We're playing?"

He leaned so close that his cheek bumped the brim of her hat and his silky baritone tickled her ear. "Until we find what we're looking for."

She slid her sunglasses off as they stepped into the darkened lobby, greeted by a cacophony of ear-piercing bells, clanging tokens, and the steady click-click-click of the roulette wheel.

Like any other casino, a visible blue gray haze of smoke filtered through the air, wafting on the sickening sweet smell of liquor. The obligatory odors of gambling. But that's where the similarities to Vegas and Reno ended.

"Pretty snazzy place," she commented, noting the soft-colored lighting that cast red and gold shadows over wide open areas between gaming tables.

She saw Luc surreptitiously scope the room, and her stomach tightened. They were really doing this. Working undercover, looking for the Plums.

"Pick something you can do while I move about," he said, so quietly she barely heard him.

She cleared her throat and smiled the way she imagined Katie Cooper, lawyer and newlywed, might smile at her husband. "I kind of like the one-armed bandits."

"Let's get some tokens and see if they like you." He cocked his head toward the right side of the casino.

That would be the west wing; exactly the spot he'd

circled when they'd studied the layout. First floor, west wing, past the baccarat tables. Her Plums were *there*.

She waited an eternity while he purchased tokens for the slot machines, her heart rate ratcheting upward with each passing minute.

This was dangerous. *Luc* was dangerous. And damn, if he wasn't just as sexy an American as he was a Frenchman. It wasn't his accent; it was him.

When he returned, they wandered further into the gaming hall, and Janine pulled her cap lower over her forehead. When they reached a row of slot machines, he put his hand on the faux leopard-skin fabric of one of the chairs and swung it around to her. "This one feels right," he said. "You do the honors. I'll watch."

She took the cup of tokens and settled into the seat. He stood behind her, placing his hands on her shoulders, and started gently massaging them.

Her shoulders instinctively tensed instead. "Relax, Katie. Just give it a whirl."

She reached up to drop the token in just as his mouth burned the bare flesh of her exposed neck.

"I feel lucky," he whispered.

Her stomach took a thrill ride, and her hand shook as she released the token. She slammed the lever down with way more force than necessary, as though she could bang out the jitters and the tingling that had taken over her body.

The wheel spun, a blur of sevens and lemons and cherries and something else.

Plums. Two of them and one lemon. She turned to

catch his eye and share the irony, but his gaze was not on the machine. He was casually scratching his cheek, looking to the right.

She dropped in another token and tugged the arm. Her heart felt exactly like the spinning wheels, whirling and twirling. Then he ran his hands possessively down her bare arms, warming her neck with his breath, and her heart slowed to a stop.

Three sevens. A raucous bell clanged as a handful of tokens poured into the brass cup. Luc kissed her shoulder; warm lips on warmer skin. She dipped her head as a shower of sparks danced down her spine and lit every nerve ending in her body.

"Told ya we're lucky, hon." He was laughing.

Laughing.

Of course. It was an act. A ruse. Katie and Dave Cooper from Chi-cah-go.

"I like to quit while I'm ahead," she said, as he kneaded the muscles of her shoulders. How long could she play this?

His long fingers extended over her collarbone, perilously close to the rise of her breasts. "Give it a few more tries. Don't make any new friends, though. I'll be right back."

She nodded, not sure of her voice. Why was she such a basket case? Were his pretend caresses playing havoc with her composure? Or was it the possibility that the Plums were within reach?

Yes. Double yes. The whole situation was electrified, with nerves and raw, unbridled craving for what she couldn't have. She wanted to shiver and scream and spin the chair around and kiss him and kiss him and . . . *have* him.

She yanked the arm again, watching the colors spin.

No plums, just a mishmash of other fruit. She glanced sideways to see where he'd gone, but there was no trace of him.

Luc rounded the corner with a quick glance into the baccarat room. He half expected to see Benazir's ugly face sitting at one of the oval tables, but the room was empty. Directly across the hall was an unmarked door, as close to the precise location as his data could get. What was behind that door?

Without knocking, he walked in. Behind a counter sat a uniformed guard, reading a book. He stood, laying the book facedown on the counter in front of him and offering a standard French glare. *"Puis-je vous aider?"*

Somehow Luc doubted this boy could help him. Noticing the tiny camera above a door on the other side of the counter, he shifted to his left and disarmed the kid with a wide American smile.

"I don't speak any French," he said in his Dr. Dave Cooper voice. "Can you get someone who speaks English?"

"I speak English," the guard responded with a heavy accent. "Do you have a safe-deposit box, or do you wish to arrange for one?"

Ah, Benazir had put the vases in safe-deposit boxes. "I just want to see if you have some available. I need one that's oversized for my wife's fur coat."

Definitely a stretch, a fur coat in May. But the rich clientele of the Parc Royal probably made far more unusual demands, and the evening temperatures easily dipped low enough in the Alps to merit fur.

"We can accommodate you, sir," the guard said. "Wait for one moment, and I will confirm what's available."

He turned, opened the door behind him with no key, and disappeared. Luc did a visual sweep of the size, shape, and simple layout of the room. Nothing to surprise him, no hiding places.

The guard returned and nodded. "I have one, *monsieur.*"

"Just one?"

"The other is being used at the moment."

By Pompadour's Plums, no doubt.

The guard scowled when Luc didn't answer. "Did you need two?"

"No," Luc said, with a quick smile. "But I gotta tell you, my wife is really worried about her coat. Can I promise her we can put it in the box ourselves? She won't want to just hand it over to you."

The implication earned Luc a disgusted shrug, which he took as a yes.

"Great, thanks a lot. We'll be back later."

Getting into the safe-deposit room would be relatively simple, and he could certainly orchestrate a way to be alone in there for a few minutes.

All they needed was a fur coat.

Janine was still feeding tokens into the slot machine when he returned. He approached her, taking advantage of their cover to caress her silky skin and tease her with a kiss under her ear. "Are we rich yet?"

She smiled at him, a cautious look in her eyes. "You tell me."

He slid his hand down her arm and clasped her fingers. "Rich enough to go shopping. How do you feel about fur?"

"Fur?" She scooped up the remaining tokens and dropped them in her cup. "Like fur you wear?"

"Precisely."

She gave him an incredulous look as she hopped off the chair. "I'm from California," she told him in a whisper. "My mother's a hippie. How do you think I feel about fur?"

He laughed and took the cup, wrapping one arm around her and pulling her into his chest. She tilted her head back so far, she had to reach up to hold her cap in place.

"You're from Chicago," he reminded her. "And your husband's a doctor. You love mink."

Her mouth opened in that perfect little O. He had to kiss her. *Had* to. But the second before he did, she kissed him first. With surprising passion. Her lips stayed open and their tongues warred in sudden, wicked exploration. With each exchanged stroke, a deeper wave of pleasure pulsed through him. He squeezed her against him, making no effort to hide his instant reaction.

When they parted, her eyes stayed closed.

"Get the girl an Academy Award," he whispered. "She's a natural."

She swayed just enough to give herself away. That had been no act.

*   *   *

This place was worse than fucking prison. Every time he got comfortable, he got interrupted.

Karim Benazir wiped the sweat from his eyes with a towel and dropped it on the bathroom floor as he rolled his girth around the hot tub to take the phone Larinna handed him. "Yeah?"

"This is Jean Claude, sir." Karim recognized the voice of the boy from the safe-deposit room. Greedy, eager, expendable. "A man came in here a few minutes ago to inquire about the large safe-deposit box."

"Did he get one?"

"No, he was simply inquiring about a box for his wife's fur coat."

"His *wife?*" So Surjeet had not been successful in Burgundy, after all.

"When I followed him into the lobby, I saw him leave with a lady."

"Did he say when he'd be back?" Karim asked.

"Not really," the boy answered. "He said, 'We'll be back later.'"

And he would, of course. The Scorpion had taken the bait—and now he would die. Along with his traveling companion.

CHAPTER
Nineteen

T his *would* be a dream honeymoon." Janine sighed, taking the chair Luc had pulled out for her at the bistro table.

"You mean it isn't?" He laughed softly, slinging a zippered bag bearing the insignia of an upscale boutique on another chair.

She studied the navy waters of Lake Geneva and the jagged, snowcapped mountains rising majestically along the horizon. "It would be heavenly just to be on vacation and drink this all in." She patted the over-stuffed plastic bag. "I'm sort of glad we had to drive over here to find this."

His sly smile dazzled in the sunlight. "I knew we wouldn't find the right fur among all that *vie-en-rose* charm of Evian. Plus, I couldn't resist showing you Thonon. I think it's one of the best-kept secrets in France."

The drive along the lake to Thonon-les-Bains had

been spectacular in itself, but Janine had never seen anything quite as picturesque as the quaint spa town perched on a cliff over Lake Geneva.

Luc nodded toward the bustling little harbor below them. "In the summer, you can ride a cable car down the cliffs to Rives, rent a sailboat, and be in Geneva in an hour or two." He looked away from the view and focused on her. "I wish I could take you."

That familiar ribbon of longing twisted through her stomach at his seductive voice. She steadied herself with a deep breath of icy fresh air, a mix of mint and spring flowers.

Since they'd left Evian that morning, they had been like this. Light, easy, flirtatious. He made it exciting to spend a small fortune for the pelts of innocent animals, for crying out loud.

"How many times have you been here?" she asked, glancing at the menu, unable to completely tear her attention away from the sight of him with the azure sky and dramatic landscape as a background. As stunning as any work of art she'd ever studied.

"A few," he said, as he opened his menu.

Topic closed. He did that a lot. His job, his family, his past—all taboo.

He'd been closedmouthed all day about why they needed a multi-thousand-dollar prop for the task ahead of them. And pretty darn evasive about what that task would be, too.

A waiter came to their table, and Luc said something in rapid French, using a dialect she'd never heard.

When they were alone again, she opened her napkin

and spread it on her lap. "I didn't get all that. What am I having?"

"For lunch? Whatever you like. I just ordered the wine."

"How do you know I want wine?"

"You're the one who wants to be 'on vacation and drink it all in.'" He grinned over his menu. "This is your chance."

She leaned forward and pushed his menu down to peer at him. "Have you forgotten why we're here?"

"I have not." His smile evaporated, but he held her gaze. "But nothing's going to happen in the next eight hours, so you might as well eat, drink, and pretend." He burned her with another sensual look. "I am."

Before she could respond, the waiter brought a bottle of wine that sparkled and fizzed when he poured it.

"Champagne?" she asked.

Luc shook his head. "No, it's Seyssel, the best white of the region." He tasted it and accepted it with a nod. The waiter filled their glasses and offered a lengthy description of the *omble chevalier,* a local delicacy that they both ordered. When they were alone, Luc lifted his wineglass.

"Santé," she said, anticipating the traditional toast.

"And to our success." He tapped her glass with his.

The wine was cool and crisp, like the mountain air. "Success depends on my knowing the plan, Luc," she said, as she placed the glass on the table. "Stop evading me. Where are they? When are we getting them, and why did we need to buy a ten-thousand-dollar fur to pull it off?"

He unfolded his napkin, an amused expression on his face. "Patience, *ma belle.*"

She narrowed her eyes and lowered her voice. "My patience is running out. And I'm not your *belle.*"

He reached across the table and took her hand. "It means beautiful." He turned her hand in his and caressed her palm. "And you are."

A shiver tap-danced up her arm as she freed her hand and slipped on her sunglasses. *So are you.* "Thank you. The plan?"

He cleared his throat and leaned on his elbows. "The room in the casino is a safe depository," he said softly. "Benazir put the real Plums in there, expecting me to go after the forgeries in his suite."

"Why the coat?"

"We need a valuable, but oversized, item to take in under the guise of renting a box. There are only two safe-deposit boxes large enough to hold the Plums, so the Plums will be in the *other* one." He raised his eyebrows in question. "Got it?"

She was starting to. "What happens when we're in there?"

"We'll have to get the guard out of the room."

Behind the protection of her sunglasses, she could look at him freely. As he talked, she took a leisurely trip over the corded muscles beneath his custom-made shirt. Imagined the feel of those arms around her. Remembered the power of his embrace. Relived the rush she got from his unmistakable response when she'd kissed him in the casino a few hours ago.

"You can do that while I open the other box," he finished.

She hadn't heard a word he said. "Sorry. Do *what?*"

He gave her that look again. Blazing brown eyes and the mysterious half smile. Could he see behind her dark lenses? "You'll get the guard out of the room while I open the other large safe-deposit box."

"How are you going to open—" She held up a hand and shook her head. "Never mind. Stupid question. Then what?"

"I'll wrap the vases in the mink, claim that the box could ruin the fur, and we're out of there."

She regarded him for a minute. He had it all worked out, smooth as silk. "When?"

"Late tonight. When the casino is full and we can get lost in the crowd."

She traced a fingernail along the enamel edge of the table, visualizing the vases and how she would use that same nail to test them once she finally had them in her hands. "What if they aren't the real Plums?"

"According to the tracking information, they are. You'll check them, of course."

Something was wrong. She took off the sunglasses and regarded him, trying to understand his logic. "Okay, we'll have the Plums. But what about the bad guy, Luc? Isn't the whole point of this to get him, too?"

"Yes, it is," he agreed. "He'll be waiting for me in his suite."

She frowned. "I don't get it."

"The real Plums aren't the bait, Janine," he said. "He doesn't know I'm after them or that I even know they're gone. That's why he has them in a safe-deposit box."

"But how are you going to get him? He'll vanish in Switzerland before we get the Plums back to Versailles."

"We're not going to take the Plums to Versailles, Janine."

She held her wineglass frozen in midair. "We're not?"

"We're not. *You* are."

An icy, familiar sense of loss slid through her. "And what about you?"

He waited a beat before answering. "I'll make sure you have someone to get you and the vases back safely."

She set the glass down without drinking. "That's not what I asked, Luc."

His gaze moved over her shoulder to the view behind her.

"You'll be long gone, won't you?" She had no idea how she knew that, but she did. There was something too enigmatic about him, too elusive. This wasn't a man who was going to stick around for Friday night dates. No matter how much she'd want him to.

He shrugged, still not looking at her. "I'm not sure what will happen."

She took a deep drink. "Well. Thanks for the warning."

Luc pulled into the hotel entrance as the sun began to dip behind the mountains. It was too early to go to the casino and too close to their lunch to think about dinner. They'd have to wait for a few hours in the hotel suite. Alone.

He glanced at Janine, her cap still in place, a flush from the sparkling wine still on her cheeks. She'd been somewhat distant since they danced around the subject of what would happen after tonight.

As they walked into the lobby, she slipped her arm

into his elbow and tugged him toward the gift shop. "Scissors," she whispered. "Remember?"

He slowed his step. He wished he could think of a way to make her stay in the room—not just to save her beautiful hair, but to keep her out of harm's way. But he couldn't verify the authenticity of the vases without her.

At his hesitation, she pulled him toward the store. "Come on, I can't wear a beret with my gown."

"Where'd you get a gown?"

"Lisette lent me one."

He couldn't imagine Lisette owning a gown that would suit Janine, but he wasn't about to argue the point. The Royal Parc Casino was damn near black-tie at night; in fact, he'd be wearing the tux that had made the rough trip through *L'Orangerie*.

He adjusted the fur coat in his arms and walked into the store with her. In the toiletries section, she picked up a sizeable pair of shears from the display counter.

"Whoa." He snatched them out of her hands. "I don't trust you with those. You're as likely to hack this mink into shreds as you are to cut your hair."

She laughed and patted the plastic covering the coat. "Those poor animals have been abused enough." Tipping the brim of her cap, she melted him with a pleading look. "Take pity on me, *Dave*. This hat's giving me a headache."

"All right," he agreed, fighting the urge to rip the cursed thing off. "Let's get these."

In the elevator to the suite, a German couple whispered to each other, and Luc moved closer to Janine, much closer than necessary. She didn't move away.

His heart drummed a steady beat as they walked down the hall. It would take next to nothing to start the seduction. He could sense her resolve slipping away, and damn if his wasn't going right down the drain, too.

He turned the key and handed her the coat. "Let me check the room first."

"What, did you leave a hair over the door, Bond?"

He laughed and chucked her chin. "Smart-ass."

A maid had been in, but his papers were untouched on the dining table. He looked in both bedrooms and the baths, to be sure they didn't have company.

"Come on in," he said, returning to the living area.

She tossed the coat on the back of the chair and whipped off the hat, freeing her hair with a shake and a scratch. "Man, I'm sick of that thing."

He stared at her, watching the tumbling tresses. "Me, too." He took a tentative step toward her, deliberately "forgetting" to return to his French accent. It was too much fun to be an American with Janine. "How much do you think you'll cut?"

She put a hand on her hip and cocked her head. "What difference does it make? You're never going to see me again."

A bitter note was buried in her tough chick act. How could he even be thinking about seduction? Her disappointment would be magnified a hundred times if he acted on his desire for her. Yet he could barely think straight for how much he wanted her.

He took a few steps closer and heard his own ragged breath. "Janine. Don't."

Her eyes widened. "Cut my hair? I have to."

"You know what I'm talking about." He reached out and grazed her cheek with his knuckles. "Don't be hurt when I'm gone."

"Hurt?" She backed away with a forced smile. "I hate to break it to you, Luc, but no one's getting *hurt*. You're imagining things."

"No, I'm not."

"Yes, you are. You're sleep deprived, you know that? This"—she waved her hand casually between the two of them—"this is just physical attraction. Some pheromones and hormones turning our brains to mush." She tapped him on the chest to push him out of her way, avoiding eye contact.

He didn't move. "Mush?"

"Can you excuse me?" She stepped to the side. "I have an appointment at the home beauty shop, and a little robbery to pull off tonight."

She picked up the bag that held the scissors and strode into the bedroom, closing the door quietly behind her.

She was so wrong. Absolutely no part of him was *mush*.

Janine had no idea how much time had passed. Ten minutes? An hour? Dressed only in the white bathrobe, she glanced at the three plastic bottles and the latex gloves spread out before her, and the two pages of instructions on the marble floor.

She had to cut, first.

She lifted the scissors for the twentieth time to a section of hair, then let them clunk onto the vanity.

Don't be hurt when I'm gone.

Why would he even say that?

And where in God's name was he going, if not back to Paris to resume his security consultant business?

Luc Tremont, international man of mystery. Why couldn't she just fall for some nice French banker or a chef?

Fall? She stared over the bottles at her reflection. She hadn't fallen, nor would she. Not ever again.

Anyway, who cared if he disappeared tomorrow? She'd tried "forever" and it stunk. She didn't have to live like a nun just because her heart was bruised from a bunch of lies and empty promises. This was now. This was real. This was—

"You need some help in there, Rapunzel?"

Exactly what she wanted.

"Actually, yes. I'm having trouble with the instructions." She could read them; she just couldn't make herself follow them. "Come on in. It's unlocked."

He opened the door and poked his head in. "What's the problem?"

Picking up one of the instruction sheets, she waved it in the air. *"Reunir?"*

"To combine." He stepped into the room.

"Appliquer?"

"To apply." He approached her chair, their gazes meeting in the mirror like a four-way showdown.

"Transformer le coleur?"

"Change the color." He stood behind her, a teasing grin softening his expression. "Your French is excellent, Janine. Why the confusion?"

"But combine what to apply where, and how long will it take to *transformer le coleur?*"

She worked to keep her voice light, in spite of the fact that his gaze was anything but. Looking at her in the mirror, his eyes smoldered as they traveled down the front of the robe and back to her face.

Without a word, he placed his hands on her shoulders, then skimmed his fingers underneath her hair. She shivered at the sensual touch on her scalp.

No, not sensual. *Sexual.*

"You've never colored your hair before?" he asked huskily.

"Never."

His fingertips trailed down to the nape of her neck, making the tiny hairs dance and her toes curl.

Trembling, she picked up the scissors and held them over her shoulder. "Here. I can't do it." She closed her eyes. "Just get it over with."

"All right," he said, taking the scissors and lifting another handful of hair. "Don't look."

But she couldn't resist. She opened her eyes when the blades scraped open, and sucked in a breath as he held them poised over a lock of her hair.

"Don't *look.*" he repeated, with a warning glare in the mirror.

She covered her face with her hands. "Yes. Now. Do it."

She felt the sudden heat of his mouth on her flesh under her ear. *She looked.*

He leaned over her, the scissor hand fallen to his side. She moaned softly and tipped her head to the other side, giving him access to her neck.

The scissors clanged to the floor.

Goosebumps rose under the terry cloth robe. "I didn't mean do *that*. I meant cut my hair."

"Really?" He crouched next to her, tangling her hair in his fingers and coaxing her around to face him. His gaze dropped to her mouth. "Maybe it's a matter of semantics, but *yes, now, do it* means something entirely different in French."

A shaky laugh escaped her. "Is that so?"

"Absolutely." He inched closer to her face. "It means stop talking and—" His kiss was hot and demanding and explicit. His tongue flicked the roof of her mouth, sending fireworks through her body.

He burned a path down her throat and into the V neck of the robe.

"Luc." Her breath caught as she buried her fingers in his hair. "We have . . . to cut . . ."

He dipped his head and kissed the rise of her breast, nudging the collar open inch by inch with one hand. "We have to do this first."

Her nipples hardened with a sudden, achy need. Sanity evaporated.

She slid off the chair, into his arms, onto the cold marble of the floor. There was no fighting this.

He fell backward pulling her onto him. "Come here, Janine. Let me feel you. All of you."

The thrill of full body contact took her breath away. She straddled him and found the natural, perfect position of her hips and his. His greedy hands opened the robe and shoved it over her shoulders.

She gasped at the force of his erection as he rocked

against her, kissing her mouth and exploring her body with his magical hands. She closed her eyes and surrendered to the delicious friction, pulsing right back into him, loving the ride against the rigid column between his legs.

A steady, natural, unstoppable rhythm built between them.

Insane pleasure licked at her as blood sang in her head and coursed through her veins. This was what she wanted. Luc. No one else. Nothing else. Just this. Just him.

She could drown in regret later—not now. She pressed her hands on the floor and arched her back, offering her exposed breasts to him. His mouth closed over her, sending white-hot flashes of blinding pleasure through her body. He sucked and sucked, laving her to an almost painful peak.

Gorgeous. Perfect. Janine.

She heard his words but couldn't think as he caressed her breasts with insistent hands. Her aching nipples pebbled against his palms, waves of stimulation shooting down, down to her stomach and between her legs as she matched his writhing motions with her own.

There was only this. Only Luc and his mouth, his arms, his chest . . . *him.* She yanked his shirt out of his trousers and fumbled with the buttons, popping one and managing to open the rest.

Don't stop. Please.

She couldn't hear anything but her pounding pulse and his rapid, uneven breathing as they kissed and tumbled against the cold, hard floor.

"Yes, yes, Luc." He rolled her on her back, on top of the discarded robe, and she struggled with his shirt, dying for the feel of his granitelike chest, almost screaming for the need of his sweat-dampened flesh against hers.

His pants scraped her thighs. Her fingers raked his back. He stroked her stomach and hips and buttocks, apparently gripped by the same urgent madness that had overtaken her.

She was blind with need; unable to speak or cry or tell him how it felt.

Every coherent thought dissolved as his hand covered her mound and his fingers dipped into the slick moisture between her legs.

I want you. I want you.

She chanted it like a mantra, he whispered it back in her ear. Dizzy, she unfastened his pants, reaching in to grasp and stroke him.

Oh, good God in heaven. Her hand felt so tiny on him. He let out a throaty growl and thrust himself further into her hand.

"Stop," he choked.

"I can't stop," she almost cried.

"I don't have—"

Protection.

Sanity and common sense suddenly reared their ugly heads. No, no, *no*. "I don't need it," she insisted.

"Good," he muttered, sliding his fingers deeper into her. "Neither do I."

She helped him push down his pants and free himself, almost afraid to look at what she held. Her two hands barely covered him.

"Let me inside you, Janine," he urged.

Yes. *Yes.* Now.

If she stopped to think and question this, she'd die. She couldn't stop. Don't stop. *Don't stop.*

He laughed softly in her ear. "Don't worry. I won't."

Kneeling over her, he bent her knees and parted her thighs, his eyes black with desire.

She reached down and encircled him, guiding him to where she needed him to be. "Please, Luc."

He dipped his head and kissed her, probing her mouth with his tongue. In and out. Teasing her. Making her beg for him to do that with his body.

Please!

He closed his eyes and plunged into her.

She grabbed his shoulders and gasped at the shock of her stretched flesh. Again he thrust, deeper, fully hilted, her hips raised off the floor by the sheer size of him. She locked her legs around his back as the pressure melted into pleasure and she matched his relentless rhythm.

Urgent. Wild. Insistent. She inhaled the heady mix of their musky, sexy scents, her teeth on his shoulder, her fingers digging into his back.

Again and again he drove into her, and she met each stroke with the same fury. Nothing mattered. Not tomorrow, not later, not anything but the sensation of being completely filled by Luc.

His face darkened with desire, his powerful chest flexed above her. He muttered her name and swore in English and shook his head so hard a bead of sweat dripped into her mouth, salty and delicious.

Every ounce of control shattered at the taste of him.

She closed her eyes as he stiffened and shuddered and quaked.

"Janine. Janine!"

An explosion ripped through her at the sound of her name, making her spasm over and over and over as he rocked and spilled helplessly into her. *"Janine."*

He fell against her, his short, desperate breaths tickling her ear. His heart hammered against her at breakneck speed, a sticky film of sweat and moisture the only thing between them.

His voice echoed in her head. *Janine.*

Not *Szha-neen*.

How very strange. Her international man of mystery made love in perfect American English.

CHAPTER
Twenty

Luc couldn't speak. His brain had sacrificed all functionality in the name of ecstasy.

Janine's tight body tremored with aftershocks around him. He was still hard. The delicious, sweet scent of her sex and their sweat filled his head as his mind slowly started to work again.

What had he called her?

Turning his head, he pressed his lips against the damp flesh of her temple and watched her eyes flutter open. No smile yet.

"That was some haircut," she whispered.

He laughed, and the movement threatened to separate them.

She put her hands on his hips and pulled him against her. "Not yet. I don't want this to be over yet."

Neither did he.

He eased some of his body weight off her, and she automatically turned with him, maintaining the contact and the connection. She positioned her leg over his hips and trained her blue eyes on him. She had to have noticed that he hadn't said a word yet.

Not in French or the natural American inflection that had escaped a minute ago. Had she noticed?

He swore in his head. He was so sick of *lies*.

"Are you okay?" she asked tentatively.

He nodded. "More than okay, *ma belle.*" There. Back to normal. "You outdid all my daydreams."

She gave him a wistful smile. "You too."

He stroked a hair off her cheek, tenderly caressing her skin. "I suppose we could find a more comfortable spot to bask in the afterglow."

"Is that what we're doing?" That wind chime laugh again. "How romantic."

His heart tripped. Romantic? Romance would include an honest exchange of emotions. Playful plans for the future. Secret revelations about the past.

Not in this lifetime.

He closed his eyes and eased out of her. She winced but still smiled.

He couldn't smile back. A sickening sensation of déjà vu teased at those numb synapses in his brain. He knew this dull ache of self-loathing; he used to get it after every job. Not that he'd exactly *stolen* this mind-blowing gratification, but he doubted it would have been so freely offered if she knew his real identity.

She touched his hand where it rested on her stomach. "Luc?"

Turning his head away, he reached for his pants and pulled them on, then picked up the scissors and cut the air with the blades. "Guess we ought to do this, huh?"

When he finally looked at her, the disillusionment in her eyes almost broke his heart.

"Right," she muttered, pulling the robe from underneath her while covering her beautiful, perfect breasts with one hand.

Oh, God. He'd completely blown this.

"Janine." He set the scissors on the bench and helped her with the robe, gently spreading it over her shoulders. "Don't—"

Her eyes flashed at him. "Here we go again. *Don't*. You're really damn good at telling me what not to do when it suits your mood, Luc."

"Please—"

She stabbed her arm into the sleeve and held her other hand up to stop him. "I didn't hear any *don'ts* out of you ten minutes ago."

He grabbed her shoulders and pulled her closer to him. "Please stop it."

She looked at him for a moment, then jerked out of his hold and made a show of knotting her robe.

"I don't want you to feel bad right now, Janine," he insisted. "I—I just wish we had more time together, that's all."

She stood abruptly. "Well, we *don't.*" Without looking at him, she left the room.

What a complete mess. He grabbed the scissors and squeezed the handles so hard they left an imprint on his palm. If he never had her again—and that was a fairly safe bet after this blockbuster postcoital performance—he'd never forget the intensity of that sex.

It wasn't like anything he'd ever known. *She* wasn't

like any woman he'd ever known. But she was the essence of every woman he'd ever wanted. Brave and strong and unwavering and *real*.

Standing up to zip his pants, he glanced at the bottles of hair dye, so out of place in her natural world.

That's what it was about Janine. She didn't have a phony cell in her body. And he? He was nothing but a pretense. A made-up name, a made-up history. As fake as the vases up in Benazir's penthouse.

How could he tell her that?

He couldn't. But he had to tell her something. Because right now, that brave, strong, *real* woman felt like shit, and it was his fault.

He found her on the balcony. Her hair was messy and tangled, blowing in the breeze as she stared straight ahead, probably not seeing the panorama of the French Alps. He stood behind her and wrapped his arms around her waist. She stiffened.

Lifting her hair, he nuzzled his mouth near her ear. He decided to go for the dead-on truth. "You are the sexiest woman I've ever met."

She didn't move.

"No matter what happens," he continued, "I want you to know that I'll never forget what just happened. I'll never forget you."

It was the best he could do. The very best.

Slowly, she turned in his arms. Son of a bitch. She'd been crying.

"I'm sorry," she said softly, wiping a tear. "I knew exactly what I was doing, and I have no right to wallow in second thoughts. That was a joint effort."

"That was no *effort*. That was a crashing success." He kissed her forehead and rested his head against hers. "And you have every right to feel anyway you want. We're in an unusual situation."

She stifled a little laugh. "Now, there's an understatement."

He lifted her face toward him. "Janine, I haven't been with a woman in a very, very long time. I live a very strange existence. If I could change it, if I could—"

"Why don't you?"

"Why don't I what?"

"Change it." Her eyes narrowed to ice blue slits. "If there's one thing I learned recently, it's to take charge of your own destiny. That's why I went after Albert's assignment. That's why I left that chapel with you after the theft."

How could he tell her that his destiny wasn't in his hands? It was a price he had to pay for his past. He couldn't. No, he *shouldn't*.

He gently rubbed the luminous skin of her cheekbone with his thumb. "Listen. I'm going to tell you something. I want you to promise me you won't ask any questions, because I can't—I won't answer them."

She frowned, but nodded. "Okay."

"When this is over, I'm not just going to *disappear*." He spoke slowly, quietly, forcing himself to say the words. "I'm going to become a different person."

She pulled back to stare at him. "What?"

He put one finger on her lips. "Shhh. No questions. After that, you won't ever know who I am or have anything to do with me again. It can never be any other way."

Her eyes darkened with confusion and disbelief, and her grip on his arms tightened. Why did he think she could comprehend this? It was unthinkable to a normal person.

She searched his face, and his heart thumped while he waited for the inevitable question. *Who are you?*

Please don't make me lie to you, Janine.

After a moment, she laid her hands on his bare chest and gave him a shaky smile. "Wow. I had no idea people like you really existed outside of spy novels."

Oh, no. His gut twisted in shame. Of course that's what she'd think—that he was some kind of crime-fighting chameleon, a hero for the good cause. Her champion.

"It's not exactly like that," he said weakly.

She slid her hands up his chest and around his neck, pulling him toward her. "Your secret's safe with me."

She didn't even *know* his secret. And she wouldn't offer her sweet mouth to him if she did. Not if she knew her "champion" was once one of the most notorious thieves that ever lived.

Unable to resist, he kissed her back, sinking into her mouth as though they'd never parted.

He couldn't change his past, but at least she would never know the truth. She could go the rest of her days imagining she'd made love to a hero—and he could go the rest of his remembering how good that felt.

Paul Dunne didn't ask too many questions. That's why he and Tristan had been partners for three years, tracking art criminals all over the world and building quite a reputation within the FBI. Even when Tristan yanked Paul from the computer for an unexplained flight to Dijon, the low-key agent was smart enough to let Tristan reveal their mission in his own good time.

"The Pompadour Plums have been stolen," Tristan announced, as he navigated the rental car onto an exit for the Côte d'Or.

Paul's attention never wavered from the scenery out his window. "Uh, I know that, Tris."

"No." He shook his head. "The real Plums. The ones Luc Tremont hid before the setup."

Paul shifted in his seat. He wasn't given to huge displays of anything. "No kidding?"

"No kidding."

"So you think they're out here somewhere in the middle of wine country?"

Tristan glanced at him. "I don't know. I have a helluva problem, though. There's a dead guy out here who knows Luc. He died the same way as the UCLA art professor who was supposed to be the curator for the exhibit. The one Janine Coulter replaced."

The only person who could rival Tristan at brain-teasers was Paul Dunne. So he laid out all the pieces as he could, holding back only one: Luc's true identity.

Maybe no one needed to know that to solve this mystery. Maybe.

They discussed it until they arrived at the little winery, about an hour later. As they pulled up to the farmhouse, a woman he remembered seeing yesterday, a younger version of the same hearty country stock as the owner, stood at the driver's door of an old station wagon. Since she'd been cleaning the kitchen, he'd assumed she was the housekeeper.

She stood at her open car door and stared at them.

Tristan climbed out and approached her, unsurprised by her distrustful glare. *"Bonjour, madame.* I am looking for Madame Soisson."

"Moi aussi, monsieur."

She was, too? *"Parlez-vous Anglais?"*

She gave that Gallic shrug that loosely translated into "if I feel like it." Well, she'd better feel like it, because he couldn't interrogate anyone in French.

"When did you last see her?"

She glanced at the car where Paul wisely remained in the passenger seat. If they needed information from her, they'd get more without ganging up on her.

"I have been here since daybreak, *monsieur,* and have not seen her all day."

Tristan frowned. "Is that unusual?"

She shook her head. "Nothing is usual these days."

Wasn't that the truth? "I need to take a look around inside, ma'am." He wasn't leaving this place until *something* lined up in his Rubik's cube of a case.

She scowled at him. "When Madame Soisson returns."

If Madame Soisson returns. He reached into his pocket and pulled out his badge. "I'm with the FBI, ma'am, and we need to get inside as part of the investigation of Monsieur Soisson's death."

Her gaze dropped to the badge, and then she looked at Paul again. Wordlessly, she turned toward the front door, and Tristan gave the nod to Paul. *We're in.*

In the front foyer, she turned on a light. *"Voilà, messieurs.* I will wait for you in the kitchen."

They looked around, and Tristan cocked his head toward the study.

"See what you can dig up on that computer, Paul," Tris suggested. "Do a search for the name Albert Farrow or Janine Coulter. I'll look through the house."

Tristan followed the woman to the kitchen, not at all sure what he was looking for. The spacious room was spotless, with no smells of cooking or food. Above the drain board hung an antique brass key. "What's that for?" he asked.

Her gaze followed his. "The wine cellar."

"Where is it?"

She pulled a chair out from the table and sat down. "Across the courtyard. Behind the shrubs."

She wasn't being totally uncooperative, and Tristan thanked her with a smile that wasn't returned. "I'm going upstairs," he announced, knowing she wouldn't follow.

He found the master bedroom, the bed evidently untouched. Of course, the housekeeper had been here all day, so that made sense. Down the hall, another bedroom. He glanced in—also untouched. But as he turned to continue his search, something caught his eye.

A trash can in the corner, overflowing with plastic and paper.

That was odd. Wouldn't an efficient housekeeper empty the trash in a guest room? He walked over and started pulling out the bags.

Boutique du Chambertin. Rue de la Liberté. Dijon, France.

Some dress store in Dijon, was all he got out of that. He dug through the bag and found a receipt. Someone had purchased about a dozen items and paid cash. Yesterday.

He struggled to translate the words. Dress. Suit. *Chapeau*. Wasn't that a hat?

Another bag from a *pharmacie* was crunched inside of it. He pulled out a receipt. *Teinte du cheveau*.

Hair color?

Adrenaline started its familiar journey into his gut. He pulled a few pieces of tissue paper from the trash can, then his hand grazed something soft and gauzy. A ball of white fabric was rolled up on the bottom.

He lifted the material with two fingers and held it out. It was torn and stained in spots, but he immediately recognized the strapless gown.

He could still see the good-looking blonde floating around Versailles in it.

"You are not going to believe what I found."

Tristan turned to the door at Paul's uncharacteristic note of disbelief, amazed how eerily it echoed his own thoughts.

Paul stormed into the room, waving a piece of paper. "The whole goddamn GPS tracking system is on that computer, and I found the Plums. Not just the ones Benazir stole—the real ones. I found a second track."

Tristan lifted the dress higher. "And I found the thief."

CHAPTER
Twenty-one

L uc was gone.
  With a tiny gasp, Janine sat up, blinking in the near darkness of the hotel bedroom. The dull ache she'd felt when they'd talked on the balcony sharpened to a point that stabbed at her heart.

Then she heard the shower and fell back on the pillow. Thank God. He hadn't vanished into the night. Of course not—they didn't have the Plums yet.

The nightstand clock read eight-thirty. In an hour or so, they'd leave for the casino. Her heart kicked at the thought. They'd steal the Plums. They'd escape with her treasures. And Luc . . . would be gone.

Where would he go?

Another country in Europe? A different part of France? *The United States?*

She laid her hand on the empty pillow next to hers and blew out a long, slow breath.

So many questions. But he'd made it clear when they'd come into the bedroom that she shouldn't ask, because he wouldn't answer. So she'd simply curled into his arms until she stopped thinking about anything but the sheer bliss of being held by him.

The bathroom door opened, and he walked in, a towel wrapped around his waist, his hair wet, his chest still glistening from the shower. More bliss.

"Hi." He sat down on the edge of the bed and smiled. "You crashed."

He sounded like Dave Cooper. She couldn't keep track anymore, so she just closed her eyes. "Mmm hmm."

"Listen to me, Rapunzel." He leaned closer, the clean, soapy smell permeating her nose as a droplet of water fell on her cheek. She moaned inwardly, reminded of making love to him, of his sweat and fury. "I have an idea."

Her stomach dipped at the possibilities. "Yeah?"

"Didn't you say you have a gown?"

She nodded, hope and anticipation evaporating with the question.

"Maybe we could cut the dress and not your hair."

She laughed softly. "Don't tell me. You sew, too."

"As a matter of fact . . ." He opened his other hand, revealing a spool of thread and a needle. "I found this and the thought occurred to me. We really only have to hide your hair. We could make a matching scarf or turban."

She smiled and reached out to him, touching his cheek. "Let me take a shower and then I'll try on the gown."

He nodded, a sexy, reluctant look in his eyes that just about melted her.

After she'd showered and dried her hair, Janine slipped on a pair of panties and took the gown from the armoire where she'd hung it. Luc waited for her in the living room. It was almost like a real date, and her whole body tingled with the same kind of expectancy. Only this wasn't a date. And they weren't a young couple in love.

They were a couple of strangers headed out to break, enter, and run.

The dress was a deep shade of blue, the very color of the lake that afternoon. Satin whispered over her skin as she stepped into it and fastened the halter around her neck. When she turned to the mirror, she couldn't help but smile. It was divine. A little roomy on her hips and an inch or two shy in length, but the bodice and waist were perfect.

The neckline plunged so deeply, it revealed her whole cleavage and the undercurve of her breasts. Hundreds of shimmering beads winked with every movement. At the waist, the material gathered into a distinctive rhinestone buckle. Below that, the skirt flared out in a fan of pleats that fell almost to the ground and back to a short train.

A train. Yes, they could cut that if she were willing to ruin this masterpiece and make a scarf.

Oh, well. This was about rescuing the Plums, not making the best-dressed list.

Leaning over the counter, she used the makeup she'd found that morning to darken her lashes and add some color to her pale skin. She ran a brush through her hair, reluctantly admitting relief that she didn't have to part with it. Scooping up the scissors and sewing kit Luc had left, she went to see what Bob Mackie could do with the dress.

He sat facing the sliding glass doors, staring straight

ahead. The lights were dim, but she could make out his handsome features, his square jaw and that heartbreaking, clean-shaven face. He wore tuxedo pants and a white shirt, the tie still open around his neck. Every feminine cell in her body did a somersault. Would they ever make love again?

The thought made her ache, intensifying the tenderness he'd left between her legs. She wanted him again. And again. Once was not going to be enough with Luc Tremont—or whoever the hell he was. She cleared her throat. "Hey."

He turned and did a double take. She resisted a smug smile and glided toward him, letting the amazing fabric float with each step.

"Oh, my God." He sounded shocked.

She paused to read his expression. This was no gaze of admiration. "Luc? What's the matter?"

The color drained from his face as he stared at the dress, the bodice, the clip. "Where—where did you get that?"

She frowned at him. "The dress?" She shrugged. "I told you. Lisette gave it to me."

Slowly, he shook his head and took a step closer. She could see the utter disbelief and confusion on his face.

"What's the matter?" she demanded again.

The pain in his eyes nearly ripped her heart out. "Lisette?"

"She said she'd never wear it." Why was he acting so weird? "She said she wanted you to see it. 'For a special evening with Luc.'"

He burned her with a look of sheer incredulity.

"Luc? What's wrong?" she demanded.

"That dress . . ."—his voice was a harsh rasp of a whisper— "belonged to my mother."

Luc couldn't stop himself. He reached out and touched the strap of the gown, his fingers floating over the sparkling fabric, down to the rhinestone *G*—for *Gabrielle*. The beads felt exactly like he'd always imagined when he looked at the picture his mother kept hidden under the paper lining of her bureau drawer.

"She didn't know I'd found it."

"Found what?" Janine asked. "The dress?"

He cleared his head with a shake and looked at her. He hadn't realized he'd spoken out loud. "No. The picture. Of my mother in this dress. With Bérnard. She kept it hidden, but I found it when I was young and . . ."

How could he explain it to her? How could he tell her that the look of happiness on his mother's face was something he'd rarely seen? That the picture of a young, carefree, innocent French girl was somehow special to him? That he treasured the photo of his mother taken before John Jarrett had scarred her with lies and deception?

Janine still looked at him like he'd gone crazy. "Why wouldn't Lisette tell me this belonged to your mother?"

"She gave you this dress for a reason, Janine." Logic fought to the top and buried the emotional eruption. "It was her way of telling me . . . something." Of telling him she knew exactly who he was. *Why?*

He took her hand and pulled her toward the sofa. "What did she say to you? Please try and remember exactly what she said when she gave this dress to you."

She frowned and bit her lip. "Nothing specific—"

"Think," he insisted. "It's very important."

"She said she wouldn't wear this dress." She smoothed the flouncy skirt and thought for a moment. "I remember that she didn't say 'again' because that's what I thought she meant."

"What else?" he demanded.

"She said she wanted you to see me in it. That I needed something to wear in the casino."

His gut tightened. He'd never told Lisette their destination. Of course, she'd seen the map with Lac Léman, but they never discussed the casinos of Evian. "Anything else?"

Her eyes widened, and she pointed her index finger at him. "Yes. She kept saying she was sorry. *Je regret.* She said it several times."

She was sorry.

Maybe it wasn't mourning and shock that made her so distant. Not that she'd ever been overfriendly to him, but she had been particularly cold the past two days. And for a while before that.

Was that because she had discovered his identity? Bérnard had kept files of information on Benazir; the man's network of crimes had been an obsession with Bérnard. Luc had told him once that Benazir had threatened Gabrielle, and that was all the old man had to know.

Was it possible that an old rivalry with his mother still brewed in Listette? Bérnard had done a ridiculously bad job of hiding his feelings for his childhood love when he was alone with Luc. No doubt his wife sensed that longing as well as anyone.

And if Lisette had discovered his real identity and turned

it over to Benazir . . . then that was precisely how Luc's cover had been blown, and why Benazir used art crimes committed by an imposter Scorpion to lure Luc to him.

Had Bérnard learned of his wife's betrayal, and been killed before he could warn Luc?

Suddenly, an unholy dread rolled through him. Had Lisette fabricated the noise in the house to get him out of the cellar and leave Janine there? If Lisette *was* the missing link between Bérnard and Karim Benazir, was any of the information she'd given him accurate?

And did Benazir know exactly who he was, where he was . . . and who he was with? "We're not going into that safe depository tonight, Janine."

"Why not?"

"Because it's a trap."

She put her hand over the rhinestone clasp and sucked in a breath. "Are you serious? How do you know?"

He was gripped by the temptation to tell her the truth. Wouldn't it be better if she knew? Wouldn't she disappear as fast as possible and get out of harm's way . . . and his?

"It's a trap," he repeated, his gaze falling over the familiar lines of the dress again. "Trust me."

Without responding, she stood, lifting the skirt with two fingers. "I want to change," she said simply.

She went into the bedroom, leaving him to replay an old refrain in his head. *It was too easy.* God, why didn't he see it sooner? Karim Benazir was a master player and a man on a mission. Of course Luc couldn't just blow into Evian, open a safe-deposit box, and walk away with a priceless treasure. Benazir was too smart for that.

"Now what?" She came back in wearing dark trousers and a top. Even in the dimly lit room, he could see the apprehension on her face.

"You have to leave." The sooner, the better.

"Excuse me?" She crossed her arms. "Where am I going?"

He paced in the other direction, refusing to look at her. There would be no debate on this.

Should he send her out alone, or get in touch with Tristan? A sick feeling seized him. Benazir would disappear at the first sight of the FBI or the DST, taking Luc's get-out-of-jail-free card along with him.

Taking Benazir's bait was a dangerous game, and Luc's future hinged on the outcome. But there was no way he'd permit Janine's life to be endangered, too.

"I'm not going anywhere without the Plums, Luc."

He stopped pacing at the cocky tone in her voice. "Janine, there's a man here who wants me dead as badly as I want him dead. He has no regard for anyone's life, including yours. I didn't think he knew my name or face, and that gave me a distinct advantage. But now . . ." Gripping the back of the divan, he looked hard at her. "He could easily get me—and you—before I get him."

"How are you planning to get him?"

Good question. He paced in the opposite direction again. "It doesn't matter," he finally said. "You'll be out of here long before I do anything. If I do anything."

He didn't even realize she'd approached him until she gripped his elbow and forced him around. "You won't even give me a chance?"

"To do what?" He glared at her. "The whole safe

depository thing is dead. We can't go in that room; we wouldn't come out alive."

She didn't say anything, and the echo of his pronouncement reverberated in the silence. Finally, she asked, "Do you still think the real vases are in his room?"

He shrugged. "I don't know. Possibly."

"What's stopping you from trying to get them?"

"Common sense, for one thing."

"Well, here's some common sense for you: if we don't do something tonight, he'll know you're onto him and he'll be gone by morning. With my Plums. And God knows how many deaths on his conscience."

Luc snorted. "Karim Benazir doesn't have a conscience."

"But he knows you're here, right? Isn't that what you're saying? What if we showed up in the casino, I got his attention, and you broke into his room?"

He shook his head emphatically. "This isn't a 007 movie, Janine, and it wouldn't be that easy. Anyway, if he saw you alone, he'd know exactly where I was, and he'd have someone blow my head off in about six seconds."

She held his gaze, her eyes narrowing in thought. "But if he saw you, he wouldn't guess where I am, would he?"

He let out a quick laugh. "Are you suggesting you'll break into his room and get the Plums?"

"Why not?"

"Because you have no idea what you're doing." He took her hands in his. "But you're brave. I like that."

"I'm not that brave." She gave him a shaky smile. "But I am a very quick study."

He gave an unyielding shake of his head. "No."

"What if . . ." She took a deep breath. "What if you got me into the room and then left to meet him?"

He stared at her, not sure whether to laugh or take her seriously.

"Listen, Luc, all we need to do is get him out of his room. Couldn't we come up with some reason to get him to, say, the casino?"

He eyed her for a minute, hating the thoughts that were forming in his head. "You might be on to something there." *Damn it*.

"What would be irresistible to Benazir?" she asked.

The Scorpion. Nothing would intrigue his enemy more than an unexpected face-to-face meeting. And the element of surprise was definitely in Luc's favor. He looked down at her, and something pulled at his heart. She *was* brave. And utterly innocent and uninvolved in his personal quest. "I won't put you in that kind of danger, Janine."

"Luc, please. We've come so far. To walk away now would be a travesty."

He smiled at her melodrama. "It wouldn't be a travesty. It would be wildly intelligent."

"Please." She grabbed both his arms. "We have to try."

God knows he wanted to. And it could work. It *could*. And if they pulled it off, everybody would win.

"Maybe," he said softly. "I have to think about it."

"Think fast."

He took a deep breath, the fragrance of her freshly washed hair and the scent he'd come to think of as *Janine* teasing him. He put his arms around her and folded her into his chest, right where it ached every time he thought about how little time he had left with her. "I'd never forgive myself if anything happened to you."

She locked her arms around his neck and looked up at him. "I'll never forgive myself if I don't get this guy and find my Plums. I promise I won't take foolish chances. Please. We can do this."

Luc's mental wheels started spinning and damn, he couldn't stop them. He'd have to contact Benazir in a way that couldn't be resisted. He'd have to make sure Benazir's room was empty, and he'd have to give Janine strict parameters. And he'd have to have a backup plan in case something went wrong.

"All right," he said. "But only if you do exactly what I tell you. If I say stop, we stop. No matter what."

"I will." She treated him to a bright, victorious smile. "Trust me."

"Get the door." Karim slammed a glass of cognac on the coffee table and adjusted himself in the overstuffed chair, a sense of unease playing around the edges of his conscious. He'd expected a phone call from Jean Claude in the safe depository for the last two hours, not a guest.

Larinna crossed the suite and opened the door to a uniformed hotel employee who handed something to her. "I've been instructed to deliver this invitation for a private game of *chemin de fer, monsieur.*"

Karim narrowed his eyes at the man. What was this all about? "Give it to me," he ordered.

As Larinna approached with the envelope, the unease

intensified to a dull pain at his temples. Karim tore it open, the sight of the bloodred ink twisting his gut.

We have unfinished business. The time has come to meet. There is work to be done.

The note was signed with a familiar sketch. He swore under his breath. Was this victory or defeat? The Scorpion had found his way here, but had a stinger ready and waiting. Or did he? Maybe he thought he deserved a second chance.

Karim had nothing to lose. He'd made sure that the vases were in a place where, if discovered, the blame would fall directly on Nick Jarrett and Janine Coulter.

There is work to be done.

He stared at the old code words they'd used in the past, then looked up and nodded to the waiting attendant. "Eleven o'clock."

Hoisting himself out of the chair, he swallowed the rest of the cognac in one gulp. "Call Surjeet and get him in here," he told Larinna. "And get dressed to go to the casino."

He'd need some assistance. And Larinna would be an excellent witness.

Or a shield.

CHAPTER
Twenty-two

Janine held her breath as the door handle slowly turned. Her heart thumped against her rib cage, her feet riveted to the floor in the middle of their suite.

"You should have had the chain lock on."

Relief nearly buckled her knees at the honeyed tone of Luc's voice. "I knew it was you," she lied, as he walked in. "How did it go?"

"The invitation has been issued and accepted." He held up a card key. "And the Coopers have a new room. Poor Dave lost a fortune gambling and has to downsize. The young lady at the front desk let us have the key for tonight, but they don't expect us to move until tomorrow."

She inhaled slowly. They were really going to do this. "It's right next door to Benazir's suite?"

He nodded.

She put her fist over her mouth and bit back a stunned laugh. "How'd you do that?"

He gave her a surprised look. "Charm. Good looks. Cash."

She had no doubt the first two went as far with the "young lady at the front desk" as the last did. "How are you going to get in his room?"

He reached into his pocket and pulled out a black tie and started tucking it under the collar of his tuxedo shirt. "That's the least of our problems. I got the cell phone page you sent, so we know my phone works."

She nodded. "Good. But I sure wish we had two cell phones."

"It doesn't matter," he assured her. "I won't be able to call you. Anyway, you'll be in and out and back here." He made a perfect bow tie, then reached for his tuxedo jacket and slipped it on. "In. Out. And back here," he repeated even more forcefully. "Got that?"

"Got it." Her voice was totally confident, though her legs were more like Jell-O. "Now what?"

"Something to carry the Plums in," he said, walking over to the mink coat. He unzipped the plastic cover to reveal the rich ebony fur. "Your wrap, *madame.*"

Janine slid her arms into the satin lining. Her skin tingled, her nerves sparked.

He pulled a pen-sized flashlight out of his pocket and handed it to her. "You'll need this. Under no circumstances should you turn on a light in any room."

She'd seen the tool before, when he broke into the château. She popped the top off to reveal the screwdriver. "Handy little thing."

"You won't need that," he assured her. "Just the light. Now, are you positive you'll remember the cell phone number?" he asked. "Even if you're . . . upset?"

She refused to think about what he might mean and

dutifully recited the number. "I know what to do, Luc. A numeric page the minute I'm back in this room. One for yes. Two for no. Three for trouble."

He walked across the room and switched off a table lamp. "Three means you need help."

"That's trouble."

"And if I'm not back by midnight?"

She cleared her throat and hugged the fur collar around her. If he didn't come back by midnight, he'd given her another number to call. A trusted friend who would get help to her in minutes. "Let's not go there."

He laid his hand on the wall switch and glared at her. "You call that number at twelve-oh-one. Do you understand?"

"You get back into this room by eleven fifty-nine, do you understand?" she retorted.

The room went dark, and she felt his arm around her. "I'll do my best," he whispered into her ear. "Now let's get in our new room before he leaves."

She paused, not quite ready to march into peril yet. "Luc?"

"Yes?"

"What happens if he comes out at the same time we're going in?"

"We're dead."

They followed a shadowy path that ran along an expansive and blessedly deserted outdoor pool and patio to get to the other side of the resort. Except for the breeze in the trees, the only sound was Janine's soft, steady footsteps as she kept pace with him.

The weight of his gun tugged at Luc's cummerbund. Every time he looked at Janine's fragile features against the black fur, at the daring sparkle that almost hid the fear in her eyes, his heart missed a beat. And every time, he fell a little bit deeper into a place he had no right to go.

At the east end of the building, they entered the lobby and hit the elevator button. As they waited, she tucked herself further into the mink, the fur collar almost swallowing her. He pushed an errant blond strand behind her ear.

"I'm glad we saved your hair," he said softly.

She gave him a shaky smile, and the elevator door opened. A young man walked out without acknowledging them. Luc guided her through the waiting doors, then touched a button on the panel.

He could feel her tense when the elevator closed and started to rise. Draping an arm over her, he tucked her against his chest. "Just do exactly what I say."

She looked up at him. "And when you're gone?"

When I'm gone, forget me. "Use your brains, Dr. Coulter. You've got plenty of them."

Her smile was tight, but reached her eyes. *We can do this,* it said. He gave her the same look back, then put a single finger to his mouth as the car thudded to a halt at the penthouse floor.

As soon as they turned the corner, he recognized the layout, a mirror image of their floor in the western wing of the resort. Around a corner, a corridor led to the rooms. The suite was situated at the end of the hall, with four other rooms on the floor. The Coopers had reserved Room

522, next door to the suite. When they reached it, he slipped in the card key.

A red light flashed once.

She sucked in a quick breath. He stabbed the key again. Still red.

An elevator car dinged gently from around the corner. The elevator doors rumbled, accompanied by the sound of a man's voice. One more time, Luc glided the card through the slot.

Green.

He twisted the handle down, careful not to make a sound, and they were in. As he eased the door closed behind them, Janine shuddered and leaned against the wall.

"Not a word," he whispered, and she nodded. After the voices and footsteps passed, he released the door handle again, testing to be certain he could open it soundlessly.

He had already studied the lock and card keys and demagnetized one of the extra keys with a credit card. Hotel break-ins were harder than in the days of metal key locks, but after five years in security, he knew the new tricks as well as the old. He wasn't worried about getting into Benazir's suite. But trusting her to get out scared the hell out of him. He'd be facing his enemy across a gaming table and unable to help her.

Janine stood stone still next to him. He propped his head against the wall adjacent to the suite, a much better conductor of sound than the steel door. How many times had he done this in his lifetime?

Too damn many.

Closing his eyes, he waited for the thin wall to res-
onate with the sound of Benazir leaving his suite. Next to
him, a tremble shook his nervous partner. He pressed his
lips to her ear and whispered, "Are you sure you want to
do this?"

She pulled back, her eyes luminous with incredulity.
That would be a yes.

Then the wall vibrated, and a man's voice carried
through the hall, gruff and low. A familiar sense of calm
settled over him as he looked at Janine and nodded once,
holding his hand up to remind her not to move or follow
him yet.

Exerting precisely the pressure he'd used before, he
turned the handle and cracked the door open, just
enough to hear.

A man said something in Sanskrit. The language of
the rebellious Benazir, who refused to conform and speak
Hindi. A woman answered, too soft for Luc to understand.

Then the gentle footfall on the hallway carpet.

Soon the elevator bell rang and the doors rolled open.
And closed.

"Don't move," Luc whispered, and slipped out the
door.

As if she *could* move. Fear paralyzed her. Her hands,
buried deep into the pockets of the luxurious coat, were
squeezed into balls so tight she could feel her nails making half-moon indentations in her palm. Her muscles
trembled. She'd damn near choked on adrenaline.

Then she heard his single sharp rap on the wall. The
signal to move. Oh *hell*.

She slipped into the hall and headed to the next door, stifling a gasp as Luc yanked her into the darkness of the suite.

"It's all clear," he whispered. "Look only in the places I told you. Don't turn a light on. Don't dawdle. If you find the vases, don't take the time to check them. When—"

"I *know,* Luc." She nudged him toward the door. "Go. Now."

He took her hands, slapping a card key in each. "Right, our room. Left, next door." He helped her shove them into her pants' pockets. "Don't go all the way back to our suite if you have any doubts that you can make it. Just page me with a four. Remember, one for yes. Two for no. Three for trouble. Four for hide out. Okay?"

She nodded fiercely. "Go." She put her hands on his chest and pushed him toward the door. "You have to get there before he does."

He pulled her face to his. His lips were hot on hers for less than a second, and then he was gone.

Her mind whirled through his instructions. First, the bedrooms. She flipped on the flashlight, and its powerful halogen beam revealed the same layout as their suite. She went straight to the master bedroom and the armoire.

She rifled through the hanging clothes and pointed the flashlight in the corners. No vases. She pulled out three drawers. Looked in the nightstand. Under the bed. Beneath a massage table. Nothing.

She darted into the bathroom and whipped open cabinets and drawers. She flung the sauna and shower doors wide open to see inside. She searched under towels and even lifted the toilet tank lid. Nothing.

Her heart pounded so hard it actually hurt her chest. She concentrated on taking steady breaths as she repeated her search in the smaller bedroom and came up empty-handed. Returning to the salon, she paused to look around. As in theirs, a china cabinet took up one wall of the dining area. She crouched down and yanked open the cabinet doors along the bottom. There was plenty of porcelain in there, but no Sèvres.

In the living room she searched the wall unit, reaching behind books and the television, kneeling down to inspect the bottom shelves. Nothing.

She tore back the sofa cushions, patting the springs for something. Anything.

Nothing. *Nothing.*

Where the hell are they?

She bit down on the frustration that threatened to undo her. She was running out of places to look. *If they're not obvious, they're not there. Don't waste time searching,* Luc had said.

She slid her beam of light across the room one more time. It landed on the refrigerator installed in the wet bar, exactly like the one in their room. The light caught on something metal on the side of the refrigerator.

A padlock?

No. That would be ridiculous. Who would hide vases in the refrigerator? But then, who would lock up their Evian?

Tiptoeing over, she trained the penlight on the industrial-strength lock. She'd never figure out the combination, and certainly couldn't force it off. She kicked at the refrigerator door, then pushed the unit to test its weight.

A trickle of sweat rolled down her back. This is exactly what Luc had warned her against doing. *Exactly*.

But her Plums could be *right here,* one lousy midget-fridge door away. Using every ounce of strength she had, she slid her arm into the small opening between the wall and the refrigerator and tried to pull it out. It moved about an inch.

Enough for her to see how the door was assembled. Six screws on metal plates down the side. She looked at the penlight-screwdriver gizmo in her hand.

Knowing full well she was breaking the rules he'd set out for her, she stuck the light between her teeth and started to unscrew. The first four came off easily. The fifth stuck, and her screwdriver slid out of her grip and down the side of the metal door.

"Come on, damn it." She used both hands, neither one steady, to find the slot again and force the screw to turn. It gave a fraction. Then a smidge more. "Yes!" she hissed, as the screwdriver made a complete revolution and then rhythmically twisted.

One more screw. She brushed a hair off her face with her forearm and crouched down to get to the last one. It was flat-out rusted.

Swearing, she knelt on the hard floor. The sudden sound of laughter nearly knocked her over. From the hall, the voices of several men—a little loud, maybe a little drunk—reverberated outside the suite. She froze.

One spoke in a foreign language. Dutch? German?

Another answered with a guffaw, then a long, unintelligible comment.

Dear God, they were right outside the door.

More laughter.

She tucked herself into a ball, biting on the flashlight so hard she thought she might break the plastic or her teeth. What would happen if Benazir's henchmen burst in and found a woman in a mink coat kneeling in front of the wet bar, breaking into a refrigerator?

They'd kill her.

The adrenaline had turned to fire, burning her chest and stomach and throat. This was it. The end. Death. She bit back a moan of pure terror.

Their voices got softer. The laughter diminished.

They were gone.

She blew out a breath and stabbed her little tool into the last screw. She would do this, damn it. She would do this. She repeated her mantra with each fruitless attempt. She. Would. Do. This. The handle dug into her skin as she wrenched with all her strength and a resounding grunt.

It budged about a millionth of a millimeter. She moaned in relief and twisted again, her biceps quivering with the effort. She was rewarded with a miniscule movement. The third time, the screw loosened completely, twirled off and clunked on the floor. Hallelujah!

With one vicious tug, she broke the suction of the refrigerator door and blinked into the blinding light.

And feasted her eyes on the most beautiful color purple she'd ever seen.

She whipped off the mink and laid it on the floor.

Carefully, she reached in and cradled the largest of the Plums, its porcelain smooth and cold under her hands. She scraped her thumbnail on the gold ormolu base. She dug as hard as she could, then squinted at the edge of her nail. Not a speck of black in the glaze. No indication of absorbed moisture. These were the real thing.

Albert would have been so proud of her. *Luc* would be so proud of her. She laid the largest inside the coat, then slid each of the smaller Plums in a coat sleeve. Cautiously wrapping the whole package in fur, she then picked it up with as much care and love as a mother with her newborn.

It was awkward, but not too heavy. Getting across the resort without looking foolish or guilty would be difficult. But there was no way she'd hide in the room next door; that was too close to Benazir.

She'd go for the security of their suite.

Adjusting the mink in her arms, she used her free hand to open the door and then stuck her head into the hall. It was empty: no laughing Dutchmen, no murderous Indian princes. No one. She squared her shoulders and marched toward the elevator as though it were perfectly normal to roll up her ten-thousand-dollar coat in a ball and carry it around. Dizzy, light-headed, and high on her achievement, she pressed a shaky finger on the down arrow and took a deep breath.

Maybe, up in heaven, a crazy old art lover with a heart of gold and an eye for beauty looked down on her. And on his Plums.

The bell rang, and she stepped into an empty car. *Thanks, Albert.*

It descended to the lobby level in one smooth run. She slipped out the door they'd come in and strode directly to the darkened path Luc had used on the way over.

Keep up the good work, Albert. We're almost home.

Her flat shoes made no sound on the concrete. The moon stayed hidden behind a cloud, and not a soul was in sight. She nearly broke into a run. Good God, she had the Plums. She *did* it!

And Luc? She took a breath. He'd come back. They'd figure something out. This was too good, too real to lose. *Wasn't it?* There was something extraordinary about that man. He made her feel whole. Alive. Amazing.

Her feet fairly flew as soon as she saw the other entrance to the lobby. The elevator was just beyond it. *You rock, Albert. Two more minutes and we're home free.*

"Janine Coulter."

She shrieked, stumbled, and almost dropped the whole bundle.

A man blocked her way, seemingly from nowhere. A gasp caught in her throat, and she backed up. Right into the rock solid form of someone else.

Her gaze dropped from the riveting gray eyes to the gun pointed straight at her.

"FBI. Don't move."

CHAPTER
Twenty-three

Luc's earlier inspection of the grounds had revealed a much faster route to the casino than Benazir would take. He had time to purchase gaming chips, order a drink, and play a hand against the house.

He won.

"I am expecting someone," he said to one of the two dealers, in his most distinct French. No Dave Cooper in this venue. Dave would call it baccarat and think it was a rich man's blackjack, roped off because the dealers wore tuxedos and the players were worth millions.

Luc knew better. He hadn't chosen *chemin de fer*, as savvy Euros called the game, because of its glamour. On the contrary. The baccarat room was teeming with casino personnel, from the two dealers who sat at the center of each table, to the caller across from them. In this particular room, a keen-eyed ladderman supervised the action from a chair above the table. Just as important as all those observers, *chemmy* was the only card game that allowed the players to deal. That was crucial to his plan.

"The table is yours," the dealer promised, looking toward the entrance. "Perhaps this is your guest."

A predatory instinct made Luc want to turn and attack, but he held it in check. He'd never met the man, but he'd certainly seen photos and watched hours of interrogation on videotape. He straightened his pile of thousand-dollar chips and remained perfectly still. The tiny hairs on the back of his neck jumped to attention, every cell in his body poised on high alert. It was Benazir. He had no doubt.

Wordlessly, a large figure settled into the seat at the other end of the oval table.

After a moment, Luc looked up and met the hooded black eyes of the man who lived to kill him. *"Bon soir,"* he said softly.

"A pleasure," Benazir responded. It would be English, then. Fine.

"The pleasure is mine, *monsieur.*" Luc looked pointedly at the exotic woman partially hidden by Benazir's considerable bulk. She wore a simple beige gown that set off her dark foreign beauty. Enormous ink black eyes looked away from him, but he purposely paid her, and her escort, a compliment by extending his careful scrutiny of her.

Benazir pushed a pile of chips toward the center, his bet a wordless indication that he would meet the house maximum and, therefore, be the banker first. Exactly what Luc wanted.

The more times Benazir slid a card from the shoe that housed the eight decks, the more opportunities Luc had to set him up. Every time his opponent hit a natural nine, it drew additional attention from security.

He shifted enough in his seat to be certain he could feel the vibration of the cell phone deep in his pocket, against his thigh, and nodded to begin the elaborate shuffling ritual. The two dealers and the caller took turns mixing the cards, then the caller held the entire deck over the middle of the table, letting the two players decide who would cut.

Luc tilted his head, granting the honor to his opponent. As Benazir reached forward to cut, he kept his unrelenting gaze on Luc, pure, unadulterated hatred in his eyes. Luc met it with a slight smile. Let him wonder. Let him worry. Best of all, let him think *there was work to be done*.

He flexed his leg muscle against the phone, as though he could somehow force it to vibrate with a page from Janine. One of the dealers flipped the top card, revealed it as an eight of clubs, and slid it to the burn pile.

A man walked in, and Luc caught a glimpse of his goatee just before he sat at another table. He remembered seeing him at Versailles, only at the gala he'd been a reporter.

So Benazir had some backup. But they couldn't back up a cheater held by security.

"Gentlemen," the dealer said, "you may place your bets on the winning hand. For the opening hand, the banker"—he nodded to Benazir—"the player"—he looked at Luc—"or a tie. The house will retain five percent of the banker's winning hands."

The four cards were dealt, read by the caller, given or passed. Benazir didn't deviate from the strict, unspoken parameters of the game and never took his eyes off Luc, except to glance at his hand. When he did, he whispered, "*Non,*" announcing that he was satisfied.

Luc lifted the corner of his card. *"Carte,"* he requested.

Benazir pulled a single card from the shoe and passed it to the dealer, who looked at it. He gave it to Luc, who barely touched the corner and knew it was the ace that gave him a natural nine. When the caller announced his victory, Luc just nodded to Benazir and sweetened the existing pot by a thousand.

Benazir didn't react to the loss. The woman stayed a few steps behind him, a mask of indifference on her face.

And his phone remained silent and still.

While Luc placed his bet on his own hand, as the rules required, an image of Janine in the room, in the dark, searching for her vases, haunted him. She was too smart to linger there. If she didn't find the Plums, she'd go back to their suite. *Wouldn't she?* A fresh wave of worry rolled through him.

An undercurrent of excitement hummed around them. Benazir's backup man spoke to one of the security guards. The ladderman peered down at Luc's table as the shoe was passed to him.

From his peripheral vision, he caught a flash of the caller's wristwatch. Eleven-fifteen. She should call within the next five minutes.

He dealt the four cards. They tied with eights.

Benazir leaned on the table and looked expectantly at Luc. "It is such a fortunate coincidence that you are in Evian," he said, impatience evident in his thickly accented voice.

He knew Benazir was impatient and greedy; this time it would work in Luc's favor.

"Evian is too tempting to resist this time of year,

don't you think?" Luc pushed the shoe back to Benazir, jostling the container just enough to reveal the tip of the second card. If Benazir saw it, he would deal seconds. He could risk that move once or twice without attracting attention; but no more than that.

"Temptation can be a downfall," Benazir said, as he glanced at the shoe.

He dealt the second card.

Luc resisted a smile of satisfaction. Benazir would cheat, but Luc would never let him know it was anything but chance and the movement of the shoe. Once every six or seven hands. By then, Benazir would have a running tally of what cards had been played. He would start to win every time.

Then he'd be under enough scrutiny for Luc to alert security.

The man at the other table had been joined by someone else. Luc sneaked a look at the dealer's watch again. Eleven twenty.

Where the hell was she?

Janine wasn't about to argue with the barrel of a gun or the steely eyes. She hugged her bundle, bit her lip, and held her breath.

"What are you doing here, Dr. Coulter?" His voice was as low as Luc's and as American as Dave Cooper's.

"Taking a walk."

He raised an eyebrow and glanced at the rolled up fur coat. "With that?"

"Is fur illegal in France?" The question came out with way more bravado than she felt.

He slipped his gun into a holster at his side and indicated the casino entrance with his head. "Come with me, please."

There was something about him . . . something familiar. She'd seen this man before. She remembered his face, his golden good looks and muscular build. She remembered him whispering into a microphone at Versailles. Of course. He was one of Luc's men. Or was he? He could have been part of Benazir's team, involved in the theft that Luc had set up.

Someone put a hand on her shoulder, and she jerked away from the unexpected touch, turning to see a bald, heavyset man. She looked from one to the other. They had both been at Versailles. No doubt about it.

This could be a setup. Or not. She cleared her throat and hugged her fur. "I'm not going anywhere until you tell me who you are and why you want me."

"I'm Tristan Stewart, FBI, art crimes division." His expression softened just enough to be genuine. "This is my partner, Paul Dunne."

"Art crimes?" She took a chance. "Then you're investigating the theft of the Plums."

"We'd like to ask you a few questions about the death of Bérnard Soisson."

She barely managed to keep her jaw from dropping.

"And the death of Dr. Albert Farrow," he added.

Relief and confusion clashed in her head, and she nearly swayed with the impact. "I'd like to talk to you about those deaths, too," she said quickly, her gaze intent on Tristan Stewart. "I think they're related and so does Luc."

"Luc?" His eyes widened in surprise. "Have you seen him?"

She opened her mouth to answer, but stopped. She'd seen the look he and Luc had exchanged at Versailles. There was no love lost between these two men. Shifting the weight of the coat, she nodded once. "Yes, I've seen him."

Tristan frowned at her vague answer and dipped his head closer to hers. His cheeks were so clean shaven, she could see the tiny pores. "Dr. Coulter, we have evidence that you have been to a château in Burgundy where a man was killed in precisely the same manner as the man who died, leaving you the opportunity to lobby, and obtain, his role as curator of the Pompadour exhibit."

Evidence? A thread of horror started to wrap around her chest. Did they think she was guilty of killing Bérnard? And *Albert?* She just stared at him, stunned. And then realized what *evidence* she held in her arms.

"How long have you known Lisette Soisson?"

She startled at the question from behind her. "A few days."

"How did you meet her?" Tristan asked.

She whipped her head back to him. "Through Luc. He took me there."

"When?" Back to Paul.

She opened her mouth to answer him, but Tristan interrupted her. "Luc was there, too?"

She didn't know whether to scream "shut up" or answer. She nodded and clasped her hands together under the fur.

"And where is he now?" Tristan demanded.

Her shoulders sank as she let out a breath of surrender. "He's in the casino playing baccarat with Karim Benazir."

Tristan paled as he looked at Paul. "Call DST. We're going over there."

"No!" Janine almost reached out to him, then remembered her precious bundle. "You can't," she insisted, gathering the fur closer to her. "Not yet. You'll ruin everything."

Paul was already dialing a cell phone.

"We're going over there," Tristan announced. "And you're coming with us."

Lisette had one chance left. It lay rolled in yards of burlap in the recesses of her husband's wine cellar, tucked on top of a shelf of thirty-year-old Pinot Noir.

She pushed the door open with the flashlight; the lock was still blackened from Luc's gunshot. The single beam of gold lit the steps to the dirt floor. Lisette followed its path, holding her breath. She had waited patiently for Arlaine to describe the visit from the American officers of the law and explain what they had taken. They'd been upstairs and in Bérnard's office. Not, bless God, in the wine cellar.

But the despicable Indian who'd left his precious bundle would be back for it. And probably for her. She'd run away for most of the day, hiding in the vineyards. Then she remembered what was tucked away in her cellar. Perhaps her last chance to do the right thing.

She let out a ragged curse. God was creative in his punishment for her sins. He'd made her pay dearly for hiding those letters from America, for burning the words of love and pleas for forgiveness that Gabrielle Sauterville sent to her childhood sweetheart. He'd made her miserable for forging the letter from Bérnard and sending Gabrielle that picture as a final farewell. He'd helped her find the information in her husband's office that gave her the idea that she could rid her world of the one most potent reminder of the past—Gabrielle's own son.

She eyed the knapsack Luc had left behind, the empty wine bottle, the blanket. All evidence that she had housed the hunted . . . or the hunters. But it was all too late; nothing would ease her guilt. And nothing would deliver her from evil.

Even her pathetic attempt to warn him with the dress seemed laughable.

Her legs sagged, and she grabbed the back of one of Bérnard's chairs. Memories lurked in every shadow of this cellar. Oh, she'd spent many hours testing the vintages in here with Bérnard. She'd never enjoyed it; but it wasn't good for her husband to spend too much time alone and drunk. It made him reminisce. But after Luc Tremont showed up, Bérnard spent far too many hours completely alone and viciously drunk. Lost in the memories, no doubt, of his first and true love.

She sighed and aimed the flashlight at the furthest alcove, taking in the bottles white with years of dust. She now owned one of the most valuable wine collections in the world, and she hated it. Every bottle, every grape, every tainted memory.

Gabrielle would have been so well suited to this life. She'd worked in the vineyard and danced at the harvest as a teenage girl. Oh, she had loved wine. Loved the process of making it, of running the vineyard, of reveling in the harvest and the tastes of their great valley.

Ancient jealousy gnawed at Lisette as she dragged the chair to the last alcove and forced herself to concentrate on her mission. She had to get to the top of the Pinot alcove. The cheap wine, she remembered, hid the valuable treasure that filthy Indian had insisted she keep hidden in her home. And that treasure had been there the entire time Luc had—a few feet from where he'd sat.

Stepping carefully on the chair, she swiped her hand over the top rack of bottles and coughed on the dust that lifted and settled around her like a cloud.

Voici! Her fingers touched the rough burlap.

On her tiptoes, she strained over the nests of wine bottles. Her fingers grazed the rough edge of the wrapping, but she couldn't quite get the grip she needed. Grunting with the effort, she stretched as far as her frustratingly short arm would go, then sucked in a breath and tried for another inch. The chair wobbled, but she held on to the corner of canvas and shifted her weight to the front of the chair to get that one centimeter closer.

She shrieked as the chair tipped, and for a sliver of time she was suspended in the air, weightless. Then she started to tumble. She flailed at the neck of a wine bottle for support, but it slid right out of its slot. The world moved in slow motion, the crash toward the ground unstoppable. In her hand, the Pinot bottle smashed against the others and exploded into dagger-sharp shards.

Her face slammed into the dirt, and something sharp

slashed her arm, just above her wrist. But she felt nothing at all. Her eyes were open, but there was only pitch black. The flashlight must have broken in the fall. She lay perfectly still, not sure what part of her old body would move. Slowly she tried to lift her head.

Then the fire shot through her arm. Pain screamed from her wrist straight into her brain. With a gasp, she grabbed the inside of her arm with her free hand. She felt hot liquid, and she nearly gagged from the overpowering smell of fermented grapes and fresh blood.

She'd cut her wrist with the broken bottle. *Au nom du Père,* she was going to die like this.

An unearthly sound came from her mouth. A gurgle, a moan, a prayer.

Mon Dieu, j'ai un extrê regret du vous avoir offensé. She began her final act of contrition. *Parce que je crains de perdre le ciel . . .*

It was a useless effort to remember the words. She'd never confessed her sins—not these sins—to God or any priest. And none would listen to her now.

It was so quiet in the cellar. So quiet, she could almost hear the blood flow from her body onto the cold dirt floor. She could smell death and wine and dirt and the faintest lingering of Bérnard's cigar. Was he watching her now?

Of course he was, watching with contempt and revulsion. With disgust, because she had let envy and petty jealousies wreck his only chance at happiness. And hers.

Mais surtout parce mes péé vous offense, mon Dieu.

But no words could clear her conscience. She was dying and going to hell for ruining Bérnard's life and for turning an innocent man over to his killer. Those sins were hers to bear.

She closed her eyes and began to sob. She tucked her gashed arm under her chest and pressed her body to the ground. When the tears finally abated, her mind went still.

She had to accept death, with no chance for reconciliation. No chance to right her wrongs. Even if she had such an opportunity, what could she do?

Oh, she knew exactly what she would do. And it had nothing to do with the bundle that had been hidden in her cellar. She would go to the office and use Bérnard's ancient phone to dial the number she'd long ago committed to memory. She would whisper the truth. And lost souls might be found again.

Salvation would be hers.

"Madame? Madame Lisette?" Arlaine's words were distant in her ears. Was that the sound of the cellar door? "Are you here, *madame?"*

A harsh yellow light burned her eyes. Was this it? The light she would walk into with her marked, sinful soul in tow? She heard the gasp as Arlaine turned her over.

"Mon Dieu, madame!"

She could still be saved. One last deed that might save her from the agony of hell.

"Arlaine," she rasped. "You must do something for me."

"Madame! You are hurt!"

Lisette shook her head and grabbed Arlaine's arm, squeezing it with the little strength she had left. "Please. Please save me."

"Yes." She scrambled to her feet. "I will call for help."

"No! My soul! Save my soul!"

Something in her voice got through to Arlaine. She halted and leaned close to Lisette. "What is it, *madame?*"

Lisette took a labored breath then, and managed to make one final act of contrition.

CHAPTER
Twenty-four

To his sheer delight, Luc had lost eight thousand dollars in less than fifteen hands. Benazir had dealt the second card and cheated at least four times. The bets were increasing, along with the room temperature and the number of security guards.

However, the silence of his cell phone had a band of anxiety crushing his chest. It was eleven forty-five. Screw Benazir and his cheating. His hands itched to fold his cards, and his legs ached to run like hell and find Janine. Regardless of the fact that he had his mortal enemy right by the short hairs, regardless of the fact that victory, freedom, and home were close enough to taste.

Where *was* she?

He calmly passed on a card. Benazir held a four and a five, taking another fifteen hundred dollars from Luc. Two of the dealers exchanged looks, and the ladderman nodded to indicate it was time for a fresh shuffle.

Benazir had made three brief attempts at clumsily

coded conversation, then stopped, seemingly content to take Luc's money, drink cognac, and bide his time. A sheen of perspiration glistened on his wide forehead, but Luc only felt a chill to his bones.

Where in God's name *was* she?

The second caller situated himself to the left of Benazir, and Luc knew his opponent would be too smart to cheat for a few hands. Luc dealt, bet on his own hand, and won a noticeably low bet from the other side of the table.

If Benazir was really smart, when he took the shoe for his next deal, he'd bet high and lose. That would take the pressure off him for a few games.

He bet low and lost. But then, he *was* greedy.

A few more people came into the room, but neither player looked away from the table. The room had grown relatively quiet, most eyes riveted on the high stakes in front of them.

The caller nodded for the next game, Luc's deal. He slid a pile of chips to the center and glanced up in expectation of the shoe.

Something caught his eye. Something bright and shiny and . . . blond.

What the—

His heart simply stopped at the sight of her. Unable to look away, he stared at her pale, shell-shocked face, and then his gaze dropped to the ebony mink rolled into her arms. The man to her left shifted and stole Luc's attention for a nanosecond.

Son of a bitch. Tristan.

Luc took the shoe and set his gaze on the cards. If Benazir saw Tristan or Janine, it was over.

He dealt, aware of every movement in the room. Tristan, his bald partner, and Janine remained in the doorway.

What were they going to do? Attack and arrest Benazir? They could. They probably would. But they didn't appear to have any backup, and he had no way of alerting them to the two men at the furthest table, who undoubtedly were armed and prepared to give their lives for the former prince.

The Indian woman who'd come in with Benazir stood next to him, motionless and patient. Benazir would use her as protection, would sacrifice the poor woman in a heartbeat.

Benazir won another three thousand dollars, then put one elbow on the table, leaned forward, and stroked his chin. "Do you wish to continue, or shall we call it a game?"

In his peripheral vision, Luc could see that Tristan had moved farther into the room, but had made no move to draw a gun. He was probably waiting for DST backup. They had their man right here, out of jail and surrounded by his bodyguards.

The other agent stepped around one of the tables, and the caller turned to look.

Damn. It caught Benazir's attention, and when he glanced up, his gaze landed directly on Janine, then Tristan. The color faded slightly from his olive skin, but he casually picked up his remaining chips in one hand. "I've had enough," he said, and stood.

Luc was up and in front of Benazir in less than a second, silencing the room as the guards jumped to attention.

"I haven't," he said.

One of the guards glared at him. Benazir cast a sideways glance at the two men at the other table, who were now standing. Tristan took three steps farther into the room, and Luc flashed him a look, but the gray eyes were trained on Benazir. Tristan's jacket moved just enough to make his target spin and grab the Indian woman. She sucked in a breath of surprise as Benazir clasped his arm around her waist and held her in front of him.

"We're leaving now," he said, as calmly as if he had just shaken hands with his opponent.

Luc felt the eyes of the other two on him. He didn't dare reach for his gun. "You're not going anywhere."

Suddenly two security officers flanked Benazir and started walking with him. Half the hotel security must be on his payroll.

"Let her go, Benazir," Luc said. "You're not getting out of here."

They continued to walk toward the door, but Tristan jumped in front of them, his gun drawn. Benazir nodded to one of the security guards, who aimed his gun at Tristan's chest. Luc didn't have time to think. He pounced on Tristan and knocked him to the floor just as the gun fired.

Luc hissed as a lightning bolt of pain sliced through him. Another gunshot rang out, and the woman screamed. Tristan and Luc struggled to get up in the riot of panicked players and trained hit men. Luc saw the goateed backup fall to the ground just as he spun around to the door.

Janine. Janine. *She had to get out of there.* One of the

guards hustled Benazir out of the room, but Janine was gone. An alarm blared just as the other FBI agent wrestled another guard to the ground.

"DST is on the way," Tristan shouted to him.

Luc wasn't about to wait around for the cavalry; they were too late. He took off after Benazir.

Janine ran in the opposite direction of the main gaming room, whizzing past a restaurant and down a carpeted set of stairs to a lower level of the casino.

She moved on instinct, fear, and with the sole objective of protecting her Plums.

She could hear the alarms and shouting from the level above her. This floor was nearly deserted, with rows of slot machines and no tables. She ran another fifty feet or so along a glass wall and stopped at a door marked for emergencies only.

Well, this qualified.

Turning her body to back into the door, she squeezed her eyes shut and waited for a blaring alarm, but the door opened without a sound.

In the darkness, she could make out a service patio surrounded by six-foot walls, thick shrubbery, and a row of overflowing Dumpsters. She stopped to get her bearings. At the far end, a pile of trash partially blocked the opening to a darkened parking lot.

Her arms burned. Her whole body trembled. The last thing she'd seen was Luc throwing himself on the man named Tristan. To save him, she was certain of that.

Through the glass wall of the casino, she saw a figure

running. She had two alternatives: trash or the bushes. She threw herself into the shrubbery, but without a free hand to break her fall, she tumbled into sharp twigs and branches and landed right on her backside.

The Plums were still in her arms.

She struggled to right herself and hide under the fur coat without dropping the vases. As she did, she saw the glass door fly open, and two men and a woman came running onto the courtyard. She recognized the men immediately: Benazir and one of the security guards from the casino.

She froze among the branches, held her breath, and clutched her fur-covered treasure.

The men spoke in short, staccato words, using an unfamiliar language. They seemed to be arguing about something, but it was clear Benazir was in control.

Benazir handed the other man something, and the man hustled back through the glass door, then Benazir grabbed the woman by the arm and started tugging her toward the parking lot.

Janine watched in horror. Should she scream, run after him?

"Don't take one more step."

She whipped her head around to see Luc striding through the door, a gun pointed directly at Benazir's chest, his hair mussed, his tuxedo jacket torn. Her heart stopped, then jolted against her ribs. All she could do was watch the showdown.

The woman tried to wrest her arm from Benazir's grip, but he pulled her closer. She let out a pleading cry to Luc. Janine squeezed tighter into a ball.

"I'm no good to you dead, Jarrett," Benazir said.

Jarrett? Who was Jarrett?

"You're no good, alive or dead." He lifted the gun higher, straight at the other man's face. "Right now, I kind of like dead."

The American accent. Pure, unadulterated American. Who *was* he?

Benazir took a step backward, still holding the woman against him. "I have the vases."

Janine hugged her coat. *Oh, no you don't.*

"I don't want them."

In the soft golden light from inside the casino, she studied Luc. Something wasn't right. His jaw was set, his eyes alert, but he looked—unsteady. The hair touching his collar was damp, and beads of perspiration covered his temples.

"You're not a killer," Benazir insisted. "You wouldn't even kill a man for a million dollars, as I recall."

Janine's throat was closed, and she could barely breathe.

"Well, I'd kill you for free." Luc took a step closer. "I want you away forever, Benazir. With a bullet in your brain or locked in Leavenworth, I really don't care."

Benazir appeared to relax for a minute. "Don't be ridiculous. If I'm free, my network is worth a fortune to you. We can work together again." A smile crossed his face. "I still need you, Nick." Janine strained to make out his thickly accented English. Did he say *Nick?*

"My name is Luc."

"You don't even have a name. Luc Tremont," Benazir

sneered. "Who the fuck is that? You only have one real name that you can live up to. You are a wanted man, my friend. And no matter how far you run or how low you scrape to please your FBI friends, you will always be the Scorpion."

Janine's blood ran ice cold. *Luc was the Scorpion?*

Luc's jaw clenched, and a vein in his neck pulsed.

Deny it, she wanted to scream. *Tell him he's wrong, Luc!*

"In two minutes the FBI and DST will be out here, and your brief taste of freedom will be over." Luc's voice was steady and low. Not indignant, not furious at these wrongful allegations. Not at all.

Benazir glanced at the door and shook his head. "You're the one who wants freedom. I know all about you. Your friend in Burgundy spilled her guts to me."

"And then you killed her husband."

"A necessity," he shrugged, yanking the woman even closer to him, as though he'd need more protection. "He had figured out where his wife's loyalties lay, and he might have warned you."

"And the professor in California?"

Janine willed her heart to stop thumping. It would give her away.

"I had to get control of Versailles, and the wise minister of culture agreed, for a reasonable fee." Dizziness threatened her, along with a black, incomprehensible fear. Claude Marchionette was behind Albert's death? "It would have been easier with one of my own in charge of the art, but the perfect replacement landed in our lap."

He tilted his head and smiled. "She was easily distracted."

Luc's eyes narrowed, and he cursed under his breath. He jerked the gun toward the casino, then pointed it back to Benazir's face. "Move. Now."

Benazir settled the woman directly in front of him. Suddenly, he flashed a knife at her neck. Janine bit back a gasp.

Benazir's hand was steady. His eyes locked on Luc. "You do not want the blood of an innocent person on your hands, Jarrett. Isn't that true? Didn't you give up your lucrative life as the Scorpion for that very reason?"

"Let her go."

The blade moved enough for a trickle of red to appear. Janine covered her mouth to keep from screaming.

"Come on, Nick." Benazir grinned, baring his white teeth. "We are both men without countries. We'll split the entire enterprise fifty-fifty."

A trickle of sweat dripped down Luc's face, for a moment, she thought he swayed. Was he *thinking about it?*

The knife dug deeper, and the woman screamed out a plea for help.

Luc lowered the gun, then threw it down. "You coward."

Benazir thrust his hostage away and held out his hand as though he wanted to shake Luc's. Luc reached for it, then yanked Benazir down to the ground with full force. They tumbled and rolled on the concrete as Janine levered herself up from the bushes and squinted into the shadows for the gun.

It lay about twenty feet away, on the other side of the

patio. As she spotted it, she heard Luc grunt and turned to see him roll under Benazir, who pinned him with all his weight. The steel blade flashed over Luc's neck.

Oh, God! She dropped the fur on the ground to slide along the back wall behind Benazir and make a dash for the gun.

She got about five feet when Luc made another sickening sound, and she froze in horror. Benazir half stood, then slammed himself into Luc's chest. Luc reached up to push Benazir off, but the bigger man managed to hold on.

As Luc lifted himself off the ground, a dark stain remained under him. Good Lord, he'd been shot! No wonder he could barely fight the guy.

Janine darted toward the gun, but her foot hit something hard. The largest of the three Plums had rolled out from the fur and lay on its side on the concrete.

Benazir's knife was an inch from Luc's throat. Scooping up the vase, Janine's hands closed over the irreplaceable porcelain.

Luc managed to push the knife away, but Benazir body-slammed him again. Luc growled from under the weight of Benazir and bared his teeth. Benazir thrust the knife at his chest, and Luc turned barely in time.

Red-hot fury quaked through Janine. She leapt behind Benazir's back and raised the vase above her head. Luc's eyes widened as he saw her. Benazir turned slightly, unwittingly offering a target.

She smashed the Plum in his face with every ounce of strength she could muster, sending purple shards everywhere and eliciting a violent howl from her victim.

Luc rolled to avoid the shower of porcelain as Benazir lunged toward Janine. Blood spurted from the cuts in his face, and she backed up with a scream.

Behind Benazir, Luc swooped toward the gun and came up in one smooth move. "Benazir!" he hollered. "Turn around, you bastard." As the big man stumbled around in a circle, Luc fired.

Janine's legs wobbled, and she stared at Luc over the body between them, vaguely aware that the door burst open and several men came running out, led by Tristan Stewart.

Her hands started to tingle, then burn, as tiny pieces of porcelain cut her palms. "Is it true?" she asked, ignoring the action around them.

He just nodded once.

Someone shouted, and a group of men surrounded Benazir's body, but Janine's gaze stayed locked on Luc. She could actually feel her heart shattering in a million pieces, just like her Plums.

Someone placed a hand on her arm. "Dr. Coulter?" It was Tristan, holding the fur. Beside him, the other agent held a vase in each hand. "Do you want your coat?"

She looked absently at it, and at the two remaining Plums. "No." She had to get out of there. "Am I free to go?"

"For the moment," he said, turning to Luc and placing a friendly hand on his shoulder. "Let's get you fixed up, man."

Luc waved him off and pinned Janine with that unreadable expression.

Only this time, she could read it. It said *run for your life*.

She nodded back once and turned to the door.

What a fool she'd been. What a fantasizing fool. And the only thing worse than a fool was a liar.

Weren't they a fine pair?

CHAPTER
Twenty-five

N ick Jarrett. The name still hit Janine like a vicious
blow to her stomach, leaving her breathless and
blinking against tears. When they filled her eyes, as they
had for an hour or more, the flickering casino lights
streamed into runny pools of yellow and red.

She stood paralyzed by the pain. It didn't matter how
long she waited on that balcony. He wasn't coming back
to this room; of that she was certain. Maybe he'd gone to
the hospital. Maybe he'd already gone to jail. Maybe he'd
gone to another country and turned into another man.

What difference did it make?

Dear God, all the clues had been there. From the day
she arrived and Simone de Vries told her the Scorpion was
alive and well and helping himself to art from the Louvre,
the clues were all around her.

Of course, she understood now that wasn't the Scorpion. That was Benazir's trap to *get* the Scorpion.

But, oh, the signs that she'd ignored. The ease with
which he stole—how else would he know how to break

into a highly secure resort penthouse? And the language. He was more American than she was, at times.

She squeezed the railing so hard that pain seared from her cut fingertips straight up her arms. It was nothing compared to the pain in her heart.

Why did his deception hurt so much?

He lied because he had to. Because he was involved in this sting operation. He let her believe he was an undercover good guy, and in a sense—in this case, anyway—he was. He hadn't seduced her against her will—that bone-melting bathroom-floor sex was as much her doing as his. So he hadn't done anything wrong in that regard, either.

The heartache was because she had fallen for him. As hard as a woman could fall, and as deep. And she wanted him to be someone else. Someone better than what he was. Someone noble and courageous and heroic.

The balcony door slid open, yanking her from her reverie, and her heart leaped.

"Hey, Rapunzel." He stood in the doorway and looked at her. "I thought I might find you on the balcony."

His hair was matted, and fire burned in his eyes. Dried blood covered most of his sleeve and shirt, with more on his face. He looked . . . *noble and courageous and heroic.*

She turned back to the water so she didn't have to look at him, didn't have to feel that ache to touch him. "I wanted to talk to the FBI, or whoever is investigating Albert's death, before I leave. That's all I care about now."

He took a few steps closer. "What about the Plums?"

She flashed him an incredulous look. "They were more valuable as a trio."

Holding her gaze, he grazed her cheek. "Is that why you're crying?"

"Of course," she insisted, backing out of his reach. "I'm crying . . . because I can't believe Albert had to die for a few vases. And because I can't believe Claude Marchionette was involved with that man." Her voice cracked, but she continued. "I still can't believe that I— I—"

He put his hand on her arm. "I can't believe you sacrificed one of the Plums to save me."

"Oh, I was just mad as hell." She gave him a shaky smile. "I get destructive when I'm mad."

"No." His eyes were as black as the lake. "You get fearless."

She brushed a hair from her face, but he intercepted her hand midmovement. She flinched.

"Jesus," he said, examining her palms. "You're hurt." He tugged her toward the door. "Let me wash these cuts."

She didn't move. "Wait . . ." *Luc? Nick?* "I don't even know what to call you."

His expression flickered with the impact of her words, but he pulled her hands close to his face and kissed one of the dried cuts on her fingers, never taking his eyes from hers.

"My name is Nick Jarrett."

She closed her eyes as he spoke that truth, and a tear escaped.

"And I owe you my life."

"What you owe me, *Nick,* is an explanation."

"*And* my life."

She slipped out of his grip. "Did you work . . . for him? For that monster? Did you steal for him?"

He blew out a quick breath. "Yes," he said simply.

The last ember of hope died. "I thought maybe . . . I'd misunderstood." She walked past him and continued straight into her bathroom, where she dropped on the vanity chair and closed her eyes.

When she opened them, he was opening the cabinets, rooting around. "There must be a first-aid kit in here somewhere."

It reminded her of her frantic search in Benazir's room. "He hid them in the refrigerator," she said suddenly.

His lips curled in a wry smile as he pulled out a white box marked with a red cross. "Very clever." He glanced at her. "And not on our list of preferred hiding places."

While he washed his hands, her gaze traveled over his bloody face and the brown stain on his expensive shirt. She could see the thick white bandage underneath.

Her stomach tightened, and she resisted the urge to touch his arm. "Were you shot?"

"Just grazed. I'm fine." He rinsed his hands and frowned at them, then lathered a second time. "What made you look in the refrigerator?" he asked.

"It was locked."

His eyebrows lifted in surprise. "How'd you get into it?"

She almost smiled. "I unscrewed the refrigerator door from the opposite side."

"Whoa." He patted his hands dry, then dampened a fresh towel. "I'm impressed."

Kneeling in front of her, he took her hands between his and avoided eye contact.

She didn't want to look at his hands—those long, masculine fingers that could spin locks and pilfer jewels. Instead, she looked at his messed black hair, at that one lock fallen on his forehead, the abrasions on his cheekbone. He certainly looked the part. Dangerous as hell.

She jerked her hand as the wet cloth touched an open cut.

"Sorry," he muttered. "Some of these are deep."

For the first time in an hour, she realized how badly the vase had cut her. She'd been too immersed in the other pain, and in trying to sort it all out.

"Why a scorpion?" she asked suddenly.

His whole body stilled for a moment, and his broad shoulders tensed. "It was my father's nickname. I wanted him to know . . . it was me."

"Your father? Why?"

He focused on her hands, inhaling slowly before he answered. "I wanted to be a spy."

She leaned back in surprise, but said nothing.

"We both did, Tristan and me."

"You—you knew him?"

He sat back on his haunches, still holding her wounded hand. "Better than anyone in the world. We got into a fight on the playground in fourth grade and I broke his glasses." He smiled. "I had to pay for them. We were inseparable after that."

"Did that launch a life of crime?"

His mouth set in a tight line. "Not a life, Janine. Just

a few wayward years. In fact, the night I got caught was going to be my last job."

She felt his pulse beat under her fingertips. "So how did the spy turn into a thief?"

"Tristan and I had big dreams. We were pretty much dirt poor, living in Southie—the South End of Boston. His father worked down at the harbor and mine . . ." He carefully cleaned a cut. "Mine was a commercial airline pilot."

Her hand relaxed under his ministrations. "Not generally dirt poor, commercial airline pilots."

"That's very true. My father, John Jarrett, had been in the air force—the U.S. Air Force." He went back to cleaning a slice on her thumb. "That's how he met my mother. At the Paris Air Show. She'd gone for fun, and he was working. They got involved, and she, well—I'm the result of it. I guess she was too ashamed to face Bérnard, and she ran off to America with the father of her baby. He put her up in a low-class neighborhood in Boston and came home on leave often enough for Claire to be conceived. After he left the air force he became a commercial pilot and invented a host of excuses for why he was never there, why we had no money, and why he couldn't marry my mother."

She had been about to ask again how all this drove him to crime when she realized what he'd said. "Your parents weren't married, either?"

"No." His sympathetic expression touched her heart. "We used his name for my mother's pride. But no marriage document was ever signed."

He laced his fingers through hers for a moment, then continued. "Anyway, I was always real suspicious of my father. He adamantly refused to marry my mother. He told her she'd be deported back to France if the government realized she'd been living in the U.S. without a visa, and she'd have to leave her children. And there were these long periods of time where he was missing."

He stood and flipped the top of the first-aid kit again, rummaging through the medicines as he talked. "When we were about sixteen, Tris and I were pretty damn sure we could take the civil service exam after high school and pass it easily."

Janine reached over and lifted a tube of antiseptic cream. "Is this what you're looking for?"

He smiled at her, leaning against the counter. He spun the lid off the tube. "We decided we needed to practice our spying techniques. I wanted to find out where the hell my father went when he disappeared, and Tristan wanted to see if we could go undercover." He let out a short, derisive laugh. "We were so stupid. We followed him to the airport after one of his pitifully short visits and managed to get on a flight that he was piloting to New York. We followed him out of the airport, expecting him to catch a cab to a hotel where the pilots stayed."

"And where did he go?"

"Home." His voice was flat. Bitter. "He went home to his wife and three daughters, who greeted him with happy kisses on the front porch of a six-bedroom house on Long Island."

She closed her eyes for a moment. "Oh, God."

He took her hands again. "This might sting a little."

She opened them, palms up, and let him work. "I still don't get it. How did discovering your father's double life lead you to . . . to what you did?"

"We broke into my dad's house that night. I wanted to see how he lived, and then help myself to what I felt he owed us." He glanced up. "No Robin Hood analogies, please. I just hated him. He had so much and we had so little. I even managed to go back and hit his house a few more times, that's how pissed I was."

"Did Tristan steal, too?"

"Only that once. Tristan remains firmly on the side of the angels." He dropped a generous amount of cream on her hand and started to massage it in. "That adventure was the beginning of the end for us."

He opened a bandage and gently pressed it between her thumb and index finger. A piece of her heart broke off, thinking of how a teenage kid would hurt when faced with that kind of lie from his father.

"Civil service requires an extremely thorough background check, especially when you ace it like I did." He spared her a cocky grin and opened another bandage. "They discovered the truth about my father in, oh, fifteen minutes, instead of the fifteen years it had taken me. I was disqualified for any government service."

"Because your father was married to someone other than your mother?" That seemed preposterous.

He sighed and applied the last bandage. "It was more complicated than that. My father's flight record was shaky; he'd been put on probation a few times. And by then I'd actually used my skills on a few other jobs, and I—I just didn't really push it. I wasn't CIA material." He shrugged, but she sensed he hadn't given up his dream easily. "Tristan aced the test and landed a job with the FBI. I couldn't afford college, of course, so . . ." He stood up and leaned against the counter, crossing his arms. "Sorry. Long answer to one question."

She had more questions. "And Benazir? How did you meet him?"

"I *met* him tonight," he said with an ironic laugh. "But years ago, he'd been one of my clients. Unfortunately, he discovered the one thing I guarded most closely: my identity. Tristan was moving up in the FBI at the time, and he had strong suspicions about me. I had become sort of an obsession with him. When Benazir tried to get me to kill a man, I refused. He set me up and I got caught. I made a deal with Tristan that put Benazir in jail, because I didn't trust the bastard who'd made threats against my mother and sister."

She jerked back in surprise. "He would have killed them?"

"Absolutely. So I turned him in, and in exchange, Tristan arranged my 'death' and helped me create a new identity. Unfortunately, I'm wanted for so many crimes that if I set foot in the U.S. without a pardon, I'd be arrested before I left the airport. So, I needed a place to live. I picked France because it was the only other culture and language I knew intimately, thanks to my mother."

"And you've spent all these years working for the FBI and trying to earn your pardon."

He shrugged. "Pardons are rare, if not impossible. The best I can do is live in the U.S. under another identity."

Would that preclude a normal life and normal relationships? "What about your mother and sister?"

"They think I'm dead." He sounded so sad, so final.

"That alone should be payment for crimes committed."

He shook his head and started to reassemble the first-aid kit. "Tris told them I'd worked undercover for the FBI and that I'd been killed in the line of duty. They don't know—no one does—that Nick Jarrett was the Scorpion."

He snapped the box lid down and gave her a questioning look. Waiting for her verdict, no doubt.

Something pulled at her deep inside. Wasn't there a noble, courageous hero living inside this former thief? Looking away from him, she studied his hands on the white box. Strong, capable, agile hands that could break locks, and hearts.

She closed her eyes to erase the image, but could still see his hands, the dusting of hair on his knuckles, the spray of tiny dark specks on his fingers. . . .

Her eyes flew open, and she grabbed his arms. "You washed your hands."

He rubbed his fingers against each other. "I did, but—"

"But . . . but they have—" *Refiring spots*. They were damn near impossible to remove. "Did you touch the other Plums?"

"Yes. I brought them up to you. They're in the living room."

She dropped his hands and ran out of the bathroom. Seizing one of the vases, she thrust it under the lamp and started digging at the base.

"The refrigerator!" she exclaimed. "The Plums were cold. The temperature must have chilled the glaze. That's why the refiring spots didn't lift when I checked them."

She held the vase out victoriously. "These are the fakes!"

"Are you sure?"

"Yes, yes! The real ones—all *three* of them—are still out there somewhere."

He took the vase and set it on the table. "Let's go, then."

"Where?"

"To find your Plums." His smile nearly dissolved her as he cocked his head toward the door. "We need to talk to Tristan. Unless you hate me too much to finish what we started here."

"I don't hate you," she said softly.

Oh, God, no. Quite the opposite.

CHAPTER
Twenty-six

"The fact is, we have no freaking idea where they are." Tristan dashed Janine's hope and excitement with one cool, quick dose of reality.

He leaned against a desk in the casino's security office, a few feet from where she sat in a stiff metal-backed chair. He unbuttoned one cuff of a blue oxford shirt, rolled it up precisely two times, tucked it, and repeated the process with the other. He seemed remarkably unruffled for a man who, two hours earlier, had been on the floor of the baccarat room dodging bullets.

"No freaking idea," he repeated. "Do we, Paul?"

"We do not." The other agent stared at a laptop computer with Luc hovering over his shoulder. "Do we, Luc?"

"Luc" looked up and caught her gaze. "We will," he assured her.

She didn't respond, but turned her attention back to Tristan. "Can you prove that Benazir was behind Albert's death?"

"We'll know more when he's alert and can talk," Tristan told her. "They'll keep him overnight in the hospital, and then we get custody. His closest henchman, Amod Surjeet, was killed in the baccarat room. He might have been easier to break than Benazir. But we'll be working with the bureaus in L.A. and Paris and Dijon to make a case."

Janine toyed with the edge of the Band-Aid on her hand, sighing in frustration.

"Everyone at Versailles is being investigated," Tristan assured her. "And the minister of culture's interrogation has already begun."

What a mess. Not only had the Plums vanished from the computerized radar, but the highest-level officials in France were under suspicion for stealing them—and for murder. The exhibit was closed indefinitely, and by morning her name would be all over the whole sordid affair.

She'd be lucky to have a basement office in the Art History Department when she got back to UCLA. Looking up from her hands, her gaze fell on Luc—*Nick*. She simply couldn't think of him as Nick. He was *Luc*, unkempt and looking more like a renegade ruffian than someone working firmly "on the side of the angels." When she turned back to Tristan, she knew she'd been caught studying him.

"Do you need names of people in the department?" she asked lamely, trying to cover the fact that she'd been ogling a wounded criminal.

Tristan shook his head. "You're both fairly useless to us," he said, and then flashed a quick, devilish smile. "I mean that in a sympathetic way, Dr. Coulter. You should get some rest. No one is going to find the vases at three in the morning. Sleep, and tomorrow we'll strategize."

"Really?" Disappointment squeezed her.

"He's right," Luc agreed, pointing at the laptop. "This isn't a programming problem with the GPS. Something's wrong in the tracking device. It's not sending a signal."

"What does that mean?" Janine asked.

Paul shrugged and clicked a key. "The transmitter's been removed."

"Not possible," Luc said. He was French again, she noticed. For the benefit of Agent Dunne, no doubt. What would it be like to live with a human chameleon, never knowing who you'd wake up with each morning?

He looked at her, and his determined expression melted when their eyes met. *"Ne t'inquiétes pas,"* he said softly. A rush of affection warmed her blood. She *was* worried, and not just about the Plums. She was worried about her heart.

Maybe she just wouldn't care about those chameleon qualities. Maybe there were more important things in life than . . . consistency.

"It's possible the Plums have been destroyed," Tristan offered.

Luc gave Tristan a harsh look. "It's also possible that they are hidden somewhere that prevents the signal from coming through. Benazir has the answers." He straightened from his position over the computer and winced in pain, absently massaging his bandaged arm.

Paul stood suddenly. "I'm going up to check on their

progress in Benazir's suite. There might be a clue some-where."

After he left, Luc took Paul's seat and started poking at the keyboard again. "Lisette's computer might still have the original coordinates," he mused, almost to him-self. "I need to get into the memory on that system."

"*We'll* look into it," Tristan said pointedly.

At his tone, Luc looked up.

Tristan repositioned himself on the desk and cleared his throat. "We'd better talk about Lisette Soisson, Luc."

"So, talk." He was American again.

Tristan glanced at Janine. "Maybe you should—"

"She knows everything," Luc interrupted him, his attention back on the computer. "Anything you want to say, you can say in front of her."

Tristan just stared at him for a minute, his normally piercing gaze wide with surprise. "Anything?"

Luc stabbed at a key and cursed under his breath. "Something is not right here." He tilted the laptop screen down and looked at Tristan again. "Yes, Tris. I trust her."

Janine's eyes narrowed. This didn't have anything to do with trust. Benazir had spilled the truth. If he hadn't, she'd have gone blithely along thinking Luc was super-man undercover crime fighter.

"We're going to have to arrest Lisette," Tristan finally said. "She's involved. We don't know to what degree, but she is involved."

Luc nodded.

"Then we have to talk to the director about your next assignment."

The two men shared a long look that spoke volumes, but Janine couldn't begin to decipher it.

"I'm in no hurry," Luc finally said, his gaze sliding to her. Something deep inside tumbled and rolled at the intensity of his look.

Tristan turned a quick snort into a cough. "Some of Benazir's men might still be out there. We don't know how much they know. The director might be in a hurry, even if you aren't. I don't think he wants you gallivanting around France with the chance that more people know . . . who you are."

Luc's dark eyes burned at Tristan, his brows locked together. "I don't *gallivant*, Tris. And the only people who know who I am—the only people who *matter*—are in this room."

Tristan eased himself off the desk and kept his **gaze** steady on Luc. "A day. Maybe two. You don't get time off for good behavior, Nick."

Nick slid his card key into the lock of the suite.

"I'd rather go find my Plums than sleep," Janine said, as she walked into the room. "Isn't there anything else we can do tonight?"

"You can barely walk." He didn't bother with a survey of the room; Benazir was in custody. "You need a shower and a long night's sleep."

She groaned softly. "Thank God for that steam room. I'm going straight in there."

His whole body tensed at the image that flashed in his mind. "You do that," he agreed quickly. "I'll just . . ." *Fantasize.* "See you in the morning."

She paused midstep, but didn't turn to him. The only sound in the room was a quietly ticking clock and the gentle hum of the refrigerator. For a fraction of a second, he thought she might . . . what? Issue an invitation to join her? He held his breath and waited.

"Okay," she said. "Good night, then."

She disappeared into the hall, and he heard her door close. But not lock.

He exhaled long and slow, then went to the wet bar for some cognac. His foot hit the bottom of the refrigerator and he paused, leaning over to examine the metal hinges on the side. How the hell did she get that door off? He smiled as he poured a generous amount of the amber liquid into a snifter.

He closed his eyes and let his imagination travel into the steam room. But the only image he conjured up was the look on her face when she held that vase over her head and gave it to Benazir for all she was worth.

And man, she was worth a lot.

He took a deep drink, willing the burning liquid to descend straight to the throbbing pain in his arm. As soon as he had a shower—a careful one that didn't soak his bandage—and a few more slugs of cognac, he'd crash and forget all about the woman sleeping in the next room.

No. The woman taking a hot steam in the next room.

He emptied the glass, poured another, and took it into his room.

The glass remained untouched on the bureau while he took a shower, shaved, and pulled on a pair of running shorts. Restless, he picked up the snifter, then put it back down. He didn't want any more cognac. It didn't dull the pain, anyway—at least not the one in his chest.

Only one thing could ease that. Janine.

Running a hand through his wet hair, he opened his door and looked across the hall. Her door remained closed. But unlocked. Maybe *she* wanted a cognac.

Holding the full snifter in one hand, he tapped on her door and waited. After a minute, he slowly turned the knob. The room was empty and dark, but for a sliver of light through the crack of the bathroom door.

He tapped on that. Still no answer. He entered. This time he recognized the hiss of the steam. This time he knew exactly where she was, how she looked. This time . . . he couldn't walk away unless she told him to.

He turned the corner. The glass door had turned opaque with white puffs of steam. He nudged it with his good arm.

"Luc?"

He could make her out on the bench, hastily snatching a towel as she tried to sit up and cover herself. "It's Nick," he said. "Can I join you? I'm dressed." His running shorts were already damp from the humidity and tented over an erection, but he *was* dressed.

She managed to wrap a towel around her.

"You don't have to put that on," he said, sitting next to her on the hot, wet marble. "I've seen you. More than once."

Her hair was slicked back off her face, and her skin glistened with steam and perspiration. A smudge of makeup under her eyes gave her a fragile, haunted look.

"What do you want?" Her voice was husky, as warm as the cognac in his hand.

He held the snifter to her. "To see if you wanted something to . . . help you relax."

Through the fog, he could see her skeptical look. "Liar." She took the glass and sipped.

He shrugged in agreement. "I wanted to see if you're all right."

She swirled the cognac and held it up in the steam. "Liar."

"Okay," he smiled. "I came in here to see if there's any chance we can still be friends."

"Liar."

He laughed out loud at that and watched her fight a smile as she took another drink, long and slow. When she finished, she lifted her face and skimmed her upper lip with the tip of her tongue. "Let's try again, *Nick.*" She leaned forward, her fist holding the towel at her chest. "What do you want?"

The room sizzled with palpable heat and translucent clouds of white steam as they locked gazes.

"I want you," he finally said.

She reached down and set the cognac glass on the tile floor, then faced him. Wordlessly, she spread her fingers and let the towel fall to the bench. "I like it when you tell the truth."

His gaze fell to her exposed body, and the sight of her hit him in the heart and fanned the fire that already raged in another part of him. Sucking in a breath of steamed air, he closed the space between them and kissed her. She tasted like the cognac, hot and sweet and potent. As her tongue probed his mouth, he angled his head to get more of her, pulling her onto his lap, her legs open around his hips. Slowly, he lay her back onto another towel.

She lifted her arms in a feline stretch, then folded them under her head. He took one of her legs, lifted it on the bench, and let the other dangle down.

With a single finger, he trailed a path over sunkissed curves and silky flesh, from her hipbone, across the concave dip, over her navel, then straight down to the golden patch between her legs. Her eyes fluttered as her muscles tightened, but she held his gaze.

"I've seen you in here before," he said, his voice raspy.

Her eyes flashed. "When?"

He leaned over and treated himself to a single kiss on the middle of her stomach. "Was it just this morning?" He shook his head at the impossibility of that. "I came into your bathroom and you were back here."

"I never heard you."

He smiled. "I'm a professional."

"So I've heard." The soft ring of her laughter warmed his heart.

With his hands planted on either side of her on the ledge, he licked the moist skin between her breasts and felt her quiver.

"What did you see?" she asked.

His tongue explored the undercurve of her breasts, loving the feel of her warm, soft flesh. "I saw you . . ."

She quivered under him. "You . . . watched me?"

"Only for a minute."

Her breath was already uneven, ragged with each touch. "I was thinking about you."

"I know," he said, twirling his tongue around the pebbled tip of her breast. "What were you imagining?"

She closed her eyes and rocked her hips toward him in a silent invitation. "This."

He suckled gently, then added pressure as her fingers curled into his hair and forced his head against her.

"And that," she whispered.

He filled his hands with her, nibbling her heated, slick skin, his mouth unable to consume enough of her. Hungrily, he made his way down, down, down to taste the essence of her.

Her fingers dug into his skull as she lifted herself toward him. He kissed the silky skin of her thighs first, teasing and torturing her until he heard her slow, pleasured moan. She tasted like honey and steam and sweet sex, bucking once before she found a steady rhythm that matched his thorough tongue's. She tightened her legs around his head, and he pulled back, sliding his finger over the pulse point of her mound.

She arched again, her fingers twined in his hair as he fondled her.

"Oh, oh." She shuddered in his hands. "You're such a magician."

He chuckled, his breath on her flesh earning a gasp of delight. Her response made his erection throb with the need to be in her, but he tasted and played and teased her until she teetered on the edge in his mouth, clutching his hair and vibrating with pleasure.

As she quaked with an orgasm, he held her hips and kept up relentless pressure with his tongue, loving the way she lost control. Slowly he kissed his way back to her beautiful face.

She was lost. Transported. Did he make her forget who he was? At least he could hope that she no longer cared.

He reached her mouth and kissed her hard and furiously, finding his place between her legs and pressing his erection against her. Only the shorts separated them, and that wouldn't last for long.

He kissed her cheek, her throat, her ear. "I want to make love to you, Janine."

Without waiting for permission, he scooped her into his arms and carried her out of the steam room. She wrapped her arms around his neck and dropped her head back, letting her hair fall over his arms.

He laid her on the sheets and joined her. As he did, she gently caressed the white bandage on his arm.

"You saved Tristan's life, you know," she said, looking in his eyes.

He bit back a surprised laugh. "He saved mine once," he responded, focusing his gaze on the mouth he wanted to taste again. "So we're even."

He leaned down to kiss her, but she dodged him with a sneaky smile. "You don't really hate each other. You know that, don't you?"

Fighting a frustrated sigh, he lifted himself to look at her. "Do you really want to talk about it now?"

She shook her head. "I just . . . I just want you to know that you're not as bad as you think."

"Thank you." He managed a half smile, although part of him wanted to throw his head back and howl with happiness. "Now if you stop talking, I'll show you just how good I can be."

She bit her lip and slid her hand down to the waist-band of his shorts, inching them lower until they were off. "Yes, please." She urged him into place between her legs, the tip of him just touching her moist flesh. "Love me. Please love me, Nick."

The name cut through his heart with the same force as the bullet that had grazed his arm. He wanted to drag this out for hours, wanted to tease her to a dozen more orgasms, but his willpower dissolved at the sound of his name on her lips.

He closed his eyes and thrust himself into her with a guttural groan. The sensation shocked him, and he froze for a second, then slid out and back in with a force he couldn't control.

"Nick. *Nick.*"

She whispered his name and dug her nails into his back and lifted her hips to meet his every lunge into her. Again and again he lost himself in the beauty of her, in the tight envelope of love she wrapped around him. Again and again she called out his name, locking her legs around his hips and grasping him with a strength he didn't know she had.

The overwhelming pull took over his whole body, blinding him, killing him with the need to release himself in her. He looked down to where they joined, her beautiful woman's curves arched to take his frantic, hungry body. It looked so right, so completely, absolutely *right*.

"*Nick. Nick.*"

The name tore at him, propelling him harder and faster toward the pinnacle of satisfaction. With his gaze locked on the place where he disappeared in her, the place where he belonged most in the whole world, he sucked in a violent breath and spilled helplessly into the one woman who knew his secret . . . and let him love her anyway.

Dawn rose over the Alps in heartbreaking shades of peach and plum. The morning hues reflected off the snowcapped peaks and into the blue black waters of Lake Geneva. They'd forgotten to close the drapes, Janine thought drowsily as she opened her eyes. She was awake too early, but the reward was a sensory overload. She smiled. Her whole body tingled with satisfaction, warmed by the powerful arms around her and rock-hard chest that pressed against her back. She listened to Luc's even breathing and inhaled the sultry scent of their lovemaking that clung to the sheets and her skin. All while enjoying one of nature's most brilliant works of art.

It surely didn't get any better than this.

Slowly, she rotated her body to face him and gaze at another of nature's fine works. Oh, yes—it did get even better.

He opened his eyes, the color of a triple espresso and just as inviting in the morning. Without saying a word, he kissed her on the mouth. "Janine," he whispered against her lips. "No regrets, right?"

She scooted into the full length of his body. "Oh, yes."

"No." He inched back, frowning. "No, you shouldn't."

"Well, I do. I have a deep and painful regret."

He lifted his head, his expression concerned. "What is it?"

"I regret that you don't call me *Szha-neen* anymore."

With a quick laugh, he kissed the tip of her nose, then her mouth, then her neck. *"Szha-neen.* Always and forever you will be *Szha-neen."*

Always and forever.

Her stomach flipped at the words, and then his relentless erection was grinding against her, making it impossible to separate her physical response from the emotional one.

And wasn't that always the case with him?

He slid his hand under the covers and did that—that *trick* again, and Janine closed her eyes and missed the rest of the sunrise. Only after they lay spent and waiting for their ragged breath to steady did she remember *always and forever.*

Did he think there could be anything like that between them? Wasn't he about to take on a new identity and disappear? *A day, maybe two?* That's what Tristan had said.

The loud double ring of the phone jarred her from her thoughts, and she stifled a moan of disappointment when he separated from her to answer it.

For a moment he said nothing, then she saw the blood drain from his face. "I see," he finally said. "Then I guess there's no rush for you to get to Burgundy."

It must be Tristan, because Nick still spoke in his American English. She wanted to snuggle deeper into the warm nest they'd made, but something about his face and body language told her that the morning cuddles had ended. She slipped out of the bed and went into the bathroom, staying long enough for him to finish the call.

When she no longer heard his clipped responses, she cinched the white robe and returned to the bedroom. He sat on the edge of the bed, staring out the window.

"What is it?" she asked.

"Lisette is dead," he said quietly, closing his eyes at Janine's tiny gasp. "It looks like an accident—"

"Not again!" Janine exclaimed.

He shook his head. "No, no. This wasn't Benazir. Tristan said the housekeeper found her on the cellar floor, her wrist slashed from a broken wine bottle. It looks like she fell. She was alive when Arlaine got to her, but didn't make it."

Janine curled her fingers around the bathrobe tie. "Oh, God."

He turned to her. "Evidently she held on long enough to give some final instructions to Arlaine."

"What is it? What did she do?"

"She left the entire vineyard and everything in it to me." His rich brown eyes had gone dull and flat.

"To you?" Janine stepped closer. "Out of guilt, no doubt."

He shrugged. "Whatever. Now I have to figure out how to sell it."

"You can't. Bérnard wouldn't want you to," she said positively.

He reached out to her with his good arm, pulling her closer. "I'm in no position to own or run a vineyard, Janine. I'll be disappearing long before the next harvest." He folded her against his chest. "But this means I have to go to Burgundy. I wanted to take you sailing on the lake. And I want to find the Plums."

She inched away, her throat constricting at his words. "Do you have to go right away?"

He nodded. "Yes, I do. I'm sorry. I'll be in constant touch with Tristan and make sure he does every—"

"Could I come with you?"

His eyes lit up, and he gave her the most beautiful smile she'd ever seen. "I'd love that."

CHAPTER
Twenty-seven

The ivy had grown so thick, it was nearly impossible to see the ancient stone walls of the château. The trees were taller, and the old yellow shutters had been painted a subdued shade of gray.

But everything else about Château Soisson was exactly as when Gabrielle had left forty years earlier. Except that Bérnard would no longer come bounding around from the back courtyard and stop in his tracks, as he always did at the sight of her.

She stole a glance toward the side yard, just in case. But all that greeted her was the ancient beech tree that threatened to burst into a verdant explosion of spring leaves. She'd climbed that tree a hundred times.

"Come on, *Maman.*" Claire took her arm and urged her toward the house. "No time to wander down memory lane."

Claire had been wild with determination since the call had come from France in the middle of the night. If her daughter hadn't been visiting for the week and answered the phone herself, Gabrielle might never have come. She would have thought she'd dreamed it.

For how else could she explain a woman who claimed to work for the Soissons, of all incomprehensible things, calling to say that Nick was alive. *Alive.* Bérnard was not, she thought with a heavy heart, but a greater gift had been given to her. Her son. Her *son.* A soft prayer sound escaped her lips, and Claire squeezed harder.

"I know, *Maman.* Come *on.*"

The mahogany front door swung open before they reached the end of the walk. In the shadows stood a weary-looking woman in a plain brown dress.

"Arlaine?" Claire asked, picking up speed and bringing Gabrielle along with her. "Are you the woman who called us? I'm Claire Jarrett. This is my mother, Gabrielle."

Arlaine nodded and indicated for them to come in. "I called you," she said, as they stepped into the entryway.

Gabrielle clutched Claire's arm tighter as memories transported her back in time. So little had changed. Furniture and paint, yes. But the house felt the same. She could almost imagine that she smelled Madame Soisson's andouillettes simmering with onions, and could taste the first bittersweet sip of the free-run juice. The unwanted wine, Bérnard had called it, but at sixteen, it had been fine for them.

She paused to get her bearings, taking in the polished wood floor covered with simple handmade rugs. The curved steps with the wooden railing where Bérnard had first kissed her. The gray limestone fireplace where they warmed themselves in the winter. Home. Or what should have been home.

They followed Arlaine through the hall into the kitchen. It had been modernized, but the coziness of a French vineyard kitchen was never lost. Gabrielle dropped into a chair at the center table. Her chair, to the left of Bérnard. She'd eaten a thousand meals in that room.

"Where is he?" Claire asked, in polite French but without preamble.

"I don't know," Arlaine answered. "He was here and he left. I told you everything that Madame Soisson told me before she . . . died."

Madame Soisson. That would be Lisette Vichey. Gabrielle had the faintest memory of the plain, chubby girl who had mooned over Bérnard during their school years at Lycée. She'd heard he'd married her, not long after Gabrielle had run away to America.

"*Madame,* we have come a long way, leaving home the instant you called." Claire had adopted her take-charge voice, as powerful in a country kitchen as she was in a boardroom. "It's imperative that you tell us everything and give us every opportunity to determine if this man— this Luc Tremont—really is my brother."

"I only know what *Madame* said to me before she died." Arlaine reached into the pocket of her drab dress. She pulled something out, glanced at it, then put a photograph on the table in front of Gabrielle. "She told me to give you this."

Claire gasped as she seized the picture. "When was this taken?"

"At the holidays," Arlaine said. "There was a small party for the vineyard workers, and Luc was here."

"Oh, my God," Claire whispered, slumping into the

chair next to Gabrielle and staring at the picture. *"Maman.* It's him."

Gabrielle opened her bag and pulled out the leather case that held her reading glasses. She slipped them on and blinked to focus as she took the photo from Claire's shaking hands.

All the blood rushed from her head, leaving her dizzy and breathless. The empty hole that had existed for so long inside of her suddenly filled with an indescribable sense of hope.

It was Nicky. Her beautiful, dangerous, precious boy. And beside him, holding a glass of wine and wearing a smile that had only gotten warmer in forty years, was the man who should have been her husband. Grinning at Nick with all the pride of a father.

For some reason, that made her the happiest of all. These two men she'd loved and lost had found each other. She looked up at Claire, whose face was wet with tears.

"Nick's alive, *Maman,"* Claire mumbled, wiping her cheeks. "He's *alive."*

"How do we find him?" Gabrielle asked Arlaine. "Where does he live?"

"All I know is that his name is Luc Tremont. He lives in Paris and visits here a few times a year. He could be in some sort of trouble, because an American law officer was here looking for him."

"In trouble?" Claire took her mother's hand, but Gabrielle just patted it.

"Don't worry. We'll help him, whatever it is." Nothing, nothing could be as bad as what they'd lived through the past five years.

Arlaine was digging around in her pocket again. "Two men were here, before *Madame* went to the basement and had her . . . accident." She pulled out a small card and handed it to Claire. "He told me to call him if Luc arrived."

"Oh, my God." Claire's face went white, then melted into utter disgust.

"What is it, honey?"

Claire let the card flutter to the table. "Tristan Stewart."

Nick reluctantly turned left on the old road to Beaune, a grimace accompanying the easy spin of the wheel.

"You're dreading this, aren't you?" Janine asked.

"Not really." He stole a look at her, watching her toy with the braid she'd let him make in her hair. "I just don't want this day to end. And I *really* don't want it to end with a trip to the morgue and a mountain of responsibility I can't even be around to handle."

"It has been a great day," she agreed. "Regardless of how it ends, it's been a great day."

They shared a smile. He could have made the trip from Evian to Beaune in a few hours as he'd done in the dead of night. This time he'd roamed country roads, and they'd indulged in a picnic in the hills above the Pouilly-Fuissé vineyards. Afterward, they'd slipped into a tour of the Château de Pierreclos, where he'd impressed Janine with his knowledge of the poetry of Lamartine, one of the castle's most famous residents. She'd countered his recital of the poem "Jocelyn" by dragging him into a museum to see a display of faience porcelain.

All day, they laughed and talked and shared memories. He told her about Gabrielle and Claire; she got choked up remembering Albert. There were no lies. No accents. No tripping around half-truths. She just had a hard time remembering not to call him Luc.

Their time together was as intoxicating as the country air, redolent with the smell of new flowers and centuries-old earth. Even more intoxicating was her presence, her easy laugh, her affectionate kisses. He ached to make love to her again. To share every intimacy with all defenses and barriers gone. They might not have a future, but they had this. *One day, maybe two.* Tristan's clock was ticking.

As night fell, he knew he couldn't drag out the journey any longer. As they pulled into the gravel drive, the first thing he noticed were the lights. Every room in the farmhouse was bright, and the lights spilled from the dormered windows onto the driveway, where two cars were parked.

"Who's here?" Janine asked, peering up to the third floor.

"Let's find out." He was relatively sure the station wagon was Arlaine's; the other looked like a rental. As he turned off the ignition, a strange sense of anticipation filled his heart. Probably because this was his, now.

He stepped into the pool of light, pausing to admire the classic lines of the old château. For a second, he thought of his mother. How she had longed to live here. How she had regretted her choices. He wished he could tell her that his strange and bizarre life had led him back to her very roots.

The door opened, and he looked up, expecting

Arlaine. But instead, a narrow-framed girl with a mass of thick, dark curls stood in the doorway. Beside her, he could see the silhouette of another woman with shorter hair. They stood arm in arm.

An eerie, mind-bending sense of something familiar licked at his senses. His breath caught in his throat as the two figures stepped out of the backlighting and onto the long patio. He froze, staring at the apparition of two women who couldn't, who *shouldn't* be standing there. His mind was playing tricks in the twilight.

"Nick! Oh, my God, it's you!" Shock and reality registered like a full body blow when Claire burst forward and flung herself into his arms. She smelled like Claire, she squealed like Claire. *Could it be?*

She clung too tightly for him to see her. Over her shoulder, the older woman approached, striding with that proud, French lift of her chin, her deep, dark eyes gleaming with joy. All he could do was stare.

"I never once stopped dreaming of this moment," she whispered with her sweet lilting accent. "Not once."

The lump in his throat burned like a heated coal, stinging his eyes and twisting his heart. With a low, long groan, he embraced them both. Over his mother's head, he caught Janine's bewildered expression.

One day, maybe two.

How could he stand to lose everything again?

When the bed dipped with Nick's weight, Janine pretended she'd been asleep. "What time is it?" she asked groggily.

He slid into the warm spot along her back and curled

a possessive arm around her stomach. "Almost dawn. Go back to sleep."

She hadn't slept a moment. Even though she'd excused herself hours ago from the bittersweet family reunion, she'd simply lain in bed and stared into the darkness, listening to the laughter and hushed conversation that drifted upstairs.

She felt like she'd spent hours as an observer, watching others enjoy a roller-coaster ride. She could only imagine what dips and thrills they were experiencing. Especially Luc—*Nick*. The highs of reuniting with lost family; the agonizing low of having to tell them the cause of his disappearance.

The women in his life knew nothing but forgiveness. His mother had cried a lot but clearly didn't care what her son had done in the past, now that he'd been returned to her. And Claire was relentless in her belief that Nick Jarrett could somehow be given a complete government pardon and be free to return to his world and his family.

After a few hours, Janine had retired to the guest room. She'd spent the time trying to examine and understand her complicated feelings for him. Could this be love? This spiraling, dangerous, heady feeling balanced by a completely unfamiliar need to connect in every emotional and physical way?

She shifted slightly against the hard planes of his chest. "Luc?"

"Nick." He tucked her bottom against him, and she felt the instant electrical jolt of their bodies touching.

"I keep forgetting," she whispered. "Nick?"

"Mmm?" His hand traveled the indentation of her waist and rested on her hip, his fingertip dipping perilously low on her stomach.

"Do you think Claire is right? Do you think you could get a pardon from the government?"

His enchanted fingers stilled. "Claire is a fireball who hates to be told no. It would take a miracle in the eyes of the FBI director."

"Could Tristan help?"

He didn't say anything for a moment. "I don't know."

"Your sister sure has a visceral reaction to the mention of his name."

"I don't blame her. He told her that he'd killed me."

She flipped around to face him. "Why would he tell her that?"

"Because she loved him. It stopped her from launching a full-scale investigation, dragging in the media and unknowingly blowing my cover. It was the only way she'd quietly accept that I was gone. Of course, it cost their relationship."

She thought of the spark in the pretty girl's eyes when anyone mentioned the FBI agent. "She's still in love with him."

"Without a doubt." His hand started its journey over her stomach again, leaving a trail of fire on her skin.

"If he's still in love with her, maybe . . ."

He gave her a quick kiss on the cheek. "Tristan would face the fires of hell for her, but Claire has no influence over his boss. In the mind of the FBI director, I ought to be rotting in a jail somewhere. I'm lucky to be free. And if I'm really lucky, I'll get to eat fast food instead of brie in my next life, and sing the right song at a sporting event. That's all."

The same niggling thought that had plagued her for hours floated to the surface. If he was going to live in the U.S., then could they be together? "Won't you—can't you have . . . someone special in your life, no matter who you are?"

He didn't say anything for a long time, and the pit in Janine's stomach grew deeper and darker. "I've never tried," he finally whispered. "But you *should* have someone special in your life, and I'm not it."

The finality of his words broke her heart. "Don't I have a say on that?" she asked, hating the way her voice caught.

"Janine." He propped himself up on his elbow and looked down at her.

"Szha-neen," she corrected, with a shaky smile.

He smiled and spun a piece of her hair in his fingertips. "You want security. You want a man who will be there for you. You want a family, a home, a curved staircase, and a grand piano. You want *legitimacy."*

The word stung, and she swallowed against the bitter lump in her throat.

"I can never give you that," he whispered. "Sure, we could be together, but for how long? To what end? How stable is life with a man who might have to move, change his identity, uproot his life at any moment?"

The pain in her heart threatened to collapse her chest.

"I won't do that to you," he said. "You deserve a better man. A man . . . without a past."

"Just tell me one thing, then," she managed to say.

"What if you were free? What if you got that pardon?" *What if I didn't care about your past?*

His lips touched her forehead, his breath warm on her skin. "I would marry you and make you the happiest doctor of art history in America." He trailed a finger along her cheek and let it rest on her lips. "But we shouldn't talk about it. Because it isn't going to happen. All we have is this time, now."

Confusion and frustration and hope rose inside her, and he quelled it all with a demanding and intimate kiss. But he couldn't quiet the echo of his words. Those, she would have forever.

I would marry you. . . .

She didn't care about his past. She didn't even care if he changed names and homes and languages like other people changed jobs. It didn't matter, because for the first time in her life, she was truly in love.

She pressed her body against him as his hands found her breasts and their kisses intensified. She slid off his shorts, he lifted her cotton nightgown over her head. She eased him on his back, careful not to hurt his bandaged arm. Then she smiled and climbed on top of him.

Driven by the now familiar ribbon that twirled her body into a knot of desire, she flattened her palms against his chest and raised herself above him. With a shake of her head, her hair tumbled down and fell around his face. He grabbed a handful and ran his fingers through it, his other hand exploring her body.

"Rapunzel." He half laughed, half moaned.

She reached between her legs and closed her hands over him, drawing him into her. When he entered her, she gasped and rocked into his hips, taking her pleasure and erasing her pain. Arching toward him, her hair tickled her backside. He grasped her waist and hips and drove into her. Slowly at first, then faster and harder. He whispered words of love in English, then French. She leaned over him, and he twisted her hair into knots as tight as the ones inside her until she felt him explode in her; then everything spun and twirled and unraveled all at once.

When Janine finally fell onto his powerful chest, exhausted and satisfied, she closed her eyes and listened to the thumping of his heart, beating in an odd three-step rhythm.

I-love-you. I-love-you. I-love-you.

Nick had his reasons for letting this love affair end, and they were real and right to him. He wasn't willing to share his life—his strange, guarded, enigmatic life—with her. She had to respect that.

And then she knew: even though she loved him, it was time to leave. There was nothing but heartache to be gained by staying any longer with a man she loved but couldn't have. Wasn't that what she intended when she decided to take charge of her destiny?

She would leave tomorrow, a richer, better woman who had finally tasted love. And twenty-thousand-dollar wine.

She didn't expect to ever have either one again.

CHAPTER
Twenty-eight

The midday sunshine broke through a stubborn cloud as Nick and Claire meandered through the vines. He plucked an unripened grape, squeezing it between his fingers.

"I like wine, but I don't know beans about grapes," he admitted to Claire.

She laughed and took the fruit from his fingers. "*Maman* could tell you what variety this is with her eyes closed."

"Gamay." He elbowed her gently. "Even I know that."

She narrowed her chocolate gaze, and for a second he thought she'd stick her tongue out at him, as if time and bad choices had never separated them.

"Yeah, but she could tell you when it would peak for harvest," Claire said. "And if it would make a decent blend."

The seed of an idea took hold as he dropped the grape and roped his arm around Claire's neck. "Mom looks good," he said. "Is she happy?"

His sister looked up at him with a sparkle in her eyes. "She is now, Nick."

He smiled. "You look good, too." He ruffled her already windblown hair. "Still a little bossy, but good." The sound of her laughter echoed across the hillside, filling him with as much happiness as he could remember since . . . last night. He glanced toward the house. They'd only been exploring the vineyard for an hour or so, but already he missed Janine, who'd declined to join them on a postlunch walk. He wanted to go back to the house, but he wanted to spend more time with his sister, too. Not a bad moment in life, he thought. Torn between two beautiful women he . . . cared about.

He tightened his grip on Claire. "No husband and babies yet, huh? Let's see, I'm thirty-nine, so you're damn near thirty-five. What's taking so long?"

She wiggled out of his grasp. "I'm married to my business."

"An auction house? Is that right?"

"Mmm." She nodded and plucked a grape of her own. "I bailed out of Sotheby's a while ago and started Claire's. It's not Christie's yet, but it's going gangbusters. I'm thinking about branching out of New York." She gave him a curious look. "You know, I'd been following the story on those French vases—the Pompadour Plums. I can't believe they brought you to me. I'd sure like to get those up on the block."

He snorted. "I'd sure like to find them. If only to make Janine happy."

"It's pretty obvious you'd like to do that."

With a grin, he pulled her back into his side. "I hate it when I'm transparent."

"Only to me."

The house was in plain view now, and he squinted into the sunshine at the figure in the driveway. Janine. She was putting something in their car. His chest constricted, and he quickened his step until they reached her.

"What are you doing?" he asked, glancing at Lisette's decrepit luggage in the backseat.

"I was hoping you'd drive me to Dijon," she said, with a decidedly cavalier shrug. "I can catch a flight to Paris this afternoon."

He stared at her, unable to speak, unable to process what she'd just announced.

"It's not a long drive," she added. "Gabrielle said she'd come along, so you don't have to give up time with her."

He shook his head, still trying to handle *flight to Paris*. "Why are you leaving?"

"I'm going to get a drink," Claire said, no doubt sensing the storm brewing.

Janine took a deep breath. "You have so little time left until . . . until you have to go."

"Precisely my point."

"It's not fair that I cut in on your time with your mother and sister. They've missed you for five years and I . . . I . . ."

"You what?"

She laughed nervously. "You're not going to make this easy, are you?"

"No. I'm not." How could it be easy to walk away from what precious hours they had? Maybe only one more night until Tristan blew into town waving a new driver's license and birth certificate.

"Luc— Sorry. Listen, I have to go. I can maybe help clean up things at Versailles or, worst case, get back to UCLA and see if I still have a job. I have to get on with my life."

"What about your Plums?" *What about us?* He bit back the inane question. There clearly was no *us*.

She waved a dismissive hand. "Yeah. Well. Let me know if they ever find them."

He caught her hand midgesture. "I can't do that and you know it. I'll never be able to contact you. I'll never see you again," he ground out.

She freed her hand and opened the car door. "Precisely *my* point," she said softly.

The rumble of a car coming up the gravel drive jerked his attention. A blue sedan rolled toward them, kicking up a cloud of dirt. It parked about twenty yards away, and in a second, Tristan slid out of the driver's seat.

Time's up.

"Did you find the Plums?" Janine asked anxiously as he approached.

Nick was tempted to remind her that three seconds ago she'd waved them off, but Tristan shook his head. Nick raced through his options, trying to decide how to break the news that the whole cover was blown. At least with some people who really mattered.

"Hey, Tris," he said, rounding the car to shake his hand. "You'll never guess who's here."

At that moment, the front door opened and Tristan looked up. To anyone else, he had no reaction. But Nick saw it. He knew that imperceptible spark in Tristan's eyes. He'd seen it every time Claire stormed the kitchen in tight jeans and T-shirt while Tristan was trying to be Mr. Cool CIA agent.

Without missing a beat, Claire waltzed out to the driveway and stopped next to Janine. "I'm going with you and Nick to the airport," she announced, not looking at either man.

Tristan pointed a finger at Nick. "You're not going to any airport."

"Can I?" Janine asked. "Am I free to go?"

Tristan nodded, and Nick almost gave in to the frustration that burned inside him.

No. You are not *free to go.*

But why would she stay here with a man wanted in thirteen states who had a criminal history as long as her legs? Taking a deep breath, he reached in his pocket and fished out the keys. He tossed them over the car to his sister, who caught them in midair.

"It's a straight shot into town," he said to Claire. "There are signs all over the place for the airport."

Claire came around to the driver's side, a foot from Tristan without even a flicker of eye contact.

"He'd better be here when I get back," she warned under her breath. Without waiting for a response, she dove behind the wheel and slammed her door shut. Over the roof of the car, Nick gave Janine one long, last look.

He snapped the mental picture of her cornflower blue eyes gazing at him, the wind lifting a strand of hair, with the sun-washed French château as her backdrop. He'd remember that vision for a long time.

"So long, Rapunzel."

She touched her fingers to her lips and tipped him a kiss in response.

With a wistful half smile, she slipped into the passenger seat. Claire was spewing gravel before Janine had the chance to close her door.

Two hours later, Tristan accepted the wine offered to him. "Thanks, Mrs. J."

"You can call me Gabrielle now," she said with a gentle smile, and then put her hand on her son's shoulder.

Tristan laughed and watched her disappear through the patio doors. Her look had told him she'd forgiven him. She somehow understood what it had cost to rearrange her wayward son's life. Claire clearly hadn't yet reached the understanding phase.

Nick held his glass up in a mock toast. "To old times."

Tristan rolled his eyes and picked up the red wine that would be far better described as black. "I probably shouldn't drink on duty," he said, holding his glass to Nick's. But after seeing Claire—and Gabrielle Jarrett for that matter—he needed it. It wasn't a show of weakness.

Weaknesses turn to strength when stared in the face.

"Is that why you're staring at me?"

Tristan jerked, not realizing he'd spoken out loud. "What can I say, Nicky? You evidently are my professional weakness."

"For which I am eternally grateful." Nick took a long

drink and settled back in the chair. "I guess 'temporary' is the operative word in the scenario you just described to me."

Tristan nodded and sipped, the berry and vanilla of the wine pulling pleasantly at his tongue. "It could last a few weeks, maybe a month or so. He just doesn't know what the hell to do with you now. The Benazir arrest carried a lot of weight, but a blanket pardon would take more than that."

Nick scowled, irritating Tristan. That wasn't the look he expected from a man who'd just been given a reprieve, however temporary. Then he remembered the look on his face when he said good-bye to *Rapunzel*.

"Why'd she leave?" Tristan asked.

"Beats the hell out of me. I think you scared her away."

"I'm sure you did that all by yourself." Tristan had no doubt he'd watched a woman in love run off to Dijon. "You're not exactly what I would call a safe bet."

Nick spun the wine cork on the table. Of course he'd start doing hand tricks; it was his favorite way to detour a subject.

"If she had just waited a few minutes, then she would have heard that I've got some time." He rolled the cork through his fingers, then it disappeared. "She could have stayed here at the château with me."

"Yeah, I'm sure that's what she'd want to do. Hang out indefinitely while the government decides the fate of one of their favorite criminals."

Nick flipped the cork in the air and let it hit the table, his look as black as the wine in his glass. "I've paid my dues, Tris. I've thwarted a dozen major heists in France over the past five years. I've made your job a hell of a lot easier as a liaison with local authorities. And I handed over a mastermind who had managed to prance out of prison when no one was looking."

"I know your résumé," Tristan said quietly. "The decision's not mine."

The sound of a car door slamming carried over the vineyard. "Claire's back," Nick said, scooping the cork in his hand and punting it with one finger right at Tristan's chest. "Drink up. Weaknesses are best stared at in the face."

Tristan speared him with a dirty look.

Nick laughed. "Or something like that."

"You shouldn't read in the dark, darling." Gabrielle reached over the desk and switched on a lamp, shedding a yellow pool over the papers and spreadsheets in front of Nick.

He smiled his thanks and didn't remind his mother that he preferred to read in dim light. She'd been babying him for a month and clearly enjoyed it. After she sat, she leaned forward and scrutinized his face.

"You don't look happy. The owner of the Rhône vineyard declined to make an offer, didn't he?"

He nodded. Although his mother was quite capable in the wine-making area and he'd assumed the administrative responsibilities, they were still searching for a buyer.

"Did Tristan have news when he called?" she asked, evidently not accepting "business" as the sole reason for his scowl.

"Not enough." The utter loss of the Plums was at the root of all Nick's angst. If he could produce them, then maybe he'd have an excuse to go to California. . . .

"What did he say?"

"Benazir still refuses to confess to stealing the Plums, and they remain firmly out of sight. They haven't shown up on the black market, and all of the usual intelligence sources are coming up with nothing. They've simply vanished." He suspected they were swept into a trash can somewhere, a million slivers of soft paste porcelain. Otherwise, someone somewhere would have seen them by now.

"What about those people at Versailles?" she asked. "They haven't offered a single clue?"

"Marchionette has been formally removed as the minister of culture, and several of his lackeys in key positions have resigned."

Gabrielle nodded thoughtfully. She'd kept up with the case every day; he'd heard her telling Claire details when she called from New York, even though Claire had been talking to Tristan often enough to know the progress on the case. And the progress on his next "assignment"—which was zero. The director had yet to place him anywhere, as anyone.

Living here in limbo was as bad as living in hell. Except the wine was better.

"And what about Janine?" His mother's face was almost expression-free, but the glimmer in her eye gave away her thoughts.

Janine tortured his dreams and invaded his days. "Evidently, the head of Versailles Security—a woman Marchionette himself put into place—has admitted to placing an unauthorized camera in the chapel, so she knew where I'd hidden the Plums. She's being charged as an accessory to the crime, and with harassing Janine to deflect the attention of the authorities. So, Tristan said Janine may have to return to France to testify." But he'd be long gone by then.

Gabrielle traced a finger along the carved edge of Bérnard's ancient oak desk. "Have you spoken to her?"

"No."

"Do you know where she is?"

"No." It wasn't a lie. He knew she was in L.A., teaching a summer course, but he didn't know if she was walking down the street, on the beach, sleeping, dreaming, crying, hoping, or simply moving on with her life. The all-too-familiar ache settled in his heart as he imagined her doing all those things.

He saw the look in his mother's eyes again. She couldn't stand to have anyone else lose love the way she had, and she'd spent a good deal of the past few weeks reminding him of that. He'd have to head her off quickly. "I have a proposal for you," he said.

She raised her eyebrows in question.

"I suggest we take the vineyard off the market."

His mother just stared.

"I'd like to keep it . . . in the family, Mom. What would you say to staying here and running the vineyard yourself?"

"Me?" She let out a giggle of delight and surprise.

"I'll help you from . . . from wherever I am. It's easy with e-mail and computers. I could find a foreman. A couple of candidates from other vineyards have sent letters and résumés."

"Do you think I could handle it?" Her eyes sparkled.

"Claire and I have been talking about it, and we know you could," he said, leaning toward her. "You belong here, Mom. And Claire will visit and, maybe, so could I. What do you think?"

She held up her hand to her mouth, her eyes swimming in tears. "Oh, Nicky, I love the idea. I've wanted to be here all my life."

He stood and came around the desk, kneeling on one knee to embrace her. "I know you have. I think you could be very happy here. What do you have in Boston anymore?"

She tried to talk, but could only fight back tears. She ran her hand over his head, as she had done a million times. "I love you, Nicky."

He smiled and leaned on her shoulder. "You've proven that." He grinned up at her. "Are you scared of ghosts?"

She laughed a little. "I welcome them. I hope that Bérnard is here, so he knows that I've finally come home to him."

Nick stood up and took her hand. "If he's here, he's down in his wine cellar."

Except to fix the vent and put a temporary bolt on the door, Luc had avoided the cellar over the past month. Only Arlaine had been inside, cleaning up after Lisette's accident. But it was time to face the past.

"Let's go get a good bottle and celebrate, Mom. That's what Bérnard would want."

But it wasn't Bérnard's ghost that seized him as he shoved aside the temporary bolt; it was Janine's memory that haunted him. He could still remember the feel of her slender frame when she fainted in his arms, the taste of the Romanée Conti on her lips, and the tickle of her silky mane in his fingers.

Playing hide and seek and spin the bottle. He smiled to himself. That was when he'd started to fall in love with her.

Holding his mother's arm, they descended the stone stairs to the dirt floor. It was exactly as when Lisette had hidden them. The table, two chairs, a single oil lamp, the rack of glasses, the alcoves of wine that had been lovingly made or collected by Bérnard. Good Lord, there must be a few million dollars in wine down here.

And now it belonged to him.

He pulled out a chair for Gabrielle and opened the new vent he'd installed, then laid the flashlight down to light the lamp. He could tell by the wistful look on his mother's face that she had her own memories of the little room.

"La Romanée, n'est ce pas?" he asked in her native tongue.

She frowned at him. "You would waste that nectar on me?"

"It's not a waste. You deserve the best."

She sniffed. "I want Pinot, Nicky. Bérnard's favorite year was—"

"Eighty-nine," he finished for her. "Believe me, I had a few with him."

"Eighty-nine? His *old* favorite year was fifty-three. I guess they've had some better vintages since then." She paused and beamed at him. "I'm so glad you knew each other. My two favorite men on earth, drinking wine together. That makes me happy."

He reached down and kissed her on the top of her head. "Good. You deserve to be happy. I'll get the wine."

"His father kept the better Pinot in alcove five," Gabrielle said, as she opened the drawer and pulled out the corkscrew. "We used to help ourselves to it occasionally."

"It's still there." Nick answered, already in front of five. "Wow. There are a lot of bottles missing."

Then he remembered Lisette's fall; at least a dozen bottles had broken in it. What had she been doing down there, anyway?

A whisper of insight chilled him. There had been plenty of wine upstairs when he'd arrived. Why *had* she gone to the cellar that night?

Slowly, he took a step back and stared at the alcove. The thick layer of dust blanketed the bottles, all the way up . . . until the top. That whole row had been wiped clean. What had removed the dust from a row of wine bottles eight feet in the air?

He reached up with one long arm, then stood on his toes and stretched as far over the top of the wine bottles as he could.

His fingertip grazed a rough edge of . . . burlap. The chill turned to ice in his veins.

It couldn't be.

He grabbed the chair and positioned it in front of the alcove.

"Be careful," his mother warned, still examining the contents of Bérnard's drawer. "That's how Lisette fell."

Oh yes. Exactly how Lisette fell.

Standing on the chair, he shined the flashlight into the alcove. It landed directly on a canvas bundle. His heart thumping but his hands steady, he closed his fingers around the fabric and carefully dragged the bundle over the top row of bottles.

He gathered it up with two hands, feeling the curved angles of the ormolu handles just beneath the material.

"What is that, Nick?" his mother asked, coming to stand next to him. "What have you found?"

He'd found a treasure. He'd found a trump card to lay on the table of the director of the FBI. He'd found *freedom*.

Nick laid the rolls of burlap on the table, then slowly folded back the layers. Gabrielle gasped at her first glimpse of the most beautiful indigo violet ever glazed onto a piece of soft paste porcelain.

"I just found the rest of my life." And he knew exactly who he wanted to spend it with.

CHAPTER
Twenty-nine

Mother Nature had outdone herself when she created a clear California sky washed by a Santa Ana wind. Janine thought of all the artists who'd tried to capture it but failed. She leaned back on one of the columns that flanked her favorite perch along the side of Royce Hall, closing her book and giving in to the beauty above her.

It reminded her of the sky over Lake Geneva, which reminded her of Luc, which reminded her that she hadn't thought of him for, oh, six or seven minutes.

A record.

Such good behavior should be rewarded with a nice juicy memory. She closed her eyes against that impossibly blue sky and pictured the perfect angles of his face when he smiled. The warm, insistent taste of his lips when he kissed. The magic of his fingers when he braided her hair. The warmth of his baritone when he spoke her name.

Szha-neen.

Oh, yes. She smiled. She could remember it perfectly.

"What amuses you, Janine?"

Her eyes popped open and she jerked forward, her heart plummeting to her stomach and her book tumbling to the ground.

She must have conjured him up. How else to explain that he stood right in front of her, with the California sky above his head and Royce Hall's red brick in the background?

"A young woman with pink hair told me I could find you here."

His eyes were real. His voice was real. He bent over and picked up her book, glancing at the cover. *"The Poems of Lamartine?"* He grinned at her as he handed it back. "Excellent choice."

She managed to find her voice. "Luc?"

He laughed softly and shook his head. "I'm Nick Jarrett." Reaching out for a handshake, he added a devilish wink. "Pleased to meet you."

She took his hand, and instantly he tugged her off the narrow stone wall, right into his chest. Sucking in a breath as their bodies touched, she dropped her head back and looked up at him.

"You *are* real."

He laughed again. "Yes, I'm real. And you're beautiful. And I've missed the hell out of you." He tunneled his hands into her hair and pulled her face toward him. "And before you say another word, kiss me hello."

All the blood rushed from her head as his lips captured hers. Her heart thumped like it would explode. He broke the kiss for air, but it didn't matter. She couldn't breathe anyway.

"What—what are you doing here?"

He cupped her face in his hand—his strong, magical hand—and studied her. "Official business."

She refused to let her heart drop. Business or pleasure, she didn't care. He was here. "What kind of business?"

"I'm looking for the world's foremost expert on Sèvres porcelain." He raked her with one of those smoldering gazes. "That pink-haired girl in the Art History office told me that would be you."

She smiled as he stroked her cheek. "What do you want to know about porcelain?"

"I'll tell you in a minute." He kissed her forehead. "Right now I want to know more about the expert."

An insane thrill danced through her and she smiled. "What would you like to know?"

Sliding his arm around her neck, he tucked her into his side. Home, she thought fleetingly. This is home.

"For starters," he said, as they started walking into the building, "I'd like to know if she is free."

She gave him a questioning look as they entered the cool, dark hall. "Free for the next hour or free for dinner tonight?"

"Free for the rest of her life."

She stopped midstep and slowly lifted her face to him. "Why do you ask?"

He shot her a smug smile and guided her forward. "Because I am."

She stopped again. "What?"

"I am free for the rest of my life."

"You mean—you mean you got the pardon?" She clamped her hand over her mouth and felt the tears burn in her eyes. "Really?"

"It's a done deal as of three days ago." He wiped a tear from her eye and touched the finger to his lips. "Don't cry, now. I told you I'm here on official business."

Nick was free. Free. Pardoned and free to go on with his life. "Shall we go in?" she asked, pointing to her office.

"No." He tilted his head toward a door across the hall. "In there."

She reached out to put her hand on his arm, but he slipped away. "That's Albert's office. It's locked. You can't go in there."

He twisted the handle and shot her a deadly grin. "Evidently, I can."

Her jaw dropped, and then she let out an exasperated breath.

He held out his hand to her. "Pink hair let me in. Now close your eyes." Pulling her toward the open door, he covered her eyes with one hand. "No peeking."

With a thudding heart and shaky legs, she let him lead her into Albert's office. She hadn't been in here since before she went to France, unwilling to face the memories.

Suddenly she felt Nick lift her hair and drop a steamy kiss against her exposed flesh, sending a shower of delight over her.

"Don't open your eyes," he whispered. "Just tell me something."

She nodded.

"Have you forgiven me for lying to you in France?"

Her legs nearly wobbled out from underneath her. "Yes, I have."

"Can you forget what I was?"

"No, but it doesn't matter to me."

She thought she heard him sigh as the softest breath caressed her ear. "Do you have any idea how much I love you?" he whispered.

Surely she would faint. No air, no strength, and her heart had squeezed up into her throat. "No." It was barely a sound, let alone an answer.

He burned her neck with another kiss and tightened his hand over her eyes. "I love you more than life. More than I thought it was possible to love another person. More than anyone will ever love you as long as you live." Another kiss, this one so tender she thought she might melt. "You are the reason I wake and breathe and eat and drink and sleep. I love you, Janine Coulter."

She dropped her head back into his chest and didn't say a word.

"Could you possibly love me, too?"

The breath she'd been holding came out in a whoosh. "I do. I love you, too, Luc."

He chuckled softly. "It's Nick, but I'll take that as a yes. Now, about our business."

Business? She was dying of love right now!

He lifted his hand from her eyes, and she blinked at the light. Then she blinked again, and brought both hands up to her mouth as she gasped.

"*Voilà, madame.* My Plums."

She took a tentative step toward them, then stopped. *His* Plums? Turning to him, she narrowed her eyes. "They belong to France."

He shrugged. "A technicality. They were found on my property, Château Soisson. Right in the wine cellar where

Lisette had hidden them. I would like you to verify their authenticity, please."

Her jaw dropped. "No! In the wine cellar?"

"Yes. That's why the tracking device didn't work."

Unable to stop herself, she reached out and carefully touched the gilded bronze handle of the center vase. Her fingers grazed the translucent enamel and the reproduction of Jeanne-Antoinette's great moment as the king's mistress.

"They're beautiful," she said softly. She tapped the base with her nail and scraped about a quarter inch of the golden glaze. "And real."

Her hand was shaking and she pulled away, afraid she might knock one over.

Nick Jarrett was free. He wanted to spend the rest of his life with her. He was here; he was real; he loved her and she loved him. And they had the Plums. What more could she ask?

"Pick it up," he encouraged her. "Go ahead."

She shook her head. "I can't." She laughed nervously. "I'm so shaky, I'm afraid I'll drop it."

"No, you won't." He took each of her hands in his and placed them on the gilded handles. Slowly they lifted it together. "Now shake it."

She glanced at him. "Shake it?"

He shimmied the vase and something skated around the bottom. Her eyes widened. "Is that the tracking device?"

He laughed. "Of sorts." Lifting the vase higher, with her hands still under his, he turned it on its side, then upside down. Something hit the desk with a clunk. "It will track my wife—if she'll wear it, and not flush it down the toilet when she's mad at me."

Janine could barely see the diamond ring through the tears in her eyes. *It will track my wife.*

He carefully set the vase down as she stared at the platinum circle with a sizeable stone. "It's—it's beautiful."

"Don't worry," he whispered, picking it up. "I bought it." He took her hand in his, held the ring poised over her finger, and locked on her gaze. "I have a lousy past, but if you'll marry me, I know I'll have a very bright future." He tightened his grip and lowered his voice. "Will you marry me? I promise, this offer is as legitimate as it gets, Janine."

And this euphoria was as good as it got. "It's Szhaneen, Luc." She slid her finger into the ring.

"It's Nick," he whispered.

And then he kissed her until they couldn't remember who they were.

Epilogue

This was overkill. One bride, one groom, five guests, and a chapel the size of three football fields. Total freaking overkill.

Tristan shook his head and smiled. He and Nick had to move heaven and earth to get the new director of Versailles to allow a private wedding in the Royal Chapel. But, once again, mountains had been moved for Nick Jarrett.

There was something about that guy.

And, there was something about his sister.

Tristan sneaked a sideways glance, knowing his attention should be on the happy couple, but it was stolen by the potent presence of the woman standing next to him.

"Isn't it gorgeous?" Claire looked up at him with that magical glimmer in her ebony eyes.

"You are," he whispered back.

They shared a smile, and Tristan turned back to the couple at the foot of the altar. Nick was beaming down at his bride, who looked like a medieval princess with her long blond braid and white lace train. After all they'd been through, he had to admit Versailles was the perfect setting for this wedding—and not just because Janine was about to relaunch the Pompadour exhibit in the next few weeks. At least she had her own private security consultant to accompany her around the world, now; that ought to keep her out of trouble.

And then they would live in L.A., with Nick running Claire's newest auction house. Janine wanted to stay at UCLA, but also planned to supervise the permanent Pompadour exhibit at the Getty Museum. In the new Albert Farrow Hall, so named by the anonymous and generous donor who'd paid for its construction.

Or not so anonymous, considering the very public recent sale of a significant portion of one of France's most valuable wine collections.

Oh, yeah, there was definitely something about that guy. Something very, very good.

He watched Nick slide the wedding ring on Janine's finger and couldn't help wondering how it would feel to do that himself someday. To take the hand of the woman he loved, to profess undying love.

Undying love was for people who believed they wouldn't die.

Claire shifted next to him, and her slender hand closed over his. He turned his palm up and weaved their fingers together.

Maybe he was wrong. *Undying love was for people who believed.* Period.

Yeah. He liked that much better.

Pocket Books

Proudly Presents

Hot Nights in Ballymuir

Dorien Kelly

Available in Paperback

March 2004

Turn the page for a preview of

Hot Nights in Ballymuir. . . .

On a spring-perfumed Tuesday morning, the devil arrived in Ballymuir, wearing a hand-tailored Saville Row suit and driving a black Porsche 911. Other than Jenna Fahey, none in town seemed to recognize him for who he was. Of course, she was the only one he nearly mowed down in the narrow street outside Spillane's Market.

Though shaken, Jenna survived. The delicate heads of organic lettuce she had charmed Mr. Spillane into holding aside for her were, unfortunately, victims.

"Two years in Ireland and you still don't know which way to look before stepping off the curb," Jenna's best friend, Vi Kilbride, teased as she helped her gather the remains of what was to have been salad at Muir House, Jenna's restaurant. "I'm thinking we'll hire a keeper for you. Male, preferably."

Jenna ignored her friend's comment. She had men enough—a kitchen filled with them, actually—talented, hard-edged, beloved lunatics.

The Porsche, whose driver she had seen with a near-death sort of clarity, had pulled into a spot uphill. Her lip curled as she checked out the high-performance, lettuce-killing machine. The car was every bit as out-of-place in this quiet corner of Ireland as she'd been when she'd arrived here two years ago, determined to make Ballymuir a bastion of haute cuisine.

A lone head of lettuce rested atop a car across the street. First looking right, then left, instead of the near-fatal reverse order, Jenna crossed. She lobbed the lettuce to Vi, who stood with a handful of people who'd come out of the market to see what the growling car and screaming woman had been about.

Before rejoining them, Jenna wiped her damp and gritty hands on her jeans. The sky was clear now, but it had rained soft and steady just before first light. Promise of even more rain clung to the jagged, purple-hued mountains that held Ballymuir hard to the sea.

Jenna pinned on a smile and resorted to humor, her favorite crutch in stressful moments. "What's the last thing that goes through a chef's mind when she hits a car's windshield?" she called from mid-street.

"This is one of those American jokes, isn't it?" asked Mr. Spillane, rubbing a hand over his thinning gray hair. "Never do understand 'em."

"Her . . ." As she reached the sidewalk, Jenna scowled, her thoughts interrupted. The Porsche's driver was jogging downhill, straight toward her. She knew his type—rich, self-important, always in a hurry. "Ass."

Black hair, dark eyes, charcoal suit, he was six feet of breathtaking arrogance come to town. Her body's reaction to his undeniable perfection was chemical. And irrelevant.

"I'm so sorry. Are you all right?" he asked as he closed in on her.

Interesting. German car, British plates, and Irish accent. Quite healthy-looking, too, though an Irishman with a tan was highly suspect—practically a crime against genetics. Irishmen burned and peeled, or weathered to a ruddy finish. They did not look as though they'd just dropped in from Cap d'Antibes for a visit. For the first time she found her "always in the kitchen" pallor problematic.

"If by all right, you mean not dead, I'm fine." She could do nothing about the pasty tone of her skin— no doubt made even paler by her brush with death— so instead she straightened her red sweater.

Not that he would have noticed. After a cursory glance that she imagined was to be sure she had no severed limbs, he had turned his attention elsewhere. This was no great surprise; she wasn't the sort of woman that men tended to linger over. Look . . . yawn . . . move on.

"I didn't even see you step out onto the road," he said, pushing back the cuff of his white shirt and checking a chunky gold watch that Jenna knew cost more than most people in Ballymuir could hope to save in a lifetime.

"How could you see anything, traveling at the speed of light?"

"Let me replace the . . ." He frowned at the crushed green stuff interred in its crate.

"It was organic butter lettuce."

His gaze again flicked over her. "Let me replace it for you."

"That's a fine offer, to be sure," elderly Breege Flaherty opined from her spot next to Vi. Trust Ballymuir's citizens to insist on being part of the action. No neutrality here, even on matters as mundane as trampled produce.

Americans had a few quirks of their own. Being born and raised in Chicago meant that Jenna's southern belle act was shaky, but how was this false Irishman to know?

"You'd do that for me?" she asked, hand neatly settled over her heart.

The eyelash flutter might have been overkill. Vi was making a sound perilously close to gagging. Jenna shot her a quick glare.

The man simply smiled. One slightly crooked eyetooth rescued him from Hollywood perfection. That, and the fact that Jenna found something very calculating about his expression.

"After running you down in the street, it's the least I can do." He reached into his breast pocket and pulled out a billfold.

Ah, cash, the great placater. She should have expected this, but something about the almond tilt of his eyes had briefly disarmed her.

"It's not that simple," Jenna said as crisp new euros appeared. "You see, Mr. Spillane, here, has to order the lettuce a week in advance, then if we're lucky, it actually makes it from Holland."

"We've not much call for the organic stuff, outside of Jenna and one or two other blow-ins with odd ideas about food," the grocer apologized.

Maybe it was because this stranger was a highly unsettling echo of everything she'd been trying to leave behind, or maybe it was because she remained ticked off over her lettuce, but whatever the reason, Jenna upped the ante . . . just to see what he'd do.

"The wholesaler in Tralee might still have a case," she said. "Or if that doesn't work, there's always Killarney. Two hours—maybe four—and we'll be even."

There, she'd called his bluff—another man of flash but no substance.

His smile didn't waver. With a graceful economy of movement, he stowed the money and flipped open a cell phone. One push of a speed-dial button and he was all business. "Margaret, I'll be needing a case of butter lettuce—"

When Jenna cleared her throat, he amended, "Make that *organic* butter lettuce delivered to—"

"Muir House," Breege's friend, Edna McCafferty, supplied.

"Muir House," the man echoed. "In Ballymuir, and no later than ten thirty, if you could." He smiled. "What would I do without you, Margaret, my love?"

"Pick up your own damn lettuce," Jenna said just under her breath.

"Sorry? I didn't catch that," he said as he returned the phone to his pocket.

She repeated the thought with sterling diction. "I

said, without Margaret, you'd have to pick up your own damn lettuce."

Their eyes met. A startling sort of awareness coursed through Jenna. She looked away first, then realized the error of her choice. One never looked away from the devil.

His smile was slow, easy, a thing of damned beauty. "Without Margaret, that, I would. Now if you'll excuse me, I'm late for a meeting. Have a grand day, everyone."

His long stride covered the incline to his car, and Jenna watched his every step.

"So that's Dev Gilvane," Mrs. McCafferty practically crooned as the Porsche disappeared over the crest of the hill.

Dev. At least his parents had recognized what they would be raising.

"I knew his mum, back when. The boy has her eyes."

Only a woman on the passing side of eighty would see Dev Gilvane as anything less than a full-grown man.

"Right, now. You can scarcely remember yesterday's supper, let alone what Kate Connelly's eyes looked like," Breege Flaherty was saying. "She's been off to Dublin thirty years and more."

Edna ignored her friend. "He's staying with Muriel O'Keefe, I hear. Paying for all three rooms so he can have some privacy, too. His name's always appearing in those London gossip columns—you know, the one filled with premieres and benefits. A prominent financier, they call him. He's nearly a star like that Bono."

"Who?" Mr. Spillane asked.

"You know, that young jackeen with his music."

"You've not seen him out your way, Jenna?"

Trapped between the warp and weft of the conversation, the best Jenna could do was blink.

"They're meaning Dev Gilvane, not Bono," Vi prompted.

Jenna was sure that even after she'd spent a full decade in Ballymuir, she still wouldn't be able to keep up with the free-for-all talk. She became too enamored by the music of the words to catch their meanings. And more and more, she found herself slipping into the cadence of their speech.

"Um . . . no. Any reason I should?"

"I've read that our boy's quite the grand man with the ladies, too," Mrs. McCafferty said. "I thought maybe he'd have brought a girl to dine—a model or actress, perhaps?"

"Sorry, but it's just the usual suspects this time of year," Jenna replied with as much sincerity as she could muster. She had no appetite for models, actresses, or playboys. She'd worked hard to escape from her high-maintenance and high-drama family.

Mrs. McCafferty remained undaunted. "We've hope yet. He's told Muriel he's just here on holiday, but she's seen him paging through the real-estate listings over breakfast. Just think of the glamorous types we'd have coming our way if he were to move home."

Breege's silver brows rose into an arch. "Ballymuir's never been his home."

"Ah, but it could be a yearning for his roots. He might be looking to settle in." Edna rubbed her hands together, as though warming to the prospect of glory and glamour strolling the streets of the village.

Breege laughed. "Have you been nipping at the *fuisce?* Just where would someone grand like Mr. Gilvane be settling in? Our manors are no more than piles of ruin."

"Well, it takes someone mad as an Englishman to bring back one of those old hulks," Mr. Spillane pointed out.

All gazes settled on Jenna.

"Not-not that I'm meaning an insult," the grocer stammered. "It's a fine thing you've been doing with Muir House. Why, I was saying to my Kathleen just the other day that—"

"It's okay, Mr. Spillane. Really."

And it would be far better for all of them if she could stop Seamus Spillane's torrent of words before he got going. He was a nice enough man, but had no OFF switch that she could find.

In any case, Jenna realized that settling at Muir House had been an act of insanity. All the same, now it was home and hearth. What these people didn't know—not even Vi—was that the place wasn't exactly hers, as they all assumed. To hear that this Dev Gilvane was sniffing around knotted her stomach.

"I suppose we'd all best get on with our days, too," Vi prompted. Jenna caught her friend's worried glance and reminded herself that she'd do well to hide any hint of emotion around Vi, whose perceptiveness bordered on the unnatural.

Mr. Spillane picked up the case of lettuce. "To the rubbish with this."

"It seems such a waste," said Edna McCafferty as she began to wrestle the box away from the grocer. "Surely with a bit of soaking, there will be some left to save."

Not more than a handful of bruised and ragged leaves, according to Jenna's practiced eye. Still, it was this sort of "something from nothing" attitude that had made Ballymuir thrive while other equally isolated villages diminished to roadside ghosts.

Breege weighed in on Edna's side of the battle. "You'd best let go, Seamus," she said to the grocer. "You know Edna can take you if she's got a mind to. Besides, it seems to me that Jenna should decide the fate of the lettuce. It's bought and paid for, is it not?"

Mr. Spillane released his grip. "Aye."

Edna held her prize tighter.

Jenna issued her verdict. "It's yours, Mrs. McCafferty. Would you like my recipe for chilled lettuce soup? It's a hit during summer teatime."

"Soup? I was thinking just to give the greens a good dollop of mayonnaise and all would be right."

Organic lettuce reduced to a mayonnaise delivery device. If that wasn't the work of the devil, what was?

"I'm sure it will be wonderful," she lied.

"What with mayonnaise isn't?" replied Mrs. McCafferty before she and Breege made their way up the street to the small house they shared next to the surf shop/bookstore.

Jenna and Vi said their good-byes to Mr. Spillane. Instead of heading toward the harbor, where her studio was located, Vi followed Jenna to her car. Once there, Jenna's friend strategically placed herself between Jenna and the driver's door.

Jenna looked up at Vi, who had several inches on her in height. What she saw didn't improve her morning. Vi's green eyes held a determined glint, that of a warrior readying for battle.

"Don't get started," Jenna warned.

Vi crossed her arms and leaned against the car. "Ah, so it's to be the standard ritual of you denying you're troubled and me prodding until you can take it no more?"

"Nothing's bothering me. I couldn't be better."

Vi flicked a lock of her long red hair over her shoulder. Nothing was permitted to stray out of line when she was in one of these moods. "Right, you are. And it's not just that Dev Gilvane crossed you, either. Though speaking of the man, I don't suppose you noticed that he was incredibly—"

"Full of himself?"

"Gorgeous, perfect, fine enough to eat."

"Says the vegetarian. Though if you think he's that hot, have at him. He's all yours."

Vi laughed, the sound rich and musical in the cool air. "In any other circumstance, I might, but he's not meant for me, you see?"

"Then who is he meant for, Edna McCafferty?"

Her friend's smile grew broader. "Are you telling me you didn't feel it? The sun shone brighter when you two spoke."

Jenna shifted uncomfortably. Vi's brand of Celtic mysticism was far more entertaining when focused on someone else. Especially because Jenna had felt something—what, exactly, her cautious heart refused to consider.

"I *feel* that I'm now twenty minutes behind schedule. I *feel* that I need to come up with a replacement for my spring salad because we both know that man's never going to get me any lettuce. And I *feel* that you're just a bit too smug for your own good."

All of which only sharpened Vi's resemblance to a sleek, contented feline, albeit one wearing a bright blue woolen cape. "Smug and optimistic, actually. I'd be tidying my bedroom for a bit of company, if I were you." She stepped aside and motioned at the car with a flourish of her hand. "Now, be off."

Jenna opened her Nissan's slightly rusted silver door. "If I didn't love you like a sister—"

"You'd hate me like one," Vi finished. "And don't be thinking I've forgotten to ask what's bothering you. I'm just waiting until I have you as a captive audience. I'll visit for a meal and a chat tonight around eight."

Vi waited for no answer before strolling away, and Jenna had none to give. She took solace in knowing that eight o'clock tonight meant closer to nine, since Vi operated on the relaxed concept of Irish Time. Still, whether Vi's interrogation was to be twelve hours off or twelve days made no difference. One bit of dissembling and Vi Kilbride would squash her flatter than the devil had her lettuce.

Dev Gilvane pulled into his parking spot at Cois na Mara. Lovely name for a house that—like many things from the 1970s—was best viewed blindfolded. Still, with the nearest hotel over twenty miles away and most bed-and-breakfasts not game for a long-term guest, the odd little place was a godsend. He supposed in time he might grow accustomed to its pseudo-gothic architecture, though he didn't plan to stay long enough to test the theory.

Dev grinned in spite of himself as he neared the strangest aspect in this landscape of the bizarre. The front garden was crowned by a replica statue of Dublin's well-endowed fishmonger and folk-song legend, Molly Malone. He hadn't quite worked up a polite way to ask Muriel O'Keefe, the bed-and-breakfast's owner, what Molly was doing in the yard. It had been bad enough when he'd asked what Cois na Mara meant.

"Why, near the sea, of course," she'd replied in tones thready with shock that an Irishman wouldn't know this.

Perhaps the fact that the sea was a faint sliver of Dingle Bay blue on the horizon had thrown Dev. Or perhaps it was because since leaving Ireland at age eleven, he'd spent no more than the occasional holiday here. His Irish was limited to the stock vulgarities that were the first words a boy learned in any foreign tongue.

All these years later he had to admit to a passing curiosity over what the Irish for "near nothing at all" might be. A more honest name for Muriel's house, if less alluring.

In a gesture rich with unintended irony, his employers at Harwood, a behemoth of a British real-estate concern, had sent him here on assignment as a reward. When settling on Emerald, they'd chosen the wrong Isle. Now, Capri or the Greek Isles came to mind as appealing spots.

Dev reveled in his career as the king of all site finders. Some souls had a nose for wine; his particular gift was a nose for sheer hedonism. He could pinpoint a travel trend and then create a resort to cater to desires a guest didn't even yet know he or she possessed.

When Trevor, his boss and mentor at Harwood, had presented him with this "marvelous opportunity to see home," for the first time ever Dev had given his superiors short shrift. Rather than fully explore a land he'd prefer to avoid, he'd traveled directly to his mother's county of birth.

True, he'd done slightly better than toss a dart over his shoulder at a map of Ireland. Mum was always waxing bloody poetic about the beauty of Kerry. And though he could remember virtually nothing of a childhood trip to Ballymuir, he'd thought that surely something here would suit his needs. And it appeared that something might. All the better for him to be quickly back to his London friends and diversions.

As Dev passed Molly, he gave her a friendly pat on her bronze bum. He bounded up the steps and entered Bric-a-Brac Central. Muriel instantly appeared, wiping her hands on a frilly blue apron she wore over nondescript trousers and top.

"And so how was your morning drive?" she asked.

Before pulling the door shut, he took a speculative glance outside, wondering if the Molly statue weren't rigged to be some sort of advance warning system. He'd never made it past the entry without Muriel materializing and her farmer husband bounding out the back door for the hills beyond.

"Rain-free, at least." As he imagined it wouldn't

do much to endear him to Mrs. O'Keefe, he kept to himself the fact that he'd nearly killed one of the locals. And for quite the same reason, he was visiting Ballymuir in the guise of a tourist. The more picturesque a location, the more hostile its residents to the idea of development.

"Can I bring you some tea, or some of my scones?" Mrs. O'Keefe asked. "They're fresh-baked, you know."

Dev pocketed his car keys and edged toward the stairway. "Thanks, but no. You filled me up with your wonderful breakfast."

Muriel cooked meals large enough to feed a legion. He'd had buttery fried eggs, rashers, toast, and juice, and enjoyed it all to excess. Both his tailor and personal trainer were going to go around the bend when he finally made it home.

"Well, if you're needing a bite later, just come to the kitchen and I'll fix you a plate," his hostess called after him.

Dev took the steps two at a time.

"Home," he muttered as he came to the door with the numeral 2 painted on its plain wooden surface.

Once inside, he slipped out of his suit coat and hung it in the wardrobe that sucked up most of the room's space and light. His accommodations were essentially a purple floral closet with delusions of grandeur. Sort of the Royal Suite for Dwarfs . . .

After debating whether to change into more casual garb, then rejecting the idea because work was work, even when conducted in a backwater, Dev grabbed his briefcase and cell phone, then made his way downstairs.

If he were staying at the Clarence in Dublin, he'd have a suite with an enormous postmodern desk and a minimum of two phone lines. Here, he had a corner of a dining table in the breakfast room. Claiming an addiction to current events, he'd persuaded Mrs. O'Keefe to let him run a line for his computer from the jack in the entryway. In exchange for the access, he'd agreed to cover her telephone bill for the time he was a guest. Muriel's appeared to be a far-flung family. Yesterday, when he'd come back from his soggy and fruitless drive, she'd been chatting it up with a third cousin in Brisbane.

Dev opened his laptop, plugged in the phone line, and got down to work. His favorite Internet search engine took less time to spew a list of results than it had taken him to type in a single name: Jenna Fahey.

Based on what he'd heard about her at the pub the prior night, he hadn't expected Muir House's chef to be so . . . feminine. Soft brown curls, a full mouth meant for kissing, and hazel eyes bright with wit weren't chief among the attributes he appreciated discovering in a potential adversary.

After noting her face, he'd permitted himself to look no lower. He was a lover of women—their scents, their laughter, their mystery. This was business, though, and he refused to regard Jenna Fahey as a woman.

He wished for an Amazonian ball-buster, bloody cleaver raised in clenched hand and invective spewing. That sort was all the easier to take in battle. Ah, but he could still defeat the pretty chef, and if circumstances compelled, he would.

Dev leaned against the straight wooden back of

his dining chair and closed his eyes. None of these were thoughts conducive to efficient business, and being in Ireland was damn distracting enough. Resolved to be done with this, he began opening links to websites and became acquainted with the seamless public persona of Jenna Fahey, a rare two-star chef, restaurateur, and daughter of a rich and privileged American family. It was what went unsaid that intrigued Dev.

He flipped open his cell phone and called his personal assistant. "Margaret, I've just forwarded you a list of websites to review. When you've finished, contact our security department regarding the background on Jenna Fahey. And I'd like a reservation for one at Muir House at eight o'clock tonight." He paused, then added, "Not under my own name. Use Malone, Molly Malone."

Dev wasn't sure what motivated this sudden yen for anonymity—not to mention egregious absurdity—but he had learned to trust his instincts. They had saved him from the fire more than once.

"Eight o'clock, it is," Margaret replied, unruffled that her employer had morphed into a woman.

He began to launch his usual "What would I do without you?" but the words died in his throat. From the depths of his imagination came a smooth American voice saying, "Why, make your own damn reservation, of course."

Instinct told Dev Gilvane that Muir House and Jenna Fahey were to be anything other than business as usual.

Let award-winning author

DORIEN KELLY

transport you to a picturesque Irish
village where passions run deep...

THE LAST BRIDE IN BALLYMUIR
0-7434-6458-3

Handsome Michael Kilbride has just been released
from prison after being wrongly convicted as an
IRA gunman. Kylie "Soon-To-Be-A-Saint" O'Shea
is a small-town Irish school teacher—and the only
woman who can see beyond Michael's hardened
facade and recognize him as the noble-hearted,
courageous man he truly is.

HOT NIGHTS IN BALLYMUIR
0-7434-6459-1

Jenna Fahey passionately loves her restaurant
Muir House, and even though the lease is coming
to a close, she isn't about to give up without a fight.
Playboy businessman Devlin Gilvane arrives in
Ballymuir intent on acquiring the property for
himself. But even as Jenna thwarts Dev's pursuit,
she can't resist his rakish charm.

**Visit the Simon & Schuster
romance Web site:**

www.SimonSaysLove.com

**and sign up for our
romance e-mail updates!**

Keep up on the latest
new romance releases,
author appearances, news, chats,
special offers, and more!
We'll deliver the information
right to your inbox—if it's new,
you'll know about it.

POCKET BOOKS